The first rank of winter wolves leaped through the flames, fangs bared and eyes glowing with eldritch blue light. Ellasif held her breath at the sight of them. They were as beautiful as they were terrible, and for an instant she wondered how it would feel to plunge her hand into that dense white fur.

Bowstrings sang in twanging chorus from the cottage lofts. A storm of arrows swept toward the fire moat. Most bounced off thick pelts, but three of the winter wolves stumbled and went down. Two rose and ran again despite the arrows protruding from their bodies. The third wolf lay twitching, a white shaft protruding from its eye socket.

Ellasif's heart triumphed as the children of White Rook made good their first volley. There would not be time for a second.

"Brace!" howled Red Ochme.

The warriors ran forward and set their pikes against the shield wall, iron points angled toward the charging pack. All the warriors, shields and spears, braced for impact.

But the wolves did not challenge the wall. To Ellasif's astonishment, the first rank slid to a stop and reared up on their hind legs. They set their forepaws on the upper edge of the shields, and at last they sang, but not to the moon. They sang to winter.

Crystalline clouds poured from the wolves' jaws, shim-mer⎯⎯⎯⎯⎯⎯⎯⎯⎯⎯⎯⎯⎯⎯⎯⎯⎯cy fog. The fros⎯⎯⎯⎯⎯⎯⎯⎯⎯⎯⎯⎯⎯⎯⎯he faces of the ⎯⎯⎯⎯⎯⎯⎯⎯⎯⎯⎯⎯⎯ound, rigid as f⎯

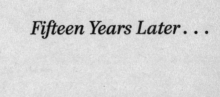

Fifteen Years Later . . .

The Pathfinder Tales Library

Winter Witch

Elaine Cunningham
with Dave Gross

Seattle

Cover art by Jesper Ejsing.
Cover design by Sarah Robinson.
Map by Crystal Frasier.

Paizo Publishing, LLC
7120 185th Ave NE, Ste 120
Redmond, WA 98052
paizo.com

ISBN 978-1-60125-286-9

Publisher's Cataloging-In-Publication Data
(Prepared by The Donohue Group, Inc.)

Cunningham, Elaine, 1957-
 Pathfinder tales. Winter Witch / Elaine Cunningham ; with Dave Gross.

  p. ; cm.

 Portion of title: Winter Witch
 Set in the world of the role-playing game, Pathfinder.
 ISBN: 978-1-60125-286-9

 1. Imaginary places--Fiction. 2. Witches--Fiction. 3. Missing children--Fiction. 4. Magic--Fiction. 5. Fantasy fiction. I. Gross, Dave.
 II. Title. III. Title: Winter Witch IV. Title: Pathfinder adventure path

PS3553.U472 P75 2010
813/.54

First printing November 2010.

Printed in the United States of America.

To Liz Courts, Crystal Frasier, Hugo Solis,
and all the creators of *Wayfinder*.

Prologue
The Dancing Hut

In the Lands of the Linnorm Kings, children seldom weep, and the hardy northern women scream only in the rage of battle. Cursing, however, is a celebrated art mastered only once a woman approaches the moment of childbirth.

Marit perfected her art while writhing on her bed, the sheets already sodden with the sweat of her agony. Her only attendant sat hunched on a chair nearby. Ellasif had just entered her tenth winter. Her small face furrowed in concentration as she committed some of her mother's more inventive phrases to memory.

When the waves of pain ebbed and Marit lay limp and panting, Ellasif dipped a cloth into an infusion of soothing herbs. She wrung it nearly dry and draped it over her mother's forehead. It was bad fortune that the child had decided to come tonight, when their mother was already weak with fever, but the midwife had not been surprised. Everyone knew that storms called to the unborn.

And such a storm! Wind howled as it stalked through the village, scrabbling at the cottage and snatching away handfuls of thatching. Shards of ice clattered against the shuttered windows. Hailstones tumbled down the chimney to die hissing in the hearth fire. The candle on the bedside table trembled as yet another peal of thunder rolled in from the forest separating the village of White Rook from the eternally wintry land of Irrisen.

It occurred to Ellasif that the distant booming she'd heard since nightfall might not be thunder. The possibility of what else the sound might be stole her breath, and her lips silently shaped one of the curses she'd just learned.

Ellasif had never given much thought to the stories village children whispered of the winterfolk, or to the maze of living fences that kept those fabled horrors at bay. But then, she had never imagined that the fences might fall.

She ran to the window and unlatched the shutter. Standing on tiptoe, she peered out into the clearing.

Rain and sleet fell steadily, a frigid downpour that clung to the roofs and trees in ever-thickening sheets of ice. Undeterred, the people of White Rook continued their work. The bonfire blazing in the village center cast a broad circle of light and—so it seemed to Ellasif—far more shadows than could be accounted for by the human inhabitants alone. There were restless spirits among the houses, long and small.

Most of the village women tended the birch grove, a natural palisade stretching north-south from the cliffs to the river. A lattice of vines connected the trees in an intricate pattern that was both maze and fence. The women went from one groaning tree to another, shaking ice from the drooping limbs. An elder birch faltered under its burden and broke with a sound like a thousand shattered mead jugs. The women scattered as the tree crashed to the ground, bringing with it several of its smaller neighbors and the web of interlaced vines connecting them.

The clatter had not yet died away when another deep report rolled across the village. It was much closer than any previous boom, and there was no mistaking the sound that followed: the slow scream of a falling tree.

Ellasif braced for the impact, her breath frozen as she counted off the moments. The ground-shaking crash signaled the death of an ancient pine, one of the pillars supporting the fence of tree-thick vines White Rook's people had shaped and tended for generations.

The outer perimeter was coming down.

They could expect no assistance from any king. Opir Eightfingers had shown little interest in defending the border with Irrisen, despite the proximity of his capital, and there were those who said he was no true king for this and other reasons. There had been a time when Trollheim declared the village part of its territory, but Castellan Freyr Darkwine had not sent his Blackravens so far south since the start of the interregnum. The men and women of White Rook stood alone against the invaders.

The village women abandoned the birch grove to guard against whatever might come through the breach. Ellasif's hands itched for the grip of a weapon as she watched the women scramble into position. She scrubbed her palms against the rough wool of her skirt and tried to push the battle-lust aside. She knew her place was here. Soon she would be an elder sister, with all the responsibility that role entailed.

But the frenzy of battle preparations proved too tempting to resist. Ellasif lingered at the window, watching as men rolled barrels of vjarik, a distilled spirit strong enough to blind a linnorm, into the stone-paved trench that formed a barrier around the village. Warriors took up positions a hundred paces behind the fire moat, weapons in hand and tall wooden shields lying ready on the ground before them. Ellasif's eyes brightened with anticipation. She'd never seen a shield wall in battle. According to the bards' tales, few foes could overcome a barrier formed of Ulfen warriors.

Spear warriors formed up a dozen paces behind the front line of warriors, weapons in hand. Several of the older boys dragged bundles of spears from the weapon huts. One had already taken his place beside his warrior, four weapons held ready to pass: two slim throwing spears, a sturdy pike, and a short spear for hand-to-hand fighting.

In the center of the village clearing, behind the warriors and their boys, three old men fed the bonfire. The storm fought them with wind-driven sleet and sudden gusts that dove down to throttle the leaping flames or hurl them up onto the thatched roofs of the surrounding houses. But the huge fire pit contained the blaze, and the circle of stone pillars supporting the conical roof and chimney of the village center kept the wood dry enough to burn. Buckets of pitch stood near the fire pit, bristling with the shafts of fire arrows.

Behind the pit, more warriors gathered, readying weapons ranging from swords to pitchforks to long-handled torches. Any child-stealing winterfolk who came through the sundered fences would have to run a gauntlet of fire and iron before they reached any of the vulnerable children or mothers. Everyone else in the village, spearman or shield maiden, would die before they let that happen.

Nor would those who survived the ordeal find the village children easy to capture. Atop every house was a loft with narrow windows nestled in the gables of each steep roof. The shutters had been flung open to reveal boys and maidens too young to wield sword or spear or battleaxe, but no less deadly with a bow.

Ellasif glanced toward the ladder that led to her family's loft. A sturdy bow of well-seasoned yew awaited her there. Her gaze shifted to the maidensword over the hearth. A sigh of longing and frustration sang through her teeth. Her mother's first weapon, despite village custom, would never be hers. Ulfen warriors were famously tall and strong, but Ellasif had always been small for her age, and seemed destined to remain so. No one of her stature would ever become a shield maiden. Never mind that the only boy who'd ever dared to taunt her about it had walked with a limp from full moon to well past new moon.

"Ellasif, come away—"

A pained gasp cut the admonition short. Ellasif spun toward the bed.

Her mother's night robe, already damp with sweat, was drenched with more ominous stains. Young as she was, Ellasif knew what this meant. The babe must come soon, or mother and child would both perish.

Ellasif knelt at the foot of her mother's bed. "I will catch the babe, and I will care for it," she said. "This I swear. Now do your part."

The ceremonial words were meant for a sister or a close midwife, but Ellasif spoke them with the assurance and conviction of a grown woman. Marit did as her daughter bade her, propping herself up on her elbows and roaring a wordless battle cry as she fought to urge her child out of the warm cavern of her body and into the cold world.

Marit's pains stopped short of their purpose. She fell back onto the bed, pale as a wraith. She clutched the damp sheets and regarded her bloody fingers. A shadow of despair crossed her face.

"Go, Sif," she groaned. "Fetch Agithra."

Ellasif shook her head. "She will not come. She cannot. Midwife or not, if she left her place now, Red Ochme would skewer her with her own spear and roast her over the fire pit."

"You, my daughter, should not have to watch—" Marit's voice broke on a ragged cough. She cleared her throat. "You should not have to watch with me, or deliver this babe."

"Who better?" said Ellasif. "Who tended the goats last summer when they dropped their kids? I lost none of them, not even the white nanny and her tangle of twins! This babe will have fewer legs and, gods willing, no sharp hooves."

A weak laugh escaped Marit's chapped lips. "Gods willing," she said. She lifted one hand to her rounded belly and traced over her babe an ancient rune of protection: a deep crescent bisected by a straight line, the footprint symbol of She Who Watches, the white raven. Most of the villagers would have called the gesture superstition or even witchcraft, but Ellasif nodded her approval. The other villagers might pray only to Torag or Desna, Gorum or Erastil, and that was well. Life would be simpler if gods were the only powers to be appeased, but when was life simple? A thousand spirits interfered with human life every year.

A blast of wind rocked the cottage. The shutter Ellasif had unlatched flew open and cracked against the outer wall. The candle flame jumped like a startled cat and vanished into the dark.

Ellasif ran outside. Sleet stung her face, and the wind whipped her skirts around her legs as she wrestled the shutter back into place. She shot the outer bolt to hold it closed and turned just in time to witness the birch grove's destruction.

Already bent low under their weight of ice, the slender white trees could bear no more. Icy gusts ripped away limbs and sent them spinning across the hard ground between grove and village. Whole trees came crashing down, leaving splintered stumps or holes clawed up by their roots. Only the strongest remained, including the enormous birch whose white trunk had been carved with the image of the bird that gave the village its name.

"The fire moat!" cried a village man. "Light the fire moat!"

Ellasif's gaze darted toward the man who'd shouted the warning. Beyond the birch grove, the forest was alive with pairs of gleaming eyes. Someone threw a torch into the moat. Blue flame leaped toward the sky and raced along the stone trench—a firewall meant to frighten the wolf pack into retreat.

"Those are no mere forest wolves," Ellasif whispered to herself. Ordinary wolves came singing to the moon. These creatures attacked as silently as they'd gathered. Great white monsters as big as ice bears, they broke from the shadows and charged the fire moat in a double line formation as ordered as any Ulfen shield wall.

"Spears away!" bellowed a female voice.

Ellasif's heart lifted at the sound. Red Ochme's command soared above the storm as surely as her raiding ships had once crested the wild waves. Nothing could vanquish the old warrior.

The warriors in the front line dropped to one knee and snapped their shields into position, edges overlapping to form a solid wall. Behind them the warriors raised their spears, ran three steps, and unleashed a thicket of death.

Ellasif's gaze followed Agithra's spear as it soared over the kneeling warriors and flew straight toward the fire moat. Twenty spears or more followed it, and all disappeared through the fire. Sharp yelps from behind the fiery barrier proved the truth of their aim.

The first rank of winter wolves leaped through the flames, fangs bared and eyes glowing with eldritch blue light. Ellasif held her breath at the sight of them. They were as beautiful as they were terrible, and for an instant she wondered how it would feel to plunge her hand into that dense white fur.

Bowstrings sang in twanging chorus from the cottage lofts. A storm of arrows swept toward the fire moat. Most bounced off thick pelts, but three of the winter wolves stumbled and went down. Two rose and ran again despite the arrows protruding from their bodies. The third wolf lay twitching, a white shaft protruding from its eye socket.

Ellasif's heart triumphed as the children of White Rook made good their first volley. There would not be time for a second.

"Brace!" howled Red Ochme.

The warriors ran forward and set their pikes against the shield wall, iron points angled toward the charging pack. All the warriors, shields and spears, braced for impact.

But the wolves did not challenge the wall. To Ellasif's astonishment, the first rank slid to a stop and reared up on their hind legs. They set their forepaws on the upper edges of the shields, and at last they sang, but not to the moon. They sang to winter.

Crystalline clouds poured from the wolves' jaws, shimmering in the firelight as they spread out into icy fog. The frost riming the creatures' mouths whitened the faces of the warriors who crashed backward to the ground, rigid as felled trees.

The second wave of winter wolves struck, hurling themselves against the shields before the surviving warriors could recover from the freezing blast. The wall jolted back, slamming into the swords the warriors raised. Savage jaws snatched away the warriors' weapons, many tearing flesh the icy breath had welded to frozen metal. The disarmed warriors reached with ruined hands for the daggers in their boot sheaths.

But the winter wolves had already retreated. As they loped away, Ellasif prayed the creatures would disappear into the forest. Defying her hope, they stopped just short of the guttering vjarik flame and wheeled about for another attack.

Ellasif caught her breath. The fallen spearfighters left gaps above the shield wall, breaches the winter wolves could easily leap through. The enemy saw their chance. On they came in a chaotic rush.

"Shields up!" shrieked Red Ochme.

The surviving spear throwers fell back, and the warriors in the shield wall stood as one, raising the wall to meet the charge.

Not all of the wolves leaped. Some came in low to attack the warriors' booted shins, while others worried the edges of the shield wall with their enormous jaws. One of the smaller wolves scrambled up the steep cliff on the village's north border, only to fall back among the pack.

In the chaos that followed, Ulfen battle cries mingled with the snarls of the monsters, but these were not simple beasts. The sound of human voices emerging from the slavering jaws of the winter wolves sent a cold drop of fear oozing through Ellasif's guts. A huge wolf bitch hung off to one side, adding to the confusion by shouting commands in mimicry of Red Ochme's voice. Ellisif had never seen the winter wolf before, but she had heard its legend. If this were the dread wolf huntress of the winter witches, then this night could surely be the doom of White Rook.

The shield wall held. Warriors stabbed at the wolves who reared over the shields. They reached down to fend off snapping jaws from below. When one warrior fell, others shifted to closed the gap. The villagers dragged away those of their wounded whom the wolves had not yet torn from their reach. Ellasif tried desperately to ignore the horrible rending sounds from the far side of the shield wall as the enemy desecrated the village defenders.

But the shield wall was shrinking, and soon it would no longer fill the gap between the cliff and the river. The warriors behind the shield wall readied weapons for the inevitable breach.

Ellasif's friend Jadrek ran past clutching a cut-off bill in his hand. Its broad head curved in a hook to one side, a perfect weapon for cutting the hamstrings of foes across a shield wall. Jadrek jolted to a stop and spun back toward Ellasif. His expression was so fierce that for a moment Ellasif expected him to throw the weapon in her face.

"Attend your task," he growled, reciting Red Ochme's first rule of battle.

A wave of shame swept Ellasif. Everyone in White Rook knew what to do in case of an attack. She was expected to be in the loft, greeting anything that crossed the fire moat with an arrow to the throat. Nothing, not even tending her mother, should have kept her from her battle task. Everyone in the village had already obeyed his or her duty.

Everyone but Ellasif.

She acknowledged Jadrek's reproof with a curt nod and ran back into the house. She barred the door behind her. Straight to the bed she strode, pausing only briefly when she heard Red Ochme call for fire arrows. She longed to be in the battle, not on its edge.

Marit bowed her back in another fit of agony. Her breath came in faint gasps. Ellasif hurried to the foot of the bed and saw that the babe was finally emerging. She cradled the crowning head and slipped her fingers around the tiny neck to make sure the cord wasn't entangled. All seemed well. There was no reason the child could not be born now.

"Once more," she urged.

Marit's eyes fluttered open. Her gaze focused on her daughter's face. Ellasif smiled with more confidence than she felt and gave her mother an encouraging nod.

Her mother gave one final effort, and the newborn slid into her sister's waiting hands.

"A girl," Ellasif exulted, holding the infant up for their mother to see.

Marit smiled and fainted dead away.

And so it happened that Ellasif was the only witness to her infant sister's first breath. What followed was not a newborn's wail but merry peals of laughter.

Shock froze Ellasif's limbs, and dread gripped her heart with fingers of ice. Everyone knew that first-breath laughter was the sign of a tiren'kii.

She stared at the bloody infant still tethered by its birth cord, still laughing. She wondered how this could be her newborn sister, this tiny creature so new to life and so soon fated to die. She was cursed.

The folk of White Rook would sooner carry a haunch of venison through a sow bear's den than allow so dangerous a child to live. No one knew exactly what the tiren'kii were, nor why they occasionally possessed Ulfen newborns, but understanding such mysteries held little allure for Ellasif's people. What they did understand was that such children were dangerous, their spirits tainted by the fey powers harbored in nearby Irrisen. No such child could be suffered to live among the Ulfen.

And yet, Ellasif thought, this was her sister. She had sworn to protect this child.

A new voice joined the chaos of storm and battle, a sound born of the unholy marriage of a beast's roar and an eagle's cry. It reverberated in the deepest recesses of Ellasif's body, chilling her liver and paralyzing her lungs. It was a sound she had heard before only from a great distance, a sound that had made her huddle under her blankets and recite the three prayers she remembered over and over until dawn.

It was the shriek of an ice troll.

Marit's eyes snapped open, the reflex of a warrior coming fully awake at the sound of danger.

"Ellasif, to the loft," she croaked. She sounded even worse than Ellasif had feared earlier.

Ellasif laid the infant down on her mother's belly. Marit gripped her eldest daughter's wrist with startling strength. Her fever-bright eyes burned.

"Take the babe to the loft," she commanded. "You swore to care for her. I hold you to your oath."

Before Ellasif could respond, her mother slipped back into unconsciousness.

Ellasif set her jaw and went to work with sure hands. Everything lay ready: a knife to cut the cord, clean linen thread to tie it off, a soft blanket in which to wrap the babe. Moments later, Ellasif climbed the ladder to the loft, one hand holding the rungs, the other clasping the bundled infant to her shoulder.

She laid the baby on the straw mattress to free her hands and dragged the ladder up into the loft. A rope and pulley attached to the ceiling secured a heavy wooden door. It was scant protection from troll invaders, but it was the best Ellasif could offer her sister.

The boards beneath her feet shuddered as the crash of another doomed tree shook the village. A moment later, the door burst open.

Ellasif's father, Kjell, lurched into the house. Blood streaked his yellow beard, and his wild gaze swept the room. At the sight of his empty hands, Ellasif knew true fear.

Her father had left his place. He'd put aside his axe before battle's end. Ellasif could imagine no surer proof that White Rook was defeated.

Kjell ran to the bed and swept his wife into his arms, blankets and all. He whirled toward the loft.

"Hurry, Ellasif!" he shouted. "The north pine is falling."

Their house stood at the northern end of the village crescent, closest to the forest. The groaning creak of a falling tree grew louder. There was no time to push the ladder back down. She could jump and roll, but not with the baby in her arms.

For the first time, Ellasif noticed the bleating of her goats outside. The byre stood separate from the cottage, but the roof and loft ran over both buildings. A second, smaller hatch led down into the pen.

She was reaching for the baby when her father's shout drew her attention back to the cottage floor. A huge winter wolf crouched in the doorway, blocking her parents' escape.

"You slew my mate," the beast said in the rough female voice so like Red Ochme's. "Now watch me kill yours."

A defiant curse bubbled to Ellasif's lips, but the oath she'd sworn forced her to silence. She clutched the baby tight to her breast and ran.

Ellasif slid down the ladder into the goat byre and waded through the milling herd. She unlatched the door and burst into the clearing amid a small stampede of panicked animals. The north pine had broken free of its halter of vines and tilted swiftly. Wind shrieked through its branches as it plummeted toward the house.

Ellasif ran through the storm, ducking under the swing of an ice troll's club as she headed for the weapon shack closest to the hot spring. It was stone-built and solid, and it would be warm inside. The baby would be as safe there as she could be anywhere in White Rook.

The tree crashed with an impact Ellasif felt in her bones. She chanced a quick look back to see if her parents had escaped.

One glance told the tale. She heard herself whimper, but was too heartbroken to be ashamed of the sound.

"I'll take that bundle, bitch cub," growled a familiar voice.

Ellasif had not heard the wolf approach. She stumbled and fell hard on one knee.

Steel swept over her head, and the wolf yelped in pain. Ellasif scrambled aside and rose in time to see Red Ochme bury her sword in the hump of the winter wolf's shoulder. The tough old warrior jerked the weapon free and held it at guard, but the sword's task was finished. The wolf's legs folded, and she fell heavily on one side. The blood pouring from the wound stopped when the wolf drew a breath. She had suffered a sucking wound, and soon her own lungs would drown her.

Bloody froth spilled from the creature's jaws and froze on her muzzle. She fixed her strange blue eyes to her killer's face.

"Die, old woman," she cursed. "Drown in a pool of your own piss. Perish, forgotten by your pack." The wolf turned her head to Ellasif, and her lips curled in a canine sneer. "Die weaponless, like the bitch cub's sire."

Something deep within Ellasif cracked, and something else slipped free. She snatched a dagger from Red Ochme's belt, thrust the baby into the warrior's arms, and leaped upon the dying wolf. With one blow she severed the plumy white tail, not caring that no one in the village, not even Red Ochme herself, had ever dared to take a winter wolf trophy. Ellasif brandished the grisly talisman at the wolf that had killed her parents.

"Die, you miserable old bitch," she snarled. "Die and know your tail hangs from this cub's belt."

"Ellasif!"

Ochme's tone told Ellasif that she'd uttered the girl's name more than once before Ellasif heard it. Ochme took her knife back and pressed the baby into Ellasif's arms. The expression on the battle leader's face was impossible for Ellasif to read.

"Go, child," she said. "Take that babe to shelter."

Ellasif ran, the wailing baby clasped to her chest. Hail pelted them as she wove a path through the ruins of the battle. Most of the winter wolves had fallen. A steaming puddle of gore told of ice trolls and fire arrows, but two of the monsters still lumbered through the village. Small packs of ice goblins ran here and there, singing cheerful obscenities as they swarmed cottage after cottage.

Ellasif darted between two of the small houses and skidded to a stop. An eight-foot-tall troll blocked her path, the monster facing off against Agithra and her spear. The creature swung its club in a pendulous arc. The blow snapped Agithra's weapon like an autumn twig and lifted the midwife off of her feet. She bent in half and dropped to the ground like a rag doll.

Three axe-wielding warriors pushed past Ellasif and converged on the troll, hacking it limb from limb. Behind them came children who picked up the smaller troll pieces and ran them to the fire pit. Not every piece of a dismembered troll would grow back into another monster, but the villagers of White Rook had learned to be thorough. Ellasif darted off to find another path.

A hand clutched at her feet. She stumbled but ran on. Her stomach clenched when she realized the hand still gripped her ankle, fingers digging into her boot leather. She set her jaw and kept going, dragging along the huge blue hand and its severed arm. The armory was just ahead.

She tucked the baby into a wooden bin and closed and bolted the hut door. Her charge secured, she looked around for a weapon. A woman's corpse lay nearby, so mangled that only her long red braids identified her as Tanja, mother of Ellasif's friend Olenka. The woman's short sword was buried to the hilt in the body of the winter wolf she'd died slaying.

Ellasif braced her free foot on the wolf's bloodied white pelt and tugged the sword free. She dragged her burden closer to the fire pit, where the battle-churned ground was as soft as summer loam, and stabbed through the blue hand. She leaned on the sword to thoroughly impale the troll limb before jerking her foot free. Lifting the skewered arm and hurling it into the fire took every bit of strength she could muster.

Oily flame leaped up around the severed arm. Perhaps twenty paces away, a blue head screamed in agony, still attached to one arm and a mangled chunk of shoulder, but little else.

Ellasif caught a passing lad by the arm and pointed at the troll's head. "Missed one," she said. The severed head had already begun regenerating a windpipe and a dark pulsing bud that would become a heart. The boy nodded and hurried to dispose of the head.

For a moment Ellasif simply stood by the pit, at a loss for what to do next. Everyone else seemed to know his task and place. Two children with pitchforks stabbed a troll hand and ran it back to the fire pit, where elders ensured every scrap of their enemies was destroyed.

Ellasif's gaze fell on Jadrek. He stood with his back to a cottage wall, knife and bill whirling as he fended off a pair of goblins. A surge of feral joy filled her heart. Ellasif hauled the sword up high over one shoulder and charged toward her friend.

Jadrek's eyes widened as he saw her approach. One of the goblins turned toward Ellasif. Her first wild thrust cut his startled cry short as she stabbed the little monster directly in the mouth. Then she turned her body and directed her momentum and the weight of the sword into a leg-slashing cut. Bright blood sprayed from his severed artery. The goblin's disbelieving expression would have been comical in other circumstances. It looked down at its wound, then up into Ellasif's face with an expression of supreme pique. Then it died and fell to the cold ground.

The second goblin wailed and crumpled, Jadrek's bill stuck deep in its craw. Jadrek knelt on the goblin's narrow chest and slit its throat with his knife.

A goblin pack boiled toward them as he rose. Jadrek offered his bloody knife to Ellasif. "Want to trade?"

Ellasif scoffed and kept her sword.

She ran to meet the foremost goblin. Her first strike knocked aside its pike, giving her an opening to kick the creature between the legs. The goblin squealed and doubled over. Ellasif's backswing missed its head but sliced the leather jerkin of the next goblin. The creature jumped back, tripping the three behind it.

Ellasif lunged, sword thrusting deep between a goblin's ribs. She was dimly aware of a knife scoring her arm, of filthy claws and fetid breath and horrible high-pitched curses, and Jadrek fighting at her side, his knife flashing again and again.

She felt as though she were in paradise. There were no troubling thoughts, no doubts, no uncertainties. She wanted to live, and to live she had to kill. Nothing in the wide world was more glorious.

When the pile of goblins lay silent—and perhaps more thoroughly slain than necessity demanded—the young warriors rose and regarded each other for a timeless moment. Jadrek's lean body shook with the exertion of his own breath. There was terror in his heart to be sure, but he radiated even more power and courage, and Ellasif felt something within her stir and move toward him. She hesitated, and their gazes locked for a moment. Ellasif licked her dry lips. Jadrek glanced away, his shoulders slumped. The moment was gone.

"It's over," said Jadrek. His voice was mingled relief and regret.

Ellasif wasn't so sure it was over. The night was filled with the muted groans of the dying, the rattle of hail against the roof thatching, the indignant demands of a toddler who could not understand why his mother would not rise to hold him. Beneath it all lay a silent, trembling energy that Ellasif could not name.

A deep thump resounded through the forest, then another. By the time Ellasif could identify the sound as footsteps, they had accelerated into a charge. She looked up at a shadow upon the snowy trees and saw a thatched hovel flying incongruously above the ground.

No, she realized. It was not flying. Rather, the hut was perched upon two enormous scaled legs. Ellasif's first impression was that they were the limbs of some emaciated golden dragon, but then she recognized the avian angle of the joints and the black talons of a chicken. This was no mere monster.

The walking hut stepped over a fallen birch and strutted into the village. No one uttered a command. No one raised a weapon. None dared defy Baba Yaga, the mother of the Irrisen queens, or whatever dread emissary the great witch had commanded to direct her dancing hut.

At the southern edge of the village, a baby wailed. The hut whirled toward the sound. Its sudden movement broke the spell. Warriors forgot their injuries and rushed to attack.

Fire arrows streaked toward the hut and bounced away without touching the shingled walls. A white-braided old warrior charged with battleaxe raised high. One enormous talon flicked him away with no more effort than Ellasif might expend on a gnat. The hut crushed two spear warriors underfoot as it stalked toward the house containing the child whose cries had alerted it.

The infant was quiet now, no doubt hushed by its siblings. The hut stopped beside the house and tilted to one side like a bird listening for worms. Faster than thought, it lifted one clawed foot and tore away half the roof.

More axe-wielding warriors closed in. A lump rose in Ellasif's throat as she recognized her father's weapon in another man's hands. The hut trampled the men into bloody ruins with its scythe-like talons as it strode to the next cottage.

A dark square on the ground caught Ellasif's eye. She stooped to pick up a wooden shingle, larger than those on the village homes. She sniffed it. It smelled of cooking smoke and herbs, old blood and the skin of reptiles. It smelled exactly how Ellasif imagined a witch's hut to smell.

She broke it in two and tossed one half onto a smoldering wolf carcass. The shingle flared into light, just as any ordinary bit of dry kindling might do.

Ellasif ran to Jadrek, who was stitching a deep gash across the face of Ivanick, his father. Waving the shingle as she ran, she shouted, "It's wood! Baba Yaga's hut is wood!"

The boy scowled and reached for a flask of vjarik. He poured some onto a rag to clean the wound.

"It's wood," Ellasif repeated. She threw the shingle at Jadrek.

He batted it away. "So? What else would it be?"

"Woods burns," she persisted. "The fire arrows can't get past Baba Yaga's magic. None of our attacks can get past. But if we send fire into the hut in a different way, we might surprise it."

Ivanick considered her for a moment, his blue eyes peering out from a mask of blood and matted pale hair. Then he took the flask from his son and removed the cork with his teeth. "I will try."

The warrior snatched a torch from a nearby stand and strode toward the walking hut. Before he could get close enough to throw the torch, the hut snatched him up in one mighty talon and flung him atop the nearest cottage. The hut tilted precipitously at the motion, and through the flapping shutters of a window, Ellasif glimpsed a strange sight. In the center of the hut, bound to a plain wooden chair, sat a tiny white-haired doll. Silver-blue eyes and a porcelain face were all the detail Ellasif saw before the hut righted itself, scratching up deep furrows in the frozen ground with its gargantuan chicken talons.

Dry thatch exposed by the hut's explorations caught fire. Ivanick staggered to his feet, limned with blue vjarik flame. He ran along the wooden roof ridge, flaming brighter with each step, and hurled himself at the hut.

He caught the edge of a shuttered window, lost his grip, and slid down the shingled wall. Somehow he found a handhold, and then another. How, Ellasif could not say. The fire surrounding him blazed furiously, its greedy flames devouring his clothes and gnawing at the flesh beneath.

The hut whirled and spun, trying to throw the man off, but Ivanick clung like a burr despite the flames surrounding him. The wood beneath his burning body blackened in the shape of his shadow.

Ellasif reached for Jadrek's hand and gripped it hard. "He'll fall," she cried, half hoping that he would.

The burning man pulled a dagger from his belt and drove it through the sleeve of his other arm, pinning himself through flesh and bone to the smoldering wall. Almost immediately he slumped, overcome by flame and smoke.

Still the hut did not burn.

Ellasif ran to Red Ochme and seized her arm. "Lamp oil!"

Understanding widened the old warrior's eyes. She shouted the order. Several women came running with vessels and hurled them at the hut. The pottery shattered against the hut's magical shields, but some of the oil splashed through. Flames licked at the hut's shingles and sped upward toward the thatch. The hut twisted away and ran, flaming, toward the river. It plunged over the steep bank and disappeared with a great splash, then bobbed to the surface, a halo of flame around the crest of its roof.

It disappeared again. A flicker of orange light touched the surface a moment later and then vanished. The villagers watched for another emergence.

It felt to Ellasif that the entire world held its breath.

Vapor burst from the gulley in a hut-shaped cloud and soared off toward the east. The storm clouds fell in behind it like obedient hounds following their master home. Hail and darkness surrendered to a silver sky crowned with a wisp of rosy sunrise.

In the silence that followed, villagers stood blinking, unable able to comprehend that the terrible night was finally over, that they had survived.

Ellasif ran to the armory, her throat tight with dread. The baby's cries brought a smile of relief to her face. She unlatched the door and swept up the red-faced infant.

"I'll milk the white nanny as soon as I can catch her," she promised the babe. "You can drink as much as you like."

She kept crooning to the baby as she joined the knot of children gathered near the fire pit. The sight of her sister—her ward now, her child—soothed some of the anguish of the loss of her parents. Some of the other children were already being led away to new homes by villagers all too accustomed to the orphaning of their neighbors' children, but there were more orphans than families to take them. To Ellasif's surprise, Red Ochme walked along the line of children, inspecting them as a war leader might eye recruits. She paused before Olenka, tall and flame-haired like her warrior mother.

Of course, Ellasif thought. Olenka is the very image of a shield maiden, everything I am not.

But Red Ochme moved on. She strode directly to Ellasif and looked her up and down. Ellasif's face flushed. She was afraid she had shamed herself before the village's greatest hero when she mutilated the corpse of the defeated winter wolf commander. Still, Ochme's gaze lingered on Ellasif's dry eyes and bloody hands, which clutched her swaddled sister.

"If you work hard, I will take you into my home. I will train you. You will become strong."

Ellasif could only stare. The dream taking shape before her was too large for any words she knew. Red Ochme saw the answer in Ellasif's eyes and sealed the deal with a curt nod. Then she added, "First you must find a home for that child."

"No." The word burst from Ellasif's throat unbidden. "You must take both of us, Liv and me together."

And just like that, her sister had a name.

The warrior frowned and shook her head. "Anngard has a babe at breast. She can feed another."

"Liv drinks goat's milk," Ellsaif said firmly. "She will not be the first warrior of White Rook to be raised on it."

"And who will tend those goats and raise this baby?" Ochme demanded. "A warrior's training is nothing easy, and you will have many chores."

Ellasif lifted her chin stubbornly. "I will do it all."

A long moment of silence passed as the two warriors, the old and the young, took each other's measure. Red Ochme shrugged. "We'll see."

Emotions too powerful to name tore at Ellasif's heart as she followed Red Ochme to the cottage they would share. She would become a warrior, trained by the village war leader. She would claim her mother's maiden-sword, and someday she would temper a sword of her own in the blood of her enemies. As a sword maiden of the Lands of the Linnorm Kings, she would be respected and feared. She could claim the place that was written in her nature, as much a part of her as a nestling bird's yearning for the sky. But how could she be glad of this—of anything—when her parents lay dead in the ruin of their home?

And what of the uncanny storm and the attack that followed? All the stories Ellasif had heard about Baba Yaga's hut suggested that its purposes might be unknowable, but not capricious. It had come to White Rook for a reason. It seemed to be looking for a baby.

She knew then with certainty that it had been looking for Liv, now her daughter as much as her sister. Liv, the child who'd laughed to welcome the tiren'kii.

Try as she might, Ellasif could find no other explanation. The tiren'kii had drawn the winterfolk's attention. They would come again, for everyone knew that once a tiren'kii possessed a child it did not leave as long as the child lived. For the safety of everyone in White Rook, Ellasif should tell the village elders what she had seen and heard at Liv's birth.

Even as the thought formed, Ellasif's arms tightened around her tiny sister. She'd sworn an oath. Her duty to Liv came before anything else, anyone else, even her own ambition.

Silence, Ellasif decided as she padded along behind the old warrior. Silence would protect her sister today.

Chapter One
The Ice Sculptures

Declan Avari squinted into the oversized spyglass mounted on the north edge of the rooftop observatory, rolling one dial after another to adjust the focus. One final tweak, and the black turrets of Castle Korvosa came sharply into view.

It was an imposing sight. Torchlight gleamed against black marble, casting long shadows down the ancient pyramid upon which the castle stood. From this distance the imps that wheeled around the towers resembled a swarm of gnats, black specks silhouetted against the rising moon.

The soft thump of wings drew Declan's attention to the grape-covered pergola on the southern end of the roof. A pale blue house drake, a recent addition to the clutch that inhabited the turret of the Frisky Unicorn, his family's inn, often followed him to the observatory. The little creature settled down amid the grapevines, folded his wings, and turned tiny golden eyes toward the castle.

My cousins are in spring flight.

This thought projected directly into Declan's mind, along with an image of small flocks of migrating dragons.

"Ah." He nodded. A flock of randy drakes near the imp nests would mean only one thing. "So the skies of Korvosa will be one big tavern brawl tonight?"

Yes. The telepathic voice sounded wistful to Declan's mind. Enmity between the imps and the tiny dragons ran hot and deep. With the possible exception of a plump mouse or a dollop of fresh butter, there was nothing a house drake enjoyed more than smiting imp-shaped evil.

"Plan on joining the fun?"

Maybe later.

The drake burrowed into the vines. Leaves rustled, and a tiny squeak, abruptly ended, announced a successful hunt. Since the little dragon would be happily occupied with his meal, Declan turned his attention back to the castle.

Now that he thought about it, he noted more activity in the night sky than usual. Imps and dragons in battle was a sight so familiar it seldom drew a second glance in Korvosa. Declan was not entirely certain what this said about the city.

He went to the astrolabe, a flat metal disk covered with intricate markings and mounted on an iron plinth. A series of dials and levers allowed Declan to set its measure upon the Grand Mastaba. The sandstone pyramid provided a foundation for Castle Korvosa and, more importantly for Declan's purposes, a known measure against which to test his skills.

After several moments of fiddling with the dials, he jotted down his figures and frowned at the result. His calculation of the Grand Mastaba's height was off by more than ten yards. If he were ever going to become a credible mapmaker, he'd need to do better.

With a sigh, Declan turned to the shallow basin of water that dominated the roof, a round reflecting pool in which tiny star-shadows glimmered. The markings along the edges of the pool, similar to those on the astrolabe, provided a second, simpler means of calculating angle and distance.

A thick book lay open on a pedestal nearby, revealing figures arranged in three columns. Declan's apprenticeship to the famed astronomer Majeed Nores had been devoted primarily to taking measurements of the stars, repeating each computation with the reflecting pool, and comparing the difference. Majeed expected him to fill the book before the next new moon.

"The nights aren't long enough for all this work," he muttered. "And I suspect there aren't enough stars in the sky to fill a book that size."

"Hello, the roof!"

Declan turned toward the stairs, glad of the interruption. His smile dimmed when he recognized Jamang Kira, a childhood nemesis he'd not seen in years.

While Declan was no more than average height and build, he stood nearly a head taller than his visitor and probably outweighed him by half. Jamang had always been small and scrawny, with a disposition that reminded Declan of the overbred lapdogs favored by the matrons of Korvosa. Some men might have rued such a small stature, but not Jamang. Declan knew that, from boyhood, Jamang had learned that when someone was busy guarding his ankles against a nip, it was easier to slip a knife between his ribs.

Jamang strutted toward Declan like a bantam cock, and his confident smile proclaimed he was sure of his welcome, not just here but anywhere in Korvosa. Jamang wore the city's colors from the red velvet slouch hat perched on his raven-black hair to his fine crimson jacket to the gleaming ebony of his boots. Riding proudly on his chest was a silver amulet proclaiming his graduation from the Acadamae, Korvosa's most famous school of magic.

They exchanged one of the back-thumping embraces common to young men and quickly drew apart. After a moment's study, Jamang offered, "You're looking well."

Declan did not miss the faint note of surprise in Jamang's voice. He nodded toward Jamang's new Acadamae amulet. "It would appear that congratulations are due."

"For many reasons," Jamang said smugly. "I have recently acquired a position with Somar Nevinoff. I trust you know the name?"

A reply was neither necessary nor expected. Everyone in Korvosa who had a passing interest in magic—and that included nearly everyone in Korvosa—knew the name Somar Nevinoff. The man was a powerful necromancer with more imagination than scruples.

"I can think of few situations better suited to developing your . . . natural inclinations," Declan said. He barely concealed a smirk.

Jamang's face brightened, and he made a little bow. "How gracious of you to say so."

Declan inclined his head politely to cover his wasted mockery. "To what do I owe the honor of your visit?"

The young necromancer's countenance settled into more serious lines, an effort at gravitas so studious that Declan suspected Jamang had practiced it before a mirror.

"Concern," Jamang said. "I'm deeply concerned about you, Avari. As one of your oldest friends, I felt a duty to speak out."

Declan gritted his teeth. Jamang's pompous intonations foreshadowed a conversation Declan did not wish to have. Still, there was courtesy to be observed.

"Speak out about what?"

Jamang swept one hand in an arc that took in Declan, the rooftop observatory, and the not-quite-fashionable Cliffside neighborhood Majeed Nores's manor occupied. He sniffed. "This is no place for a wizard of your talents."

Alarms chimed in Declan's brain. Flattery had never been among the weapons in Jamang's arsenal, and Declan doubted it was a skill he had learned at the Acadamae. Whatever had brought Jamang here was something he wanted badly enough to overcome his scorn for the innkeeper's son.

"I'm afraid my master shares your opinion of my ability," Declan said, deliberately misunderstanding the compliment, "but since my apprentice fee is paid in full and he is not inclined to return it, he bears with me."

"My point precisely," Jamang said. He stabbed a finger in Declan's direction for emphasis. "You are still an apprentice, and to an astronomer."

"It's an interesting study," said Declan.

The necromancer shook his head sadly. "Such a waste! You, who set out on a wizard's path—although why you chose to study magic at the Theumanexus confounds me, considering that the Acadamae holds thrice the prestige and many times the opportunities . . ." He frowned, seeming to have lost his train of thought.

"I'm not interested in fame and fortune," suggested Declan.

Jamang's laugh was as sharp as a dog's yap. He shook his head as if he'd just heard the most ridiculous joke. Of course, Declan thought. In Korvosa, avowing one's disinclination toward fame, wealth, or power would almost certainly be perceived as a deliberate absurdity.

"You could almost persuade me of that," Jamang said. "The Theumanexus was bad enough, but why you would leave it in favor of the university is beyond my comprehension."

"The University of Korvosa has a fine art school."

The necromancer pursed his lips. "I suppose I can see your attraction to art, all things considered, but why astronomy?"

"Why do you care?" Declan said.

"Perhaps I presume upon our friendship," said Jamang. "That alone would not excuse my curiosity, but something your brother said preys upon my mind."

"What about my brother?" growled Declan.

Jamang was oblivious to Declan's mood, or pretended so. "Asmonde took the study of magic seriously. He once told me that you both swore to pursue the art—swore at your mother's deathbed, no less."

Declan clamped his mouth shut. That was not a subject he wished to discuss with anyone, least of all Jamang.

Undeterred, Jamang pressed on. "You are not the sort to abandon an oath, I think. Where have you been studying, and with whom?"

Declan folded his arms. "My situation is exactly as it appears. I'm learning the entirely unmagical art of reading the night skies."

"But why? Art? Astronomy? What on earth do they have in common?"

"Maps," Declan said.

Jamang frowned in puzzlement.

"Korvosans are known across Avistan as an adventurous breed. Adventurers require maps, and I intend to provide them. Knowledge of the stars is a necessary part of my training in cartography."

"Cartography!" said Jamang. "You're learning a *trade*?" He blanched at the last word, as if he had bitten into an apple and found half of a wriggling grub.

Declan shrugged.

He watched in silence as Jamang's face contorted in a struggle between disbelief and distaste. Declan noted the soft rustle of vines and glanced toward the pergola. The house drake perched on the edge of the lattice roof, his eyes bright with avarice as he studied the newcomer.

Declan knew what the little creature wanted. Dairy farmers had cats, and Korvosan innkeepers had house drakes. His family ran the Frisky Unicorn, a small inn famous for its tall, slim turret and the drakes that nested there. More curious than cats and more acquisitive than ravens, the tiny dragons gathered in places frequented by strangers, where jewels were worn and coins exchanged. For the most part, the Unicorn's winged residents left the guests in peace, but some of the creatures were accomplished thieves. This little blue dragon, a relative newcomer, could make the slickest pickpockets weep with envy.

Declan brought to mind an image of Jamang's silver amulet and gave the little drake a subtle shake of his head.

The drake's whimper of disappointment echoed through Declan's thoughts.

Want, he said emphatically.

Can't have, Declan sent back. *It is unwise to steal from a necromancer.*

Nasty necromancers.

Declan could not dispute the assessment.

"It's about your brother's death, isn't it?" said Jamang at last. Before Declan could answer, Jamang placed a ring-laden hand on his shoulder. "There's no stigma attached to you, if that's what concerns you. Many of the students who begin at the Acadamae don't survive to graduation. This is not only inevitable but necessary."

Declan stepped back. "I certainly hope you don't intend to assure me that Asmonde's body was put to use in the necromantic laboratories."

The necromancer raised both hands in a placating gesture. "You know how things are done."

"I don't want any part of 'how things are done' like that."

"Instead you want to draw maps?" Jamang sneered. "Perhaps you fancy yourself a Jeggare?"

The name was one of Varisia's oldest and most famous families, but in this context Declan understood it to mean an adventurer in the style of Montlarion Jeggare, someone who left the civilized world behind to stamp his name on wild and unclaimed lands.

"My aspirations aren't so grand," Declan said, "but thanks for the compliment."

"It wasn't intended as a compliment," said Jamang. "Old Montlarion died a pauper."

The sound of light footsteps interrupted their argument and drew their eyes toward the stairwell. A young woman stepped onto the roof, a tall but delicate blonde clad in a green kirtle worn over a chemise of unbleached linen. Her gaze fell upon Declan's visitor and she paused. For a moment she stood poised between speech and flight, like a forest nymph startled to have walked into a hunter's camp.

The sight of Silvana lifted Declan's spirits and clenched at his heart with an intensity that would be painful were it not so poignant. She was the most recent and by far the prettiest of Majeed's constantly changing staff of servants, and she provided the only bright spot in Declan's apprenticeship. He'd hoped she would come to the roof tonight. She often slipped upstairs to indulge in her private vice, a fragrant little pipe delicately carved from some sort of ivory.

Declan beckoned her over. "Silvana, may I present to you Jamang Kira, an old . . ." he balked at *friend* and settled on ". . . acquaintance."

The necromancer's eyes lit up. He took Silvana's hand and raised it to his lips. "I begin to understand Declan's sudden enthusiasm for astronomy," he oozed. "Had I known Majeed Nores possessed so lovely a daughter, I might have taken up stargazing myself."

Silvana cast an uncertain glance at Declan. She said, "I work in Master Majeed's kitchen."

Jamang froze. "Oh," he said flatly. He dropped her hand and turned back to Declan.

"As I was saying," he continued, "you yourself had nothing to fear from the trials at the Acadamae. You are far more talented than your brother."

"And far less tolerant of bad manners," Declan snarled. "If you wish to remain, you will treat Silvana with courtesy."

The wizard looked puzzled. "What?"

Behind Jamang's back, Silvana shook her head and flicked one hand as if brushing away a small insect. She lifted her little pipe and tipped her head toward the far side of the roof, where she retreated.

Declan turned a cool stare to his visitor. "What do you really want, Jamang?"

The necromancer reached into a satchel hidden beneath his crimson cloak and produced a slim book bound in blue leather.

Heat flooded Declan's face as he recognized the volume as one of the bawdy trifles he had created in his Theumanexus days. He barely refrained from snatching it out of Jamang's clutches.

"Where did you get that?"

Jamang ignored the question and opened the book to reveal an ink drawing of a voluptuous courtesan on the sole page of the book. "I must say, it's marvelous work."

As they watched, the drawing began to move. The courtesan rolled her hips in a sensuous walk along a popular Korvosan street known for its various entertainments. "Nothing like this is taught at the Acadamae, nothing even remotely similar. Who taught you this?"

"No one," said Declan. That was true. He liked to explain that the magical animation might have been the residual effect of a curse placed on the creature whose hide became the leather cover. In reality, he had replicated the magical effect in two other tomes with completely different bindings. The truth was that he had no idea how his attempt at composing a flip-page novelty had transformed from nearly two hundred pages of sequential drawings to a single fat sheet on which his caricatures moved of their own accord.

Revealing his own ignorance to someone like Jamang Kira was like dumping chum overboard to draw sharks before jumping in for a swim, so Declan merely shrugged and said, "It's a spell of my own creation."

An expression like relief flared across the necromancer's face. "Truly? This is remarkably original work. Even so—" Jamang pursed his lips and studied Declan as if calculating how much he could reveal without tipping his hand. "This particular application of magic," he said at last, "is something I've not seen before. It is not an illusion. If it were, the spell would affect the person viewing it, but here the ink itself moves."

Declan shrugged. "So it's a transmutation."

"No, I tested, and it isn't," Jamang said. "Don't bother listing the seven ancient schools for something that seems to fit. I've examined this thoroughly, and the answer is not what one might expect at first study." He snapped the little book shut and raised it like a priest presenting a holy artifact. "This is necromancy."

"There's no need to be insulting," Declan said.

"I'm serious," Jamang insisted, once again oblivious to Declan's mockery. "The spell you crafted animates the ink itself. It brings the dead organic matter of the ink back to a semblance of life."

"So?"

"So?" the little man echoed. "While the story plays out, the characters you drew are alive. Well," he amended, "not 'alive' as most understand the word, but certainly in the more inclusive sense that defines a necromancer's art. Observe."

He opened the book once more. The image started to move—gracefully, realistically, with a lavish sashay of the sort Declan had spent many happy hours observing as the young women of Korvosa took their evening promenades. The courtesan strolled past an open-air tavern where a uniformed member of the Sable Company sat drinking. She paused to cast a look of unmistakable invitation back over her shoulder. The marine gestured, and the drawing's perspective pulled back to reveal a broader vista and the sight he wished the courtesan to observe: his hippogriff mount, an enormous eagle-headed, winged horse tethered to a rail in the tavern side yard. In response, the beast arched his wings to reveal a saddle long enough for two. The courtesan's lips curved and she sent her new client an arch, sidelong glance.

"I have seen this," Declan said. "Remember, I drew it."

"Wait and watch," the necromancer insisted.

Declan watched as the familiar scene played out. When the marine's hippogriff began circling Castle Korvosa and the courtesan's legs encircled the soldier's waist, Jamang pulled a jeweled pin from his hat and jabbed the page.

The hippogriff reared up, wings back-beating the air and beak flung wide in a silent shriek. A stream of ink-dark blood stained the white feathers of its breast. The riders slid from the saddle and tumbled toward the distant city, limbs flailing. Discarded bits of clothing drifted down after them like autumn leaves.

Jamang snapped the book shut and affixed Declan with an expectant stare.

Declan realized he was gaping and shut his mouth with an audible click of teeth. "You killed my hippogriff."

"I admit that I have tried," Jamang said candidly. "But short of burning the book, I don't think I could have any lasting effect on the spell."

He handed the book to Declan. "Go ahead. Open it."

Declan cracked open the book. The courtesan began her undulating stroll anew.

"You see? The magic remains intact."

"That's a relief," Declan said in a voice heavy with irony. "I'd hate to redraw all the sketches that became this one page."

Jamang waved this consideration aside. "You could easily hire someone else to do the drawings. It's the magic that interests Somar Nevinoff."

At last Declan understood Jamang's motive, and he suppressed a smile as he said the words he knew would foil the man's scheme. "In that case, I'd be happy to talk with him. Set up an appointment."

"One does not just 'set up an appointment' with Somar Nevinoff," Jamang said. "Tell me how the spell is done, and I will relay the information."

"Let me guess," said Declan. "You passed the book off as your own work. Is that how you got your position with the necromancer?"

Jamang's face reddened. "What matters is that this discovery could be very good for both of us. If you show me how the spell is done, you will be well paid."

"And if I don't, you'll be turned into a newt for promising more than you could deliver. Out of curiosity, what is the price of newt prevention these days?"

"Fifty crowns," Jamang said. "In addition, in exchange for this spell, I will undertake to teach you the necromancer's art. You obviously have a gift and would benefit from the knowledge I have gained at the Acadamae. After a few months of my tutelage, you won't even know yourself."

"And that," Declan said, "is precisely why I must decline your generous offer."

Spots of angry color rose high on Jamang's cheeks and his eyes turned hard. He moved to stand toe to toe with Declan. He reached for the book, but Declan held it tight against his chest. He knew Jamang lacked the physical courage to take it by force.

"Your brother's body was tossed into a vat of urine and simmered for two days," Jamang said. "That process dissolves the flesh from the bone. The resulting sludge was fed to the creatures that scour the Acadamae sewers. His bones were added to those of camels and asses to create skeletal amalgamations—difficult to animate, but the results are amusing to watch."

Vengeance uncoiled in some dark corner of Declan's heart. He let it fill his eyes as he held the necromancer's gaze.

Uncertainty flickered across Jamang's face. He covered it with a sneer before he spun away with a swirl of his crimson cloak. He paused at the head of the stairs and swung dramatically back.

"Keep it," he spat. "I have others like it, and from them I will learn the secret on my own. But you will pay dearly for the time and effort that costs me. Before I'm finished with you, you will wish that you'd sold me the spell."

Declan tipped his head to one side and considered. "Not a particularly original threat, but the delivery was authentic. Marvelous prop, the cloak. One might mistake you for a proper villain if only you could grow a sinister mustache."

The necromancer's face twisted with rage. He hissed. "This isn't over."

"No, I suppose not," Declan agreed. "There's still the question of your explaining yourself to Somar Nevinoff. To be a fly on the wall of that room . . ."

For an instant, stark terror replaced Jamang's furious expression. He mastered his countenance with all the grace of a grocer stuffing a sack with cabbages.

"Master Somar is a reasonable man. He wants the spell. It will be of little consequence to him whether he gets it from me or peels the secret from your animated corpse."

He tipped a mocking bow toward Declan and started down the stairs. "It's a surprisingly effective means of inquisition," he called back. "You might be surprised by the secrets your brother's corpse revealed."

On impulse, Declan hurled the book after Jamang. The tome flew over the necromancer's head by a comfortable margin and smacked solidly into the pergola. A startled feminine gasp and an equally startled but telepathically silent *squawk* reminded Declan that he was not alone on the roof.

The drake flew toward Castle Korvosa, no doubt to join his fellows in chasing the imps. Silvana emerged from the pergola and picked up the book. She opened it, and her eyes widened.

Declan skirted the reflecting pool at a run and took the book gently from her hands. "Pay no attention to that. This trifle isn't worthy of your eyes."

"Not worthy of a kitchen wench?" she teased. "I doubt your educated friend shares that opinion."

Silvana's voice suited her delicate appearance. It was high and light, with a pretty lilt that sounded more like personal affectation than any accent Declan could identify. Despite his embarrassment, Declan found it easy to return her smile.

"Jamang is an ass," he said. "Having perfected this art among the living, he trained as a necromancer so that he could annoy the dead."

Silvana rewarded his wit with a smile. She said, "Your necromancer friend was right about one thing. The magic in that book is clever."

Declan shrugged. "It's a trifle. Just a silly little trick to amuse boys. I was only a boy when I did it. Years ago. I would never think of such a thing now."

"A silly little trick?" she laughed, ignoring the rest of his halting equivocation. "Those are words seldom spoken in Korvosa. Magic is so very important here."

Her imitation of Jamang's overwrought tone was spot-on. The unexpected mockery sent Declan into a spasm of laughter. When their shared mirth faded, an uncertain expression rippled across Silvana's face.

"Have you made a drawing of me?"

"No!" he said. "Certainly not. Not anything like this," he added. "That would be . . . I would never do that."

"But you have drawn a picture of me?" she persisted.

Declan had never intended to show her the painting, but under the circumstances he didn't see how he could avoid doing so. He reached for the silver chain he wore around his neck and pulled the miniature from its hiding place beneath his tunic. He pulled the chain over his head and handed it to her.

Silvana stared at the tiny painting, her face the essence of puzzlement.

Declan wasn't surprised by her reaction. The likeness was true, but he'd taken certain liberties. For one thing, he'd depicted her standing in front of a many-paned window overlooking a springtime garden. The pale hair she always pulled back in one braid spilled to her waist in a rippling cascade. She wore a pale blue gown trimmed with pearls, a garment much finer than anything Silvana might own and extravagant even by the standards of Korvosan nobility. Declan had drawn it from memory and imagination, calling upon a child-hood story of a fey princess for inspiration. To his eyes, the fairy tale image suited Silvana. No other woman had ever made him remember ancient stories so vividly.

After a long moment, Silvana lifted her gaze from the little oval frame. "This is how I look to you?"

The awe in her voice gave him courage. "The elves of Kyonin make the truest pigments, but no elf alive can do justice to hair the color of ripe wheat, or eyes that shame the winter sky."

"Now you're teasing me." She flushed, turned half away from him, and then with an adder-quick thrust pushed him backward into the brisk water of the scrying pool.

The shock of cold water stole his breath, if not his ardor. He climbed back to his feet, surrounded by scattered fragments of starlight reflected from the rippling pool. A wicked grin curved his lips as he reached for her. She darted beyond his reach, laughing.

Declan sloshed over the low wall and chased her. They circled the scrying pool twice, Silvana pulling away with each fleet step. She ran for the pergola and nimbly climbed the trellis. Declan started to follow, but the lowest wooden strip snapped under his boot, letting him know beyond question that the pergola would not hold his weight.

Silvana scrambled to the top and sat on the edge of the pergola's roof, feet swinging just out of reach. As she watched him, the playful expression on her face shifted to one of chagrin.

"You're shivering," she said. "The wind off the bay is chilly. I should have thought of that."

Now that she mentioned it, Declan realized that his teeth were chattering like a gaggle of schoolgirls.

"I can endure a little hardship in pursuit of . . ." He was running out of poetry, even the cheap stuff that had seemed successful a few moments ago. He winced as he said, "beauty."

She shook her head. "You must get warm and dry at once, or you will be sick."

The concern in her voice warmed Declan. "My room is just off the bathhouse. If it will make you feel better, I promise I'll take a quick steam to warm up."

"That's a good idea." Silvana climbed down from her perch and walked toward him, holding up the painting. "I have no mirror, and even if I did I would never appear so fine. May I keep this? Not the chain, of course," she added.

He pressed the trinket back into her hand. "It's the picture I value, but I can always paint another."

Something flickered in her eyes, an emotion Declan couldn't identify. She gave him a shy smile. "When you are warm and dry, perhaps you will return to the roof?" she said. "I thought I might wait here until Skywing returns."

"Skywing?"

"The little blue dragon," she explained. "That is what I call him. He seems to like the name."

"He talks to you?" Declan said, secretly pleased. House drakes could communicate by projecting their thoughts, but they deemed few humans worth the effort. He wondered what it meant that Skywing had determined them both worthy. He decided it was a good omen.

Silvana nodded. "It took a while for me to learn how to think out loud so that Skywing could hear me. But let's talk about it when you return." She shooed him away with both hands, a charming gesture that solidified his faith in good omens.

Declan ran for the stairs, curving his path only far enough to surreptitiously pick up the dirty book from where it had fallen next to the reflecting pool. The last thing he wanted right now was for Silvana to get bored and open it again for a longer stretch, revealing his indiscretions in earnest. With it tucked safely under his arm, he took the stairs three at a time. Two floors down, a narrow corridor led past the servants' quarters into the turret that housed his room. He seldom came this way, but Majeed would not thank him for dripping on the carpets that covered the lower floor.

Something odd caught Declan's eye. He skidded to a stop and frowned at the arched, many-paned window overlooking Majeed's garden. It was the same window he'd painted in the miniature of Silvana, but he had never been conscious of its inspiration for his painting. Stranger still, he'd never noticed such a window in Majeed's manor, nor had he viewed the quince tree that appeared in the miniature painting from any window at all.

Declan shrugged and continued toward his room. He had never paid particular attention to the corridor. He didn't remember seeing the window, but not noticing something was not the same as not seeing it. Some memories lingered in the mind like piles of drawings locked in old chests, out of sight but not entirely forgotten.

He hurried to the small bedchamber Majeed had assigned him and collected a simple muslin tunic and trousers, both in the warm brown hues he favored. After a moment's consideration, he tossed aside the tunic and rummaged in his trunk for his best shirt, a white one with a bit of blue at the cuffs and collar. Perhaps he would invite Silvana to a late performance of *The Scarlet Raven* at the amphitheater. Silvana deserved better treatment than she received in Majeed's household, and far better than she'd suffered from that insufferable ass, Jamang.

It occurred to Declan that Silvana deserved better than he could offer, as well. An occasional flirtation, a miniature portrait, an evening's entertainment in nowhere near the best seats Kendall Amphitheater had to offer—this was the best he could provide. Perhaps there was something to what Jamang said, despite his ulterior motives and despicable behavior. Perhaps it was time Declan strove to rise in the world.

Declan shook off that chain of thought. Odd, how the contemplation of a pretty woman could disrupt his thinking. The pursuit of wealth and fame and power didn't interest him in any other circumstances. He didn't believe they were necessary to happiness. In fact, he'd seen enough in his twenty-four years to believe they took a man down the opposite path. He was enchanted by Silvana, and she seemed to enjoy his company. In his saner moments, he would consider that enough to build upon.

Deep in thought, he buried the moving-picture book deep beneath his other clothes, then straightened and strode into the bathhouse. A startled oath brought him abruptly down from the clouds.

Majeed Nores, one of the most renowned astronomers in Korvosa, glared at him from his seat at the far bench. The astronomer was naked to a degree that few men could duplicate.

Declan had noted Majeed's bald head and his curious lack of eyebrows, but he'd never followed their clues to their logical conclusion. Apparently some quirk of nature, or perhaps a spell gone awry, had left Majeed as hairless as a fish. With his egg-shaped belly and short, fleshy limbs, his pale skin flushed pink from the steam, the famed astronomer resembled an enormous, angry baby. The sight was a startling change from the images of Silvana that Declan had enjoyed on his walk to the bath.

Few men could appear intimidating under such embarrassing circumstances, but Majeed managed through sheer ill temper.

"So, you've discovered a new comet," he said, in a voice so acidic it could melt plate armor. "Congratulations."

"Actually—"

Majeed cut him off. "A new comet," he repeated. "I know this because only a fool would burst in here like a fox with its tail afire on a matter of lesser import. The only greater folly would be assuming I might wish to hear about such an unimportant matter."

Declan mumbled an apology and ducked out. He retraced his steps to his room and changed into dry clothes. When he tied his coin bag to his belt, it felt a little lighter than he had hoped. He'd need to do another job for Basha soon or, better yet, persuade the map merchant to pay him for the last few jobs.

He climbed the stairs to the roof two at a time and paused a moment just before reaching the top to catch his breath. He did not wish to appear overeager, although to be honest with himself he had to admit he'd probably crossed that line earlier. A faint herbal scent perfumed the air, courtesy of Silvana's ivory pipe. The woman herself was not within sight, but the dim light of the rising moon gleamed on the drake's iridescent scales. The creature sat on the pedestal that held Declan's logbook, his tiny shoulders hunched.

Declan approached the dragon. "Skywing, eh?" Declan had to admit he was a little jealous that the little drake had shared its name with Silvana before him.

Skywing lifted his tiny head. *Silvana went away*.

Declan stopped cold. He'd assumed that she waited for him under the pergola. "She left?"

She went away.

Something about the drake's telepathic voice sounded wrong to Declan. There was a sense of sorrow. "Skywing, where did Silvana go?"

Fetch a light. Go to the vine cave.

He took the torch from one of the stands ringing the roof and absentmindedly muttered a cantrip that would set it aflame as he carried it into the shadows under the pergola. Skywing fluttered in behind him and perched on the bench. Firelight glimmered on the glass statue of a tall, slender woman that resembled Silvana.

Declan moved in for a closer look. Yes, the statue was definitely modeled on Silvana. In fact, the likeness was remarkable, right down to the kirtle she'd been wearing and the little strand of hair over her left ear that always seemed to work its way free of her braid.

He reached toward that errant lock. To his horror, the instant his finger touched the sculpture, the entire structure shattered onto the roof.

Declan stooped to pick up a shard. It was cold and so thin that it melted on his fingertips.

"This is ice," he marveled. "Skywing, what happened?"

Skywing arched his wings, a gesture that seemed to Declan much like a human shrug. He leaped from the bench and winged off into the night.

Declan sat back on his heels to consider the possibilities. A hollow ice sculpture of such complexity was obviously the work of magic, but who had cast this spell? Declan thought instantly of Jamang, but despite the necromancer's promise of revenge, he did not seem the likely culprit. He was a necromancer, not an ice mage, and he had always been one to nurture a grudge for days or weeks before retaliating. No, it had to be someone else.

The more important question was whether Silvana had been harmed, or worse. No, thought Declan. It was pointless to imagine the worst without further clues. Silvana was not, could not be, dead.

This mystery might not equal the discovery of a new comet, but in Declan's opinion it warranted a second trip to the bathhouse. Majeed was not a wizard, and it was unlikely that he could shed much light on this matter, but any prudent man would surely wish to know when strange magic manifested in his own home.

As he started to rise, Declan noticed that Silvana had left her little white pipe on the bench, as well as a bag half full of herbs. He tucked both objects into his coin bag and ran for the stairs.

He hurried back down to the bathhouse and knocked on the door, grimacing as he steeled himself for Majeed's abuse. A faint grunt was the only response.

Worried, Declan swung open the door. Majeed hadn't moved from the bench. His wrathful expression was reassuringly familiar, but something in his rigid position seemed wrong.

"Master Majeed?"

The astronomer made a sound like that of a gagged man trying to scream. The sound was muted behind his immobile lips.

Declan crossed the bathhouse and tapped the astronomer's plump pink shoulder. His fingertips clicked against a hard, cold surface.

Majeed was encased in ice.

Dread pooled in the pit of Declan's stomach. He tapped again, harder this time, and again harder still.

Unlike the frozen replica of Silvana, the ice surrounding the astronomer proved unbreakable.

He considered dragging Majeed closer to the fire pit but discarded the idea. The steam in the bathhouse had dwindled to a few stray wisps, but the rocks on the grate over the fire still glowed red. The air in the bathhouse was hotter than midsummer.

"Why aren't you melting?" he wondered aloud.

As soon as the words escaped his mouth, he realized Majeed was doing exactly that. Within the cage of ice, the entrapped astronomer was slowly fading away.

Declan slammed his fist into the ice again and again, afraid his master was dying. Yet it did not look as though Majeed were in pain. Instead, Declan had the distinct impression that Majeed was falling away or actually traveling, perhaps through magically twisted space. His only thought was that if he could break the shell, perhaps he could drag Majeed back from wherever he was being taken—which had to be the same place Silvana had gone.

Majeed continued to fade like a painting carried away through the mist. One moment the astronomer's form was there, the next, Declan's fist met empty air. The icy construct had simply vanished, leaving a large, spreading puddle on the bathhouse floor.

Declan stepped back, running one shaking hand over his head as he tried to make sense of what he had seen. Majeed Nores was well known and, although not fabulously wealthy, certainly not without means. He was parsimonious when it came to sharing his expertise, but kidnapping seemed an extreme road to take in the pursuit of knowledge. It was more likely that someone had taken him for ransom.

"Or possibly revenge," Declan murmured. "He certainly is a bit of a bastard."

Regardless of which scenario held true, there was reason to be concerned about Majeed, but Declan felt far more worried for Silvana. A famous astronomer had an obvious value; a servant caught up by mistake did not. If the unknown kidnappers were willing to cast the strange teleportation spell until it found its intended target, they were unlikely to show much regard for any other fish the magical net might catch. He had to find Silvana, and fast.

Declan spun and ran for the stables. Majeed's hostler was as ill-tempered as his master, but Declan planned to offer the man a choice: nod and smile while Declan took the fastest horse the astronomer owned, or be cut up into small pieces and fed to the barn cats.

Dim lantern light glowed above the half-door of the stable. Good. The hostler was not yet abed. Declan shouted his name, but the man did not appear.

Just as well, thought Declan. He took tack down from the wall and saddled Majeed's gray stallion. The horse accepted bit and bridle without protest, perhaps sensing the urgency Declan felt. Without another thought, Declan vaulted into the saddle, slapped his heels against the horse's side, and galloped off into the night.

Chapter Two
The Necromancer's Familiar

A night's lodging in the narrow boarding house near Korvosa's Acadamae cost more money than Ellasif had seen in her first twenty-five years of life. But the last year had brought many changes, including a fat purse. She'd been renting the attic room for several nights now, and her new coin bag was still nearly full.

The boarding house occupied a side street where a few old homes stood besieged by the small shops and taverns that had sprung up like mushrooms around the famous school of magic. The house had never been grand by the standards of Korvosa, and over the years it had earned its share of drafts and creaks. Ellasif had reason to be grateful for both. The night wind made the heat of this southern city a little more bearable, and the creaking of the third stair from the top announced that someone was approaching her attic bedchamber.

"Someone big is coming," she called out in her native Skald. She rose, fully dressed, from the narrow bed. "Someone big and clumsy." She heard another step and sniffed loudly. "Smells like someone treacherous. Who could that be?"

She reached for her sword and crossed the small chamber in two strides. After sliding back the bolt, she stepped back and rested the sword casually on one shoulder. "Come in, Olenka."

The door swung open, and a tall woman ducked her way through the low doorway, an Ulfen warrior with flame-colored braids and full lips pressed together in a grim line.

They stood regarding each other for a long moment. "Next time," Ellasif advised, "try bracing your hands on either side of the stairwell as you climb. And wash yourself, woman. I can still smell the winter's bear fat on you, which means a southerner can smell you a day before you arrive."

"I was not concerned with stealth," said Olenka. Ellasif had every reason not to be glad of the sight of her former friend, but still it was good to hear someone else speak her native tongue in this foreign land.

"You've come a long way if you're looking for a fight," said Ellasif. "And you arrive at a most inconsiderate hour."

Olenka sighed through clenched teeth. "You know why I've come."

"Is White Rook so secure, and are the raiders of Irrisen grown so tame, that the elders send you hundreds of miles to meddle with matters that no longer concern them?"

"If you cared about the village, you would come back with me and answer for what you've done."

"What I've done?" Ellasif repeated incredulously. "You betrayed my sister, and in doing so you betrayed me, your oldest friend!"

Faint color suffused the woman's face. "It was a needed thing. The elders decided. I simply did my duty.

Whatever you might think of me, I came here out of friendship."

"A few years ago, I might have believed that."

Ellasif took a step closer. Olenka's hand flashed to the hilt of her knife. The reaction drew a grim nod from the smaller woman.

"We know each other better now, do we not?" Once Olenka had been her dearest friend. It was to Olenka that Ellasif had confided her deepest secret when she could no longer carry it alone. For years she believed it would do no harm, but eventually the weight of the secret was too great, and the elders learned the truth. Olenka needed no reminder of the cost of her betrayal, but Ellasif gave her one anyway. "I trusted you, and so did Liv."

"She heard things before they were said, saw things before they happened."

"You should have seen that for the gift it was!"

"Some did. The raiders from Irrisen have besieged the village for years. When Liv departed White Rook, they left us in peace." Olenka's face softened. "Come back, Ellasif. Now that the witch is no longer—"

Ellasif's fist slammed into Olenka's jaw. The taller woman rocked back a step and spat bloody foam and a broken tooth into her palm. Her muscular body tensed and then relaxed.

"I deserved that," she said. "My words were poorly chosen. But look beyond our quarrel, Ellasif. Now that . . . things are back to normal, the council of elders wants you back."

"What possible reason could they have to summon the witch's sister?"

"Red Ochme is dead."

Silence fell like a funeral shroud over both women. Ellasif saw her own grief reflected on Olenka's freckled face, and they mourned together in silence. There was no denying that Red Ochme was an old woman, well past the age any warrior expected to live. The news shouldn't have come as such a surprise, but somehow it still stabbed a cold knife into Ellasif's heart. "How?" she asked.

"A wasting sickness. In just one winter she faded away to rag and bone. When her time neared, she rode to the sea and hired on with a captain she knew from years ago. They went raiding. Later, the captain sent word back to the village. Red Ochme wanted it known that she'd died with her feet on a ship's deck and a sword in her hand."

Ellasif pushed thoughts of her own loss aside to accept the end her foster mother had chosen. "A good death."

Olenka nodded.

"So now the council of elders needs a new battle leader."

"They want you."

Ellasif tapped at her chin with one finger and pretended to think it over. There had been a time when her most selfish desire was to lead the village defenders as Red Ochme had done. Her dream had always been to emulate the woman she had admired above all other heroes of White Rook, a village whose warriors' names were sung all across the Lands of the Linnorm Kings. And yet they were the same villagers who had reviled her sister, Liv, whom Ellasif had practically raised as a daughter. What they had done to her, Ellasif could never forgive.

"Tell me, Olenka," she said. "Does my black billy goat Satyr yet live? The one who tried to cover everything from a sled dog to a she-bear?"

Olenka frowned. "I believe so."

Ellasif smiled a knife. "Then tell the elders I'll come back to White Rook after they line up inside Satyr's pen, drop their pants, and grip the fence."

"Ellasif!" Olenka never blanched at crude insults, but it was heresy to apply them to the village elders. "There's no time for foolishness. My orders are to return with you and serve under your leadership, or else to claim that honor by bringing home your body."

"I must inconvenience you," said Ellasif. "I am still using it."

"I don't want to kill you," Olenka whispered. "To be honest, I don't think I could."

"Now that," the smaller woman said approvingly, "is the first sensible thing you've said tonight."

"So you'll come with me? You'll come home?"

The pleading note in Olenka's voice touched a place in Ellasif's heart that she'd thought long frozen over.

"I will think about your offer," she said. "How long can you wait?"

Relief washed over Olenka's face. "I am expected back by the next new moon. If we leave tomorrow and ride hard, we should be able to make it."

"You'll have my answer tomorrow at dawn. If I decide that you will not be traveling alone, I'll arrange passage for two on a northbound ship."

Olenka offered her hand. They clasped each other's wrists to seal the agreement. The big woman started to say something more but then shook her head and left the cramped room.

Ellasif listened as her visitor descended the stairs. When she judged that Olenka was well away, she opened the latch on the bedchamber window and slipped out into the night.

After the first day spent stalking her quarry through Korvosa, Ellasif had learned that the quickest way across the city could be found on its rooftops. More than a series of paths over connected buildings, the Shingles were a district unto themselves. Many Korvosans, not just the indigents who slept in ever-moving shanty-towns, took to the rooftops. Business of all sorts could be conducted there, high above the patrolled streets. It was not the safest path through the city, but Ellasif had earned a certain reputation in her short stay, and no one bothered her as she headed back toward the Heights of Korvosa.

She had to act quickly. A wizard was what she needed, and she had a good idea where to find one that might suit her purpose.

The moon rode high in the sky by the time Ellasif stood in the street behind the astronomer's manor. She hugged the garden wall, watching from the shadows as a dark-haired young man not much taller than she busied himself with chalk and candles and small fetish objects that appeared to have been harvested from a butcher's garbage bin. He started to walk around the circle he'd drawn on the ground, chanting sharp-edged words with each step. When the chalk markings took on a faint red glow, he backed away and began a second, softer chant.

Rats came to the wizard's call, slinking out of the shadows by the score. He snatched up four of them by their tails, two in each hand, and threw them into the glowing circle.

Something flashed, something without sound or color or even light. Until this moment, Ellasif would never have imagined that fire could be so dark, but "black fire" was the best phrase she could conjure to describe the ethereal tongues that consumed the rats.

The fire disappeared as suddenly as it had flared. In its place stood a single monstrous rat, the size of the four rats the wizard had sacrificed combined. Its eyes were unnaturally large and bulbous, and they glowed with evil red cunning.

"Declan Avari," the wizard said. "Remember that, Vexer, for it is the name of your quarry. Take his soul if you can get it. Eat his liver if you can't."

The rat-thing smiled.

A shudder rippled down Ellasif's spine. There was no mistaking the nature and origin of the spirit housed in the enormous vermin. Everything she'd seen since arriving in Korvosa deepened her opinion that this city stood on the gateway to Hell. The fey-haunted forests of her homeland had not prepared her for a place where swarms of imps were as common as ravens, and where anyone who hoped to become a wizard must learn to summon devils.

In such a city, it seemed certain that everyone who could afford a bit of magic would ward their houses against infernal creatures. And that, Ellasif decided, explained why the necromancer had clothed his evil servant in the flesh of the most mundane of creatures. As a rat, perhaps the little devil could slip past the manor's magical defenses and do as the wizard bade.

Ellasif reached for the special weapon hidden in a small pouch Liv had sewn into the hem of her tunic. She watched as the wizard toed a gap in the chalk circle. The fiend slipped through the opening. This seemed to break the wizard's second spell, as well, for the swarm of rats scattered and slunk off into the night.

As soon as the wizard turned away, Ellasif climbed the wall that separated the back street from the astronomer's garden.

The giant rat was quicker. It scrambled up one side and down the other and sped toward the manor, silent as shadows.

Ellasif raised the tiny silver whistle to her lips and blew.

No sound emerged that her ears could hear, but the rat-fiend convulsed and came to a sudden, twitching stop.

Ellasif leaped to the ground and continued blowing the whistle, reaching over her shoulder for her sword as she ran.

As long as she blew, the giant rodent writhed in pain, but the moment she stopped to draw breath, the creature whirled toward her and reared up on its hind legs. Malevolent red witch light gathered between its paws, which looked more like clawed human hands.

Ellasif's sword slashed down and lopped them off.

The rat-fiend dropped to the ground and attempted a hobbling escape. Ichor flowed from the severed limbs and left a steaming trail on the mossy path. Ellasif followed, raising her sword high. She overtook the creature in a few quick strides and chopped down hard. The heavy blade split the abomination's black hide and bit deeply into meat and bone.

Black fire flared from the carcass. Ellasif reeled back, one hand clapped to her nose to ward off the searing stench of sulfur.

The black flames took the shape of a tiny devil with bat wings and a hideous face crowned by long, curling horns. The imp circled Ellasif as if trying to decide which part of her might be the tastiest.

Something fast and pale swooped from the sky like a diving hawk. Ellasif spun away, sword sweeping up in a protective arc.

But the attacker—a pale blue dragon about the size of a young rabbit—did not concern itself with her. It slammed into the imp, sending the devil spinning through the air to crash face-first into a garden statue.

The imp slid down the sculpture and tumbled onto the gravel path. It came up in a crouch and hissed like a deranged cat before leaping into flight.

Imp and dragon met in midair, jaws snapping as they scrabbled at each other with their sharp talons. Their barbed tails lashed and stabbed, dueling like a pair of limber swords in a contest seemingly independent of the battle of tooth and claw. The creatures broke apart, dropped to the ground, and rose again to fight on the wing like territorial birds.

Another time, Ellasif might have been charmed by the tiny, sky-blue dragon, and certainly she would have been fascinated by the living poetry of morning and midnight battling for possession of the sky, but she was in a hurry. Again she blew the whistle.

Imp and dragon jolted away as if equally pained by the sound that Ellasif could not hear. They hovered for a moment, wings beating as they glared down at her.

A sizzling sound drew Ellasif's attention to the rosebush beneath the imp, which wilted and drooped from the ichor dripping from the creature's wounds. The dragon, on the other hand, appeared unscathed.

She was not surprised when the imp gave up the battle and darted off into the night sky. The little dragon followed in close pursuit.

Ellasif nodded, satisfied that she'd found the right wizard for her purposes.

Tracking him was not difficult. Remnants of the chalk from the summoning circle lingered on the sole of his boot long enough for him to reach a nearby tavern. Ellasif followed him into the smoky room and sat down uninvited at his table.

The wizard's gaze swept over her, taking crass and obvious inventory. "Are you for hire?"

"Are you?"

Surprise reddened his face, but it was swiftly replaced by amusement. "No one has ever asked me that question before. It's quite an interesting notion," he said with a leer.

Ellasif rolled her eyes. "Please. That silver medal tells me you're a death wizard, and I need to be dead for a while."

"Ah." He leaned back in his seat, his expression contracting to a supercilious little smirk. "I am a necromancer, yes, but even for someone of my considerable skill, 'dead for a while' is a tall order."

Ellasif ignored the mockery in his voice. "I need to appear to be dead. Can you make a corpse look like me?"

"Did you have a particular corpse in mind?"

"I'm not particular, as long the corpse is close to my size and there's plausible reason for it to be a corpse."

Curiosity nudged the scorn from his face. "Close to your size," he repeated. "Any particular reason for this?"

"There are stories of amulets, items that can be enchanted to make a corpse look like another person. A transformation," she emphasized, "not just an illusion. I require a death wizard to put something of mine inside such a locket and cast the spell."

The necromancer lifted one eyebrow. "You are well informed, for a barbarian. But had you actually studied the art of magic rather than relying upon traveler's tales, you would know that such items are quite expensive. Even ignoring the spell for the moment, a necklace of sufficient quality to be worthwhile as the focus is probably worth more than—"

He cut off as Ellasif raised a shining locket to dangle in front of his face. It was a tiny silver cage rendered in layers of elaborate filigree.

The necromancer feigned casualness, but she could see he was suddenly taking their exchange more seriously. "A pretty bauble," he said. "How did you acquire it?"

"I enjoy shopping," she said. "Can you cast the spell or not?"

"Yes. Yes, of course." He licked his lips, a gesture that was both nervous and greedy.

Ellasif tucked the amulet into her tunic. "Say the words."

He blinked. "What?"

"The spell. Say the first three words."

"Am I to understand," he intoned ominously, "that you want me to audition?"

Ellasif placed both palms on the table and leaned forward as if she were about to rise. "I don't have time to waste. If you can't do the spell, I need to find someone who can. And just so you know, I've heard it cast before. I'm no wizard, so I can't speak those words, but I remember the sound of them."

The necromancer stared at her as his pride battled his greed. Finally he threw up his hands and muttered a sibilant phrase.

Ellasif nodded and leaned back in her chair. "You'll do."

"You're too kind," he said bitterly. He cleared his throat. "There remains the small matter of my fee—"

"I plan to use the amulet tomorrow morning. Afterward, you can keep it."

"Agreed," he said. From the speed of his acquiescence, she gathered that necromancy didn't pay as well as she'd thought. At least not for this one.

She rose. "Let's get on with it, then."

He leaped from his chair and fell into step beside her, clearly buoyed by the good fortune that had fallen into his lap. When they reached the street they argued briefly about where they should go to cast the spell and the mode of transport needed to get there, but Ellasif knew she had him hooked.

The necromancer was surprisingly agile when it came to climbing a drain pipe to reach the Shingles. They hurried across the city's rooftops without speaking and ducked into the window of her attic room with several hours to spare before sunrise.

The necromancer looked around the tiny chamber. "I'll take that personal item now. A lock of hair will do."

Ellasif drew a knife from her belt and sliced off a strand of her hair. She coiled it around her small finger and put the honey-colored circlet in the little silver cage.

His gaze lingered on the coin bag tied to Ellasif's belt. "This is not an inexpensive spell. The casting of it requires certain things of considerable value."

"We had a deal," she reminded him.

"And I will honor it," he said smoothly. "We agreed upon my fee for casting the spell. The cost of the necessary materials is another matter. The brimstone, for instance . . ."

The last time Ellasif had seen the spell cast, the wizard involved had used nothing more than a lump of wax. This one was either trying to rook her or else was significantly less skilled. Either way, it didn't matter. She placed a peridot on the bedside table, a gem the color of early spring leaves and the size of her thumbnail.

"That should cover you," she said. "And you already have all the brimstone you need. I smelled it when you cast the summoning spell behind the astronomer's manor, and the stink's still on you."

His eyes narrowed. "I didn't see you there."

"You weren't intended to."

"Neither did my infernal servant."

"Oh, it saw me," Ellasif said. When the wizard raised an eyebrow, she added, "It probably didn't consider me much of a threat."

"Yes, that's probably it. Now, about the cost of the other components . . ."

Ellasif curled the fingers of her right hand around the hilt of her dagger. "Two choices: You can cast the spell as agreed, or I'll send you to a place where you'll find brimstone in surplus."

The little necromancer shrugged as if to indicate that he expected this outcome but felt compelled to bargain as a matter of custom. He flipped back one side of his crimson cloak and unbuckled the satchel strapped over his shoulder. He sat down on the edge of the bed. After a moment of rummaging, he put the satchel on the floor and rose with a half-burned candle and a lump of acrid yellow coal in one palm.

Ellasif dropped the amulet into his extended hand and watched impatiently as he cast the spell. It was not, as she understood such matters, an exceptionally difficult feat of magic, but the necromancer performed

the spell as theatrically as if he envisioned himself surrounded by leaping flames and a choir of grim-faced
men chanting in a forgotten tongue.

"And here you have it," he said at last, handing her
the amulet with a flourish. "When you find a suitable
corpse, put this around its neck."

Ellasif took the filigreed locket, gave the chain a twirl
around one finger, and let fly. It opened into a circle as
it spun toward the necromancer and settled around his
neck before he could move away.

He gazed down at his prize with a satisfied smirk. The
soft hiss of a weapon sliding free of its sheath drew his
gaze up to Ellasif. Terrified understanding dawned in
his eyes.

Ellasif hurled the knife at the necromancer. It spun
once and buried itself deep in his gut. She stepped
close, yanked the knife out, and plunged it in again,
under the ribs and angled up to pierce the heart.

The necromancer was dead before he hit the cot.
Ellasif knew this for a certainty when his face gradually transformed into the likeness of her own.

For a moment she stood over the bed and regarded
her double. To her relief, she'd judged the weight cor-
rectly. She was small, but solid with muscle. The wizard
was slightly taller but almost certainly weighed a little
less than she did. That was important. She'd heard that
if the corpse were significantly larger than the person it
was intended to mimic, the spell took what was needed
for the transformation and left the extra flesh behind.
A pile of surplus meat, she reflected, was precisely the
sort of detail that prompted people to stop and think
more than was convenient for her present purposes.

A glance at the open window revealed a night sky
fading toward the deep sapphire of early dawn. Time

was running short. She went to work setting the scene, first cutting away the wizard's rich clothing and stuffing it into his satchel. She uncorked a bottle of cheap wine she'd bought from a Shingles vendor and splashed some around. An empty coin purse, embroidered in the Ulfen style with a circle of entwined wolves, she dropped on the floor. She followed it with two small copper coins, one of which she toed under the bed to make it appear that it had dropped and rolled when someone hastily emptied the purse. On the bedside table she left a scrap of paper that guaranteed passage for two on a northbound ship due to set sail from Korvosa around midday.

She left the knife in the necromancer's heart.

To be stabbed by a robber while sleeping off city wine was no way for an Ulfen warrior to die. Ellasif wasn't sure whether Olenka would find this end tragic or appropriate.

She picked up the wizard's satchel and slipped out the attic window. After pulling herself up onto the roof, she crouched in the shadows of the chimney and scanned the roofs, the streets, and the skies for anyone or anything that might have followed the wizard. Apart from the imps and dragons that occasionally whizzed past, intent on their skirmishes, the only sign of life was a trio of students staggering down the street, arms draped over each other's shoulders as they sang a drunken hymn to brotherhood. They sang with gusto, despite the fact that only one of them seemed to know the words.

Across the street, a second-floor window banged open and a scowling, white-bearded man leaned out to heave a chamber pot at the singers. The pot shattered against the street cobbles, splattering the students' robes with urine.

A shouted exchange of insults ensued, giving Ellasif all the cover she needed to scramble down the back side of the building to the second floor and then drop onto the roof of a large dovecote, a rounded tower with many tiny arched doorways on each nesting level. From there her climb was easy, and the only sound that marked her passage was the murmuring whirr and coo of the birds inside. It was, in her opinion, considerate of Korvosans to provide housing for the city's doves, not to mention convenient handholds for those who wished to come and go unobserved.

Ellasif circled around to the Jittery Quill, a public house that stayed open throughout the night. The few patrons who'd lasted to this hour wore the strain of their efforts. Men with faces dulled by too much ale and too few proud memories slumped back in their chairs. Students and scribes drooped over their books and parchments and steaming cups of bitter-smelling brew, their fingers stained with ink and the shadows under their eyes as dark and hard-won as bruises. All were too deeply steeped in their chosen libations to take much note of her. She chose a seat that put her back to the wall and gave her a clear view of the lodging house.

Olenka entered the house at sunrise, as agreed. After a few moments, she returned to the street, "Ellasif's" body rolled discretely into the bedchamber's carpet and slung over one shoulder.

Ellasif smiled. When the transformation spell wore off, the ship would be well on its way. The elders of White Rook would not be fooled, but she would be rid of Olenka for the foreseeable future.

Now all that remained was arranging secure passage to the northlands for herself and the other wizard for whom she had plans, one Declan Avari.

Chapter Three
The Rare Magic

Declan's pell-mell ride through Korvosa came to a halt a few blocks from Kendall Amphitheater. In his haste, he'd forgotten there would be a midnight performance and crowds of theater patrons thronging the streets.

Empty carriages streamed past him as drivers, having dropped off their wealthy patrons, headed toward taverns and alehouses for a different sort of entertainment. Up ahead, small parties of riders dismounted and handed their reins to the theater's yellow-clad hostlers. Many of the patrons came on foot, and the crowds were especially thick near the Janderhoff Gate, an entrance for people who could not afford the full price of a ticket and were willing to risk sitting directly over the spot where dwarves labored to shore up the cavernous sinkhole beneath.

The clock in the castle's Epochal Tower chimed. Declan turned the stallion northward toward Midland. The open-air market would be closed at this time of night, and the roads clear.

His reasoning might have been sound, but it fell short of reality. Declan's impatience grew as he wove a path through carts trundling down the roads, drawn by sullen donkeys or pushed by sweating servants. He had to move off the road completely while a small caravan of ice carts rolled past, the precious cargo packed in straw and sawdust against the heat.

Finally the south bridge came into sight, a broad ribbon of light over the blackness of the Jeggare River. No shadows moved through the bright circles cast by the lanterns spaced along its length. By some happy turn of fate, it appeared that Declan would have the bridge entirely to himself. He shook the reins over the stallion's neck and urged the horse into a gallop.

A squad of city guards, conspicuous in baggy red trousers tucked into low red boots, emerged from a side street just before the bridge. All were afoot, and Declan knew they would saunter in front of him, claiming the road for themselves just to show they could set his pace for him by dint of the uniforms they wore. On any other day, he might have tolerated it, but he was in a hurry. Declan gauged the distance and decided he could gallop past them before they could fan out and block his way.

As the gray stallion thundered toward the bridge, one of the guards stepped forward and raised a wooden wand. A short burst of light pulsed from it, and Declan's borrowed horse stopped in midstride.

Declan, unfortunately, did not.

Time slowed to the languorous pace of dreams. Declan flew over the stallion's neck and floated down toward the street at a speed that recalled the flow of treacle from a jar. Despite the oddly slowed descent, he hit the cobbles in a bruising tumble. He rolled to a stop and lay staring at the spinning stars, idly wondering if it might be prudent—and for that matter, possible—to draw another breath.

The flow of time resumed its normal pace. Guards gathered above him. Their faces swam in and out of Declan's vision, but he was pretty sure the wand-carrying wizard among their ranks was smirking.

Two of the men dragged Declan to his feet. He cast a quick glance at the gray stallion. It stood frozen in mid-stride, balanced precariously on its back hooves, front feet stalled out in the act of kicking powerfully down.

Declan blew out a long breath, the closest he could come to an incredulous whistle in his current condition. Holding spells were common enough, but seeing a galloping horse suspended in midair was still impressive.

"Last I heard, the law prohibited magical attack against citizens of Korvosa," he said.

"Magical detention is permitted if that citizen is engaged in a crime," the wizard intoned, "or otherwise endangering the populace."

"Or looks like he's trying to avoid us," chuckled one of the other guards to his companion.

Declan looked pointedly toward the empty bridge. "What populace? There was no one in my path."

"The law forbids riding recklessly through the city streets," the wizard said.

"Giving your horse free rein on an empty bridge is not reckless." Declan looked to the guard wearing the captain insignia on his jacket. "With respect, sir, unless you had good cause to stop me, you're acting outside of your charter."

"Zimbidge didn't stop you," the captain said, reaching out to clap the wizard on the shoulder. "He stopped your horse. Dangerous beast."

His squad seemed to find that amusing.

Declan hissed a sigh through gritted teeth. "Time is not my friend, gentlemen. I need to consult one of my professors at the magic school on a matter of great urgency."

Most of the guards suddenly misplaced their smirks, but the wizard's face twisted in doubt.

"If that's true, you're riding the wrong way."

"I'm not going to the Acadamae," he said. "I studied at the Theumanexus."

"Oh." A droll expression crossed the wizard's face and he rolled his eyes toward the squad captain. "The law does make some allowance for the feeble-minded."

The captain shrugged. "A wizard is a wizard. He's done no harm. I say we let him go."

Zimbidge spun back to Declan. "You have your Theumanexus medal, I trust? Or at least your student papers?"

"I turned them in when I left the school," Declan said. "And I have no medal because I didn't complete the training, which is why I need a wizard's counsel now."

"Did you by chance study with Canalora Rivista?"

"Everyone who enrolls at the Theumanexus studies with Lady Canalora," Declan said. "Lady Lore teaches the principles of magic, and she tests first-year students on their mastery of basic spells and cantrips."

"That is true," the wizard admitted. "But it's also widely known. You could have heard that from anyone. Cast a simple spell, and I'll let you go."

Declan shook his head. "I left the Theumanexus because I didn't wish to become a wizard. In fact, I have sworn off the use of magic."

"Isn't that convenient," Zimbidge sneered. The wizard's attitude was not the most vexing thing Declan had experienced since nightfall, but it touched his honor in a way the other indignities had not.

"Forgive me if I misjudge your intent," Declan said coldly, "but it sounds as if you were calling me a liar."

"I most certainly am," the wizard retorted. "One moment you employ magic to cushion your descent from a spell-stopped horse, and the next you tell me you've sworn it off altogether?"

"But—"

The protest that leaped to Declan's lips died unspoken. There was no denying that his fall from the horse had seemed too slow and his landing too gentle. It certainly wasn't painless, but a holding spell placed on a horse in mid-gallop should have flung him harder and farther.

The wizard took a small, tightly rolled parchment from a tube hanging at his belt and swept it over Declan's head. He unrolled the parchment, glanced at the runes that winked into being, and cast an accusing, sidelong glance at Declan.

"According to this, you've also cast two other spells in the past few hours. A cantrip to light a fire and a defense against enchantment."

Declan remembered taking the torch into the pergola to look for Silvana.

"Now that you mention it, I do recall lighting a torch," he admitted. "That's a routine bit of magic any first-year student could accomplish. Since my mind was preoccupied, I did it without thought. But a defense against enchantment? That takes considerable effort. I think I'd remember casting such a spell, and I do not."

"Maybe he was in a warded building?" one of the guards suggested. "If he was in such a building when the wards were triggered, would the lingering effects of that spell cling to him?"

"Only if he cast it," the wizard said. He considered Declan. "Did you by any chance set warding spells around a building? Activating those wards might read as casting a spell."

"Sworn off the use of magic," Declan reminded him.

"Perhaps you set these wards before you developed these mysterious and convenient scruples?"

He folded his arms and met the wizard's accusatory stare. "No."

"And you did not knowingly cast the slow-falling spell?"

"I have already told you that I did not."

The wizard tapped the parchment. "Then how do you explain the result of this scanning scroll?"

"Inferior workmanship?" Declan suggested.

The rustle of wings drew the guards' attention upward. Skywing fluttered down to perch on the frozen horse, settling on the saddle's pommel like a falcon. The little drake stared balefully at the wizard. Declan could not hear what the dragon was telling Zimbidge, but the wizard's face reddened.

"There's no need to take that tone," Zimbidge said stiffly. "Of course I have heard of Mareshka Zarumina, although I have never heard that she took apprentices."

A few more moments of charged silence passed between the drake and the magic-wielding guard.

Finally the wizard gave a curt nod and sent a glare in Declan's direction.

"You're free to go. But walk your horse through the East Shore, or you'll be stopped again."

As Declan walked toward the stallion, he wondered whether the horse's awareness had been frozen along with its body. If not, the experience would be terrifying for the animal, worse that being caught in a trap or cage.

The wizard raised his wand and flicked it toward the horse in a sharp, dismissive gesture. Immediately the stallion burst into motion. Within a few strides, however, the horse checked, whirled, and headed back at a trot. White rings showed around the stallion's brown eyes.

Declan caught the reins and wrestled the horse to a stop. The wizard backed away during the struggle. Just as Declan was getting the stallion under control, Zimbidge raised his wand.

A wet sheen like thin mucous sprang into existence all over the wizard's body. For one terrifying moment, Declan thought the guardsman was being encased in ice the same way Silvana and Majeed had been.

Then the wand squirted out of Zimbidge's grasp. His feet followed, windmilling on the slick stone cobbles as if they had been greased—which, of course, they had. He went down in a tangle of arms and legs. His fellow guards looked uncertain whether to laugh or attack.

Skywing, however, had no such qualms. The dragon's amusement sang through Declan's thoughts—not laughter, exactly, but a happy, high-pitched hum.

When at last the slime faded and disappeared, the wizard gathered the shreds of his dignity and stomped toward Declan.

"I suppose you didn't do that, either," he snarled. "Don't bother denying it, and remember that commanding a familiar to cast a spell is no different from casting it yourself."

I told him I'm your familiar, Skywing explained.

Declan had never known the little drake could cast spells, but it made sense if Skywing were someone's familiar. But he wasn't Declan's familiar, which led to the question of what wizard he served. Declan sent the dragon a look that promised more discussion on this matter later. "My apologies. Until tonight, I was unaware that . . . my familiar could cast spells."

The wizard opened his mouth as if to argue, then grimaced and shook his head. "If you can't control your familiar, I suggest you turn the creature over to a wizard who can."

Declan nodded and hauled himself into the saddle. The horse swung its head back toward the wizard and made a noise suspiciously like a snicker.

He reined the stallion toward the bridge. Once they were beyond hearing distance, he shook his head at Skywing.

"My familiar?" he repeated. "Apprentice to Mareshka Zarumina? I never even heard that name."

Neither had the wizard. He just didn't want to admit it.

Declan let out a bark of laughter. "Brazen and inventive—just the qualities I'd want in a familiar, assuming that I wanted a familiar. But I don't mean to sound ungrateful. What happy coincidence brought you to the East Shore bridge?"

No coincidence. I'm protecting you. The little dragon puffed out his chest. *Someone needs to.*

Declan considered that answer. "So it really was you who cast those spells?"

Protecting you, the little creature repeated emphatically. *I chased off an imp the necromancer sent to attack you.*

"Jamang didn't wait long, did he?" Declan was impressed that he had taken action so soon. "I suppose he'll keep trying."

No more trying. The necromancer is dead.

Declan froze, astonished and more than a little horrified. "Skywing, you didn't—"

No.

It seemed to Declan that the little drake sounded regretful. Even if it were true he had not slain Jamang, Skywing looked as though he wished he had. Declan decided not to examine that insight too closely. "How did it happen?"

A bad person, the dragon opined.

"Ordinarily I'd agree with that assessment, but killing Jamang might have been an act of self-defense, or at least a well-deserved retaliation. How do you know he was killed by a 'bad person'?"

I know, the dragon insisted. *I watched this bad person follow you for more than three sleeps and sunrises.*

"Someone has been following me for three days?" Declan demanded. "And you're telling me this now?"

Telling you now, yes.

Declan cast a quick glance over his shoulder before he realized the futility of such precautions. If he hadn't sensed the presence of this "bad person" over the course of several days, he doubted he'd have better success going forward. Whoever the stalker might be, most likely he possessed a command of magic far beyond what Declan had mastered at the Theumanexus.

He didn't see the benefit of magic that could turn a pile of drawings into a single animated page, but apparently its novelty gave it value. If Jamang's reaction was typical of his peers, competition to own the animated books and decipher the spell would be fierce. Apart from its current impact on his safety, Declan frankly didn't care about the book magic. In fact, the sooner someone decoded the spell and claimed authorship, the sooner his part in this nonsense would be forgotten.

On the other hand, he did care about this unknown stalker. Jamang claimed he had others books like the one Declan had left on the observatory roof. Since Declan had made only three such books, Jamang's wording suggested that he possessed the other two. If the stalker Skywing had followed killed Jamang, most likely the killer now had those books in his possession. Assuming the killer was a wizard of some sort and could figure out the magic on his own, Declan had no reason for concern.

That was unless the books' new owner decided to eliminate anyone who might otherwise lay claim to the spell.

The thought prompted Declan to pick up the pace. He trotted the gray stallion down the quiet streets. Along the way he rode past two patrols of the city watch and several members of the Sable Guard. All of them noted the little dragon perched on his saddle and let him pass unhindered. Skywing was a useful companion in more ways than one.

Soon the gate to the Theumanexus loomed up ahead, a massive barrier of intricately wrought iron. A fence of similar design surrounded the estate upon which the university had been built. The iron, as Declan understood it, was intended to hold back the fey. Apparently the gnome who'd built the gate had made some enemies in the First World. It was a story Declan hoped to hear someday. At present, however, he was more concerned with the gate's ability to keep him out.

Declan dismounted and gave the bell pull a few vigorous tugs. The bell itself hung in a window of a tiny stone building just beyond the fence. The guard stumbled out, scowling and scratching sleepily at the stubble on his chin. His expression became considerably more respectful when he noted the drake on Declan's saddle.

"Master Avari," he said respectfully. "So you became a wizard after all! No surprise to me. I never thought you were as hopeless as the professors claimed, never once." He grimaced and raised one hand to his bald pate. "Except maybe for the time you accidently set my hair afire, but no lasting harm done, eh? Even the All-Seeing Eye of Nethys would overlook a passing doubt now and then."

"Of the two of us, I'd say you have more cause to remember that unfortunate incident," Declan said with a rueful smile. "If you'd be so kind, I have business with one of the professors."

"At this hour?" The guard huffed incredulously. "They're long asleep."

"Including Paddermont Grinji?"

"Well, no," the guard allowed. "Probably not him." He tipped back his head and sniffed the air like a hunting hound. "Ambergris and sulfur. Oh yes, he's still at work."

He swung open the gate and took the stallion's reins. Declan had a brief and silent exchange with Skywing, who grudgingly agreed to stay with the horse.

Declan hurried past the manor house that was the main building of the Theumanexus and made his way to Geezlebottle Hall.

The building resembled a large tree stump out of which grew many large and bizarrely shaped mushrooms. Its rambling walls had been shingled haphazardly with dark wood. Oddly shaped turrets rose here and there from the roof, and an occasional dormer window jutted from the gables. The strangest aspect of the building, however, was its scale. It had been designed for the size and comfort of gnomes and halflings, few of whom pursued the study of magic in Korvosa. The building had been half completed before someone pointed this out to the gnome patron. As a result, half the building was scaled for humans, the other for shorter folk.

Declan ducked his way through the main door and veered into a corridor that led into the gnome-sized section of the building. Hunched down to spare his head a banging on the lintels, he followed his nose toward the worst-smelling workroom in the hall. Billows of foul red smoke roiled out of an open door. Declan took a deep breath and plunged through.

The air inside was breathable, and the room itself had a mercifully high ceiling. Declan straightened and looked around the workshop.

A long row of tables placed end to end stretched down the center of the room. Shelves lined all the walls. One of these walls resembled a floor-to-ceiling wine cellar, but the compartments held dusty scrolls rather than bottles. Every other available space was crowded with books, vials, bottles, crates, casks, and every conceivable sort of container needed to hold a veritable dragon's hoard of spell components.

The room's only occupant was a gnome, a chubby little man with curly green hair. He stood with his back to Declan, and he seemed intent upon pouring a blood-red liquid, drop by drop, into a steaming basin. Several strangely shaped glass flasks and vials stood near at hand, holding liquid in shades ranging from clear turquoise to sunshiny yellow and bilious green sludge. Some vials shimmered with light. A few bubbled ominously. A vial filled with something pink swayed back and forth in time to the melody it whistled. Declan thought he might have heard the tune at one of the Kendall's musical events.

He cleared his throat. "Pardon the interruption, Master Paddermont, but I'm in urgent need of your expertise."

"Which one?" the gnome inquired without turning around.

"Rare and obscure spells."

The gnome harrumphed. "To the untutored, magic of any sort is a mystery."

"It's a type of magic that isn't taught in the Theumanexus, or even in the Acadamae."

"And you'd know that how?"

"I suppose I don't, but it involved ice."

Paddermont Grinji turned around, revealing a round, rosy face begrimed with soot from a recent explosion. "You have my attention."

"It appears to be a teleportation spell of some sort, one that's cast from a distance. It encases a living person in ice. That person fades away inside the ice and leaves behind a thin shell."

The gnome stroked his pointed green beard as he thought this over. "A shell of ice, you say. I'd like to know the thickness. Was there an aura of crystalline motes around the subject when the spell was cast? Was anything nearby frozen? And the object of the spell, did he disappear slowly, or all at once?"

Declan suppressed a sigh as he glanced toward the gnome-sized window. It was not daylight but close to it. Years of acquaintance had taught him that Paddermont Grinji was capable of asking questions for hours.

"Do these particular details really matter?"

"Probably not, but I won't know which details are important and which not until I hear them, will I?"

Declan nodded and drew a long breath. "Here's everything I know: The object of the spell disappeared slowly. I couldn't break through the ice to free him. When he disappeared, the ice melted immediately. He wasn't the first person taken. I found an ice casing, very thin and fragile, after my friend Silvana had already vanished. The most obvious difference in these two cases," he added, because he knew the gnome would ask, "was location. One was taken from a steamy bathhouse in Cliffside, the other from its rooftop."

"Interesting," Paddermont murmured. "Ice spells. That's a strange choice for Korvosa. And the spell was cast from a distance, you say?"

"Presumably, since there was no one there that I could see. Naturally, I have no way of knowing what sort of distance was involved."

"No, of course not." The gnome tugged at his beard and gazed off into nowhere. After a moment, he said, "Most likely the work of the jadwiga, I'd say."

"The jadwiga?"

"Northern witches," the gnome answered. "They're humans, more or less, descended from Baba Yaga. Notorious for snatching people when the mood suits them. They're seldom known to travel, so most likely the spell originated from Whitethrone."

"Whitethrone? But that's in—"

"Irrisen," Paddermont finished. "Anyone captured with an ice spell would almost certainly have been whisked off to Whitethrone, the royal seat. It's quite an accomplished spell, you see. Well beyond the grasp of any but the most powerful of witches."

Declan dropped heavily into a gnome-sized chair. "Irrisen. A witch stole Silvana away to Irrisen. And not just any witch, but a descendant of an evil goddess."

The gnome pursed his lips. "That's a rather narrow assessment of Baba Yaga, but not entirely inaccurate. And I dare say this Silvana you mention wasn't the target. You humans are always marveling about finding things in the last place you look, but once a thing is found, what's the point in continuing?"

"That much I'd figured out on my own. The witch kept casting the spell until she got the person she wanted."

"Or possibly until she ran out of spells," Paddermont suggested. "Either way, it seems apparent that she wasn't trying for the girl and probably won't have much interest in keeping her. That's good news for you, assuming you intend to get her back."

"Of course I do!" Declan said. "Uh—any suggestions as to where I should begin?"

Exasperation skimmed the gnome's face. "The first logical step would be to tell me who was taken next."

"Oh, right. Majeed Nores, the astronomer."

"In that case, the observatory would be the obvious choice. Whitethrone has a rather famous one. Unless he was taken for revenge, I assume they brought him to Whitethrone for his expertise, in which case he'll be quite safe for as long as he's useful. But the girl?"

The gnome grimaced and hissed in sympathy, revealing tobacco-stained teeth.

"Do you think they'd consider taking ransom for them both?"

"I suppose it's possible." The small wizard pursed his lips and studied Declan. "Since you're coming to me, I assume the astronomer has no family to make inquiries on his behalf. Has he wealthy friends or patrons to contribute to a ransom?"

Declan shook his head. "To the best of my knowledge, he has no friends of any sort."

"Then you'll need to scare up the coin yourself, and plenty of it." The gnome sucked his teeth as he thought this over. "Does the astronomer pay you well enough?"

"No," Declan said glumly. "In fact, I'm paying him. I'm his apprentice, not his assistant." He brightened. "But Basha still owes me for several maps."

The gnome raised one green eyebrow. "You had treasure maps to sell? And you didn't give me first refusal?"

"You wouldn't want these," Declan assured him, "unless, of course, one of your spells requires a pile of hippogriff dung."

"Ah." Paddermont nodded sagely. "The maps were your work. In that case, you gauged my interest precisely."

Chapter Four
The Cunning Mouse

A bright rim of sunlight crowned the eastern hills as Ellasif sauntered into the Varisian merchants' camp. Just north of Korvosa's city walls, broad meadows stretched out on either side of the road, offering fodder for the caravan's draft beasts and a level camp ground for merchant caravans whose members, for one reason or another, preferred not to entrust their goods or well-being to Korvosan law. Korvosans regarded full-blooded Varisians with suspicion, so Ellasif wasn't surprised to learn that many Varisian caravans opted to stay outside of the city.

The camp hummed with activity, and Ellasif paused a moment to take it in. Bright colors barded the horses that nipped at the tall grass beside the road. Mostly red and purple, Ellasif noted, a color choice also reflected on the clothes of most of the sun-browned men who moved goods from sturdy wagons to smaller carts suitable for traversing city streets. She also saw flashes of emerald green and deep, brilliant blue. Varisians liked any bright color, but they seemed fondest of those that mimicked gemstones.

The morning meal, a thick soup that smelled of fowl and onions, simmered in a vast black pot hung over an open fire. Two dark-eyed women knelt nearby, deftly patting down balls of dough. The fragrant circles of completed flatbread heaped a brightly painted wooden tray on the ground between them, and several more loaves baked on the hot rocks surrounding the fire.

The traveling community included not only whole families but also their animals, from dogs to chickens to goats. The barking and clucking and bleating made the camp sound exactly like a farmyard, but Ellasif noticed with some pleasure that it did not smell the same. Such Varisians who wandered from city to city rarely spent more than two or three nights in the same place.

Near the edge of the camp, one of the men strummed a triangular gusli as he sang a ballad about a clever fox and a gullible farmer. Ellasif had heard versions of the song all her life, although the verses changed from town to town. "The farmer's yard is guarded by a fence of wood and stones," sang the musician. "But Foxy knows a secret path that winds beneath the bones." The man's Varisian accent gave even the common tongue an exotic lilt.

A wistful smile stole onto Ellasif's face as she listened. Like the Chelaxian-descended citizens of Korvosa, Ulfen viewed the far-traveling Varisians as vagrants and thieves, but she had enjoyed the few occasions when bands of them passed through White Rook. They told such fascinating stories and sang such lively songs. Liv loved few things better than a well-sung tale.

The thought of Liv froze Ellasif's smile and then let it melt upon her face. She forced the memory to strengthen her resolve and focused on what lay ahead of her rather than the infuriating betrayals of the past.

Ellasif looked around for the caravan leader, one Viland Balev. A tall, black-bearded man stood near the center of the camp, directing the surrounding activity with sweeping arm gestures and bellowed commands. Ellasif strode toward him, raising a hand to shape the gesture the Varisians knew as a warrior's hail. He responded with a grave nod, but his mustache twitched with amusement. It was the same reaction, Ellasif noted sourly, that he would likely have upon being approached by a precocious child.

"You have only fourteen caravan guards," she said without preamble. "You could use more before you travel all the way across Varisia and back."

The big man propped his hands on his hips and gave her a long, assessing stare. "And how do you know so much about my caravan?"

"I can count. And since I know the land between here and Irrisen, I have a pretty good idea of how many guards you'll need to protect a caravan of this size."

"Not all of the guards are wearing weapons," he mused, "and some of them are reloading the goods. Yet you were able to tell the guards from the workers and merchants?"

"Warriors move like warriors."

"So they do," he said. "You have a good eye. If you recommend a guard, I will consider hiring him."

"Her," Ellasif corrected. She spread her arms wide to present herself.

The captain burst out laughing. His laughter stopped abruptly when the point of Ellasif's sword materialized at his throat.

Silence fell over the camp. The captain motioned away the men who crept toward them, weapons drawn.

"You are quick, little one," he admitted. "What is your training?"

Ellasif fell back a step, keeping her sword at low guard. "I am a shield maiden from the Lands of the Linnorm Kings."

His face contorted in disbelief and his gaze slid down Ellasif's small, compact form. "Were you hexed as a child?" he asked. "I have seen Ulfen women before. One traveled with this company some years back. She was taller than me, twice your size."

"At least twice her size," one of the captain's men echoed, cupping his hands several inches from his chest. This drew laughter from the other guards.

Ignoring his man's joke, the captain pointed to the biggest fellow in the camp, a massive Varisian who wore his black hair in four long braids and his beard in two. The big man went shirtless beneath a short cape of brilliant blue, and his brown torso bulged with muscle.

"This is Gisanto. He is a fine swordsman, and, as you can see, not a small man. Do you think you could deal with him?"

Ellasif looked Gisanto up and down. "Yes."

"How?"

She shrugged. "I'm more cunning than I look."

Gold glinted in the captain's smile. "Show me."

Ellasif gathered a handful of her long amber hair with her free hand. "I wasn't expecting to fight. I'll need a moment to prepare."

"Take all the time you like," Gisanto said with a grin. "It will change nothing."

She sheathed her sword and reached into a pocket for a leather thong. She plaited her hair into a single long braid. After securing the end with the thong, she shrugged off her travel cloak and took a few moments to check the broad dagger she kept strapped to one forearm and the knives in her boot sheaths. In her experience, four weapons struck most people as an excessive number for one small woman to carry. Drawing attention to them led most people watching to assume they'd seen all there was to see.

While she prepared for the fight, Gisanto put on a show of his own. He circled Ellasif with his sword drawn, his cloak swirling as he moved through an elaborate display of lunges and feints.

"Are you ready for me, mouse?"

Ellasif picked up her own cloak and wrapped it around her arm with a flamboyant swirl. "Shall we have music for this dance?"

A few of the other guards snickered at her confidence. "Timoteo," shouted Balev. The skald—Ellasif reminded herself that the name for such singers was "bard" or "minstrel" so far south—needed no further instruction to strum up his gusli. As the company began to clap in time to the music, irritation flashed across Gisanto's face, but Ellasif smiled as she recognized the tune she'd heard earlier.

With a growl, the Varisian rushed toward Ellasif.

She sidestepped the charge with room to spare. They whirled to face each other, cloaks swirling, and both attacked high and hard. Swords clashed and held. The big Varisian leaned into the crossed weapons heavily enough to demonstrate his superior strength.

"Too easy," he said.

Ellasif's sword slid away first. As she backed off, one of the guards barked a laugh.

Gisanto sent him a glare, eyes demanding an explanation for the outburst. The laughing man pointed to Ellasif, and Gisanto looked at her.

She'd tossed aside the cloak, which had obscured a small blade. In addition to the hidden knife, she also held one of Gisanto's long black braids. His hand flew up to palm his head, where he found the frayed stump of his braid. He bellowed and charged again. Ellasif wheeled back from her feigned retreat and counterattacked.

They exchanged a flurry of blows, sharp and fast and ringing. But the Varisian could not keep his gaze off of the braid in Ellasif's hand. Distracted, his attacks lacked force and focus. Ellasif deflected and returned them with ease.

Gisanto's temper cooled after a few clashes. He tried to shift the battle's pace to one that favored his strength over the smaller fighter's speed. Ellasif pressed him, staying inside his reach and keeping her attacks coming so fast that he was forced into small, quick defenses.

Finally they broke apart and began to move in a circle, stalking each other while searching for an advantage.

Ellasif noted the amulet hanging over Gisanto's heart. It was a small wooden disk upon which was painted a crude image of a firepelt cougar. There was no knowing what meaning the big man ascribed to it, but Varisians were a superstitious folk who felt strong affinities with totem animals. Ellasif smiled as a new ploy formed in her mind.

She began to sing, improvising words to the tune Timoteo played. Instead of the clever fox outwitting the farmer, she sang of a little mouse turning the tables on a fat, stupid cat.

"The cat is fat, and slow at that," she sang, snapping Gisanto's ample belly with the whip of his own hair. "The mouse is quick and cunning!"

Gisanto's face darkened as he covered the distance between them with three long strides. Their swords met again and again in an angry metallic clamor.

"She hears his big old belly thump," she sang, retreating. "And through the grass goes running." Ellasif slapped Gisanto hard on the buttocks with his braid.

The big Varisian's eyes blazed. He drew a long, curved knife from his sash. Sunlight glinted on the keen edge. The man's sword was designed to thrust or bludgeon, so he'd need that curved knife if he planned to retaliate in the manner she expected. He would also need a free hand.

Sure enough, Gisanto thrust his sword point-down into the ground. He feinted low with the knife. When Ellasif parried, he reached over their crossed weapons and seized her braid with his sword hand.

Instantly he jolted back, staring with disbelief at his hand. The palm was bright red, and his fingers were already starting to swell.

"Swamp nettles," Ellasif explained. "I hid a few in my hair when I braided it. Worse than hornets, don't you agree?"

A few chuckles came from the watching Varisians, along with some angry muttering and one lone whistle of admiration. Ellasif nodded toward Gisanto's sword. "Need more instruction?"

Gisanto tried to grasp the weapon, but his swollen fingers refuse to close around the hilt. He gave up the effort and brandished the curved knife in his off hand.

"Knives, then," he said.

"That's enough." Balev strode between the combatants and put a restraining hand on Gisanto's shoulder.

"You are the best fighter in the camp, even with one hand. Perhaps you want to know what other tricks the Ulfen knows, but I do not. Let them be a surprise for any who seek to waylay us on the road."

"You've won your place," said Balev, turning toward Ellasif. His eyes held some admiration, but no love for her.

Ellasif realized she might have flaunted her cunning too much. Taunting Gisanto was valuable, but humiliating him was a mistake if she wished to remain safe in this company. An apology would only make things worse here before all his peers, so she avoided his glowering stare and nodded at Balev.

"If you have business in Korvosa," said the caravan captain, "conclude it quickly. We leave at dawn tomorrow."

Chapter Five
The Unexpected Treasure

When he emerged from Geezlebottle Hall, Declan saw no sign of the impulsive Skywing. Probably the little drake was chasing imps again, or—considering the excitement of recent events—more likely he was curled up in a morning sunbeam, dreaming of hordes of field mice fleeing from his shadow as he swooped down out of the sun.

The market bustled with activity by the time Declan made his way back to Midland, the section of Korvosa where much of the city's business took place. His weary horse pressed through the crowded streets, the slow clop of hooves a counterpoint to Declan's troubled thoughts.

Silvana was in danger, and he was determined to rescue her. That part was simple. But how did an apprentice mapmaker launch a rescue expedition? If he could persuade Basha to settle their account—and that was a very large "if"—he might have enough to cover his travel expenses to Irrisen, assuming he continued to borrow Majeed's horse rather than purchase one of his own. Raising a ransom was another matter.

Gambling was a possibility. He played a decent game of cards, and his dice seldom took a dislike to him. In theory, his chances stood as high anyone's, but he was beginning to wonder whether he cast spells subconsciously somehow. Jamang's reminder of his animated caricatures and Zimidge's insistence that Declan had cast some sort of ward against enchantment had him wondering what was wrong with him. Whatever it was, if it happened at the gaming table, it would mean big trouble.

High-stakes games generally had a wizard present to ensure that no magic was cast to influence the game. Laws against magical cheating were strict, and violators paid fines far heavier than their prospective winnings. But not, Declan noted glumly, heavy enough to deter people from trying. He suspected the laws were designed to allow certain people to cheat and still make a small profit, the better to fill the city coffers. On the other hand, Declan couldn't be certain that he wouldn't end up owing a cheater's tax, which he couldn't possibly pay.

He wouldn't try to influence the game, but he hadn't set out to create the spell Jamang had valued so highly, either. His goal had been a flipbook, a popular trifle with pictures drawn in small stages of movement, so that when the pages were swiftly riffled the drawing seemed to move. But when he'd stacked the completed drawings, they'd melted together into a single page. If he could create a magical animation without meaning to, who knew what might happen in a game of chance?

And of course he could always lose the game outright.

Putting gambling aside, his options were few. He owned nothing of value to sell. Borrowing money was out of the question, for he had nothing to put up as collateral for the moneylenders. His friends would help him if they could, but their circumstances were similar to his own—they were students and artists, earning their way, but only just. After paying for their training, their room and board, their books and paint and brushes and so forth, they were lucky to hoard enough coins for an occasional evening at a tavern or theater.

In the tales Declan had read as a boy, the hero would simply set out on his journey. He'd find a sword along the way, win a wild hippogriff's trust by removing a caltrop from its hoof, maybe slay a dragon or two to finance the venture.

In real life, he noted glumly, things were seldom so easy.

The deeper Declan rode into the marketplace, the slower his progress. Finally he decided he could move faster on foot. He left the stallion at one of the tent stables and pushed into the crowd thronging the heart of the market.

Booths and tents lined both sides of the street. Declan edged past a stout woman who was eyeing a gray-and-white rabbit in the pen outside a curtained butcher's shop. Just beyond, a flock of hens scratched outside their movable coop, a brightly painted miniature wagon that reflected the common image of a Varisian vagabond caravan. Declan waded through the flock and waved away the enterprising merchant who was handing out slices of fragrant pink melon.

An overturned fruit cart blocked the street ahead, and the argument between the vendor and his apparent competitor was swiftly moving toward a brawl. Declan ducked through the makeshift grape arbor one of the merchants had set up to showcase enormous bunches of scarlet grapes. In the alley just behind, a stained wooden press stood nearby to crush the grapes for fresh juice. Declan wiped the back of his hand across his damp forehead. If the day proved as warm as it promised to be, the juice would be vinegar by sunset.

The sun was nearing its zenith when he finally came to Eodred's Walk, a dozen or so permanent structures arranged in a semicircle. The shops were constructed of whitewashed wood, with upper floors that overhung the street and provided some protection from the sun. The scent of smoked meat filled the air, reminding Declan that he hadn't eaten since the previous afternoon.

He pulled up short near the fortune-teller's door, just missing a collision with the well-dressed man leaving. Behind him, a plump, white-haired woman smirked as she counted a handful of silver coins. She caught sight of Declan and slipped the money into her pocket. Planting her hands on her ample hips, she stepped into his path. "Back so soon?"

"Don't sound so surprised, Bettina," he said as he sidestepped her. "Surely you knew I'd be coming this way."

A quick grin twitched Bettina's lips, and she adjusted her stance to match his. She did not act too proud with Declan, who had always treated the theatrical fortune-teller with teasing affection. Bettina was not a true Harrower, nor even a Varisian, but one of the many native Korvosans whose forebears had immigrated from Cheliax generations earlier. "I see plague and pestilence, gloom and doom. You are too young for such fates as I dispense."

Declan suppressed a sigh and resigned himself to an exchange of pleasantries. He inclined his head toward the departing client. "That gentleman looked happy enough."

"He should," she said complacently. "His future shines like the stars on a moonless night."

"If I were a cynical man, I'd suggest you reward those who are in a position to return the favor."

"Ha! True enough," she said. "And in that spirit, if you can get Basha to repay me for his share of the street sweeper's fee, I'll tell you what tomorrow has in store for you."

He shook his head. "I thank you, but I've had enough bad news for one day."

The fortune-teller cackled appreciatively and waved him on his way.

Basha's Maps stood at the end of the crescent. A massive door of dark wood with many small panels heralded an interior that resembled a gentleman's library. Basha claimed to be a retired adventurer who'd walked the world enough to judge the value of his wares. In truth, most of his maps were works of fiction. He sold enough real maps, however, to interest serious travelers, and to keep those with stars in their eyes coming back when the "ancient treasure maps" they purchased didn't quite pay out.

The proprietor stood on a ladder propped against a tall shelf, staring into an old and dusty tome. He jolted and looked up when the shop bell jangled. His mustache lifted in a disturbingly wide grin.

"Well now, look who's come!" he said heartily. "I was hoping you'd visit today."

Declan huffed with surprise. "You weren't happy to see me two days ago when I stopped by for my fee. Speaking of which—"

"Say no more, my dear lad. Say no more!"

Basha scampered down the ladder, nimble as a ferret, and bustled over to the strongbox. He unlocked the latch and rummaged inside.

Coins clinked for longer than Declan would have thought necessary. He was nearing the end of his patience when Basha slammed the strongbox and held up a leather coin sack of substantial size.

"You may keep the purse," he said munificently.

Declan regarded the old bag. The leather was worn shiny in spots and smelled faintly of old sweat.

"At the risk of sounding ungracious, I'd rather have the full payment."

"It's all in here," Basha said, soundly affronted. "Full payment for every map you've ever drawn for me, those that have sold and those still in inventory. There's also an advance for your next job. It's a real map, so you'll need to travel."

Declan studied him for a moment. The merchant seemed to be serious. "You know I've never left Korvosa, much less mapped unfamiliar terrain. I'm not sure anything I'd draw on this trip would reflect reality."

The merchant snorted. "You're worried about this now? The last map you drew for me, the one that was supposed to be the interior of a Katapeshi harem? Funny how the layout resembled the floor plan of the Jeggare Museum."

Declan shrugged. After all, the man had a point. "What do you want me to map?"

"An inland route through the Sanos Forest." Basha rubbed his hands together in unabashed greed.

"Merchants will gladly pay good money for such a map. The Varisian caravans travel through it all the time."

"And they're notoriously secretive about their paths."

"That's why you're perfect for the job!" Basha said triumphantly. "You're not a known mapmaker. You're not a wizard. You certainly don't fit anyone's idea of an explorer. No one will suspect you."

"They might, when they see me taking measurements and making drawings."

"Let them see you drawing other things," the merchant persisted. "They'll take you for a naturalist or— Abadar forgive you—an artist."

Basha took from the shelf a slim volume bound in blue leather and opened it to display the moving ink on the book's single page.

"Make another of these. That should distract them."

Declan's jaw dropped. "Where did you get that?"

Basha splayed one hand over the place his heart would reside, assuming he possessed one. "My dear boy, surely you don't think I would betray a confidential client. My impeccable sense of propriety forbids it."

"I've seen no evidence that you possess any such scruples."

The merchant pointed to a basket holding several battered scrolls. A small handwritten sign proclaimed them to be *Rare Maps—Recovered from a crypt deep below the Mindspin Mountains*.

"Now suppose I told prospective buyers, 'Those are just some sketches Declan Avari worked up in his free time.' Where would we both be then, hmm?"

"That's different."

"Different how?"

"Well, to start with, I'm fairly certain that the last person to own that book was murdered last night."

The color drained from Basha's face. "That is a significant difference," he admitted. "But wherein lies the degree of uncertainty? That there was a murder or that the murdered person owned this book?"

This struck Declan as a reasonable question. Jamang had implied that he owned the other two "living" books, but Jamang had never been celebrated for his honesty. For that matter, Declan couldn't be certain that Jamang was dead. He had no reason to believe that Skywing would lie to him, but it was possible that the dragon's assessment of the situation was optimistic. Necromancers were supposed to be difficult to kill.

After a moment, Declan said, "If you won't tell me who sold you the book, perhaps you'll tell me whether anyone else came looking for one like it?"

"Perhaps," Basha said cautiously.

"A man of my years, about this tall." Declan held out one hand, palm down, to measure Jamang Kira's height. "Black hair, fine clothes. He was thin and wore a necromancer's amulet from the Acadamae."

"No such person has entered this shop." The map merchant again placed one hand over his heart. "You may believe me, my boy."

"So you were outside the shop when you spoke to him?"

Basha burst out laughing. "Oh, very good! As the saying goes, a keen ear is better than a quick tongue."

"Thank you. You know the curious thing about compliments? They're frequently employed as evasions."

The merchant sobered. "True, but that was not my intent. I have never laid eyes on the man you described. Is he the one you fear is dead?"

Declan nodded. "If I knew who sold you the book, I'd have a better idea who else might be looking for it."

"That I doubt," the merchant said. He went to a table and showed Declan a small, dusty satchel. "A street urchin found this and brought it in early this morning, hoping to sell me the book. I recognized it as your work."

Declan froze in the act of reaching for Jamang's satchel. "You did? How?"

Basha sent him a long-suffering look. "You signed your artist's mark to it. The same mark, I might add, that I have to scrape off your maps whenever you forgetfully inscribe it in the compass rose."

"Sorry," said Declan, genuinely contrite. It was his one concession to vanity in his artwork, although he tried to remember not to include it on his fanciful treasure maps.

The merchant waved this away. "So, will you take the job?"

"Let's start with the book."

Basha handed it over without comment. "It will help convince the Varisian merchants that you're a traveling artist." He grimaced. "And if you are right about the short man's fate, I've no desire to keep such a book in my shop."

"So where do I find these merchants?"

"Just outside of the city, in the meadows beyond the north gate. The captain's name is Viland Balev. He travels the length of Varisia, all the way to Jol in the Lands of the Linnorm Kings. Tell him you're a bored student in search of novelty, or an artist in search of inspiration. Offer him money for passage and protection."

It did not escape Declan's notice that the merchant was talking a little faster than usual, as if he was uneasy.

And when he spoke of the merchant caravan, his hand went to his throat. Most likely, Declan reasoned, Basha wanted him and the troublesome book out of his shop as soon as possible. Under the circumstances, that was prudent.

The job offer, on the other hand, was downright peculiar. It was too good to be true, sending him exactly in the direction he wanted to go mere hours after he'd realized he wanted to go there. Still, Declan didn't see how he could turn it down. He needed to get to Irrisen, and a job that would move him closer to his goal suited his needs.

"Anything I should know about this Viland Balev?"

"He likes to be paid," Basha said bluntly. "Offer him a good fare, and he'll treat you well and leave you alone."

"About this fare . . ."

"Ten gold will content him."

"As well it should," Declan said. "That is, coincidentally, the very amount you owe me."

"It's in the bag, along with forty crowns for this job."

Declan blinked. "You're paying me forty crowns to draw this map?"

"In advance."

Forty platinum crowns would pay a skilled workman for the better part of a year. The fee struck Declan as too good to be true—which, of course, indicated that the job would be far more dangerous, unpleasant, or complicated than Basha was letting on.

But how could he refuse his best chance of rescuing Silvana? Even a fraction of this small fortune would almost certainly be viewed as fair compensation for the services of one accidentally acquired servant, leaving him plenty to pay for any expenses incurred on the trip there and back. As for ransoming Majeed Nores . . . well, he would deal with that question later. He dared not tempt Desna, the goddess of luck, to reverse the incredible good fortune she had just bestowed upon him by asking for more so soon.

The shop bell jangled. A beaming nobleman rushed in, a middle-aged man in a waistcoat and monocle straight out of a portrait of Montlarion Jeggare. He seized Basha's hand and pumped it enthusiastically.

"Splendid investment, Basha, simply splendid! My friends scoffed at the notion, didn't they? But we showed them, eh? Eh?"

If Basha was as puzzled as Declan, he gave no indication. "Of course, my lord," he agreed.

"Not what I expected, of course, but that's part of the adventure, isn't it?"

The man's eyes swept the shop. "You have others, I hope? I'll buy everything you have. Old treasure maps, the older the better. If just one of them pays out like the last, by gods, I'll be more famous than Aximondi Har." He chuckled, "Richer, too!"

"Sir, am I to understand that you found treasure using one of Basha's old maps?"

The nobleman adjusted his monocle and affixed Declan with a glare. "Young man, the offer is on the table. Don't think to outbid me. I won't allow it."

Declan raised his hands and took a step back. "I'm not a competitor, sir. I'm just interested in hearing your story."

"Well, then." Mollified, the noble harrumphed and began. "The map took me deep into the Mindspin Mountains. Deep into them, mind you. Found a small cache of Osirian treasure, mostly gold and lapis jewelry. Wonderful find."

"That's . . . hard to imagine."

"Quite, quite." His brow furrowed. "Odd thing, though. The box was surrounded by dun-colored sand. Just what you'd expect from something that came out of the desert, but the soil in that area is a combination of rock and heavy clay. Odd thing." He shrugged and smiled. "Truth be told, I enjoy the mystery almost as much as the treasure."

"Here you are, my lord." Basha reached into the basket and handed him four scrolls, all of them stained, well-weathered parchment. Declan could account for the stains and the weathering, seeing that his were the boots that had stomped them and he was the one who'd steeped them in a pan of weak tea until they appeared suitably battered.

The man took the maps with avid glee. "This is the lot?"

"For now." Basha sent a furtive glance in Declan's direction. "But I'm hoping to acquire more from the same source in the near future."

"Send word when you have them, and I'll race your messenger back to the shop," the man said in a jovial tone. He tipped his hat to Basha and gave Declan an amiable nod before rushing out of the shop.

After the door shut behind him, the map merchant turned to Declan. "About that map . . ."

"It was one of mine, wasn't it?"

Basha raised both hands and shook them as if importuning the gods. "How in the name of Abadar did you find an Osirian treasure in the Mindspin Mountains, thousands of miles north of Osirion?"

"I haven't a clue," Declan said. "But if those other maps turn up something interesting, let me know."

"Why would I keep such a thing from you?" Basha said, eyes wide with feigned innocence. "Surely you know that I would embrace any opportunity to pay you twice your current rate."

Declan picked up the old coin bag and dropped it into Jamang's satchel. "I'm off then."

"A real map," Basha reminded him. "And don't delay. The caravan leaves at dawn tomorrow."

The merchant held his smile until the door shut behind the young man. He raised his hands high and away from his body, as if to indicate that he held no weapon.

"Well done," said a feminine voice behind him.

Basha slowly turned to face a small woman and her sharp sword, which she held with its point a few inches from his belly. "Was he right?" he asked. "Will others be looking for that book?"

The woman shrugged. "Maybe, but no one has reason to look for it here. Unless, of course, you give them a reason."

"I won't speak of a word of this," he babbled. "Any of it. This whole episode is already forgotten."

"Then we're done here."

As she strode past, Basha impulsively reached out to stop her. "That treasure map," he said. "Is this about the map?"

A thoughtful expression crossed the woman's face. "You know, I think it might be."

Chapter Six
The Last Goodbyes

The clack of a wooden loom beckoned to Declan long before he reached Isadora's shop. He paused in the open doorway for a moment to watch the weaver at her work. Slim and pale, her dark hair pulled back from a round, pretty face and tied with a bit of ribbon, she didn't look much different from the girl who'd tagged along at Asmonde's heels for as long as Declan could remember. And since he'd done a great deal of tagging after his brother himself, Isadora felt more like a sister to him than a friend.

"One shadow, two parts," he said.

The woman's gaze darted to his face, and a welcoming smile bloomed on her own. She immediately pushed away from her work and ran into Declan's arms.

He held her close, overwhelmed with a familiar sense of relief and gratitude. She could have hated him for what his brother did to her, or refused to have anything to do with him. That she did not was a constant marvel to Declan, and a blessing.

"You're smothering me," she said into his chest.

Declan released her and stepped back. "Where's my little girl?"

"Sleeping." The word came out on a sigh.

Declan noted the shadows under Isadora's eyes. Her daughter had always been wakeful at night and difficult to rouse during the day. Declan had never heard that this was common among hellspawn children, but it seemed logical to him that infernal blood might result in a deep affinity for night.

"You can't sleep when she does, and work while she's awake?"

A wry smile lifted one corner of Isadora's lips. "That would be difficult with any five-year-old, much less a hellion like my Rose."

She spoke matter-of-factly and with considerable affection. It seemed to Declan that her description of Rose was nothing above what any fond and harried parent might say.

"Can I look in on her?"

Isadora tipped her head toward a curtained alcove in the rear of the shop.

He didn't bother to walk softly. If the thump and clatter of a loom didn't wake the child, footsteps were unlikely to disturb her slumber. He edged the curtain aside and gazed at the stocky little girl sprawled on the cot.

Some hellspawn could pass for human, but a single glance told the truth of Rose's heritage. Her broad face reminded Declan of an unfinished sculpture, all sharp angles and hard planes, and her skin was a deep pink that verged on crimson. Long, glossy curls of the same hue spread across the pillow. Except for her coloring and her strangely beautiful hair, Rose would not look out of place crouched amid a roofline gallery of stone gargoyles.

Isadora came up behind Declan and rested her chin on his shoulder. "She's beautiful, isn't she?"

From most people, such words might have been ironic, or at best, a plea for reassurance. Isadora meant what she said.

Declan let the curtain fall. "She'll never outshine her mother, but who could hope to?"

"Liar," Isadora said in his ear.

"I prefer 'charmer.'"

"Same thing."

She stepped away and poured two cups of water from a sweating pitcher. Declan accepted his, drained it gratefully, and held it out for a refill.

Isadora lifted one eyebrow. "Long night?"

"Very, but debauchery played no part in it." He emptied the second cup. "I'll be going away for a while, Izzy."

The woman nodded and raised a hand as if to tuck a stray lock of hair behind one ear. She caught Declan watching her. Too late, he smoothed the pained grimace from his face.

"I keep forgetting that ear is gone," she said lightly.

Declan would never forget. Nor would he ever forgive. "Sometimes I regret that Asmonde is dead—"

"I always regret it," she said. "I always will. And that is all that needs to be said."

There was no time to tread this path again—and, Declan had to admit, there was no point. He accepted her sentiment with a nod and reached into his pocket for a small red leather bag he'd purchased on the way.

"This is for Rose."

Isadora took the gift with a smile, which froze when she heard the chink of coins within.

"We're doing just fine, Declan. I don't need your money."

"I hope you'll accept it anyway."

The woman huffed out a sigh. "You're not responsible for me and Rose. You're not responsible for your brother."

Declan wasn't so sure about that, but he responded with a shrug and an easy smile. "I had the money, and it pleases me to give Rose small gifts from time to time."

"You will spoil her."

"Spoiling Rose is entirely within my rights as her uncle."

This coaxed a reluctant smile from Isadora. "In that case, thank you."

"It's not much, but there should be enough for a wooden practice sword and five or six lessons with my old sword master. If Rose takes to the sword as I think she will, he will happily teach her all he knows and never ask for another copper pinch."

"That would suit her." She paused for a fleeting smile. "It might even reconcile her to a few hours of daylight. Again, thank you."

Declan accepted a sisterly kiss on each cheek and left the shop. The gray stallion raised his drooping head to send Declan a reproachful glare. Whatever enthusiasm the horse had held for the unexpected midnight exercise had long since faded.

He patted the beast's neck. "Just another couple of errands, and we're off to find the merchant caravan. It won't leave until tomorrow, so you can have a good long rest."

The horse blew and stamped as Declan swung into the saddle, but he trotted along briskly enough. He even had enough energy to eye with interest the matching pair of roan mares hitched to the guest carriage waiting at the gate of the Frisky Unicorn.

Declan tied the stallion to the rail a safe distance away and started down the flower-lined walk. He nodded to the large, fussily dressed matron who sailed toward the carriage, a small pelisse clutched in one plump hand.

She drew up just short of Declan and flapped her free hand at him in a shooing motion.

After the first startled moment, Declan realized she was looking past him. He turned to see Skywing perched on the iron fence.

"One of the Unicorn's resident house drakes," Declan assured the woman. "This is Skywing. He's harmless."

"He's a thief," she sputtered. "All of them are. I've no idea why this . . . this rookery came so highly recommended."

Good cheeses here, Skywing noted. *Plenty of mice, too.*

Don't help me, Declan pleaded silently. To the woman he said, "Are you missing something?"

Her expression snapped tight with haughty annoyance. "I don't see how that's any of your concern."

Declan bowed. "My father, Nagashar Avari, wants to hear of any trouble a guest might experience."

Or create, Skywing added, echoing Declan's own thoughts.

"I'd be happy to escort you to him. If there's cause for complaint, the matter will be handled, I assure you."

The guest's gaze darted toward the carriage. "That will not be necessary. If you would be so kind as to let me pass, I'm expected at the Kendall."

"You may wish to consult your calendar," he said. "Yesterday's midnight performance of *The Scarlet Raven* was the last. There are always a few days between, to allow for scenery changes and rehearsals and so on. If something of yours has gone astray, there's plenty of time to check your room. I'll summon the housekeeper to assist you."

Before she could protest, Declan reached past her for the bell pull hanging on the shaded porch. Immediately the door opened. A middle-aged woman with iron-gray hair and the eyes of a tax collector came to stand beside Declan. He got the distinct impression that she'd been on her way well before his summons.

"Allow me to take that for you," the housekeeper stated as she reached for the pelisse.

The guest handed it over. Declan was not surprised. He'd met sea captains whose presence aboard their own ships was less commanding. If the Frisky Unicorn's housekeeper told a Hellknight to hand over his armor, he'd probably strip down to his smallclothes before he thought to question her.

"Now, is there something I might help Madame with, before she settles her account?"

Resignation flitted over the guest's round face. "No, nothing."

As the housekeeper herded the would-be skip into the inn, Skywing flew over to perch on the ornate wooden trim that fell like lace from the roofline of the porch.

Can't find Silvana, he mourned.

"I think I know where she was taken. Tomorrow morning, I head north."

The dragon leaned forward, ready to leap into flight. *Want to come.*

Declan shook his head. "The trip will be long and dangerous."

Want to help, Skywing insisted.

"You can keep an eye on things here for me."

The little creature arched its wings and hissed. Declan grimaced.

"You've already helped," Declan said, "chasing off the imp, dealing with the city guard. I don't know what I would have done without you, but I think I can take it from here."

Skywing did not form a comment, but the doubt that washed over Declan's mind was far more eloquent than words. The dragon leaped from his perch and winged up toward the inn's turret.

"The benefit of low expectations," Declan grumbled as he climbed the stairs, "is that one so seldom disappoints."

The familiar scent of polished wood welcomed him to his childhood home, and as he hurried down the hall he caught the spicy aroma of the cakes for which the Unicorn was famous. The cook's latest creation stood on a flower-decked table just outside of the dining salon. A thin layer of fondant, artfully cut into a design that mingled flowers and stars, overlaid the dark icing. It was a far cry from the edible art his mother used to fashion, but still fine enough to carry on the reputation she had established.

He walked quietly past the study and on to the narrow, circular flight of stairs that climbed to the inn's single turret. Out of long habit, he counted the stairs as he climbed. The dust began to collect around fifty-three. No one, not even the inn's otherwise fearless housekeeper, could find a compelling reason to enter the drakes' lair.

Skywing awaited him there, along with several drakes Declan had known since boyhood. Most of them basked in a patch of afternoon sun, but a few raised their heads and sent silent greetings. One, a little red female, hopped to the floor and spread her wings protectively over a small heap of shiny objects.

Didn't steal, she said defensively. *But mine now.*

Declan looked toward Skywing.

Courting, the drake said matter-of-factly.

There was no time for a lecture on house rules. Declan removed an empty nest from one of the window seats that ringed the turret room. He raised the lid to reveal the small wooden chest inside. As he'd expected, the lock on it had been broken.

He opened the chest and stared at the contents, a single book. It was small enough to slip into a pocket, inexpensively bound in boot-quality leather and secured with a small strap and lock. In short, it was the sort of thing a traveler of modest means might use to jot down his observations, or a young girl her romantic daydreams. This lock, too, had been broken.

Declan reached for the little book and rifled through the pages. There were more spells than he remembered inscribing, but still hardly enough to interest a wizard nearing the end of his Acadamae training. A wizard's spellbook was his most valuable possession, yet when Asmonde had looted the chest of assorted detritus Declan had accumulated during his years at the Theumanexus, he'd left his younger brother's spellbook behind. Asmonde had found the animated flipbooks of greater value.

Declan wondered whether Jamang had killed Asmonde for these books. Unlikely, he decided. Most likely Jamang was simply the first scavenger on the scene. Asmonde's ambitions were too high, and the risks he took too large. Declan had little doubt that his brother's fate, whatever it had been, had come down to drinking the ale he'd brewed.

Wizard book, Skywing observed, his silent words rounded with surprise and respect. *Yours?*

"Not anymore." Declan tossed the book back into the chest. "I'm not going down that path again."

The path that leads to Silvana?

The dragon's comment was not, Declan suspected, either as arch or as accusing as Skywing could have made it. Even so, it hit him between the eyes.

He sank down onto the window seat and dug both hands into his hair.

No more magic. He'd sworn a private oath the day he'd found Isadora, nearly dead from what happened in the aftermath of Asmonde's botched summoning. That his brother would attempt such a binding was bad enough. That he would abandon Izzy when it failed was unthinkable.

Declan reminded himself again that he was not the same as his brother. For one thing, he didn't have half of Asmonde's talent. The study of wizardry was never easy, but Declan had struggled with it as he never had with any other discipline. If great temptation came only with great talent, he should be safe enough.

And even if he was not, wasn't the end worth the risk? For that matter, it seemed to him that turning away from Silvana to save himself would destroy any remnant of the virtue he was trying to safeguard.

A conundrum, Skywing agreed.

Declan glanced up sharply. "I wasn't talking to you."

How could I know that? You were thinking very loudly.

"Since we're discussing this, do you have an opinion?"

A prediction, the dragon said. *You will do what you need to do, whatever that is.*

Declan could find no argument for this impromptu aphorism. He retrieved the spellbook from the chest and slipped it into his pocket.

He retraced his steps to the main floor and tapped on the door of the study. His father glanced up from the ledger he'd been contemplating.

Most people would consider Nagashar Avari a handsome man. Tall and solidly built, he possessed an abundance of wavy black hair and a strong face dominated by a proud aquiline nose. He was also an older, slightly thicker version of his elder son. Declan reminded himself that it would unreasonable to hold this against him.

The study was a tidy room, the opposite of those in which Declan's teachers had made their lairs. While the wizards and astronomer were masters of clutter, their desks surrounded by pinnacles of stacked books and ruins of knick-knacks and half-eaten lunches, Nagashar's chamber was both clean and spare. On his desk lay only an accounts ledger and an inkpot upon a blotter. The room's sole lamp hung unlit above the desk, but sunlight poured in from a high window to reveal that every corner of the room was free of dust and cobwebs. Against the wall stood a closed sideboard where Nagashar kept the inn's records and his personal papers.

The only nod to decoration was a pair of exquisite papercraft landscapes, each framed and mounted under glass upon a field of dark silk. Each was composed of hundreds of hand-torn paper scraps that Declan's mother had made by boiling discarded ledgers, contracts, and letters. Every piece was a different shade of white, often with a fine thread or speck of slivered glass mingled with the reconstituted paper. The art was in the selection and shape of each hand-shredded strip, pasted and layered upon a background of pure white vellum. Both landscapes depicted snow-swept hills that grew more ethereal in the distance. Declan felt a shiver each time he looked at them. They were the finest things in the inn.

"I'll be leaving the city for a while," Declan told his father without preamble.

Nagashar settled back in his chair. "Oh?"

"I've been offered employment that requires travel."

His father's brows rose. "Drawing maps?"

"Yes."

"How so? You don't have a guild license, or any real experience, for that matter. You haven't even finished your apprenticeship with the astronomer!"

"Basha doesn't seem to care."

"Yes, I've heard about Basha's Maps," the senior Avari said darkly. "Working for that scoundrel will do nothing to build your reputation."

"This is a legitimate map and a good opportunity. I intend to take it." Declan folded his arms. "You've been telling me for years to be practical. One would think you'd be pleased."

"I'm not displeased, exactly." His father's face took on a familiar, wistful expression. "Still, it was your mother's wish that her sons undertake the study of magic. You promised to do so."

"Asmonde made the promise for both of us," Declan reminded him. "I was ten years old at the time. Anyway, I wasted several years in the Theumanexus."

"The Theumanexus," Avari said with distaste. "Asmonde went to the Acadamae."

"And died there," Declan shot back. "One of many who become corpses rather than wizards."

"Young soldiers die in battle, young wizards burn in magic's flame. It is a tragic fact of the ambitious life."

"If you ask me, the true tragedy is that so many survive the training."

Nagashar rose from behind the table, trembling with rage. "That is a despicable thing to say."

"Is it? Name one wizard whom you admire. And not because of his power or wealth or fame."

"All of those things are admirable."

"Very well then, name one arcanist of any sort whom you could trust. Just one."

"Your mother!" Nagashar roared.

The argument broke. For many moments, neither man could gather enough shards to fashion them into thoughts, let alone words.

The older man sank slowly down into his seat. Declan felt none too steady himself. This revelation did not accord with his memories of his mother, and he'd had too many props kicked out from under his boyhood assumptions of late to welcome another. More importantly, he understood that in Korvosa, one did not hide magical ability without good cause.

"Is it true?"

"Yes," Nagashar said slowly. "But it should have remained unsaid."

"Why?"

His father simply shook his head. As he often did in times of high emotion, he reached for a delicate porcelain vial that hung from a chain around his neck. The vial contained his wife's bone dust—a ghoulish keepsake, in Declan's opinion, which by unspoken agreement remained a family secret.

"Your mother wanted you to learn to use and understand magic," said Nagashar. "She had her reasons."

"I'm sure she did. No doubt they are similar to the usual ones: power, wealth, respect."

"Do you blame her for wanting these things for her sons?"

"Not at all. Mother knew better than most how difficult is it for artists to earn a living in Korvosa. She, who could create that"—Declan gestured toward one of the framed paper landscapes—"was known as a cake decorator."

"And you would be known as a mapmaker."

"Korvosans might not be generous patrons of any art but the theater, but they value maps and pastry. Like my mother before me, I'll do what I must to make my way in the world and spend the hours remaining to create art that pleases me."

"And that is the sum of your ambitions?"

For a moment, Declan was tempted to tell his father about Silvana and his determination to rescue her. Nagashar would call it a fleeting madness. Declan knew all too well where that conversation was likely to go. So he merely shrugged.

"What more can I tell you? I am, after all, Pernilla Avari's son."

Nagashar brandished the little vial. "That's precisely what I'm afraid of."

Declan considered his father for a long moment. "What are you not telling me?"

The older man made a visible effort to collect himself. "The bane and blessing of reaching my years," he began, "is coming to know that most of life's regrets focus not upon the things that one did, but the things one failed to do. This is something I would spare you if I could. Your mother believed it was important for her sons to gain mastery of magic. I agreed with her. I still do."

Declan sighed. "With respect, Father, you need to let it go. I am not my brother. I loved Asmonde, but I despised what he became. And that is my last word on the matter."

He turned and strode toward the door.

"Exactly where do you think you're going?" his father demanded.

"Whitethrone." Declan tossed the answer back over his shoulder and shut the door firmly behind him.

Chapter Seven
The Imp's Revenge

Sunset tinted the sky as Ellasif returned to the Varisian camp. Men and women finished the last of their suppertime chores before darkness confined them to the borders of their campfires, where they took turns standing watch at the edge of the darkness. The smell of bubbling stew spread out over the company, and an old Varisian man with a curling mustache stood ready with a mallet, watching Balev for the nod that would signal permission to remove the bung and tap the ale keg.

Ellasif saw no sign of Declan Avari, nor of the tall gray stallion she had seen him ride to and from the mapmaker's shop. Before her encounter with Declan's necromantic rival, she'd spent several days following the Korvosan mapmaker, learning his habits and taking his measure. When Silvana was snatched away, Ellasif assumed that Declan would want to rescue the girl, and she'd made sure he had the means to do so. But these careful preparations could not dismiss Ellasif's sense of foreboding. There was always the chance that

Declan would find other uses for the small fortune that had come his way. If he did, Ellasif would drag him to Whitethrone herself, but for now it was far easier if he went willingly.

As Ellasif dismounted from her new steed, several of the Varisians hid their smirks behind their hands. The pony was a shaggy little beast, her thick coat a white-dappled gray that looked almost blue. A thick white mane hung over her eyes, disguising the evil-tempered gleam that had caught Ellasif's attention, and the ribbons someone had braided into her tail lent an air of harmless innocence.

A young man, shorter and slimmer than his companions, nodded amiably to Ellasif and came over to take the pony's reins. He jolted back with a curse as the beast snapped at his hand.

He flashed a wide, white smile at Ellasif. "I see you have found a kindred spirit."

His jibe surprised an answering smile from her. "I like northern ponies. They're sturdy and strong, and there's nothing like them in battle. They'll carry you willingly into the worst of it and fight like cornered badgers."

"And you don't need a stepladder to get into the saddle."

"There's that," she agreed, since his jest sounded more friendly than challenging.

The youth touched his forehead and sketched an elaborate bow. "I am Camillor Vamoni, delighted to make your acquaintance."

"Ellasif," she said. "Before you waste your time and obvious charms, I'm here to fight, not to flirt."

His brows peaked. "I see. You would not be the first to look upon us Varisians as vagrants and thieves, unworthy of the attentions of a mighty shield maiden."

"That's not it," Ellasif said absently. She scanned the road. Still no sign of that blasted Korvosan. If he didn't show up, all her hard work would be for nothing.

"Have I offended you? Tell me and let me make it up to you."

She turned her attention back to the young man. He gazed at her with an earnest expression. He seemed pleasant enough, and her task would be easier if someone in the caravan was kindly disposed to her.

"You've done nothing wrong," she assured him. "But like this pony here, I often give people the wrong impression."

"Small, cute," he said, "but with sharp teeth."

"Exactly," she said, pleased that he could grasp the salient point so quickly.

The clatter of hooves drew her gaze to the road. A tall gray stallion drew up to the camp, and Declan Avari swung lightly down from the saddle.

He was not a big man, no more than average in height and frame. His skin was as fair as Ellasif's, but unlike most dark-haired Korvosans, his slightly shaggy hair was a light brown. His eyes were like none Ellasif had seen before. His irises were a peculiar shade of slate blue that in some lights held hints of purple. His features were pleasant enough, and unlike the men of her village, he kept his face clean-shaven.

Camillor followed the line of her gaze. "Ah," he said, as if he'd solved a mystery, and not altogether to his satisfaction.

Ellasif shrugged and handed him the reins. To his credit, Camillor could take a hint. He led the pony toward the deep grass where the other animals were tethered.

Ellasif wandered over to the cooking fire and accepted a piece of flatbread from a woman of middle years and unfriendly demeanor who was sitting with her daughter.

"Ellasif," she said by way of introduction.

The older woman's eyes narrowed. "Gisanto's mother," she said. She inclined her head toward the younger woman. "His sister."

"Nadej," the young woman said with a smile. She ignored her mother's scowl and handed Ellasif a plate heaped with fried fish and herb-scented potatoes. "I never laughed so hard as yesterday. Gisanto gets too big for his own boots. He should be reminded from time to time that a man also fights with what lies between his ears. You are welcome here."

Ellasif doubted that everyone shared Nadej's opinion, but she thanked her with a nod and wandered closer to Avari. He was speaking with Timoteo. The bard pointed Avari toward the captain.

Declan approached the caravan leader. "Viland Balev?" he inquired.

Balev turned toward him. "You are free with my name."

"And mine as well," said the mapmaker. He held out one hand. "I'm Declan Avari. I'm looking to travel north, and I hear you might be willing, for a fee, to let me ride along."

After a moment's hesitation, the Varisian took the offered hand. "You are Korvosan. Old blood Korvosan, if those eyes speak truth."

Ellasif noted the flash of irritation on Avari's face. That, she could understand, having had her own coloring remarked upon for her whole life. Most Ulfen had hair that was fair or red. Hers was neither. It was not brown, exactly, but a color that found the exact point where brown and red and blonde intersected. Jadrek used to say that it was the only indecisive thing about her.

Not that she cared about anything Jadrek had to say. Not anymore. She turned her attention back to the discussion of Declan Avari's supposedly ancient heritage.

"Only half Korvosan, I suppose. My mother came from northern folk."

Balev's gaze swept Avari. "Shoanti?"

He shrugged. "I never met my mother's people."

"So, being of barbarian stock and open mind, you are not afraid that we will rob you and throw you to the carrion birds?"

Declan blinked. "Well, I'd certainly prefer you didn't."

For some reason, Avari's tone amused the merchant captain. His bearded face relaxed into a genuine smile. Ellasif listened as Declan repeated the story the map merchant had suggested to him. As he spoke, he pulled a small book and a charcoal pencil from his pocket and made a few deft markings. He showed it to Balev, who roared with laughter and clouted him companionably on the shoulder, albeit with enough force to make the young man wince.

When the men concluded their bargain, Balev pointed to the cooking fire and strode off. Ellasif went over to the captain and exchanged a few words to establish the next step of her pretense.

She walked over to Declan and gave him a curt nod of greeting. "I am Ellasif, a shield maiden of the Lands of the Linnorm Kings. I'm to be your guard for the trip. The captain thinks that you will not trust a Varisian."

Surprise flitted over Avari's face, followed by a rueful smile. Apparently he thought he'd made a better impression on the Varisian captain.

"So I'm to believe that no Ulfen ever takes anything that didn't rightfully belong to her."

"Not by theft," Ellasif said. "Perhaps at the point of a sword."

Avari's smile broadened into genuine amusement. He looked her over, his eyes lingering on the long winter wolf tail that hung from her hip. It was her oldest and most treasured trophy, and it pleased her when others noticed it.

"I'm picturing you on the deck of a longship," he said.

"And you find that amusing?"

He was saved from answering by the swift approach of a rider. The man wore a servant's livery, but his horse was a fine red mare with white stockings and blaze. Avari sighed, his shoulders slumped.

He excused himself and walked over to meet the servant. They spoke quietly, but Ellasif caught the gist of it. The servant carried an urgent message from Avari's father, demanding that he return. He must not go to Irrisen, the servant stressed. It was far too dangerous.

The message appeared to prick the young man's pride, and he curtly dismissed the messenger, who reluctantly returned without a reply.

Ellasif wandered over. "Your father is right to be concerned. The northlands are dangerous."

"I'm not worried."

"You really aren't, are you?" she said. "You must be either a fool or a mighty wizard."

He raised a suspicious eyebrow, and she silently cursed her clumsy ploy. Fortunately, rather than ask why she made that assumption, he said, "Is there any difference?"

"Do you know how to use a sword?"

After a moment's hesitation he replied, "In theory."

It was her turn to raise an eyebrow.

"I had a sword master in my youth. In Korvosa, that's typical for most young men and many women. But I've never been in a real fight. I suspect that's rather different."

"You're unlikely to find out unless you carry a sword. We're stopping in Baslwief. You can buy one there."

Camillor walked past in time to catch the last comment. "You lack a sword, Master Avari?" he said. "Permit me to lend you one of mine."

The two men fell into conversation like old friends, discussing blades and fighting preferences. From what Ellasif overheard, Avari knew more about technique than she had expected, but his lack of experience would be a problem if he ended up facing so much as a lone goblin. It would do her no good if he died on the way to Whitethrone.

As Ellasif walked away from the men, she heard Camillor ask Declan whether he had any prior claim on the affections of a certain petite northern woman. Declan assured him he did not.

Ellasif rolled her eyes and kept walking.

The caravan left at dawn the following morning. The captain set a brisk pace, and Ellasif soon found herself uncomfortable in the saddle of her rough little pony. Avari rode well, with an ease that spoke of training and practice.

The morning's travel passed with no incident more exciting than the occasional wave of a farmer driving his produce toward the city markets. Now and then Timoteo sang a riding song, and most of the company joined in. After the third time, Ellasif realized he was marking the hours, and after the sixth the caravan paused for a midday break. The afternoon passed the same way, with the addition of a much shorter break for water and a stretch of the legs.

When they stopped for the night, Avari removed the horse's bridle and brushed it down, drawing nods of approval from some of the Varisians and puzzled frowns from others. Ellasif was certain that everyone in the caravan knew to the copper what fee he'd paid and how much his horse and gear would fetch in market, but he was not acting like a snooty Korvosan student indulging himself with a trip to northern parts. She had seen him pause now and then, surveying the territory and sketching in his little book. He was taking his own ruse seriously, unaware that it was all part of Ellasif's design.

Despite her triumph over Gisanto, or perhaps because of it, the Varisians seemed far less impressed with Ellasif. She returned a couple of friendly nods from Nadej and Camillor, and even the bard Timoteo tipped her a wink as he helped erect a tent, but the rest of the company turned away when she tried to make eye contact, or else found something more interesting just past her shoulder. Her offers to help set camp gained her curt requests for water or firewood. The Varisians had hired her, but still they did not welcome her. Once more she worried whether she'd gone too far in demonstrating her "cunning" against the big warrior. She wished he'd take his revenge sooner than later, preferably in some harmless prank. Perhaps then she would be more welcome in the caravan.

Avari was experiencing the opposite problem, Ellasif saw as she returned with a double armful of deadfall for kindling. He sat between a pair of teenage Varisian girls, peeling and dicing vegetables for the stew pot while the girls took turns asking him flirtatious questions about his life in Korvosa. A third was dancing a Varisian welcoming dance that Ellasif herself had not been offered, not that she cared. Avari enjoyed the attention but accepted it with a casual attitude, as though he were used to receiving it. Still, despite his smile and open face, he was holding something back from the Varisian girls. It wasn't that they were homely or graceless. Rather, it appeared that Declan's mind was half reserved for some other matter.

It had to be Silvana. Good, thought Ellasif. The more dedicated he is to rescuing her, the easier it will be to get him to Whitethrone. Yet as soon as the thought formed in her mind, there was something unsatisfying about it. Ellasif was cunning in more than battle, but for the first time since she began to devise her rescue plan, something about it gnawed at her stomach. So much depended on the cooperation of others who had no idea of her true intention. So much depended on later improvisation. So much could still go wrong.

After the sun set, Ellasif munched on a sweet apple and paced a perimeter just outside the campfire's light. Balev had assigned pickets at four points, but Ellasif's watch did not begin until the small hours. She knew she should catch her sleep soon, but she felt restless, and walking helped her digest the thick venison stew the Varisians had shared in generous helpings. Unless the caravan saw some action soon, this job threatened to give her a merchant's paunch.

Before she'd stretched her legs enough to settle onto her bedroll, Ellasif noticed one of the girls who'd been flirting with Avari kneeling beside his packs and bedroll. She remembered hearing Timoteo call the girl Vira earlier. Avari remained near the fire, now flanked by another pair of chatty women. Despite all of his city education, Avari had fallen for one of the world's oldest ruses. The proof of his fallibility in such matters brought a smile to Ellasif's lips. As she moved quietly toward the girl opening one of Declan's packs, her smile turned grim.

"I can't imagine how Varisians developed this unfair reputation as thieves," she said.

Vira startled and froze. Ellasif saw in her eyes that an excuse was already taking shape in her mind. She opened her mouth to voice it, but Ellasif silenced her with a disapproving cluck of her tongue.

"You were merely making yourself ready to surprise him as he came to bed," Ellasif suggested. "Or you were going to wash his clothes as a favor. Maybe you left him a flower as a symbol of your esteem."

Vira smiled ruefully. She said, "One of those, yes." She closed the flap on a familiar leather traveling satchel and patted it wistfully.

"Balev took the Korvosan's coin," said Ellasif. "Yet I saw their color glow in your eyes."

"Do not tell Balev," said Vira. "I beg you."

That was reassuring. If Vira feared the captain's reaction, Ellasif could count on some semblance of discipline within the caravan. The question now was whether it was better to rely upon Balev's authority or to place her confidence in this clumsy little conniver. It was really no choice at all, since Ellasif carried so little weight with the captain.

Ellasif sighed. "If Avari finds anything missing—"

"He won't," promised Vira.

Ellasif shot a hard finger into Vira's belly. Vira gasped, but not in pain. Ellasif's finger struck the rigid, flat surface of a book hidden beneath the Varisian's shift. Ellasif put out a hand, and Vira sighed again before removing the stolen book and surrendering it.

"Don't let me catch you sniffing around things that aren't yours," said Ellasif. Remembering how she'd stung Gisanto, she added, "You little squirrel."

Vira smiled as though Ellasif had called her by an affectionate nickname. She darted away.

Ellasif opened the book and found that it still contained only a single illustrated page, as it had when she'd left it for Declan at Basha's shop. She returned to her own pack, looked around to be sure she was not observed, and removed the other book. The distant firelight was barely enough to make out the images. The subject matter was different—one depicted a lonely milkmaid, the other an adventurous noblewoman—but both were notable for their lascivious subject matter and their magical animation. This was one unusual wizard she had been sent after.

She casually wandered over to Avari's spot and slipped the book back into his pack. Satisfied she had done so unseen, she returned her own copy to her pack and moved her bedroll to gain a clearer view of the spot Declan had chosen for himself. If Ellasif understood Vira as well as she hoped, the little squirrel would soon chatter all to her sisters. If they had half the good sense Vira had demonstrated, they would realize Avari's purse was off limits for the duration of the trip. Just in case, Ellasif would keep an eye on the young wizard.

On the next day the meadows gave way to rolling foothills. The morning dawned warm and clear, but strong winds stirred around the hills. Hawks wheeled overhead while ravens called their fellows to join in a feast of carrion. The tall grass was full of grouse. From time to time one of them danced away from the caravans, dragging a wing to appear easy prey. Foolish birds, Ellasif noted, to nest so near the road.

As the thought formed, a grouse burst out of a cluster of grass ahead.

Ellasif strung her short bow.

"Do you plan to hunt?" Balev asked.

"Something scared up the grouse."

"A merchant caravan, perhaps?" Balev's suggestion held a hint of sarcasm.

"And the bird flew toward us, not away."

The captain considered her point. "Perhaps a few of the guards should ride ahead."

"Just two," Ellasif said. "This could be a ruse to lure the fighters away from the caravan."

Balev nodded his approval. "Choose one fighter to accompany you. Anyone but Gisanto."

Ellasif beckoned to Camillor. The young Varisian looked to his captain. Balev shrugged. "Do as she says."

They rode forward. When they reached the spot where the grouse had emerged, the caravan lay yards behind them. A gentle cooing came from the grass, a sound as sleepy as a lullaby. Camillor grew drowsy, dull-eyed.

Ellasif leaned over and swatted him on the cheek. Camillor barely registered her touch, so she slapped him smartly. He blinked and shook his head, but not in time.

A tiny black creature shot up out of the grass. Ellasif snapped her bow up and got off the shot.

The arrow tore through the imp's wing and sent it spinning to the ground. The pony snorted an equine battle cry and stamped at the imp.

Ellasif recognized its wicked little head. It was Jamang's familiar, the fiend he'd called Vexer.

The tiny devil snatched one of the pony's legs and climbed, talons digging into the thick blue hide. The pony screamed and reared back. Ellasif dropped her bow and gripped the pony's mane to hold on.

Vexer leaped up at Ellasif, raking at her with teeth and talons, hot spittle spraying from its savage little jaws.

They fell from the saddle and rolled into the grass. Ellasif pinned the creature and drew a knife from her belt. She drove it down hard, but the blade plunged only into the grassy soil.

The imp had vanished.

Ellasif heard a cackling taunt from above. She looked up to see the black imp hovering with some difficulty due to its injured wing. It jabbered in some tongue Ellasif could only presume was spoken in the depths of Hell, and jerked its fingers, arms, legs, and tail in the most spectacular show of vulgar gestures she had ever witnessed.

If she did not wish so badly to rip the little monster in half, she might have grinned at the sight.

As it was, it was all she could do not to gape when she glimpsed a flash of blue swooping toward her foe. The interloper was almost the same color as the blue sky, and when it struck the imp it knocked the devil tumbling to the ground only seven or eight feet from Ellasif. She rushed forward, sword high to dispatch the foe, but then she saw she was too late. Its scrawny body lay limp and headless.

Camillor ran up beside her, sword in hand. As Ellasif withdrew from the stench emanating from the imp's mortal wound, Gisanto and Timoteo arrived, along with Declan Avari. The mapmaker turned his face away as a sky-blue house drake flapped frantically upon his arm like a startled falcon returning to its master. The little drake spat out a glistening black lump. As it hit the ground and bloodied the surrounding grass, Ellasif recognized the imp's head.

"I was wondering whether you'd show up," said Avari. The dragon's response was a constant thrusting of his blackened tongue while he gagged and spat. Avari tried and failed to swallow his laughter, and the indignant drake flew away to perch on one of the Varisian wagons.

Gisanto shot Avari a curious look, then shook his head and turned to Camillor and a matter he understood. "You were slow to attack."

"It's not his fault," Ellasif said. "The imp's magic slowed him."

"It had no effect on you."

"I'm obstinate," she said with a shrug. "And I've dealt with such imps before. It may be that I've built up immunity, as one does when one lives near snakes."

"Or swamp nettles," Timoteo observed. Behind him, the rest of the caravan approached.

There was a general laugh at Gisanto's expense. The big warrior gave the singer a good-natured punch in the arm and climbed back into the saddle. He gestured for the others to follow him back to the caravan, leaving only Camillor and Avari with Ellasif.

"It was kind of you to excuse my failings," Camillor said.

"What failings? Once I had the imp engaged in battle, its power over you faded. If I'd needed help, you would have given it."

"Most gladly," he said. He offered her a gallant little bow and a smile that trod dangerously close to a leer.

"But she did not need your help," Avari said. He sounded irritated, and Ellasif could not imagine why.

A shadow passed over Camillor's face. "Viland Balev hires only competent fighters. Obviously, this shield maiden is no exception."

"No, she isn't." The emphasis on "she" was just subtle enough to leave some doubt as to whether or not Camillor had been insulted.

"I have no need to prove myself to you," Camillor said.

Avari stepped closer to Ellasif and sent Camillor a level stare. "That matter we discussed the first evening? I believe I've changed my mind. Thanks for your offer to respect my claim. It makes things simpler."

The young Varisian's face darkened, but he gave a curt nod and vaulted into his saddle. Ellasif watched him ride away.

"What was all that about?" Ellasif concealed her disgust at Avari's presumptuous claim. She knew perfectly well what they were talking about, but she was wise enough not to let on that she'd been eavesdropping.

"I just wanted a private word with you."

"It must be important, to risk angering the one person in this company who likes me."

Avari wrinkled his nose as if he'd smelled something rank. "The imp you chased off. It's likely it was following me."

Ellasif had already come to that conclusion, but she wanted to know how he'd learned of the necromancer's death.

"Why would an imp be following you?"

"I failed to obey the wishes of a certain necromancer. He was a vengeful sort."

"Was?"

"I have reason to believe he is dead," Declan said. "But before his death, he sent an imp to attack me."

"That must have been frightening," ventured Ellasif.

"Not really," he said with a shrug. "Someone chased off the imp. I heard about it only later."

Ellasif considered this news. If someone had witnessed her fight with the imp and told Declan about it, he might also know of her involvement. But if he did not, pressing the matter might make him suspicious.

"Since you have enemies, you should be prepared to fight them. When we stop, let's see what you can do with that sword."

He eyed her dubiously. "I'm not sure that's a good idea."

The rest of the caravan caught up with them. Gisanto clapped Declan on the shoulder. "Don't worry, brother. There is no shame in fighting a woman. This one can handle herself."

"That's what concerns me," Declan said, drawing a chuckle from the nearby Varisians.

By the time they stopped for their midday break, Avari pretended to have forgotten her suggestion, so Ellasif fetched him and nearly dragged him to a clear spot. She'd hoped they could work in private, but it was no use. Before they had even drawn their swords, Gisanto and half a dozen others arrived to form an audience. Ellasif noticed that the big Varisian warrior had cut the rest of his hair short since the loss of one of his braids. She thought of telling him the new cut looked good, but that was as likely to spark new anger as to soothe his hurt feelings.

After a few initial exchanges, Ellasif was pleased to see that Avari's parries were strong, if a little slow, but he did not counterattack as often as he should to disrupt his foe's advantage. She showed him a few simplified alternatives to his existing repertoire. To become good with them, he would need only practice.

"Go ahead, Mouse," said Gisanto. Ellasif sighed, hoping that name would not stick to her. "Show him some of your cunning."

The other Varisians shouted agreement, and Avari lifted an inquiring eyebrow. "Your cunning?"

"You would call them dirty tricks."

Avari nodded. "I'm game," he said, but then a thought darkened his eyes, and he stepped close. "On the other hand, since you got off on the wrong foot with some of these men, perhaps you'd rather keep them a surprise."

"Don't worry," she said. "I have plenty of tricks."

"All the same," he said, but before he could continue, Balev bellowed the order to resume travel. Gisanto and his friends groaned in disappointment, but they moved quickly when the captain called. Avari and Ellasif did the same, and she made sure to ride beside him.

"I see you can use a sword. What else can you do to help the caravan?"

He shrugged. "Out here in the wild? I can do this and that. I can read the stars a little. I know how to catch a fish and sail a small ship. I know which mushrooms can be eaten and which should be avoided."

He said not a word about the spells she knew he could cast or the strange moving art he'd created. She knew she had the person the winter witch had demanded, but Ellasif could not understand why Avari, or anyone for that matter, would pretend not to wield such powers.

"These are useful talents," said Ellasif. "I did not expect a wizard to have learned such mundane skills."

"I'm not a wizard."

"That little dragon," said Ellasif. "I assumed he was your familiar."

"Ha!" said Declan. "He assumes that, too. But no, he's just a neighbor. More like a friend of the family, really."

"But you do know magic, don't you?"

Avari sighed. "I studied for a few years, but I'm done with that." Before Ellasif could ask why, he anticipated her question. "Let's just say I've learned enough about magic not to put my faith in it."

Ellasif grunted approval at Avari's philosophy. No matter how dearly she loved Liv, she had no love for the magic and the fear of it that had made her sister a pariah among their own people. The irony that she required a wizard, then, to rescue her witch sister was not lost on her. Ellasif supposed she could understand why Avari might prefer to be known as a mapmaker. "If that is how you feel," she said, "then you are smarter than you look."

Chapter Eight
The Tangled Skein

A few days after leaving Korvosa, the caravan passed the village of Harse by the Falcon River. The settlement was small and of no particular interest to Declan, but he was relieved to have the break. He was unaccustomed to riding more than a couple of hours at a time, so three days of travel had left him stiff and sore. He was glad he had decided to travel light, and he was sure his horse felt the same way. His pack contained only two sets of spare clothing, a pair of thick woolen blankets, and a tin cup and plate. In addition, Declan had brought along Jamang's satchel, which he had recovered from Basha. It now contained the caricature book, a sheaf of fresh parchments for sketches, a small parcel of charcoal sticks, a sketchbook, and the small spellbook he had retrieved from the Unicorn.

Ferrying the caravan across the river, two carts at a time, took the better part of the afternoon. The Varisians used the time to good effect trading for Korvosan goods. By the way they stood so close to the locals and shared a smoke afterward, Declan guessed they were selling flayleaf and perhaps thileu bark. He did not know whether such drugs were legal in Harse, but he decided to stay well away from the traders just in case. The last thing he needed was an excuse for some greedy constable to confiscate his purse as a fine.

He recalled from some otherwise forgotten university course that Harse was founded by a mapmaker, and his legacy remained in one of the finest map and folio shops Declan had ever seen. He selected equipment he would need for his own work: a small astrolabe and sextant, ink, quills, parchment, and a waterproof bag to hold them. It was about time he began doing more than rough sketches from time to time. Even the Varisians, whom he suspected kept their own maps on the parchment of their memory, would suspect his ruse given enough time.

The Varisian caravan continued until after dusk, when they made camp just outside the city. Declan was beginning to realize there would be few opportunities to spend the night in a soft bed, for the Varisians preferred their independence—and freedom from taxes, tolls, and levies—to the comforts of a city. Despite the fatigue that had burrowed down into his bones, he remained awake long enough to make a few rough calculations from the position of the stars. Without the proper equipment, he was able to make only the crudest of approximations, and he resolved to correct that problem as soon as he could.

Two days later they reached Baslwief, a mining town beneath a fortress on the Sarwin River in the foothills of the Fenwall Mountains. Declan was greatly relieved to hear they would spend a few hours in the village. Among the Varisian and Chelish humans, Declan noted a higher proportion of halflings than he had ever seen. Unlike those few who lived in Korvosa, these halflings walked with a proud demeanor suggesting that here, if not in other human settlements, they were equal partners in the community. Declan liked that notion. Such a town promised safety and a line of shops willing to barter.

"You should buy a sword." Ellasif's voice surprised him, for he hadn't realized she had followed him from the Varisian camp.

"You've been following me," he said, sounding more offended than he'd intended. Since Skywing's arrival at the caravan, the little drake had refused to communicate with him. Declan wanted to think the dragon was sulking simply because of the lingering taste of imp head, but he had noticed Skywing casting baleful stares at Ellasif. What was it about the Ulfen woman that the drake disliked? There was no way of knowing unless Skywing decided to speak with him, but it made Declan wary of her.

"It's my job to protect you," said Ellasif. "Besides, I rarely have the opportunity to go shopping."

"You don't strike me as the sort of woman who—"

"What?" She cut him off with a wry smile. "The sort of woman who buys things?"

"That's not what I meant," he said, but he gave up on making further excuses. He had the feeling he'd said something stupid but wasn't sure how to correct it. Ellasif let him off the hook by gazing past his shoulder. He followed her gaze through the shop window toward a seamstress's shop across the street.

"I'll be right over there," she said. "Don't try to lose me. Balev won't thank me if you get yourself beaten up by some of those shady-looking halflings."

Declan nodded dumbly, unsure whether she was mocking him or flirting with him. When she was gone, he paid for his purchase and followed her across the street.

Ellasif stood admiring a shallow shelf of bright silken thread, skeins of each color in their own compartment. Declan had never seen so much variety before, not that he made a habit of browsing seamstress's shops. It surprised him to find such selection in what was essentially a frontier mining town, but he supposed the minerals brought the small community relatively great wealth, and where there was gold, there would be merchants of every luxury.

Declan noticed that Ellasif's tunic, while dusty, was decorated at the hem with an elaborate design of fine embroidery. Entwined within the northern knotwork were exquisite little animals: stags, timber wolves, hawks, foxes, geese, and others he could not see without spinning Ellasif around. He had a sudden impulse to take her by the elbows and do just that, but he weighed the chance that she'd welcome the gesture against the probability that she'd punch him in the mouth and chose to restrain the urge.

He realized she had turned to see him looking at the embroidery, which to her must have appeared as though he were staring at her hips. She arched an eyebrow.

He cleared his throat and pointed at her hem. "That's pretty work. Is it yours?"

She laughed, and he could not tell whether she believed he had been admiring the clothes. "I'm definitely not the sort of woman who does such needlework. I can mend a tear or fix a button, but no more." Her humor faded, and she added, "My sister made this for me."

"She has a talent. You should bring her some of this thread."

A wistful expression flittered across Ellasif's face. "Some other time."

"Families are complicated," suggested Declan, sorry he'd touched a bruise. "I have a niece. Sort of."

Ellasif tilted her head with interest. When he did not immediately speak, she led him out of the shop by the elbow, bought a pair of sweet lemon ales from a chubby halfling, and sat him down on a sagging bench beneath a canvas awning. There the story spilled out of him: Asmonde summoning a devil, a powerful being far beyond his skill, and losing control of it. He implied without explicitly explaining the price Isadora had paid for his ambition and arrogance.

"That's why I'm no wizard. That was not the first fiend my brother summoned. With each summoning, he changed."

Ellasif frowned, and Declan added, "The imp you fought. It reminds me of the necromancer who may have summoned it. Dealing with wicked creatures, summoning spirits—after a time people become just as wicked."

"You don't know what you're talking about," said Ellasif. Abruptly she stood and stalked off, the wolf tail wagging from her hip.

Once again, Declan was dumbfounded. Perhaps he had shared too much, but the way she had reacted made him think he'd hit a nerve. He hoped he had not ruined what might have been his first friendship outside of Korvosa. On an impulse, he returned to the seamstress' shop and bought several small skeins of thread and put the wrapped package in his bag. Before returning to the caravan, he obeyed Ellasif's advice and perused the blades offered by the local smiths. He finally chose one engraved with the image of a dragon in flight. It made him think of Skywing.

In the weeks that followed, Declan recorded the caravan's journey with the basic skills he had learned from Master Nores. He could not restrain the impulse to add an artful flourish here and there, adding a sketch of Melfesh and its enormous drawbridge where the odd little village straddled the Yondabakari River on piers the size of castle turrets. Near the spot indicating Ilsurian, he drew a tiny fisherman lifting a trout from the Skull River, and he illustrated the page on which he detailed the Sanos Forest with capering gnomes, although he spied none on their passage. Perhaps that was because of the Varisians' precaution of leaving pails of goat milk and bundles of spiced bread at the four corners of their camp each night they spent beneath the canopy of that enchanted wood.

Every day, Ellasif found Declan and badgered him into another practice bout. They exhausted him, especially when she caught him in the mornings, and he tried to beg off with the argument that he was a paying customer of the caravan, not her apprentice. Ellasif would hear none of that. After the first week, he stopped trying to avoid her, knowing it was pointless to escape. She was relentless in her insistence that he must be able to defend himself should some savage bugbear make it past her to crush his skull. Declan doubted that would happen, in part because the caravan's journey had seen nothing more alarming than a drunken insult around the campfire, which Gisanto settled with two swift clouts across the offender's cheeks.

By the time they reached the pass between the Iron Peaks and the northern range of the Malgorian

Mountains, virtually every member of the caravan had made some excuse to lean over Declan's shoulder while he was sketching. At first he was oblivious to the ulterior motive behind their compliments—"What a fine likeness of the town," one might say, or "That gnome is the spitting image of my great uncle Vledosk"—but eventually he caught the hint, and by the time the caravan passed north of Ravenmoor, the approximate halfway point of their journey across Varisia, Declan had sketched half the members of the caravan.

But not Ellasif. The shield maiden had been conspicuously absent from the occasional circles of appreciation that had gathered around his sketchbook in the waning hours of daylight. While Viland Balev and a few of the other older members of the caravan had declined to let Declan draw their portraits, he suspected for superstitious reasons, only Ellasif had actively avoided him during those sessions. She had to know what he was doing. He often spied her watching from a distance as he drew. Within a week he had sketched everyone who asked for a portrait, but the demand did not end there. Now he was working from the Varisians' description of a favorite pet dog that had run away, or their recollected description of a revered late grandmother.

At first the praise for these latter sketches flattered Declan, but soon he began to suspect that the Varisians were far more sentimental than he had imagined. The tears streaming down the face of a Varisian widow at the sight of her late husband's face made Declan distinctly uncomfortable. When she clutched his sleeve and blessed him for his "magic," he struggled not to tear himself away and flee. It was impossible that he had captured more than a general resemblance of the man he knew only from the widow's few sentences of

description. To believe her, however, he had drawn him
in perfect resemblance, down to the mole at the corner
of his eye.

Was it possible? Declan wondered. Much as he hated
to think on the matter, there was no denying that he
had a mysterious talent for magical illustration. First
the animated caricatures, then the business with the
maps he sold Basha, and now this inexplicable phe-
nomenon. He knew it had to be related to his magical
studies in some way, but he was a wizard, not a sorcerer.
When he cast a spell, it was because he had studied its
arcane ingredients, its secret gestures, and the obscure
syllables that were powerless on the tongue of those
who did not comprehend the relationship between
these components and the intangible arithmetic of the
spell's invisible shape, its incalculable form. Declan
sometimes thought of this elusive quality as the spell's
soul, for lack of a better term.

Sometimes Declan wondered whether all the wizards of history had overlooked the simple if prepos-
terous notion that spells were living beings, their lives
briefer than those of butterflies. Conjurations, for
example, were said to bring forth creatures from other
places, but Declan could not help but suspect that the
imp produced by a conjuration had not been plucked
from Hell but was the incarnation of the spell itself.

Speculation like that had contributed to Declan's
flunking out of the Theumanexus.

Finally the requests tapered off, and one night Declan
found himself free of promises to draw the house in
which someone was born, or a first love, or the pony
that a father had raised from a foal for his firstborn.
At last he could return to what was ostensibly his job:
mapping the Varisians' path from Korvosa to Irrisen.

He had finished his calculations soon after the caravan halted for the night. All that was left was to illustrate the trail between camp and the Lampblack River.

On a whim, Declan decorated the otherwise barren plains with what he fancied to be a Shoanti totem atop a short obelisk that vaguely resembled ruins he'd seen illustrated in volumes of ancient history. Pleased with the result, he returned his art supplies to his pack and strolled just outside the camp. He found a comfortable spot on which to recline and gaze toward the impending sunset. For a while he watched as Skywing floated on the summer breeze like a hunting kite, at last to plummet without warning upon a hapless field mouse.

After recovering from the noxious taste of the imp's head, the dragon had presented Declan with a double talonful of stolen jewelry. To Declan's skeptical inquiry, Skywing asserted with a tone of wounded pride that none of it had been taken from guests at the Frisky Unicorn. Grateful, if dubious that a handful of jewels would be enough to pay the astronomer's ransom, Declan secreted the small treasure in his jacket pocket. There was no sense tempting the Varisians further than he had already.

Since delivering the ransom, Skywing had become uncharacteristically solitary, spending most of his time on the hunt or perched upon a caravan wagon. From time to time Declan noticed the little drake gazing watchfully at him, especially while he was practicing swordplay with Ellasif. He sensed Skywing was jealous of his new protector.

Smiling, Declan let his eyes close to slits, and—for the first time in days, he realized with a start—an image of Silvana came to his mind.

Rescuing Silvana was the reason he had left home and embarked upon this journey. He felt like a traitor to realize she had entirely escaped his mind. And Majeed Nores still needed ransoming. Yet here was Declan, lying on a bed of soft grass with no greater care than that the Varisians with whom he traveled had finally given him an evening's rest from drawing sketches.

Some hero he had turned out to be.

It should have been Silvana's image he drew night after night. He had not even replaced the one he had given her back at Majeed's home, and she was the woman he—what? The woman he loved? Now that it had been so long since he had last seen her, the word seemed intimidating, too big to express his actual feelings. He liked her, fancied her obviously. He wanted her to fancy him. Was that enough to send him halfway across the world to save her from where he guessed she had been taken? Frustrated by such absurd doubts, he cursed aloud.

"Sorry," said Ellasif from behind him. "If you want to be alone—"

"No, no," said Declan, spinning around to sit facing her. "I was just thinking . . . well, I don't know what I was thinking."

Ellasif considered that and sat down. "Perhaps you need a distraction from all that thinking. That is, if you have any pages left after drawing the entire company and all their dead relatives."

"You want me to draw your portrait," he said with a nod. She had just been waiting her turn.

"No," said Ellasif. "Not mine. My sister's."

"Ah," said Declan. He hoped it was a noncommittal sound, but the truth was he had been wondering when the shield maiden would tell him something more about her past. He had to admit that he had been avoiding her as much for shame that he had told her too much about his own as to escape daily sword practice.

He went to his saddlebag to fetch paper and charcoal. As he removed them, the book of animated caricatures he'd retrieved from Basha dropped to the ground. It opened as it fell. He picked it up and glanced at it before he tucked it away.

His gaze flew back to the page, and his brow furrowed in puzzlement. This was not the volume he'd received from Basha. This was the third book, which he had not seen since his university days.

Before his death, Jamang had implied that he had all three of the books. One had been left with Declan at the astronomer's manor. The second had ended up in Basha's shop, and Declan had claimed it along with a job offer for which he was not qualified—one that coincidentally led him in exactly the direction he wanted to go. Declan recalled how nervous Basha had been, particularly how his hand went to his throat when they discussed the merchant caravan.

Ellasif seemed the type to do most of her negotiating at sword point. Who else could have placed the book in his pack, and why would she have made such a clumsy exchange? Was there a reason other than jealousy that made Skywing shun her?

Declan looked to make sure he remained in sight of the Varisians. He wanted answers, and if Ellasif didn't feel like giving them, he didn't know how she would respond. For the first time in what seemed like ages, he wished he had prepared a potent spell to defend himself should she attack him. He returned to her and showed her the book from his pack.

"There are three books like this one," he said. "But this one is not the one I left in my pack."

He watched for a reaction, but her face betrayed no sign of guilt.

"Until now," he continued, "the third had not been accounted for. Did you kill Jamang Kira?"

"Could be," said Ellasif.

"What?" said Declan. "Don't you record your kills?"

He was half-joking, but she shrugged again.

"My foes don't always introduce themselves."

"Short fellow, skinny, likes to wear a red cape," said Declan. "Wanted to kill me. Conjured that imp."

"Very well," said Ellasif. "Yes."

"Yes, you killed him?" Declan asked. "Why?"

"You said it yourself. He wanted to kill you."

"But you didn't even know me—" He remembered what Skywing had told him before they left Korvosa and stopped short. "You're Skywing's bad person."

It took Ellasif a moment to realize the drake had identified her as the necromancer's killer. "That's one way of looking at it," she said. "Surely the man I killed found me bad. But from his intended victim, I would have expected something more like gratitude."

"Then why didn't you tell me before?"

"I didn't want to frighten you off of your quest," she said. "You still want to rescue your fair maiden, don't you?"

"Of course I— How did you— That's beside the point! You put Basha up to sending me to Irrisen, didn't you? You've been spying on me and manipulating me this whole time. I want to know why."

"I haven't made you do anything you didn't already want to do," said Ellasif. "I only made it possible."

"I still want to know why."

"It's . . ." Ellasif trailed off. She glanced toward the setting sun, now only a sliver of molten gold above the dark blue line of the western horizon. Skywing shot past them both, wheeling once around the Varisian camp before fluttering down onto the perch he'd claimed atop a wagon. "It's complicated."

Something about that phrase rang a bell, but Declan couldn't remember why. He was too angry and confused.

"I don't like it," he said. "Who are you to decide what I do?"

"I didn't decide," she said. "I simply helped."

"I didn't ask for your help!"

"You certainly needed it," she said.

"I know nothing about you," he said. "You seem to know everything about me, but I don't know why you're doing this or even whether I can trust you."

"That is wise," she said. "Sometimes you find that even people you have known all your life cannot be trusted."

Something about her tone diverted Declan's anger toward curiosity, and he remembered why *it's complicated* sounded so familiar.

"Tell me something," he said. "Something about your life. Anything."

For the first time that day, Ellasif's expression lost its granite composure. A flicker of emotion crossed her face and then vanished with the last of the day's light. "Let us return to the camp," she suggested. "I will tell you about my sister."

An hour later their bellies were full of roast rabbit and buttered turnips, as well as the herbed Varisian bread served at every meal. Declan wondered how he would ever be content with the white loaves of over-milled grain he had once enjoyed in Korvosa. These Varisians found a way to enliven every aspect of their lives, particularly their food.

Ellasif examined the portrait of her sister for what must have been the seventh or eight time. She shook her head in astonishment. "It's her," she muttered. "It's Liv."

The shield maiden had told him only that her sister looked much like her, but ten years younger and with lighter hair, straight and soft as the fuzz on a fawn. She mentioned the color of her eyes, the absence of the freckles that dotted Ellasif's face, but little else. Instead she told Declan how she felt when she first held her baby sister, the fear that she had come on an ill-omened night, and the misery that her parents had not lived to see the child grow so much as an hour older. She told of how Liv had never truly fit into the community at White Rook, demonstrating no talent as a warrior and little interest in the games the other young girls played. And then, shortly after Liv reached puberty, she—

Ellasif would say no more, but she marveled over the likeness.

"How can you know her face so well?" she asked Declan.

He shrugged. "I have a knack," he said. "And you describe her very well."

Ellasif thought on that for a moment, and then the corner of her mouth curled in mischief. "Did someone describe the woman in your little book for you?"

Declan colored. He had hoped but not really expected that Ellasif had not peeked inside his lascivious illustration. She had explained the mix-up without identifying the thief she had found rifling his pack. Normally he would have found that a good reason to distrust her story, but for some reason he believed her anyway. That she had decided to protect the would-be thief from Balev's discipline gave him hope that she was more of a hero than a schemer, no matter how much she had deceived him so far. Perhaps she really did have his best interests in mind.

He cleared his throat in hopes that she would take the hint and drop the line of inquiry.

"Or did you draw her from life?" she persisted.

"I just made it up," he said. "A little joke to amuse my friends."

"Is that so?" she asked. "Or do the men of Korvosa require instruction in the activities you illustrated?"

"No," he said, a little more indignantly than he had intended. "I do not, anyway."

Ellasif laughed. "I am glad to hear it," she said. "Although I suspect there are a few young women among the caravan who could be persuaded to offer you some of that . . . instruction."

Declan scoffed. "No," he said. "They're not my type."

"No," agreed Ellasif. "Your type is kitchen maids, I think. What is her name?"

"Silvana," he said. Saying it aloud to another woman, even a tough little shield maiden, took some of the magic out of it. Now that he thought of it, he was sure he did not consider Ellasif beautiful. Not exactly, anyway. A better word was pretty. Ellasif's small, heart-shaped face, pointed little chin, and nose that turned up a little at the tip brought to mind an oversized pixie. She wasn't graceful in the feminine sense, but she displayed the purposeful economy of motion that he associated with trained fighters.

"I should like to see how you draw her face," said Ellasif.

Declan hesitated, then shrugged and picked up his charcoal. He had meant to replace the portrait he had given her with one for himself. Just as he had drawn the first one from memory, he sketched out the borders of Silvana's face. There were her delicate cheekbones, there her elegant chin. Two curves for the cascade of her silken hair, and then a pair of faint ovals where her eyes should be.

That wasn't right, he thought. He studied the lines and realized they did nothing to evoke Silvana's face. He smeared them away with the heel of his hand and began again, but his second attempt was worse than the first. He had not experienced such difficulty recalling a face since he was still a child drawing on the backs of his father's old ledger.

He frowned and scribbled over the failed effort. He turned to a blank page, but Ellasif lay a hand upon his arm to stay him.

"You are tired," she said. "Best to get some sleep and begin again tomorrow."

Declan had to agree. More than anything else, he wanted a fresh start in the morning.

Chapter Nine
The Nolanders

Ellasif released a breath she did not realize she had been holding when Balev ordered the caravan to skirt the dense thickets of the Churlwood.

On her journey to Korvosa, Ellasif had avoided the dark woods on the advice of a peddler, who warned her of both bandits and unnaturally large vermin who preyed on lone travelers. Despite the strength of numbers in the Varisian caravan, Ellasif kept her bow strung until they approached Roderic's Cove, where the caravan captain ordered the company toward a barge dock east of the town. There Balev bartered with a bargeman to carry the wagons across the Chavali River without entering the town itself. Ellasif overheard Avari inquire as to the reason they did not visit, and Balev made the sign of the evil eye toward Roderic's Cove and muttered, "Haunted."

Ellasif felt a smile blossom on her lips, but it died after an instant. She had appreciated the Varisian's superstitious caution when it coincided with her own aversions. She would trust that Balev knew far more than she about the land she had crossed only once before.

The captain was less shy of the larger harbor of Riddleport, a notorious haven for pirates. Still, the caravan did not enter the city but set camp outside, where they were met by merchants eager to trade for goods from Korvosa and the communities they had passed along the way.

As men and women from the city arrived, the entire company came alive. While merchants bartered with Balev, the caravan's young women danced for coins tossed by eager young men, and the older women—who painted their faces to appear older still—sold ointments and herbal remedies, or else told fortunes for a handful of silver. As for the Varisian men, those who did not encourage the visitors to drink a little too much wine and ale prowled the edges of the campfire, and more than a few of the city men returned without their purses that evening.

Even Avari allowed the festive mood to suffuse his heart, spending the last hours of daylight sketching the Cyphergate, a magnificent stone arch that spanned the city's harbor, and later annoying the city men with questions about the monument. His enthusiasm was a welcome change from his recent mood.

The wizard—or mapmaker, as he pretended to be—had been unusually quiet for the past few days. Ellasif had initially thought that the revelation of her manipulating Avari had passed as well as could be expected, especially after their campfire talk on the night he drew her sister's portrait. But after the next morning, when they passed a strange ancient stone decorated in Shoanti fetishes, Avari had become withdrawn, and she feared she had lost what little trust she had won from him. The drake that had followed from Korvosa had even lit upon Avari's shoulder, and by the way they exchanged frequent glances, Ellasif was certain they were communicating silently. Their expressions suggested some sort of debate, and Avari's reactions were often so comical that Ellasif felt assured he had learned nothing that would jeopardize her plans. He was surprisingly gullible for a wizard, and he underestimated the intelligence of those around him.

For instance, how ridiculous it was to pretend he was not a wizard when everyone could see his familiar!

Ellasif knew that wizards, witches, and others who dealt in arcane matters could communicate with fiends and beasts. Such tales were common enough from the elders back in White Rook on cold winter nights. And to their minds, there was only one way to deal with a witch—as Ellasif had learned to her everlasting grief when they dragged Liv to the river and cast her into the icy water.

Ellasif wished she could do the same to all of them, especially her former friends. Her betrayers.

Such thoughts made Ellasif even more sullen and introspective than Avari had been. For days she did not even bother to drag him off of his blanket for sword practice, and he said nothing to her until the caravan was halfway through the Velashu Uplands. By then the caravan guards were too busy keeping watch for the territorial horse lords who claimed dominion over all the wild horses for which the region was famous.

Upon her first passage through the region, Ellasif had encountered three poachers hanging from a barren tree, the pronouncement of their guilt marked by an old horseshoe tacked to each man's chest. She would never forget the drone of the plague flies that formed a black halo around their corpses. That night she had walked three hours after sunset to put distance between her and the gruesome site before she lay down to sleep with no supper.

This time, Ellasif spied no such warnings, but she could tell that the Varisians needed none. The cheerful banter so common during the past weeks of their journey had vanished, replaced by solemn conversations among the guards, who rode closer to the wagons. Even the scouts remained in sight at all times, and Balev assigned that duty to his senior men, including Gisanto. Ellasif could not help but feel slighted that he had not chosen her, but it was better for her that she remain free to keep Avari in sight.

The caravan traveled north to the foot of the Red Mountains, where they made camp. The peaks formed a range that seemed low compared to the soaring peaks of Varisia's interior, but still they made a grand spectacle with the Velashu River coursing down their rocky valleys and into the plains below. A wide pass marked the end of the Uplands and opened up to a rugged expanse whose reputation Ellasif had known since she was a child.

For untold generations, it was to this shunned territory that her people banished cowards and traitors, rapists, murderers, and other useless men. When the Shoanti whose tribes roamed the lands south of the mountains learned of the northerners' practice, they adopted it as well, sending their most reprehensible criminals north to mingle with the dregs of the Ulfen. There the unwanted men soon fell prey to their predecessors or else demonstrated enough strength and guile to join one of the dozen or so bands of raiders who preyed on travelers and each other. Cast out of civilized tribes, these men were called the Nolanders, and their foremost reputation was for cannibalism.

It was to pass through the Nolands more than any other reason that northbound Varisian caravans hired armed guards, and it was here that Ellasif expected to earn her pay. Yet she did not feel fearful as much as she felt alert. She had, after all, passed through this same territory just over a year earlier without spying another living person. The chances of encountering a band large enough to overcome an armed caravan had to be small, and yet Ellasif understood the economy of banditry. The provisions from traders like Balev's company could sustain a group of twenty men for months. Here, food and clothing were worth more than gold.

Balev addressed the guards on the night before they entered the Nolands. They would steer clear of Brinewall, as Ellasif expected. She had seen the place only from a comfortable distance because she had heard its legend, and having heard it, begrudged Balev none of his superstitious caution.

Over twenty years ago, a Chelish emissary had arrived to find Brinewall—both the village and the fortress for which it was named—completely abandoned. Initially the empire blamed Ulfen raiders or a coordinated attack from several bands of Nolanders, but there were no bodies to be found, and not the slightest evidence of violence or looting. Even the ships remained at moor in the harbor, the emissary's men said, untouched by weapon or flame. Speculation turned toward supernatural causes, and soon everyone from Ulfen raiders to Shoanti shamans shunned the place.

To respect the taboo and minimize the time spent in the Nolands, Balev chose a course that led them northeast, toward a point where they could ford the Steam River out of sight of the accursed castle. He wanted to be on the other side before dark, and that meant hard driving without rest. Everyone would take a turn at watch tonight, giving each guard as long a sleep as possible. Balev wanted everyone strong and sharp-eyed on the morrow.

Before turning in, Ellasif caught Avari sketching a map by the light of a single candle he had affixed to a stone that formed a makeshift desk. She recognized the general outline of the Nolands region, and the silhouette of a lonely fort that could only be forsaken Brinewall. Avari glanced up as she approached. He offered a distracted grunt in greeting before adding an arching bridge over the Steam just east of the forbidden site.

"There is no such bridge," said Ellasif.

"Are you sure?" he asked.

She nodded. "I saw it from a distance, but I am certain."

"That's too bad," said Avari. He lifted a thumb to rub away the bridge, but then he shrugged, rolled up the map, and stuffed it into his pack. "You'd think a town of that size would have a bridge. And it would have been convenient, if Balev weren't so frightened of the place."

"It would be more convenient for all of us if you were to use the remaining candlelight to prepare your spells," she suggested. "There are shamans and witches among the Nolanders. It would be good to have a wizard among us if they—"

"I've told you I'm no longer a wizard," snapped Avari. He sounded as testy as an old man.

"Then why do you carry that little book of spells?"

Avari set his jaw, but he swallowed whatever retort he had been about to unleash on her. Ellasif knew he was still angry that she had opened his pack, even if he believed it had been only to return the book that Vira had stolen.

"You plan to use magic to rescue your lady," said Ellasif. "That's it, isn't it?"

Avari did not speak for a moment, but then he nodded curtly. "If it is necessary, then yes, I will use spells," he said. "But magic is a dangerous thing."

"Like a sword," said Ellasif.

"No," said Avari. "A sword is good or bad depending on who holds it, and in that way it is the same. But a sword does not corrupt its wielder."

"No?" said Ellasif. She could not have poured more condescension into the word with a bucket.

Avari frowned at her.

"That was a bad analogy," he said.

"No," said Ellasif. "It was good. I just hope that you will decide that the people of this caravan are as valuable as your fair maiden. What is her name again?"

"Silvana," he said.

"Well, then Desna send you sweet dreams of this Silvana, Declan Avari," she said. "Now I go to sleep so that tomorrow I can protect you from the savage Nolanders." She turned to walk away.

"Ellasif."

She paused just at the edge of the candle light.

He hesitated as if reconsidering what he had been about to say, then said simply, "Good night."

The next morning they broke their fast on last night's cold loaves while breaking camp in the dark. Even Avari was up before anyone needed to slap his feet, his yawning dragon stretching his wings nearby.

They put a mile behind them before dawn gilded the western peaks and began to spill into the valley. The sunlight raced down the western slopes to escape a coal-black storm front encroaching from the north-west. Tangles of weeds and patches of scrub grass no bigger than the foundation of a barn colored the land here and there, and a few stands of malnourished trees clung to the rocky soil, but otherwise this section of the Nolands was an expanse of red clay. The summer heat had baked spiderweb cracks into the earth, but it would take only one good shower to turn it all into an impassable mud field.

Ellasif saw Balev eyeing the approaching storm. If Desna should smile upon them that day, the storm would blow north across the Steam River. The Varisians drew the wings of the goddess over their breasts and kissed their fingers, but they also slapped the reins and threatened their donkeys with dire punishment should they tarry. The goats bleated protests as they followed the merciless tug of their leads.

At noon, Balev called a halt to water the animals. Ellasif scanned all directions for any sign of Nolander raiding bands. Unbidden, Avari had joined the ring of guards, and Skywing flew a spiral high above them. Apart from a few distant eagles scanning the ground for prey, the dragon was the monarch of the sky, swooping down now and then as if launching his own attack on the caravan. Avari looked up and nodded at the tiny drake as if receiving a silent report. Ellasif caught his eye, and Avari nodded confidently—all clear. The moment the water pails reached the last of the donkeys, Balev shouted a command, and they resumed their journey.

An hour later, Avari turned his horse and galloped toward Balev. Ellasif followed, arriving just in time to hear the caravan captain ask, "Are you certain?"

Avari thought about it for a moment. "No," he said. "But I think it's strange."

Balev lifted his mustache with a heavy sigh, a sight that might have appeared amusing under other circumstances. "Thank you," he said. "Please, keep him watching."

Avari nodded, but Balev had already kicked his horse's flanks and rushed along the caravan, urging everyone to pick up speed.

Ellasif made her inquiry with a raised eyebrow.

"One of the eagles flew away," Avari said. "Straight away, to the east. Skywing thinks it might be a spy for a Nolander band."

"Skywing thinks this?"

"He's smarter than he looks." Avari gave her that casual smile she'd seen him throwing at the Varisian girls when he arrived. Even if it were an appropriate time for such foolishness, his charms would not work on her.

Ellasif left him to return to her place. Soon she tasted the storm on the wind. The gusts snapped open the painted canvas walls of the wagon carrying, among other supplies, the chickens. Handfuls of feathers blew out with a clamor of clucks, and twin ten-year-old boys emerged to secure the canvas with the agility of veteran sailors.

Two hours later, Skywing descended from the heights, driven down to the caravan by increasingly powerful gusts. He perched on the horn of Avari's saddle, and together they rode toward Balev. This time Ellasif joined them just as the Korvosan relayed Skywing's report.

"Riders from the east," he said. "Forty-two of them."

Balev glowered at Avari as though blaming him for the news.

"Skywing counted twenty-seven with bows, and all of them carry other weapons. Two are Shoanti with tattoos on their faces."

"Shamans," said Ellasif.

"What else?" asked Balev.

"That's all," said Avari. "Perhaps you can barter with them."

Balev looked at the Korvosan as if he had pulled his beard. "These men do not barter," he said.

"Perhaps if we left some goods behind," began Avari, but he saw that Balev was no longer interested in his counsel.

Ellasif would not have believed the caravan could travel any faster, but a combination of imploring and cursing the donkeys urged them to speeds that threatened to smash the wheels from the wagons. Balev led them northwest, toward the approaching storm. Soon the thunder rolling down the western mountains was louder than the rumble of their wagon wheels. Deep within the black clouds, lightning crackled with dire mirth.

Within half an hour, one of the rear guards called out that he spied their pursuers. All at once, the quiet with which they had entered the Nolands fell beneath an avalanche of curses and prayers. When one of the goats fell and was dragged, a girl of no more than seven years leaned out of the back of the wagon and cut the beast's tether. The beast tumbled and stood, bleating its indignation. It trotted after the wagons that steered to avoid it, and then it was left behind.

It was foolish to think the raiders would be content with a single goat, but Ellasif hoped they would at least pause to capture the animal. With any luck, it would slow one or two of them as they secured their prize. She looked back to see whether they would take the bait, but a wake of dust had risen behind the caravan. Gusts from the storm stabbed holes in the opaque wall, but only for an instant before it closed again.

A cry from one of the rear guards heralded the first volley. The arrow stood straight up from his leather spaulder, and the man slapped away the shaft as if shooing an insect, leaving the arrowhead stuck in his armor like a bee's stinger. It was a lucky shot, the other missiles falling short or harmlessly near the other caravan guards. At least the wind favored the caravan, thought Ellasif.

An instant later, the rain began.

Ellasif nocked an arrow and waited for a clear shot. The rain thinned the wall of dust, and for a few moments Ellasif could see their pursuers. They were big men with ragged silhouettes, like the rough sketch with which Avari began most of his drawings. Some were fair-haired with long, braided beards, their clothing made of bear and otter pelts. They bellowed dire promises, mostly stolen away by the wind. Others in buckskins kept their heads and faces shaved but wore paint or tattoos over most of their exposed skin. They whooped ululating war cries of no words Ellasif understood, but the threat was no less horrible.

In one smooth motion, Ellasif stood high in her stirrups, turned, and fired an arrow. It struck a thick wooden shield bolted to the half-severed arm of an

Ulfen man. He stared at her as he rode on, his black-toothed grin promising personal revenge. Ellasif nocked another arrow.

Her second shot appeared to miss, passing near the head of a Shoanti warrior. A few seconds later, the man fell backward off of his saddle, a dark plume rising from his throat.

The other guards were less successful. Only one other raider fell to their arrows, and he leaped up immediately to run after his mounted companions.

A bolt of lightning struck nearby, for an instant turning the world black and white. Horses screamed, and the back of the chicken coop wagon flew up over its front, crashing upside down over the backs of the animals. One of the twins flew from the ruined vehicle and tumbled to the ground. Ellasif rode to him. Timoteo and one of the guards rushed to the wagon as she reached down to lift the stunned boy onto the saddle before her. She looked up to see what else she could do. The driver of the wagon was obviously dead, his neck broken.

The Nolanders were less than twenty yards away as Timoteo stood between them and the guard lifting the other twin from the wrecked wagon. Ellasif moved toward them, but Timoteo caught her eye and waved her off. "Go," he said. "Take him away from—"

Another bolt of lightning fell, this time directly upon Timoteo and his horse. For an instant Ellasif saw them outlined like withered skeletons, and then the blinding flash was gone. In its wake, man and steed stood like a grim statue, burned black and red. Then they tipped as one into a jumble of flesh and bone.

The surviving guard's horse screamed as the man swung back into the saddle, pulling the other twin up before him. He kicked the beast into motion, and they galloped toward Ellasif. She was already turning, but one of the approaching raiders caught her eye.

The man was a tall, emaciated Shoanti. He wore a bone breastplate and held a feathered wand above his head, his face lifted to chant to the storm. A nimbus of electricity crackled around his fetish. Ellasif knew he had slain Timoteo, and she felt a hot surge of vengeance fill her heart.

"Come!" cried the man carrying the other twin. "Hurry!"

Ellasif weighed the warm mass of the boy against the cold weight of her anger. She rose in the stirrups and shot one last reckless arrow toward the shaman. She turned and kicked her pony into a gallop the instant after she saw it enter his open mouth and emerge with a gory little plume above his skull.

The raiders' horses were faster, and in seconds the thunder of their hooves was louder than the storm. Ahead of Ellasif, Avari had turned to stare at the oncoming raiders. His mouth was an O of shock or disbelief.

"Run, you idiot!" shouted Ellasif. She could not risk losing Avari, especially not after traveling so far for him. How could he just stand there gaping?

Avari lifted his palm as if showing something to the Nolanders, but his hand was empty. His lips moved, and Ellasif realized he was not gaping but speaking. As she passed him, he completed his incantation and turned his palm outward. A brilliant cone of colored light shot from his hand and enveloped the nearest four riders and their horses. Without a scream, the horses tumbled to the ground, their riders falling with or over them. Men and beasts lay stunned or dead, crushed beneath their falling mounts.

A volley of arrows from the caravan guards slowed the next ragged rank of attackers, but still they did not stop. Leaving their companions on the ground, they charged ahead.

Avari chased after Ellasif, the long legs of his horse soon overtaking her pony. He gestured with one hand and spoke more of the arcane words that were powerless on the tongue of anyone but a wizard. Ellasif heard the snap of bowstrings behind them and cried out a warning, but Avari had heard it too and pressed himself flat against his steed, as did she. An arrow skimmed her shoulders and caught in her cloak, but neither she nor the boy was hit. Avari cursed like a sailor, and for a moment Ellasif thought he had been hit.

"Lost the damned spell," he shouted at her. She sympathized, knowing how difficult it was even to shoot an arrow while riding full tilt.

Ellasif and Avari reached the rest of the caravan, but the raiders were already among them. The other guards had closed in with the wagons, interposing themselves wherever possible between the Nolanders and the non-combatants. Gisanto had already cut halfway through the neck of a red-bearded Ulfen man, and the blood spray covered the Varisian's face. He looked like a demon as he screamed curses at the attackers, wheeling left and right to cut off any who dared approach the wagon he defended.

Balev rode up beside Ellasif and grabbed the boy, who cried out, "Uncle!" Thus freed, Ellasif drew her blade and looked for Avari.

The mad fool was standing up in his saddle, making himself the best possible target in the caravan. The Nolander archers had already marked him, and their arrows formed a black crescent as they fell toward him.

"Get down!" cried Ellasif. Avari had to have heard her, but he continued to cast his spell. He completed it just as the arrows struck, but none of them touched his flesh. Each of them—and there had to have been more than a dozen—flinched away as though striking an invisible wall a few inches from his body.

Avari's new spell materialized among the Nolanders, a roiling green cloud of noxious gas. Even from twenty yards' distance, the stench curdled Ellasif's stomach. The effect on the raiders touched by the cloud was instantaneous. A couple turned their horses away, leaning over the beast's necks in convulsive vomiting. One or two more crumpled to the ground within the miasma, disappearing in the distance. Two more rode through the cloud, choking and gagging along with their horses.

Avari had slain no more than one or two, but he had slowed them. In the resulting confusion, the nearest of the Nolanders spread out through the caravan. A one-eyed Shoanti warrior dragged a screaming woman from the driver's seat of a wagon and rode away with his prize. Camillor began to ride after her, but Balev bellowed at him to remain with the caravan.

Another Shoanti shaman, this one with a pale green snake entwined along his arm, raced toward Avari while shaking a serpent-headed staff. Avari snapped off a few syllables and made a lewd gesture. The spell sent quakes of uncontrollable laughter through his attacker's body. The shaman veered away, barely able to grip his horse's mane, much less direct his mount toward the foe.

The guards repelled the raiders, but only for a moment. Balev shouted encouragement for all to keep riding, but behind them Ellasif heard the Nolander leaders rallying their forces to continue their pursuit. With the mud growing ever thicker, they would be upon them again in minutes.

Avari cast another spell, the results of which were invisible through the veil of rain. A moment later, the screams of horses and the curses of their riders told her he had somehow impeded their path.

"Go!" Avari cried. "Balev, turn us toward Brinewall."

"No!" shouted Camillor. There was terror in his voice, beyond that which Ellasif knew every member of the caravan already felt.

"They won't follow us there," yelled Avari. Ellasif had to acknowledge he had a point.

"To Brinewall!" she shouted. To her surprise, Gisanto added his voice to their plea.

Balev made his decision. "Follow me!" he roared, his voice challenging the thunder for command. No one could disobey that voice, and so they ran northwest.

They were much closer than Ellasif had realized, and the next stroke of lightning cast the fortress of Brinewall into stark silhouette. She could make out no details, only the crenellated edge of a wall that seemed to rise naturally out of the riverside cliffs. There was a village on the other side, but Ellasif had hoped never to see its abandoned homes, nor whatever lay within the haunted walls of its castle.

The Nolanders drew close again. If the sight of the fortress frightened them, they showed no fear of it. They were bloodied now, their prey grown more precious for the blood they had spilled in pursuit of it.

Lightning flashed again, casting the outline of the forbidden place against blanched clouds.

Queerly, the lightning cast the shadow of the castle down upon the caravan and beyond them, throwing a shadow over the Nolanders. One of the attackers screamed. Others grew desperate in their threats. "We shall retrieve your corpses in the morning!" cried one.

They were not alone in their fears. Mothers driving the wagons and warriors riding beside them wept openly. None desired to spend a moment, much less a night, in Brinewall.

"We cannot go in there," shouted Gisanto, his face etched with an agony of indecision. He had supported the suggestion to flee here, but could not force himself to enter.

"We don't have to," replied Avari, with a brassy note of triumph in his voice. "Look!"

All eyes turned in the direction where he pointed. East of the castle, a bridge wide enough for wagons spanned the Steam River. Each flicker of lightning made its granite stones gleam under the rain.

Rain tickled Ellasif's tongue, and she closed her mouth. The others were gaping, too, but Balev wasted no time wondering who had built the structure, or when. He kicked his horse and led the charge.

The storm swallowed the last of the daylight, and they rode by the intermittent flashes of lightning, encouraged by the sight of the inexplicable bridge. At first the Nolanders faltered and fell back, but then they too saw the span. At least the far side would provide a bottleneck for defense, Ellasif thought, but after the grueling chase, she doubted the Varisians' ability to fend off the savage men.

They flew across the bridge, and just as Ellasif would have done had she been in command, Balev ordered two of the wagons turned to provide cover, while the guards stood behind them, bows in hands. Ellasif joined them, but Avari did not. He stood nearby, digging through his pack until he found the map she had seen him drawing the night before. He rubbed at the bridge he had drawn, but neither his finger nor the rain made so much as a smudge on the page.

The first of the Nolander's horses touched the opposite side of the bridge. The raiders paused, waiting for their full strength of numbers to arrive before resuming the assault.

"It's no good," murmured Avari. "But it can't have been coincidence."

"What?" shouted Ellasif. She wished the wizard would either join the defenders or get his city-bred skin behind the wagons.

Declan ignored her. "It has to be the map," he whispered. "And if I can just erase . . ." His gaze sharpened at the sound of his own word, and he spoke a few more in an arcane tongue. Upon the last syllable, he passed his palm over the map, rendering the parchment completely bare.

In the darkness between the thunderbolts, the sound of two large splashes came from across the river. Men shouted in alarm, and one voice traveled downriver, its screams growing more and more frantic as it moved toward accursed Brinewall.

When the lightning flashed again, Ellasif saw no bridge. There was only the black expanse of the Steam River flowing between the caravan and the Nolanders.

Chapter Ten
The Stalkers in the Pines

Declan had always thought of the Lands of the Linnorm Kings as a snowy wasteland, but in summer it was greener than the pastures surrounding Korvosa.

It was also a rugged land, but even across its stony hills, bright patches of lichen and brilliant wildflowers made it appear more like a faerie land than the forbidding territory of the dreaded Ulfen raiders. In just a few days he had come to realize the Ulfen were far more diverse than the reputation of their pillagers would suggest. Since their narrow escape at Brinewall, the surviving members of the caravan had passed farms tended by men and women who, while big and hardy, resembled the seafaring marauders of their country as much as Korvosan stable boys resemble Hellknights.

When Balev sent Camillor ahead to ask permission to approach a dairy farm in hopes of camping nearby, the man of the house welcomed the entire caravan to water their beasts at his troughs. The grateful Balev haggled only halfheartedly while trading Taldan linen and skeins of embroidery thread from the bazaars of distant Katapesh for chickens, milk, flour, and a pig that the Varisians roasted that night to share with their hosts. Gisanto's mother told a fortune of marriage and many children for the farmer's daughter, but no one danced, and no one sang. There had been no music since Timoteo died.

Balev had wept openly when Gisanto's mother led the women in sewing a gray shroud around the bard's gusli. Declan felt himself choke up, but he was surprised to see Ellasif wiping away tears before she fled the ceremony. While she had rarely chatted with the bard, she seemed to grieve as deeply as any of his kin since his passing.

The men dug a shallow grave, and Gisanto's sister Nadej placed the instrument inside. Balev praised Timoteo's talent and courage before saying a prayer to Desna, imploring the goddess to send happy dreams of their lost friend to all who loved him. Then Gisanto's mother prayed to Pharasma to speed him to his final rest, and tossed a handful of earth lightly upon the "body."

Declan was relieved to see that, after all others walked away from the grave, the men assigned to fill it gently removed the shrouded instrument before closing the hole. Later he spied one of them placing the gusli inside one of the Varisian wagons, where Declan guessed it would remain until one of the children demonstrated a talent for music.

Later, as Declan peered through his sextant to find a bearing on their current position, Ellasif approached. "Is that where your magic comes from?" she asked. "The stars?"

He jotted down the figures he had gained before she could distract him further. "No, this isn't magic at all."

"How does it work?"

He hesitated, wondering how much a warrior bred in the Land of the Linnorm Kings would comprehend basic arithmetic, much less the calculations required to determine longitude and latitude. "Basically, I measure the height of the stars from the horizon, and that tells me where we are."

"But the stars move."

"Not exactly," he said. He explained that the rotation of the planet made the stars appear to move, and that the pole star could always be trusted to indicate north. She knew the latter fact and scoffed that he could assume otherwise.

"All right," he said, raising a hand for peace. "The basics are simple, but the details can be complicated. If you get them right, you can not only figure out where you are, but you can plot a course to where you want to go."

Ellasif made a point of identifying eight or nine constellations to show him that he wasn't the only one who knew something about the night sky. A few of the names were different, but she had learned them almost as well as he had, and without the benefit of a university education. Once she had made her point, they said their goodnights and retired to their beds.

After the night spent at the farm, the mood of the caravan recovered, if only slightly. Balev was only the first of many to thank Declan for his help fending off the Nolanders, but he walked quickly away after expressing his gratitude. Even the young women who had once greeted him so flirtatiously now cast their glances from a distance. They were more curious than ever, but now they were also a little frightened of him. Knowing a man could cast spells was different from seeing him do it, and Declan suspected the Varisians were equally attracted to and wary of wizards. In Declan's opinion, the latter was the wiser reaction.

After several years of eschewing the skills he had learned at the Theumanexus, it had felt strange to cast spells so freely. They came to him much more easily than they had in his student days. He was not sure whether that meant he had learned them better than he realized or that fear of death had inspired a certain excellence. Much as he regretted the need to cast them, he was glad he had listened to Ellasif.

While he could not bring himself to trust her fully, the little Ulfen woman had given him good counsel. If only he knew more about her and why she was guiding him toward Whitethrone, perhaps they could be . . . what? Friends? Trusted colleagues at the least, he hoped. He had to admit that he liked her, despite—or perhaps because of—her refusal to tell him much about her past. With her skill at arms, not to mention her cunning, Ellasif would be a valuable ally in ransoming or rescuing Silvana and Majeed Nores.

That was assuming, of course, that Ellasif meant to be helpful. The closer they came to Irrisen, the more Declan needed to understand what motivated her. After fighting and running for his life, and watching good folk die, Declan felt a keener appreciation for his own life. If Ellasif's scheme included putting him in danger—more danger than he intended to put himself in, anyway—he wanted to know. He was far from his home in Korvosa, and with every step they moved closer to Ellasif's homeland, which he understood poorly at best.

Before approaching Ellasif, Declan consulted Skywing. During the battle with the Nolanders, the feisty drake had disabled two of the attackers with his narcotic stinger. He had not, now that Declan thought about it, cast any spells. Declan sent Skywing a telepathic question. It was becoming easier to send his thoughts as they communicated more and more often since leaving Korvosa.

Spells to protect you, the little dragon explained. *Was expecting you to fall off your horse again.*

Very funny, thought Declan. Despite the badinage, Skywing's telepathic message included a strong sense of chagrin, so Declan believed him. It occurred to him then that he had never asked Skywing how it was he could cast spells at all. Was Skywing the familiar of some other wizard? Before he could ask, the little dragon interrupted his thought.

I know only a few spells, Skywing sent. *Not a wizard like you.*

I am not—! Declan thought before giving up. If he had proven nothing else in the flight from the Nolanders, it was that he was undeniably a wizard.

And possibly something more. The incident with the Shoanti monolith and then the vanishing bridge had confirmed that fact. Somehow, his powers of magic were mingling with his knack for art. Whatever it was, it was not a power he evoked consciously—although to be honest, he had the notion of an easy river crossing at the back of his mind when he first sketched the map of the Nolands from Balev's descriptions. The question was whether it was a power he could use intentionally.

Do you trust Ellasif? Declan asked Skywing.

There was a long pause before Skywing replied, *Maybe she is not a bad person.*

Maybe?

Usually I am right the first time, the dragon said. *Takes time to adjust.*

Declan's laugh attracted the attention of the nearest Varisians, but when they saw Skywing circling above, they shook their heads and looked away. The ways of wizards were strange.

Declan spent the better part of a day devising conversational strategies to coax Ellasif into revealing more of her past and plans. The Ulfen city of Jol lay just south of the Grungir Forest, another day's travel to the north. It was there the caravan would end its journey, trading the remainder of its southern goods for fine northern pelts and ivory.

Despite her return to the Lands of the Linnorm Kings, Ellasif did not behave as though she were looking forward to the homecoming. Declan had overheard her conversing with Viland Balev. The caravan captain had tried to persuade her to accompany the Varisians back south after he had finished his business in Jol, but Ellasif remained adamant that she would continue her journey north with Declan.

It irritated Declan to hear her speak for him, as though they had come to an understanding. He had never agreed to travel with her beyond the caravan's route, despite her assumption that she was here to protect him. And he would not agree, not so long as she failed to explain why she had surreptitiously guided him along this path.

The prospect of traveling from Jol to Whitethrone alone or in the company of a hired guard, however, was not exactly appealing. The truth was that Declan could think of no one else he'd prefer to accompany him on a dangerous trek, if only he knew that he could trust her.

After Ellasif left Viland Balev, Declan rode up beside her. She greeted him with a curt nod, and they rode in silence for a time while he mustered the nerve to start an innocuous query that would gradually wind around to his real question. Yet he found himself unable to begin. It all seemed so deceitful that at last he blurted out, "Exactly what are you leading me into?"

Ellasif opened her mouth, her pointed chin jutted as if to deliver a defiant retort, but nothing came out. Declan seemed to have caught her flat-footed, so he pressed the unexpected advantage.

"I mean, we've fought side by side now," he said. "We've seen people we both care about die on this journey, and you still haven't told me why you cleared my path to join this caravan."

Ellasif shut her mouth and stared steadily ahead. To the north, a distant forest cast a thick blue line on the northern horizon. The caravan passed more and more stands of fir trees as they followed a network of ox trails and fields so full of stones that a romantic might have mistaken them for ruined plazas.

"So that's the way it is," said Declan. "I'd just hoped I'd earned a little more of your trust after all the time we've spent together."

"You can spend your whole life with someone and still have your trust betrayed," Ellasif said.

Her tone was so bitter than Declan could almost taste it. He sensed she wasn't talking about him or anyone else in the caravan. Whatever she was talking about, it still tormented her. Unfortunately, he had no better course to follow, so he asked, "Who hurt you so badly?"

Ellasif's eyes moved from the north to the east. "My closest friends," she said.

"Could it have been some sort of misunder—?"

"No."

Declan sucked air through his teeth. It would have been easier to let it drop and try again later, but he was running out of time.

"I have to think that in my position, you wouldn't trust you," he said.

Ellasif said nothing to that.

"And perhaps it would be better for me to strike off on my own," he said. At an empathic protest from Skywing, he added, "With only a sarcastic house drake to protect me."

"You would be eaten by trolls within two days," Ellasif predicted.

"Making me of no use to you."

"You don't know how to reach Whitethrone," she said. "You wouldn't even make it past the dancing huts."

"The what?"

"One of them nearly destroyed my village when I was a girl. Hundreds of them stand sentinel around the borders of Irrisen, ready to tear apart any intruders in their gigantic talons."

"How did you get past them?"

"Stay with me," she said, "and I will show you."

"Not until you explain why you need me," he said firmly.

She frowned as if considering his ultimatum. Declan wasn't sure how convincing he had sounded, and Ellasif made some good points about why he needed her help. Skywing was an excellent scout, but Declan doubted the dragon and he could fend off a band of goblins, much less a pack of wolves. And, anyway, what the hell was a dancing hut?

"You are not the only one who wishes to rescue someone from the winter witches," Ellasif said. "I need your help as much as you need mine."

"But why—"

"You do wish to rescue your Silvana, do you not?"

"Well, of course, but—"

"Then it is settled," she said. "When the caravan stops in Jol, the two of us go to the rescue together."

Skywing chirped a protest.

"The three of us," said Declan.

Their conversation did little to help Declan understand the shield maiden, but he let it go for a while as they marched ever northward. The path they followed led through stands of woods no bigger than a Varisian village, and the dark outline of the Grungir Forest still lay thick and blue on the horizon. There was at least another day to discuss the matter further, depending on whether they waited for the Varisians to finish their business in Jol. If Declan and Ellasif had not come to a full understanding by then, he would have to spend a little more of his small fortune to hire one of the full-sized Ulfen bodyguards that southern nobles favored.

He prayed it would be just a little more of the money, because he still was not sure how much it would take to ransom Silvana and Majeed Nores. If his purse was too light, would he have the courage and skill to rescue his "fair maiden" and his astronomer master like a hero from a story? Alone, he certainly would not. But perhaps with the help of Skywing and Ellasif . . .

The fanciful notion brought a smile to his lips, and he immediately regretted it. This was the sort of arrogance that had led his brother down a path of self-destruction. And worse, Declan reminded himself, thinking of

Isadora and Rose. He hated the cliché of the evil wizard most of all because he knew how much truth there was to the idea. The fear and admiration he'd received from the Varisians ever since using his spells to fight the Nolanders was exactly the sort of thing that put a man's foot on the wrong path. He'd enjoyed it, both the respect afterward and, to be honest, the thrill of the fight itself. And that was exactly why he had to be careful how and why he used his magic.

There was still the matter of the mystery bridge. He was certain now that he had created it himself when drawing the map, and equally sure his drawings had created both the seemingly ancient Shoanti monument and the incongruous Osirian treasure trove on the ostensibly phony treasure map Basha had sold for him. The implications of such a power were staggering. Already he thought of ways to make himself a fortune, become a lord of his own domain. And yet he had no illusions as to what would become of him if someone else learned of his ability. In a moment he could fall from noble to slave when one more crafty and powerful than he decided to bend that power to his own designs.

Such thoughts made it more difficult than ever to place his full trust in Ellasif. She had seen him erase the map at the Steam River. The Varisians had not, although they all credited his magic with the disappearance of the bridge. Ellasif was the one who was most dangerous to him. Declan let out a little roar of frustration.

An instant later, from the shadows in the woods, a huge beast echoed his roar. The sound lifted the boughs and shook the needles from the pines. The guards started and cast astonished glances at Declan. Even Skywing sent a wordless inquiry.

"It wasn't me," Declan stage-whispered.

Ellasif and the other guards strung their bows. Gisanto and Camillor were in the lead, with Ellasif and Declan ten paces behind them. Declan made a quick mental inventory of the magic he had prepared. Thinking of the woman he had seen carried off by the Nolanders, he had replaced a few of the spells for slowing pursuit with a deadly invocation and a couple of useful enchantments. He doubted any of them would be potent against something large enough to make that sound.

Balev gave commands in a low voice, and the guards passed them along the line. They increased their pace but did not yet break into a full run. Declan wondered how much strength they had left since the flight from the Nolands.

Another roar sounded in the woods, this time from the opposite side of the road.

As the company turned together toward the new sound, Declan saw something drop from the trees ahead of them. It looked like a man.

He appeared an inch or two shorter than Ellasif. As his feet struck the path he crouched, steadying himself with one long-fingered hand. His ragged cloak slapped against his back with a clatter of bone fetishes tied along its hem. He looked up and gazed straight at Ellasif, his bulging eyes dominating a face that retreated down to a vanishing chin. He grinned, displaying teeth that had been filed to sharp points.

"Sweet child," he said. "How I have hungered for you."

Ellasif cursed and raised her bow. Her arrow flew swiftly, but he was already gone. In his place, a wall of thick white webs blocked the path. Ellasif's arrow shot deep within them to hang trembling where the man's face had been.

Declan knew a charm to dispel conjurations like this one, but he had not prepared it. The curse of the wizard's life was the need to predict the future, with or without benefit of divinations. Declan was definitely without divinations. He considered casting a minor fire invocation, but before he could decide, a terrible sound exploded behind him.

He turned to see an enormous troll bursting through the ruins of one of the wagons. The Varisians scattered, panicked by the sight of the ten-foot-tall brute. Its green-gray flesh glimmered with sweat, and bits of wood, honey, flour, and other detritus from the demolished wagon stuck to its skin. The monster snatched up a cask rolling past its clawed feet. It sniffed once before hurling the container at the nearest pair of Varisian guards. The barrel knocked one man from his horse and crushed the other to the ground, bursting open over his corpse. Golden ale mingled with blood in an expanding puddle.

Camillor screamed bloody vengeance and charged the troll. At the last moment, his horse balked, sending him hurtling toward the monster. Camillor gripped his sword in both hands and let the momentum of his flying body drive the weapon deep into the troll's arm. The beast bellowed its pain and grabbed the Varisian with its uninjured hand. It squeezed, and Camillor's death rattle was followed by a fountain of blood.

Two more guards and the survivors of the destroyed wagon fell upon the beast, but Declan watched the other side of the road for the proverbial second shoe. He saw the trees bending and heard the thunder of the second troll's footsteps before he saw the thing.

It was even bigger than the first, as tall as a cottage. Fearful of the consequences, Declan conjured a patch of slick grease in the troll's path. The brute's first step onto the slippery field took its leg out to the side. The troll plummeted forward, sliding toward Declan as fast as it had been running.

Frantic, Declan shaped the figure of a large globe in the air before him, intoning the words to evoke a channel from one of the elemental planes. A moment later, he hurled the ball of fire toward the troll, which was only just standing up. The flame engulfed the monster and climbed up its massive body, evoking howls of terror and pain.

Ellasif appeared beside him, saw what he was doing, and gave him a surprised, "Good! More fire." She ran to help the other defenders, but the enemy reinforcements had also arrived.

From the rear, a horde of jabbering goblins ran out from their hiding places in the trees. Emboldened by the troll's assault, they rushed the wagons, howling and singing insipid rhyming profanities. Despite their disorder, they concentrated their attacks on their most hated foes, the horses.

The first of the little terrors ran toward Gisanto's steed, only to die a second later under the horse's hooves. The second leaped up to slash the man with a crudely forged sword whose blade was drilled in several places to lighten the weapon for its tiny wielder. Gisanto beat the weapon aside with his own blade and grasped the goblin by its scrawny throat. He throttled the creature to death in three hard shakes and dropped the twitching body to the ground.

Declan chased the second troll with his flaming ball, directing the conjured fire with a simple gesture while searching his surroundings for any sign of the wild man who had begun the assault. Clearly he was a wizard or warlock of some sort, and it was only a matter of time before he revealed himself with another spell.

Ellasif interposed herself between the first troll and his target, another wagon on which Nadej and Gisanto's mother defended themselves with a cooking cauldron and a sharp iron spit. Ellasif hacked at the troll's thigh, and her third blow staggered the monster as the blade cut its hamstring. The monster reeled away from the wagon, and Nadej grabbed the reins to urge the panicked horses away from their attacker.

Ellasif pressed the attack, hacking at the troll as it crawled away to buy time. Dark blood oozed from half a dozen shallow wounds on its legs, hip, and shoulder. With a deafening roar, the troll stopped and lashed out at its tormenter, slamming Ellasif with a wide back-handed blow. The impact lifted her from her feet and threw her back against the retreating wagon.

A trio of goblins saw Ellasif fall and ran to swarm over her.

Declan let go of his ball of flame and flung another spray of glaring magical colors at the goblins. All three went down, knocked unconscious by the blazing illusion. Sparing only a glance to ensure the troll was not approaching for its revenge, Declan rushed past Ellasif and stabbed each senseless goblin through the throat. Then he turned back to her, but she was already rising, shaking the stars and comets from her vision. She looked toward the spot where her foe had fallen and shouted, "No!"

Declan braced for an attack, but instead he saw an immense Ulfen warrior raising a warhammer for a second strike at the troll's crushed skull. The man screamed in such controlled fury that Declan knew without being told it was not an expression of emotion but a war cry. The man was some sort of berserker, more dangerous than any common raider.

The man looked at Ellasif, and a shadow of pain crossed his face. He turned away from her and barked at Declan, "Fire, man! Bring more fire."

Without pausing, the berserker swung his hammer in a great underhanded arc, lifting a charging goblin off its feet and crushing its ribcage with an audible crunch. A swarm of the little monsters followed, but Declan did not think for a moment that the big man needed his help.

More Ulfen warriors overran the camp, wading into the fray with their hammers, axes, and swords sweeping through goblins like scythes through barley. Soon their battle shouts were drowned in high-pitched screams of terror as the goblins realized they were no longer attacking a simple trade caravan.

Declan had expended his only proper fire spell, but he ripped the sleeve from his shirt and wound it around his sword. Once it was tied off, he grabbed a few pieces of wood from the shattered wagon and ran to the fallen troll. There he ignited his makeshift torch with a cantrip and lit a fire upon the monster's corpse.

He looked up to see a tall Ulfen woman with dark red hair standing before the troll he had briefly frightened off. The beast opened its maw to roar into her face, the force of the blast lifting the braids from her shoulders. The troll's tusks were as long and thick as an ox's horns, and the monster must have weighed half a ton, but the woman stood fast, her greatsword held high.

The troll smashed a fist the size of a rain barrel down at her, but the woman stepped nimbly aside and slashed the brute's arm. She was not quick enough to avoid the second fist, which knocked the breath from her lungs and sent her sword spinning away behind her. She scrambled to retrieve it as two of her kin rushed to her aid.

Behind him, Declan heard a clash of steel and Ellasif shouting curses. Impossibly, she was beating back the Ulfen who had slain the first troll. The man was twice her size, and he'd already slain a troll and a small mob of goblins, but she was driving him away.

"Stop!" shouted Declan. "He's helping us!"

"Lower than a dog!" screamed Ellasif, hacking at the man's head.

"Wait," the man shouted. He raised his hammer in a two-handed grip just in time to save himself from a mortal blow.

"Ellasif!" said Declan, but he knew he couldn't stop her with words. She had lost her mind, perhaps falling into one of her people's berserker rages. He reached out through the intervening space and let the now-familiar spell flow through him. Suddenly Ellasif's hands and blade were covered with slippery grease. Her grip was strong, but her surprised clutching worked against her, and the blade slid from her grasp.

She half-turned to follow the path of her weapon, and when she saw Declan concluding the gesture that had stolen it from her, she understood what he had done.

"You idiot!" she shouted. She said no more, because just then the big Ulfen man clouted her on the head and knocked her unconscious to the ground.

As he watched the shield maiden crumple, Declan realized he might have misjudged the situation.

The big man touched Ellasif's throat and nodded as if relieved she were still alive. As he lifted her limp form in his arms, he saw Declan preparing to cast another spell.

"Don't be a fool, boy," he said.

The insult struck Declan as absurd, since he was sure the man was little or no older than he. Sure, the beard made him appear older, but the point was that he was kidnapping Ellasif. "Just put her down," he said, not entirely certain how he would enforce his demand.

"Listen," said the big man. He took one step forward and his eyes rolled up into their sockets. He sighed and fell to the ground. Mercifully, Ellasif fell atop him rather than being crushed under his bulk.

All around them, trolls were fleeing into the woods. Declan saw one run off holding Camillor's limp form. He moved toward Ellasif, but a knife flew down and hovered a few inches from his face. He heard a mad giggle, and the caped wild man floated down from the heights.

"Have a care, boy, unless you want to go into the pot tonight!"

Declan gritted his teeth. He had already expended his strongest magics, and he doubted he was a match for this weird stranger with the sharp teeth. He darted to the right, but the floating knife followed him. He stopped less than five feet from the wild man. The smell of the thing's unwashed body was sickening, but worse was the stench of rotten flesh from his warm breath.

The wild man clucked and waggled a finger at Declan, who felt a sickening knot of pain form in his stomach. "Not so quickly, my tender morsel. I will return for you another night, when my boys are hungry. But I see I have one less belly to fill, so you can live another day or two." He roughly shoved aside the unconscious form of the big barbarian—whose strange fainting was now clearly the result of magic—and lifted Ellasif in his arms.

"No," said Declan, raising his sword. The floating dagger darted toward him, and he had to take a step back to parry it.

The wild man cackled, and the pain in Declan's belly grew stronger.

"Patience," said the wild man. He rose up into the air, clutching Ellasif's limp form. "We will sup soon enough, you and I. Soon enough."

And with that he flew away through the pines.

Chapter Eleven
The Footprints in the Frost

Ellasif awoke to the peculiar scent of pine sap and rotting corpses. Even before opening her eyes, she recognized the sweet stench of Hell.

Her head felt worse than it had the night she had celebrated her first raid with enough mead to drown all of the goblins she had slain. She licked her cracked lips, but her tongue was dry and swollen. Nausea wracked her hollow belly, and she felt as though she had not eaten or drunk for days.

Tough wooden manacles gripped her wrists and ankles, pinning her to a wall of trees grown so close together that they formed the circular wall of a huge house. Through the gaps between the trunks, the wind whistled a sinister tune.

Above her, the trees bowed toward a central chimney gap, their bristling branches trailing like the beards of ancient elders who leaned their heads together for a whispered conference. Through the opening Ellasif saw stars in a clear sky, and from the silver-limned boughs, she knew the moon had risen.

The cool wind stirred long ropes hanging from the upper boughs. Each length was woven of human hair, most of it the red, blond, and brown of Ulfen warriors. Bones and whole scalps were entwined in the ropes every five or six inches, and at the base of each strand hung a skull filled with coins. The gold glimmered in the eye sockets and rattled in the breeze.

Beneath the chimney, a fire crackled in a pit bordered by blackened rune stones. The flames tickled a chain of lumpy sausages, each link the size of Ellasif's forearm. Beyond the pit stood a table carved out of a single massive pine trunk. Light from a dozen red candle stubs cast gruesome shadows against the wall. Ellasif recognized the fragments of severed human limbs. Over the edge of the table jutted a human foot.

Ellasif turned her face away lest she recognize some sign confirming what she feared: that the dead man was one she knew, perhaps Camillor or Declan. If the caravan had been overwhelmed after she had fallen, it could have been almost any of the men. The foot was too small to have belonged to Gisanto. If there were any justice, it was Jadrek's.

Ellasif would have thought the idea of Jadrek's demise would be a relief compared to the loss of one of the others, but she felt a pang of despair just the same to imagine him suffering such an ignoble fate. Even after what had happened between them, Jadrek deserved better. In the heat of her vengeance, sometimes Ellasif had imagined that she would be the one to kill him, but even in her most violent fantasies, she granted him a warrior's death.

Ellasif knew she was in the house of Szigo the Man-Eater. She had seen it before, over a year ago, but then she had approached only close enough to glimpse the interior through an opening she could not perceive from her present vantage. Perhaps there was no opening until the warlock desired it. Ellasif looked for some other way to escape.

Along the wall of pine trunks hung the helms, shields, armor, and weapons of the heroes who had come before, each hoping to claim the title of witch-slayer. Gnarled fingers of wood grew out of the pines to clutch each prize. She recognized the sword of Laughing Erik, a man whose reckless courage she had admired when she was a girl. His flying blade had sung the dirges for an entire cohort of goblins and dozens of trolls and human thralls sent by the witches of Irrisen to cross the border and pillage their own kin in the Lands of the Linnorm Kings. Erik had left White Rook one day boasting he would return with the head of Szigo, the warlock of the Grugnir Forest. Now his enchanted weapon was one of the warlock's trophies.

As was Ellasif.

She rued the hour she had departed this house without taking the head of its master. Szigo had given her the opportunity. His trolls had been too far away to save him if she had simply drawn her sword and cut his throat, and Ellasif would have gambled that his mistress would have only cackled as she watched him die. Yet Ellasif had not come to Szigo's grove that day to slay the warlock. She had gone there to find her sister's body.

No matter how often she tried to bury the memory of that futile quest, thinking of it always evoked the sensation of Jadrek's strong hands on her naked skin, his breath warm upon her shoulder. She had never been able to separate the ill memories from the good, and every time she thought of Liv's fate, Ellasif also remembered that day, over three years ago, when she and Jadrek had finally made love.

They had stolen away from the village on the first day of spring. No one would follow them, for everyone in White Rook knew they had been making the long, slow dance of a courtship once thought impossible, each afraid to be the first to make a wrong step. And no one saw where they went, except for a pair of foxes still half-snowy in their hoary winter coats.

Jadrek led her to a shallow cave from which the village warriors had driven one of the monstrous bear-owl creatures the previous autumn. The beast had returned, daring even to approach the village, unaware that the perpetual incursions by the forces of Irrisen had honed the warriors of White Rook into the deadliest of defenders. The monster's carcass had provided nights of feasting, and the candles from its tallow still lit the houses at night.

When Ellasif saw that Jadrek had covered the floor of the cave with fresh straw, she understood his intentions. It had taken him years to come to his senses and give up on Olenka, who despite her long legs and red hair was hardly the right match for the strongest man in the village. Jadrek needed a woman whose fighting heart was equal to his own. Or even stronger.

Most of her romantic rivalry with Olenka had sparked to flame in the practice circle, where Ellasif was rarely defeated. When the two most skilled shield maidens of the village faced off, Ellasif always remarked, "I am shorter than you. Thus, I am meaner than you." More often than not, she followed up her jest by knocking the tall redhead on her ass and touching her chin with the point of her sword. Olenka took her defeats in stride, realizing only near the end that she was also losing the battle for Jadrek's heart. She was the last to notice that when Jadrek offered his arm to lift her from the ground, his eyes strayed toward the victor.

Eventually Jadrek broke off his dalliance with Olenka, and after a few days had passed, he began to appear as if by coincidence whenever Ellasif was on watch. Sometimes she would find him rambling through the woods where she was known to take her solitary strolls. They walked together, talking of their dreams of glory, their plans for carving their names into the legend of their village.

He broke her name over his lips as lovers do, and she did not object. "Sif," he murmured into the hollow of her neck. When she did not protest, he took her hand in his, holding it until they returned to the village. This continued until Ellasif began to feel the impatience of uncertainty. She was not averse to making the first move. She had done so often enough with other men and boys. This time, however, she wanted to feel what it was to be the prey, not the hunter.

At last, she thought as they approached the cave. At last Jadrek had finally gathered the courage to do more than hold her hand or nuzzle her neck outside the light of the village fires. Today he would chase her to ground.

Jadrek lifted her chin to kiss her mouth. She almost smiled as she tasted the spearmint he had chewed to sweeten his breath, but then she surrendered to the pleasure of his embrace. His straw-blond beard was still soft as a rabbit's pelt, and not yet so long that he could braid it as the older men did. She ran her fingers through his beard and clutched it tight as she took control of the kiss. As big as he had grown, as brave as he had proven himself in battle, Jadrek still shivered at her touch. His boyish reaction released a thrill deep inside her.

It was the first time for neither of them, and both knew it. None of the jokes about the ironic title of "shield maiden" mattered, not among the tight-knit band of White Rook warriors. Yet for Ellasif, it was the first time the physical union had felt inevitable. Fated, as the skalds would sing as they sat beside the hearth and unfolded tales of great loves. All of them were fated.

Looking back on that day, Ellasif realized she should have remembered the other thing those fabled loves had in common: they were all doomed.

Afterward, when they lay panting on the damp straw, Ellasif heard the distant cry of a bird she could not identify. It was not a crow, but the shrill tenor of its voice spread a cold unease through her belly.

"Do you hear that?" she asked Jadrek.

He cocked his head to one side. "What is it?"

Ellasif did not know. "Probably just a goose fallen behind its—" A nameless fear filled her stomach with ice. She felt something was wrong back at the village, and she wished now that she had told Liv where she had been going. She pulled her clothes back on, ignoring Jadrek's questions until he also dressed and followed her as she ran back to the village.

White Rook was empty. Not even a lone sentinel remained.

"Where is everyone?" asked Jadrek.

Ellasif ran the perimeter of the village. When he saw what she was doing, Jadrek did the same, running the opposite direction. Ellasif found the footprints and called out to him, still believing he was as mystified as she, a ruse for which she would later hate him all the more.

The footprints led directly to the river. The path was so wide that Ellasif knew every adult and child from White Rook had gone together. In a rush of certainty, she knew why they had gone.

"Liv," she groaned, her voice dying in her throat.

She ran along the path of footprints. Jadrek followed, calling for her to wait and tell him what she was doing. With his long gait, he soon overtook her, but he did not try to stop her. He knew better.

They met the villagers on the way.

They shuffled back toward White Rook, most of them with their gazes fixed on the ground a few feet ahead. Only the elders held their heads high, but their eyes were fixed on the horizon behind Ellasif. Even they could not look in her eyes.

Standing tall among the crones and crookbacks was Red Ochme, her posture unbowed by the years. Her hair was more gray than red these days, but in her blue eyes shone the strength that in her younger days had made her the hero of White Rook. Her clothes were drenched from the chest down, as were those of two of the stronger old men.

Ochme's gaze wavered at the sight of Ellasif. Her frown deepened, but she did not look away as the others did.

"What have you done?" cried Ellasif.

"It was a needed thing," said Ochme. Her voice, so strong in the fray, cracked as she added, "Daughter of my heart, you knew this day would come. We could not allow a witch to live among us."

"She did nothing wrong!"

"One day, she would have."

"You could have sent her away," said Ellasif.

"And you would have gone with her," said Ochme. "You are too valuable to the village. We cannot lose you. One day you must take my place."

Ellasif ran past the villagers. She followed the wake of their footprints. Most of them stopped far from the water's edge, but four pairs went all the way to the bank and into the water. Only three returned.

Ellasif ran along the bank, calling for Liv. The river ran fast in the spring thaw. Her eyes sought any sign of her sister, but she saw nothing but the water.

What had Liv been wearing that morning? Was it the gray woolen robe? That would be difficult to spy under the iron-colored water. Why hadn't she worn the yellow or the white?

Ellasif knew the answer to the absurd question: It was because Liv had woken that day with the expectation that the people of her village—her neighbors, her kin—would drown her. And she'd gone with them rather than fight against the inevitable.

Tears blurred Ellasif's vision, but she kept running along the bank. She heard Olenka call her name, but refused to turn back. Olenka's shouts grew closer and closer, drowning out her own cries for Liv. The red-haired warrior grasped Ellasif's shoulder and spun her around.

Ellasif hesitated when she saw the anguish in Olenka's face. They had been fast friends since childhood, and their rivalry for Jadrek's affections could not have changed that. Then a horrible realization struck Ellasif deep inside, a staggering blow on a day when she thought she could endure no further pain.

She understood that Jadrek had never broken off with Olenka. It had all been a ruse to distract her while the rest of the village murdered her sister. In all her years of keeping Liv's secret, Ellasif had confided in only one person, allowing Olenka to help shoulder the weight of that terrible knowledge. And now her friend had clearly betrayed her to the village elders, telling them about the tiren'kii.

"Come back," said Olenka. She held out her hand.

Ellasif kicked the woman's knee hard enough to crack the joint. Olenka hissed in pain and fell as she tried to step back. Ellasif drew her sword and raised it high.

"Sif, don't!" Jadrek ran toward them, but he was too far away to stop her. All she had to do was strike once, and at least one of her betrayers would pay.

Yet Ellasif hesitated. Something meaner than any trick she had ever used in battle growled up from the pit of her heart. She held the sword in both hands, the point inches from Olenka's throat as she locked her gaze to Jadrek's.

"Stop," she said, and he obeyed. "Go back, or I will kill her in front of you."

"Sif—"

"Never call me that!" she yelled.

His mouth moved, but he backed away, his eyes on Ellasif's face until the last moment, when his gaze fell to Olenka, who lay staring at the sky, awaiting her death. He turned and ran back toward White Rook.

When he was out of sight, Ellasif stepped away and sheathed her sword. Olenka could crawl back to the village, but with her wounded knee, she would not be able to follow her former friend. Ellasif turned and ran along the river.

She ran no more than a quarter of a mile before she saw the marks beside river. For a moment she dared to hope Liv had not only survived the drowning but retained the strength to pull herself onto the bank, but no. She saw from the signs that someone had pulled Liv out of the water here. There were footprints approaching from the north, not so large as those left by the biggest of the Ulfen warriors, but probably those of a man rather than a woman. Here he had knelt beside a swath of wet grass that could only be where he had pulled Liv from the water.

Could he have revived her? Was he a healer? It was a faint hope, but to Ellasif it felt like the sun appearing from behind winter clouds.

The man's tracks returned the way they had come, only this time they were accompanied by a trail of irregular gaps in the frost that Ellasif took for water dripping from Liv's robe.

She followed the trail a mile farther. How long had it been since they threw Liv in the river? Why had Ellasif not yet overtaken a man carrying a woman whose clothes were drenched in river water? He was not unduly large, judging from the footprints. Ellasif should have spied him already, but soon she found the reason. Liv's rescuer had met something on his return.

The newcomer's tracks were clawed and four times larger than a man's, each leaving an inch-deep depression in the hard spring soil.

It could only be a troll.

After an instant of despair, Ellasif realized there was no blood. She prayed that her sister was yet uneaten. Perhaps Liv's rescuer had summoned the monster to convey her elsewhere—but of course one who could summon a troll was not likely to be a village healer.

The man's tracks had vanished, so Ellasif guessed that the monster carried him as well, or else he had some other means of travel. Perhaps flight, if he were a witch, as Ellasif was beginning to suspect and even to hope. How strange to hope for a witch, when all her kin were set on slaying witches, even those born to their own village.

Ellasif ran after the troll's footprints. If it came to a fight, she knew she was no match for such a monster, not without half a dozen warriors by her side. But she also knew she would rather die avenging her sister than return to beg for help.

She traveled all day, running when she could, trudging along the river when she could not. When the edge of the sun touched the horizon, she fell to the ground. She lay there until long after the last of the reflected light evaporated from the western clouds, and then she rose and followed the tracks by moonlight. The morning sun had melted the last of the spring frost by the time Ellasif entered the easternmost reaches of the Grungir Forest and followed the troll's path inside.

She smelled the place before she saw it. The wholesome odor of roasting flesh mingled with the stench of an open grave. She spied the withered remains of butchered corpses impaled on pine stakes, each little more than a skeleton and a gauze of skin dancing on the breeze after cannibals harvested the meat. The gruesome totems formed a wide ring around a clearing.

Around a central fire pit stood two massive tables, each stained with blood and scarred with axe-strokes. A pair of lean trolls crouched over a cauldron hanging above the fire. One of them peered inside, smacked his lips dismissively, and stalked away into the western woods in search of fresh prey. The other poked a long wooden spoon into the pot, stirred it once, and coughed before laying its misshapen head upon its crossed arms. Whatever lay within the vessel was unappealing even to such monsters.

The smell of roast flesh came from a tight cluster of pine trees that lay on the far side of the clearing. Their trunks grew together in a rough oval that could not have been arranged by chance or nature. Some powerful druid or witch had commanded them into such an array, forming what Ellasif imagined was an enormous house, larger than the mead hall at White Rook. The trunks were bare of branches until a height of perhaps fifteen feet, where the boughs formed a continuous eave around the perimeter. The ground beneath the overhang was covered in a thick layer of bark harvested from other trees. If not for the bone wind chimes dangling from the high branches, Ellasif might have assumed it was the home of a druid or fey creature.

Ellasif felt certain Liv was inside the house of pines, but there were no windows through which to spy the inhabitants. She prayed her sister was still alive. The thought that Liv might be the source of the savory odor emanating from the house made Ellasif feel sick to her stomach.

A simple bell pull emerged near a crease on the side of the odd house nearest the fire pit. The trunks bulged to either side of the crease, like bruised lips just beginning to turn green at the edges. Ellasif had never witnessed any magic more spectacular than her own sister's intuitions that one of the village girls was pregnant before the girl herself knew, but she knew this was a magic door. Some charm or magic phrase would open it. Perhaps it was simply a matter of pulling the bell, but she could not even do that before dealing with the troll that remained beside the fire.

The scheme, such as it was, came to her in a flash. She crept as quickly as she dared around the grove, confirming her first impression that there were no obvious entrances to the house of pines. To the northeast the ground declined into a shallow gully that became a sharp ravine farther to the north. A huge, gnarled bristlecone pine gripped the edge of the embankment, its hollow bole forming an ideal hiding place. Ellasif picked up a few of the previous year's cones from the ground, each as heavy as a stone. She slipped back to just within hearing of the grove.

She grunted like a rooting pig.

She paused to listen but heard nothing but distant birdsong. She repeated the guttural snort, adding a flourish of boar-like snuffling.

The iron cauldron rang against the stones of the fire pit, and she heard the troll's first heavy footfalls move in her direction.

Ellasif ran along the gulley. There was no need to pause and listen, for the troll's steps drummed the ground and shook the needles from the trees. As she reached the point where the gully sank into a ragged-edged crevasse, Ellasif uttered another loud porcine grunt and flung the first of the pine cones ten yards or so ahead of her. She darted inside the bole of the tree.

The troll crashed into the ravine, landing just a few feet from Ellasif's shelter. There it paused, sniffing the air. Ellasif wished she had bathed before attempting this ploy, but she resisted the urge to smell herself. She held her breath and thought a silent prayer to Desna: *Lady Luck, please let this stupid monster run farther.*

And so it did, taking a few tentative steps along the ravine before stopping to sniff again. Ellasif knew it had to have caught a whiff of her. She watched as the brute's squat head rotated left, then right as it scanned its surroundings. She leaned as far as she dared out of her shelter and lobbed the second pine cone high above the troll's shoulder. It descended in a perfect arc, narrowly avoiding a bare pine branch to crash noisily in the ravine ahead.

The troll lunged toward the sound, leaning forward to run four-limbed on its knuckles. Something ahead bolted from cover and ran to the north. It did not sound like a boar, but the troll was past caring. The monster careened through the forest, knocking the younger trees aside in its reckless course.

Ellasif ran back to the charnel grove. She struck the swollen crease in the tree with her hand. She kicked it. She drew her sword and thrust the point into the crack. She did not think these crude efforts would succeed, but she had to try something before trying the obvious, stupid option. She pulled the bell string.

Seconds later, the pine trunks parted like a blossoming bud. A balding man dressed in rags put his face close to hers and smiled. His teeth were filed to perfectly triangular points, and his breath was rancid. He said something in a sibilant voice, but Ellasif looked past him. Inside his strange house of living pines, bound to the opposite wall by thick, finger-like branches, was Liv. Her gray gown had dried upon her, and she sagged helplessly in the grip of the enchanted wooden manacles, but her slender chest moved with respiration.

Ellasif's sword was in her hand, but before she could raise it to separate the warlock's head from his body, a voice called out behind her. Not a voice, exactly, but the human-like cry of a bird. Against her better judgment, Ellasif turned to see the source of the cry.

An enormous white raven perched at the edge of one of the butcher tables. Ellasif blinked. It was not a bird, but a white-haired woman of forty or fifty years. She wore a snow-white gown with pale blue bracers at each wrist. Bronze discs, each set with a blue gem, hung from a chain draped around her shoulders. On her hip hung a heavy dagger sheathed in thick blue hide, and she held a staff carved with the head of a bearded Ulfen warrior wearing a horned crown.

"The sister," she said in a tone of pleasant surprise. Her eyes were fixed on Ellasif's face, her lips half parted as she smiled. She lifted her arm, and Ellasif's sword was suddenly in the raven-woman's hand. She admired the blade as if she recognized it. "Ellasif Maritsdotter."

"You are free with my name," said Ellasif. She tried not to let her astonishment show on her face. Before she could think of something else bold to say, she felt the warlock's breath on her neck and kicked his insole. As he reached for his foot, she smashed his nose with her elbow. She grabbed his neck and threw him to the ground before him.

"Mistress," groaned the warlock, writhing on the bark floor. "I have captured the girl as you bade me."

The white witch threw back her head. Her laugh was the tinkle of shattering ice. "So I see," she said. "You are pathetic, Szigo. But today you have served me."

"Served you how?" demanded Ellasif. "Who are you? What do you want?"

"I am Mareshka Zarumina," said the woman. "And what I want, your barbaric tribe casts away. Your sister belongs to me now."

"No," Ellasif stated firmly. She heard Szigo whispering at her feet and kicked him in the belly, stifling whatever spell he had been trying to utter. "Let my sister go, and I'll release this dog of yours."

Mareska laughed again. Despite the creases on her face, her voice was youthful. Then her blue eyes turned the color of frost, and she rapped her staff upon the ground. Thick antlers grew from her brow as the blank eyes of the staff's head blazed white. Ellasif took a step toward her, but Mareshka uttered a single syllable, and Ellasif froze in place.

A cold sheath of ice encased Ellasif's body. She could not budge a muscle, and all the forest sounds were muted, as though she were submerged in water. She could still move her eyes, and she watched as Mareshka stroked Szigo's balding head and stood him up beside her. The warlock leered at Ellasif, licking his lips as his eyes stroked her body not with lust, but with hunger.

The witch whispered something in his ear, and the warlock's expression changed from imminent satisfaction to horror and hurt.

"But I'm hungry," Szigo whined.

Mareshka's only answer was mocking laughter. She raised an arm above her head, and from the corner of her eye Ellasif saw—or thought she saw—the wing of an enormous white bird. She could not turn her head to see more.

Ellasif felt herself pulled down into a cold and breathless darkness. She imagined this was how Liv had felt when she had been thrust into the icy currents of the river. The difference, Ellasif knew, was that no one would come to her own rescue. She would drown alone.

Chapter Twelve
The Charnel Grove

Wake up, sent Skywing.

Declan raised his head with a start. His chin had been on his shoulder, and without the dragon's warning, he was certain he would have woken only after he'd slid off his saddle. That Skywing might have cast a spell to protect him from cracking open his skull was small consolation. Since he was the only one mounted after a full day's hard travel, the humiliation alone might have killed him.

Since they had left the Varisians, Declan had been riding Majeed Nores' gray stallion, but the Ulfen warriors ran on either side of the horse, seemingly tireless. Declan marveled at their endurance, not to mention their size. Even Olenka was an inch or two taller than he, and the red-haired warrior woman was the shortest of the band. Ellasif must have felt like a gnome among these giants. No wonder she had become such a cunning warrior. What she lacked in mass, she more than made up in dirty tricks.

The six Ulfen had remained with the survivors of the Varisian caravan only long enough to help bandage the injured. They ignored Viland Balev's furious demands for an explanation until his anger dissolved into grudging thanks for their intervention. Only then did Jadrek speak to the captain in the common tongue, his words lilting with his Ulfen accent.

"Now that Szigo has taken her, the trolls will trouble you no more," he said. "Think no more of her. We will find her."

"What do you want with Ellasif?" Declan demanded before Balev could reply.

Jadrek looked down at the Korvosan. He paused as if considering whether it was worth his breath to answer, but then he said, "To bring her home. To her people."

She doesn't want to go home, thought Declan. She wants to find her sister. But he didn't need another look at the stern faces of the Ulfen to realize it was better not to say so. Instead, he said, "I'm going with you."

One of the Ulfen warriors barked a laugh of disbelief, but Jadrek frowned and reappraised Declan with a hard stare. "Why?"

"Because she needs rescue," said Declan. "Because she is my friend."

Jadrek considered that answer while Declan said his goodbyes to the Varisians. Balev was as gracious as he could manage under the circumstances, but Declan sensed he was glad to be rid of the other stranger in his midst. If Ellasif had been the cause of the troll attack, he had to be wondering what trouble the Korvosan wizard might bring them.

Life was much easier when he wasn't a wizard. Declan wondered whether he could ever shed that name again, especially now that he planned to run into the northern woods in search of a warlock with trolls for minions. There was no way he could succeed without using every last spell he could cram into his brain.

The seven Ulfen warriors were having a heated debate in their own language. Whatever its substance, the others reluctantly accepted Jadrek's decision.

"Try to keep up," Jadrek said. He turned and ran toward the east.

Declan mounted his horse and grasped the reins of Ellasif's pony. He almost smiled at Jadrek's challenge, but within moments he realized it was no boast. The Ulfen warriors traveled lightly, their packs half the size of one of his. They set a quick pace through the trees, loping away toward the east. Declan could barely keep them in sight as he guided the stallion and led the pony through the wood. Once they were clear, Declan urged the horse into a gallop across the rolling plains to catch up with them. Even afterward, he had to keep moving at a brisk trot for the rest of the day. He kept expecting the pony to balk, but the feisty thing seemed more than willing to come along. All the while, the northerners ran steadily, their eyes fixed upon the edge of the Grungir Forest.

When Declan asked where they were headed, the Ulfen threw him dark glances. They muttered prayers to Gorum, the Lord in Iron, as they touched the hafts of their weapons. One drew the wings of Desna over his heart, and Declan realized that one, at least, did not trust his battle prowess alone to overcome whatever it was they expected to find in the forest.

Shortly before dusk, Jadrek made a sign, and the band veered north toward a creek trickling into the forest. Half of the Ulfen threw themselves prone to drink while the other three scanned the gloaming horizon. Declan slid down to stretch his legs.

A squirrel ran up a nearby tree. Declan had seen plenty of wildlife throughout the afternoon. Geese had passed above them, honking as they rose from one pond to find another. Does and their fawns raised their heads as the humans crossed the fields where they grazed, never so close as to startle the beasts to flight. Far to the west, a trio of boars rooted for yams at the edge of the forest.

Skywing flew down to perch on the saddle horn. Instantly, two blades sang out from their scabbards, and Jadrek lifted his warhammer above his head. The Ulfen that had been drinking leaped up into defensive crouches, their hands on their weapons. All were poised to strike the little drake.

"It's all right!" Declan called out, raising his hands to beg for peace. "This is Skywing. He's my . . . pet."

Nobody's pet, sent Skywing with an emotion like indignation. Under different circumstances, it might have made Declan smile to have ruffled the drake's pride, but something had held him back from repeating the ruse that Skywing was his familiar. Despite employing spells in defense of the caravan, he was not quite ready to go around introducing himself as a wizard.

"What manner of beast is that?" asked Jadrek.

"A little drake," said Declan, avoiding the word "dragon." He did not trust that the Ulfen would believe Skywing would grow no larger. "They are common in Korvosa."

Olenka spat a few words in Ulfen. Declan recognized one of them: jadwiga.

"I am not a witch," said Declan. Jadrek raised an eyebrow at him. Declan had first heard the term only

a couple of months ago, but it had remained prominent in his memory. He knew the northern people were
particularly suspicious of spellcasters, especially those
they deemed witches. Recalling the troll attack, Declan
wondered whether any of the Ulfen had witnessed his
casting spells. Possibly the big one, Jadrek, had seen
him directing the rolling fireball. He was not certain
enough to attempt a direct lie. "I am a mapmaker."

His pronouncement began another skirmish of arguments among the Ulfen, but Jadrek silenced them with
a chopping gesture from his open hand. There was no
further discussion. After everyone including the animals had drunk from the creek, they set off again.

They did not stop after sunset but continued running
through the night. Several times Declan wished to ask
when they would stop to camp, but soon he realized
the answer. Every hour or so, they slowed to a walk, but
they did not stop. He gave the stallion a rest and rode
Ellasif's pony for a while, but his offers to let one of the
Ulfen ride the stallion were curtly dismissed.

After the moon disappeared beneath the horizon,
they paused to drink from the water skins they carried. This time, half of the Ulfen lay on the ground for
less than an hour before trading places with those
who stood watch. Declan removed the steeds' saddles
and brushed their trembling flanks before lying on
the ground without bothering to unfurl his blanket. It
seemed only moments later that one of the Ulfen men
kicked the bottoms of his feet to wake him.

They traveled all night. Even the chase from the
Nolanders had been less exhausting. It was afternoon
when Skywing alerted Declan that he was falling asleep
in the saddle again. By then even the northern warriors
were beginning to show signs of fatigue, and Declan

thought it a wonder his stallion had not yet collapsed. Though bigger and stronger than the pony, the stallion had far less grit and stamina.

He dismounted and led the animal by its bridle, wishing he had a reward to offer it. Olenka overheard him apologizing to the beast while he stroked its muzzle. She produced a double handful of dried oats and fruit, which vanished the instant she held them to the stallion's mouth. Before she could wipe her palms, the pony nosed her for its share. She scoffed, only half amused, before surrendering the rest of her trail rations. She did not reply to Declan's thanks, but the gesture touched him. He began to believe their hearts were kind as well as brave.

When at last Jadrek halted the warriors and directed one to build a fire, Declan moved as though in a dream. He barely noticed two of the warriors running deeper into the forest at Jadrek's command. He did not recall tending to the stallion and the pony, but he must have done so, for he awoke with a start some time later with his head resting upon one saddle, his feet propped on the other. Nearby, a fire crackled unattended. A short distance away, the Ulfen were arguing more fiercely than before. The scouts had returned.

Declan could hear every word, but understood none of them. He sat up, disturbing Skywing as he bumped the slumbering dragon with his foot. Rather than impose on what appeared to be a private debate, Declan retrieved his spellbook from his pack and began to study a new array of spells to replace those he had cast in defense of the Varisian caravan. With the principal weakness of trolls in mind, he allowed some others to slip from his thoughts and replaced them with fire invocations.

"Come," Jadrek called to him, then turned back to the group. "This man is a friend to Ellasif. He should have a say."

One of the other warriors interjected, but Jadrek cut him off with a raised hand. "Speak a language he can understand, Uwe," he said.

The other man sighed heavily. He was at least five years older than Jadrek, who seemed to be about Declan's age. Thick braids ran through his ruddy blond beard and hair. "He is not of White Rook," Uwe said. "He has no voice here."

"Let him speak," said Olenka. "Even the words of an outsider may hold wisdom."

Uwe muttered something in his native tongue. He spat. "Jadwiga."

All eyes were on Declan. He felt like one of those insects Paddermont Grinji kept pinned on cork panels in his laboratory. He summoned his most confident smile, but it felt like a flimsy mask. "What exactly is the problem?"

"The warlock Szigo has taken her to the Charnel Grove," said a black-bearded warrior Declan had heard referred to as Gunnar. He was missing several of his upper teeth. "It is the lair of his trolls, where they take their captives to be butchered."

Declan felt a lump rise in his throat. He had seen the warlock fly off with Ellasif. By now she might already be dead and eaten.

"This is why we must attack at once," said Jadrek.

"No," said Uwe. "We were sent to ensure that Ellasif returned or that she was dead. Now she is certainly dead."

"Not certainly," said Jadrek. His eyes sought out Olenka's for support. She nodded—somewhat reluctantly, Declan thought. "We leave no comrade in the hands of such monsters. Are we not warriors of White Rook?"

His triumphant tone was lost on the others, who turned their stony gazes to the ground between them.

"Ellasif was not banished," a grizzled man named Ingver conceded. A winter frost had bitten off the tip of his nose and gnawed his ears down to stunted mushrooms. "She is still one of us."

"Why did she leave?" asked Declan. Immediately he regretted the question, as the silent glares of the Ulfen weighed upon him. "It was something to do with her sister, wasn't it?"

Jadrek nodded slowly. "Ellasif's sister was cursed."

"She was a witch," said Uwe. "Every year she lived at White Rook, the jadwiga sent their monsters to claim her."

"So what did you do?" asked Declan.

No one spoke at first. Jadrek frowned at Olenka, who turned away. Eventually Ingver broke the silence. "We gave her to the river," he said.

"You drowned her?" Declan's voice was a whisper.

"It was a needed thing," said Ingver, but like Olenka he turned away.

"It was needed," insisted Uwe. "She would have had absolute power over us had we let the jadwiga take her. Blood calls to blood, and the warriors of White Rook will never be thralls to the witches of Whitethrone!"

"And Ellasif must not be prisoner of their minions!" countered Jadrek.

"There were four trolls within the clearing," said Saxo, a bald warrior whose beard was braided into a long rope he slung around his neck. "Who knows what else the warlock keeps inside that house?"

"All the more reason to slay the warlock," said Jadrek.

"Better men than you have tried," said Uwe.

Jadrek rose to the bait, stepping forward and jutting out his chest. The smaller man stood his ground, his hands loose and open at his side. He looked up at Jadrek's livid face and said simply, "Erik."

The name was a charm to soothe the rising tempers. Jadrek turned away, and all the Ulfen shifted slightly, as if casting their thoughts back to an ill but solemn memory.

"Who is Erik?" asked Declan.

When no one answered him, he sought their eyes. At last he caught Olenka returning his inquisitive gaze, and she said, "Laughing Erik was the last hero to go to the Charnel Grove to slay the warlock Szigo."

"But there are six of you," said Declan. He drew his sword and held it before him. "There are seven of us."

"Erik had the strength of ten warriors," said Saxo. He continued in a bard's meter: "His sword would sing the song of blood. His shield of wood, now sundered lies."

"Erik is dead," said Jadrek. His voice was full of mourning for an argument he knew he had lost.

Declan couldn't believe what he was hearing. Either everything he had ever heard about the heroes of the Lands of the Linnorm Kings was wrong, or else . . .

"Did that cannibal unman the lot of you?" he said. The men turned toward him with disbelieving sneers. "I mean, did he cast a spell that made your balls disappear?"

"You dare?" said Saxo, slapping away Declan's sword.

Declan let the weapon fall away. It took an effort not to flinch away from the man. His physical threat was daunting, but his smell was even worse. "Dare what?" he said. "Dare question the courage of men who will not aid their fellow warrior?

"I'm sorry," he said, waving a hand in mock apology, but also to dispel the miasma of Saxo's body odor. "I got the wrong idea. When I saw Jadrek slay that troll back at the caravan, I thought heroes had come to save us."

"Who are you to speak to us this way?" demanded Uwe.

"Me?" said Declan. He retrieved his sword and said, "I'm the one who isn't going to leave his friend to be eaten by trolls."

He turned on his heel and marched away, pausing only to scoop up his packs and sling them over his shoulders. He realized a moment later that he probably should have tethered the horse and pony to a tree, but he didn't want to spoil his dramatic exit. If he lost his nerve before he reached the forest's edge, he only hoped the Ulfen would be gone.

Behind him, the Ulfen returned to their own language, mostly in dismissive and mocking tones. Uwe yelled after him, "You will be in Szigo's cauldron before we reach home!"

"I'll say hello to your balls," Declan shouted back. Despite his bravado, his shoulders slumped under the weight of his realization that he was on his own.

Skywing? he thought. When he received no reply, he despaired that his last friend had abandoned him. Or perhaps the drake was still asleep. Maybe that was for the best. There was little or nothing the drake could do to protect him in a fight with trolls. If he were to have any hope of success, Declan would have to be cunning, like Ellasif. But despite his book-knowledge, he had to admit that he just wasn't that clever. He was being a fool.

Jamang's satchel rose off of his shoulder. He turned to see Olenka hefting it onto her own shoulder. She looked down at him and said, "You are a fool."

Before Declan could respond to her apparent reading of his thoughts, he felt the weight of his own pack rise off the other side. There was Jadrek. "Don't worry," he said. "It means she likes you."

The cheer of camaraderie was fleeting. The other Ulfen had chosen to return home, leaving them with only three against at least four trolls. The arithmetic of the situation gnawed at Delcan's belly as they crept through the dark woods. When Jadrek put a heavy hand on his shoulder, they crouched and peered ahead. There was the dull light of a campfire in a clearing. Three trolls huddled around a cauldron upon the fire. The flames cast their enormous shadows upon the towering walls of a queer house formed of pine trunks.

"Let us hope Ellasif is in the house," said Olenka, "and not in the pot."

Jadrek turned toward her. Even though Declan could not discern his expression in the gloom, he could practically feel the admonishment radiating off his face.

"One for each of us," said Jadrek. He thumbed the grip of his sword and murmured the name of Gorum, the Lord in Iron. As Olenka did the same, Declan sketched the wings of Desna over his heart, expecting his survival would depend more on the whims of Lady Luck than on his meager fighting ability. He supposed he should have prayed to Nethys, but the two-faced god of magic just didn't give a damn.

The Ulfen warriors began to creep forward, but Declan hissed, "Wait. What's the plan?"

Olenka said, "We break their skulls, you burn them."

"That's not a plan," said Declan. "Your scout said there were four trolls, but I see only three. That means we need to lure the fourth one back to the others, so we aren't surprised."

"Good," said Jadrek. "What else?"

"Well . . ." Declan hesitated. He hoped Jadrek already suspected he was a wizard, and more than that he hoped both of them understood there was a difference between a wizard and a witch. If they wanted an explanation of the difference, he realized he didn't know where to begin. "While I am definitely not a jadwiga, I can cast a few spells."

The others were silent, but Declan sensed that Jadrek was nodding, his suspicion confirmed.

"After our last fight, I prepared more fire, but not enough for four trolls," he said. "Unless you two can gather them up for me."

"Very well," said Jadrek. "What's the plan?"

Declan told them, and they considered the many ways it could all go wrong.

"You'll need to run fast to get out of range," said Declan.

"I know," Jadrek said. "But as long as we get Ellasif out of there, I don't care if you burn the forest down."

Olenka sighed. Declan sympathized. She and Jadrek were taking most of the risk.

"Good plan," Jadrek decided. He clapped Declan on the shoulder. It was a heavy blow, but not, Declan thought, outside the bounds of Ulfen affection. "We go now."

Declan felt a moment of panic, and he almost called out for them to wait. But there was no point. He was as ready as he could be.

Olenka and Jadrek ran around either side of the clearing. They moved quickly, making just enough noise to be sure the trolls could hear them, but not so much that it was obvious they wanted to be heard. Declan kept his eyes on the clearing, where one of the trolls rose from its squat beside the cauldron and snuffled at the air. An anticipatory grin creased the creature's bestial face. It nudged one of its fellows with its knuckles and grunted out a few words in their monstrous tongue. All three rose and turned to face the woods in three directions. Declan guessed the brutes had been hoping for a rescue attempt.

The fourth troll bellowed to the west of camp, the direction where Olenka had gone. The three trolls by the camp turned as one in that direction. In the same instant, Jadrek streaked across the clearing. He swung his hammer down to smash the thigh of the nearest troll. The beast wailed louder than a pack of wolves. Jadrek ran past, turning his body to sweep his warhammer in a horizontal arc. He struck the second troll with an audible crack to the spine. The beast opened its massive maw toward the sky, but no sound emerged. It clutched at the small of its back.

The third troll reached for Jadrek just as Olenka burst out of the forest. Behind her, the pines bent to either side as her massive pursuer shouldered them out of its way. Shadows flickered over the troll's gray-green skin, giving it the appearance of a foul pond into which someone had cast a load of garbage. The troll's claws, each big enough to grasp Declan around the waist, clutched for Olenka. For a second, Declan feared the troll would grasp the warrior's long red braid and reel her in like a fish.

"Run," Declan whispered. "Hurry up and run!"

Jadrek and Olenka ran into each other, shoulder to shoulder. They turned together, his hammer and her sword striking low. Jadrek smashed a foot, sending his troll into a spasm of barking and hopping. The point of Olenka's blade swept up, trailing a crimson plume, but the troll's claws slashed down across her jerkin, taking with it a thick swath of leather and a spray of blood. She cried out, a sound more angry than fearful, and spun away to flee beside Jadrek.

They ran five or six steps together, then Olenka stumbled. She stood to run almost instantly, but she was a few steps behind Jadrek and only a few steps ahead of the nearest two trolls.

Startled and confused, the other two trolls hesitated. Declan worried that Jadrek had injured them too badly for the ploy to work. The big warrior must have shared his fear. He taunted them with shouted insults and vulgar gestures. They came after him, but Declan feared they were still spread too far apart. His timing had to be perfect.

He cast the spell when Jadrek was about ten yards away. He estimated it would just miss Olenka, but as the spell slipped from his mind and took form in reality, one troll lunged forward and grasped the shield maiden by the ankle.

A chaotic network of silvery gossamer formed between the trees nearest the trolls. It glimmered for an instant, barely real, before clotting to form a dense, sticky barrier. The weight of the trolls stretched the webs and bowed the trees. Their roars blew like storms through the conjured barrier, but the webs held fast.

So did the grip of the troll holding Olenka's leg.

Declan uttered a curse so vile he surprised even himself.

"Do it now!" Olenka shouted, kicking with her free foot. It was no use—the troll's grip was far too strong to break. It dragged her into the webs, and she sat up to hack at its wrist.

"I can't," said Declan. He knew she would be caught in the blast.

"Do it," demanded Jadrek, skidding to a stop beside him. He ran back toward Olenka, placing himself in the same deadly spot. "Hurry!"

"This is a bad idea," muttered Declan, but the next words he uttered were those that evoked the most powerful spell he knew. He squeezed his hand tight and felt the prick of heat upon his palm. It was no use waiting—it had to be now. Declan cocked his arm and hurled a fiery orb no larger than a pebble toward the webbed trolls. As it flew toward them, it blossomed, expanding to engulf the entire mass of webs.

The explosion blew Declan's hair back from his face. He felt the heat on his skin as he closed his eyes against the blinding flash. The plan had been to follow the first spell immediately with another, but he dared not hurl another fireball until he could see Jadrek and Olenka. He blinked and peered into the brief inferno.

It had vaporized the webs and blasted the bark from the trees. Flames danced up the pines to hiss in the oily fir needles. Pinecones popped and spun down from their bows, spreading the fire to the neighboring trees. Below them, silhouettes of the trolls capered in pain and terror. Two ran into each other, falling in a tangle of long limbs in their desperation to escape the flames. Another turned, blinded and amazed, just before emerging from the flames. The fourth ran howling toward the house of pines, jabbering for help from within.

Declan could not see the Ulfen. "Jadrek!" he shouted. "Olenka! Where are you?"

"Again!" shouted Jadrek. Declan saw him stumbling away from the blast, one arm under Olenka's shoulder. Flames guttered in their hair and died in a nimbus along their arms and shoulders.

Declan threw another of the fireballs, enveloping the three panicked trolls and the surrounding trees. When the flash subsided, one of them was gone save for a pile of oily cinders. The other two monsters staggered out of the blast, flesh shriveled by the flames. They staggered toward the clearing, tall black skeletons, and fell burning to the ground.

Jadrek and Olenka stood beside him, both still patting out flames on their clothes or hair. Both had angry red burns on their arms and faces. Olenka favored one leg, but she stood without help. They looked past Declan at the surviving troll, his skin blistered and oozing from the fire. The monster beat upon the pine house and begged to be let inside.

Declan raised his hands to cast another spell, but Jadrek put a hand on his arm. "Save it for the warlock," he said. He and Olenka charged the monster, their weapons raised high. The beast turned to face them, but its death was swift and bloody.

Jadrek dragged the carcass to the cooking fire and fueled the flames from a nearby stack of firewood. Olenka stripped off the rest of her armor to expose two long, deep claw marks running from just inside her left breast to the middle of her belly. Declan winced as he saw the extent of her wounds, but when he moved forward to offer his help, she waved him away.

The door, sent Skywing. Declan felt that the drake was somewhere above him, but looking up revealed only the pine boughs encircling the weird tree house.

"Where?" he said aloud.

Right in front of you, sent Skywing anxiously. *Hurry, getting away.*

Declan had seen no opening on the pine house, only a long leather cord that might have been a bell pull. He tugged it and heard a clatter of bones or wood inside.

"Open up," he shouted. "Let us in, or we'll burn the place down."

"Hurry," called Ellasif from inside. Declan heard cackling laughter followed by a shriek of surprise and a few choice curses. Moments later, he felt a strange sensation as of a powerful spell being cast nearby.

He beat upon the walls, and then Jadrek was beside him.

"Stand back," said the big warrior. He raised his warhammer, but stopped when they saw the trunks pull apart like the mouth of a drowning fish. The warlock Szigo crawled over the threshold, hugging himself with one arm as he dragged his body toward them.

Declan drew his sword and simultaneously began to trace a spell in the air, but he saw that the man was no longer a threat. He had painted the floor behind him with a wide swath of blood, and his guts spilled out over the arm he held to his belly.

Behind Szigo, the cluttered interior of the house appeared completely uninhabited.

"Where is she?" asked Declan. He punctuated his question by pointing the tip of his sword at the warlock's eye.

Szigo giggled, a foam of blood oozing out from between his teeth as he grimaced in pain. "Gone," he rasped. "Gone to Whitethrone. Gone to Baba Yaga's kin, to be flayed and ground to powder in the Bone Mill."

Chapter Thirteen
The Spring Palace

On that day long past—before Korvosa, before Declan Avari, before anything except a desperate need to rescue her sister—Ellasif had gasped for breath as the ice vanished from her face. White light dazzled her eyes, glinting at her from all directions. The air was so humid that she could barely breathe, and a powerful sense of vertigo shook her brain in all directions. In an instant she realized she was not suffocating but falling. She dropped into surprisingly warm water.

Her startled gasp took a mouthful of sulfuric water into her lungs. She sank fast, her woolen clothes sodden and heavy. She thrashed in panic and reached for a hold that was not there. Then her buttocks struck the flat bottom of the pool. She put her feet beneath her and stood up, choking and coughing up water.

She stood in a steaming oval pool. Once she had spit up enough water to breathe freely, she smelled flowers, their perfume strong enough to overcome even the stench of the mineral bath. To either side were thick green walls of foliage, at the base of which flowered strange blossoms. Their thick petals were lush as the flesh of a freshly scaled salmon, golden and pink and pale white with stamens of bright reds and yellows. Above them floated odd insects, similar to the butter-flies that lived for a few brief days in late spring, but with too many wings. High above, the ceiling and walls were all of glistening glass.

No, she realized—not glass but ice. The sunlight warmed the panes enough to wet them, and Ellasif saw steady rivulets trickling from the highest reaches. Even as she followed their paths, one dropped upon her brow, cool as the spring thaw.

"Welcome to Whitethone," said a voice that flowed like liquid silver.

Ellasif turned to see Mareshka reclining upon a chair carved of mammoth hide and ivory. The tusk of one such great beast curved up behind her to lend the seat the air of a throne, and the way the witch held her horned staff across her lap seemed to Ellasif the very image of a monarch. She guessed that was no coincidence.

From somewhere above them, a strange creature fluttered down and took up a perch between the horns of Mareshka's staff. It looked like an emaciated ver-sion of the Korvosan necromancer's imp, but rather than fire-blackened flesh, its skin was the translucent blue of deep river ice. The thing slowly waved the bony framework on its back, like a newly emerged butterfly drying its wings in the sun, and the webbing between the finger-like wing struts cracked and fell away with a tinkle, allowing it to fold them down against its body. Ellasif couldn't stop herself from staring.

"My familiar," said Mareshka. "I called it out of the rime beyond the world. It's not a proper elemental, but it suits me better than a toad."

"Don't be so sure about that," Ellasif said, with as much acid as she could muster with her wet hair plastered to her neck. "Who are you, anyway? The queen of Irrisen?"

Mareshka's mouth opened in a half-smile, but her eyes darted left and right at the servants who stood to either side of her chair. A man fanned Mareshka while a woman stood beside a sweating ice pitcher containing a beverage the color of ripe strawberries. Both servants wore simple garments of white and pastel blue. When Mareshka was assured that neither of them had blinked at Ellasif's remark, she replied, "I take that as a compliment, but do not repeat such a thing, even in jest. Elvanna is our glorious queen, and I am but her loyal servant."

"So it is for Queen Elvanna that you kidnapped my sister?"

"Kidnapped?" Mareshka sounded genuinely insulted. "You should thank me, both for her sake and for your own. My minion pulled her from the river and breathed life back into her frozen body. For that he deserves your thanks. He would have taken his reward himself had I not intervened. It has been many months since he last tasted the flesh of a warrior of White Rook."

"Had you not interfered, I would have put an end to his ghoulish ways myself."

"Do not underestimate Szigo," said Mareshka. "He will not even lift a hand to defend himself in my presence, except by my command, but his powers are more than sufficient to prepare a little barbarian like you for the oven."

"Where is my sister?"

Mareshka sighed. "Before we continue this conversation, would you mind climbing out of the spring and donning some dry clothing?" She waggled a finger at the male servant. He set aside his fan and fetched a stack of thick cotton towels and a robe from a table with legs formed of three human thigh-bones bound in copper wire.

Scowling and feeling more ridiculous than intimidated, Ellasif clambered out of the pool. She let the servant stand there while she stripped away her sodden clothes. She was secretly pleased to see a tic develop under his eye as she got down to her bare skin and plucked a towel from his arms. A bead of sweat dribbled down his cheek by the time she snatched the robe away and wrapped it around her body.

"That is much better," said Mareshka. She nodded toward a chair the other servant had brought close to her own. "Now let us sit and enjoy a civilized discussion."

Ellasif sat, ignoring the cold sorbet the servant proffered. "Where is Liv?"

"She is nearby," said Mareshka. "I do not think she is quite ready to face the sister who allowed her own people to cast her into the river."

"I didn't allow it!"

"Yet you failed to prevent it," Mareshka continued. "Whereas I, within moments of her arrival in Szigo's grove, appeared to convey her out of that filthy den. Once she realized her new circumstances, Liv was overjoyed to find herself among people who appreciate her talents."

"Her curse," said Ellasif.

"Mm," said Mareshka. "That is how primitive people interpret those gifts they do not understand. What they do not understand, they fear. And what they fear, as you know, they seek to destroy."

"My people only defend ourselves against the monsters your people send to attack us."

"Come now," Mareshka said, "if your tribe would only submit to the rightful rule of Queen Elvanna, you could join us in civilized society."

Ellasif was no sage, but she knew Mareshka was twisting history to her own ends. A thousand years ago, maybe two thousand, the lands now known as Irrisen belonged to the Linnorm Kings. Then the ancient crone Baba Yaga appeared as if from nowhere. Some claimed she flew down from the moon in an enormous mortar, while others said she was from another world entirely, like the elves. Wherever she came from, she brought an army with her, a vast horde of fey creatures led by norns and cold riders commanding snow goblins and ice trolls. Within a month, the territories of the Linnorm Kings—the mightiest warriors of Avistan—were cut in half. Baba Yaga installed one of her daughters as the queen of her new nation and departed the world. Once every century since then, the undying witch returned from whence she had come to claim the monarch and take her away, installing a new queen in her place.

Ever since the witch's conquest, the lands of Irrisen had been locked in a perpetual winter. With no great harvests to feed its citizens, the nation's population had withered, clustering around its few cities, including the capital of Whitethrone. Somehow the country survived, its human population forever augmented by monsters. They had some trade to the south, and the queens of Irrisen had come to an uneasy truce with the Mammoth Lords to the east.

They had never made peace with the Linnorm Kings. Irrisen constantly sent raiding parties to harry the nearest communities of the west. Those warriors they captured became slaves to the ones called jadwiga, the nobles of Irrisen, all descended of witches. The children they stole met a darker fate, although no two elders agreed exactly what that was. Some believed the witches raised them as their own, teaching them the arcane arts. Others feared the newborn souls were captured to give life to the dreadful dancing huts that stood vigil along the Linnorm Kingdoms' border. For countless generations, White Rook had been one of many villages that repelled the attacks from Irrisen. Since Liv's birth, however, Ellasif knew they had been attacked far more than any other border village.

"What you call civilization—" began Ellasif.

"Yes, yes," said Mareshka. She tossed her drink carelessly toward the servant. The woman caught the glass, but the sorbet splashed upon her tunic, staining it red. Ignoring the mess she had made, Mareshka stood and beckoned to Ellasif. "Come with me. It is time you saw what civilization looks like."

Ellasif stood. The witch clutched her arm, and Ellasif stiffened at her touch. Mareshka lifted her staff in her other hand and raised it above her head, sending the weird ice creature the witch had called her familiar scrambling to a new perch on the back of the throne. The two women began to rise off the floor.

Ten feet above the pool, Ellasif saw that the level on which she had arrived was one of many beneath a vast dome of ice. Including a central pool exuding a constant cloud of steam, there were six tiers of pools and streams, many filled with nobles and attended by servants. From these pools, the water flowed out through walls of clear ice into what appeared to be fields in an enormous, all-encompassing greenhouse, nourishing wide plots of grain and vegetables, as well as flowering fruit trees and berry bushes.

"You are fortunate to see the inside of the Spring Palace," Mareshka noted. "Few but the nobility of Irrisen ever step into the Hidden Gardens, let alone the baths that form their steaming heart." Ellasif didn't bother dignifying this triviality with a reply.

They were still rising. Now the walls of the surrounding greenhouse structure were falling away, and they were left with nothing but an incredible dome of ice arcing up overhead. Through the transparent dome, Ellasif saw the blurred outlines of Whitethrone. She had never seen the capital of Irrisen before, but there was no other place it could be. Within a vast hexagonal enclosure stood hundreds, perhaps thousands, of buildings. There were buildings in all directions, their intricate designs lost in the refraction of the thick dome. Some were larger than fortresses, others barely larger than a house in White Rook, and between them the streets teemed with motion.

Most of the city was bone white, but here and there were spots of brilliant color, especially where the crowds moved. Ellasif saw domes and towers such as she had only heard described in bards' songs, and she could not even begin to imagine what sorts of people had built them, much less what they did in such a fabulous place.

"Look," said Mareshka, pointing to the south.

From a frozen harbor rose a colossal spire of ice. At the very top, hundreds of feet above, a glittering palace sparkled in the spring sunlight. Far below, the waters of the lake flowed, if only for a few hundred yards before the permanent winter froze them solid once more.

"This is civilization," said Mareshka. "Taming a savage land to serve its people rather than allowing a harsh climate to reduce them to frightened, dangerous animals."

Ellasif felt Mareshka was wrong, but the spectacle of Whitethrone had stolen her voice.

"This is home for those who would shape the world," said Mareshka. "I can teach Liv to use the spirit within her to work great spells. She will be my apprentice. This is where she belongs."

"No," said Ellasif. "She belongs with me."

Mareshka sighed and looked down. They floated sixty feet or more above the stone floor. Ellasif knew the witch could kill her simply by letting her fall. The faint smile upon the witch's face told her Mareshka knew what she was thinking.

"Kill me, and Liv will know," said Ellasif. "She will never forgive you for that."

Mareshka's smile widened. "I was right to deny Szigo his supper," she said. "You are bold and resourceful, and I admire you very much. It is a pity you do not share your sister's gift. Still, you could be of service to me."

"I will never be your slave," said Ellasif.

"That is not in question," said Mareshka. "But perhaps we could make a bargain. There are others with gifts even more promising than your sister's. Bring me one of them, and I shall let your sister go with you."

"Where could I find such a person?"

Mareshka nodded as if they had struck a bargain.

"I will show you."

It had seemed a simple bargain at the time—travel to Korvosa, locate a certain young wizard-turned-mapmaker who had recently come to Mareshka's attention, and then bring him back to Whitethrone to take Liv's place as Mareshka's new apprentice. But it appeared now that all Ellasif's efforts had only led her back into the clutches of the cannibal Szigo. When she heard the guttural voices of his trolls from outside the pine house, she knew she had little more time to live. Soon they would butcher her body and throw it piece by piece into their stewpot.

Or would they? She wondered why they had kept her captive so long. The way her stomach felt, she knew it had been at least a day since Szigo captured her during the attack on the caravan. If there were survivors . . .

She hated to think that way. She was not like Declan's fair maiden, waiting helplessly for someone else to come to her rescue. As for Jadrek and Olenka, she would almost rather end up in Szigo's belly than be indebted to either of them for help. She could expect no help, and in truth she wanted none. She would find a way out of this charnel house, even if she were entirely alone.

But she wasn't alone.

Less than ten feet away, Laughing Erik's sword winked at her, or so it seemed as the candlelight flickered across the gold dragon on its crosspiece. While there was no denying the man himself had earned his legend, Erik's sword was almost as much a hero as he. They said it sang to him in his sleep, and that he whispered his dreams of glory into the blade, that together they would turn them into reality upon a mound of enemy corpses. They said he could hurl the sword across a battlefield, and after it had cut the throats of his enemies it would fly back to his hand.

Come to me, thought Ellasif.

The sword remained in the firm grip of the wooden fingers that grew out of the pine trunks.

"Come to me," she said aloud. Still the blade did not move.

Ellasif sighed. Her fleeting hope now felt ridiculous. It was Erik's sword, not hers, after all. Perhaps the magic came from the man, not the blade. Even though he was her kinsman, there was no reason to believe the weapon would serve her the way it had its former master. Even if she could summon it to her hand, she could not use it to cut herself free from her tight bonds.

She wrestled against those bonds, but they only tightened their grip around her wrists and ankles as she squirmed. A shudder passed through her body as she considered whether the surrounding pine trunks were alive and aware of her. If so, then she was already inside a monster, and that was a bad omen for escaping the warlock's cooking pot.

The magic door opened wide, and Szigo stepped through, wiping his running nose on the back of his hand. His balding pate glistened with sweat, and Ellasif could smell his sour stink from across the room. Under his arm was an enormous, wart-covered toad, which he tossed casually to the floor, allowing it to make its own way to a nest of bone and hair on the warm stones near the fire pit. When the warlock saw Ellasif was awake, he grinned, showing off his pointed yellow teeth.

He hummed a childish tune as he went to the butcher's table, making a show of taking inventory of the ghastly objects there. He casually tossed the severed foot over his shoulder and pretended to study a wet lump of brown flesh in a clay bowl. Ellasif struggled to keep her face impassive, but she caught him peeking over his shoulder for a horrified reaction. He frowned, disappointed. He lifted a curved butcher's knife from the table and honed it with a rasp.

Despite his foolish theatrics and her memory of beating him to the ground a year earlier, Szigo's refusal to speak first began to unnerve Ellasif. Before fear could put a cold grip on her spine, she ventured, "Mareshka must be impatient for my arrival."

Szigo swiveled his head toward her, eyes bulging like a lizard's. He said, "She cared more for what you were sent to fetch for her."

"Then she will be angry with you for delaying my return."

"The one she sent you to recover was traveling to Whitethrone with or without you," said Szigo. "Once he arrives, Mareshka will have no further need of you."

"So you were driven off before you could capture Declan for yourself," she said.

Szigo smiled, and Ellasif realized she had said something he had hoped to hear. Perhaps he was more dangerous than she had credited him. Szigo had not known Declan's name until she said it.

And yet Szigo was privy to her agreement with Mareshka. The only reason she could imagine the jadwiga would share her scheme was if she had given Szigo some task to help further it. Probably he was watching for her arrival, or perhaps one or both of them had been observing her progress all the while. Ellasif had heard more than one tale of witches spying on their enemies through mirrors or pools of water. Yet if Szigo could do such a thing, no doubt Mareshka could do it for herself. Ellasif wondered what task the powerful jadwiga would give to a henchman she so clearly scorned. Furthermore, why would she not have told Szigo something as simple as Declan's name?

Ellasif realized the answer: Mareshka had not instructed the warlock to attack. Perhaps she had told him nothing of her bargain with Ellasif, but he had somehow gleaned the knowledge for himself through spying or his own witchcraft. Szigo was acting on his own, probably to avenge his rough treatment at Ellasif's hands during their first encounter. Yet he had not yet taken his revenge, which meant he was still uncertain whether he could do so with impunity.

"Mareshka did not send you to attack us," said Ellasif. "Probably she did not even order you to spy on us. Oh, imagine her displeasure."

The warlock's smile melted away. He stabbed the table with the butcher knife. He tried to tug it out again, but hadn't the strength.

"You haven't worked up the courage to report to her, have you?" she said. "What will you say when she learns I am no longer with the caravan?"

"You weren't there," he said, with the timidity of a child learning to frame a deception. "Perhaps you had already perished on the journey. Caravan guards often do not arrive at their destinations."

"Very clever," said Ellasif. "How did you know where we were? Probably some spell you learned from your mistress."

Szigo smiled as if she were praising his resourcefulness, but then her other meaning sank in. His mouth became a tiny O in the weak triangle of his jaw.

"That's right," said Ellasif. "If you were able to watch the progress of our caravan from this hut, would it not be child's play for her to watch yours from the comfort of Whitethrone?"

Szigo's parchment-colored flesh paled. "She would never spy on me," he said hopefully. He giggled, trying to laugh away the suggestion. Ellasif laughed with him, smothering his voice with her own. It was then she felt a tickle in the back of her throat and a warm tingling upon her palm. She heard a distant scrape of steel on leather, and she felt her eyes drawn toward the far wall.

There, the pommel of the sword shone far brighter than possible in mere candlelight. It had not heard her earlier call because she had not spoken the language of its former wielder.

Laughing Erik.

Ellasif threw back her head and roared her mockery into the warlock's face. Szigo paused, confused and increasingly angry. Behind him, Laughing Erik's sword shifted in its scabbard. Three inches of untarnished steel flickered and glowed in the candlelight. The blade was laughing, too.

Come to me, Ellasif thought as fiercely as she could. As if in response, the trolls outside began to hoot and howl. She shouted her feigned mirth, and her hand felt hot and cold.

On my way, said an unfamiliar voice in her mind. Oddly, it felt as though it came from above, not from the direction of the sword. Ellasif redoubled her laughter, both to distract Szigo from the commotion outside and to call to the sword.

Szigo grasped the handle of the butcher knife in both hands and lifted his feet off the floor, using his full weight to pry the blade from the block. No longer laughing, he turned and leered at Ellasif, raising his weapon. He lurched toward her.

A deafening explosion rocked the house of pines. A light brighter than dawn briefly illuminating the chimney hole above, dazzling Ellasif's eyes. She blinked up at the opening and momentarily thought she spied a winged shape descending from the sky.

Too many things were happening at once. In a second, Ellasif's feigned laughter became real. She laughed at the danger. She laughed at the insanity of her situation.

Erik's sword flew across the room. It struck the blade from Szigo's hand and sank into the wall by Ellasif's right hand, severing the bond that held her fast. She reached for the sword's grip, but after so long a confinement, her arm was weak and numb. She slapped it against the wall in a frantic effort to beat the sense back into her half-dead limb.

Szigo let out a little shriek and whirled around to face the interloper he imagined had thrown the sword. He jabbered a spell and stroked the air before him, his fingers leaving trails of purple flame in their wake. He hesitated, seeing no foe where he believed one must stand.

Tiny claws scrabbled over Ellasif's left wrist. There was Skywing, tearing away her other manacle.

Hurry, came the voice in her mind. She realized it was the little drake that spoke. *Declan is coming.*

The news brought a thrill to her heart. She was not alone, and Declan had not been slain. The instant Skywing freed her other hand, she reached forward and grasped Erik's sword. As her tingling hand closed around the grip, she felt the mad lust of battle fill her heart, and then the sword sang through her.

Two quick strokes freed her legs, and she stepped toward the warlock. Another explosion thundered in the grove outside, and Ellasif stumbled over her own sleeping legs to the dirt floor.

At the sound of the blast, the warlock cocked his head once more like a startled bird. "What's happening?" he shrieked.

"You brought this on yourself, you miserable worm," said a familiar voice.

Szigo and Ellasif both spun around. Behind them, Mareshka stood tall, her staff crackling with ice. The warlock threw himself prostrate in fear for his life.

"Mistress . . ." he uttered, but there was nothing else he could say. His guilt was plain.

"My plans do not include having the boy discover me here, like this," the white witch shouted at her cringing lackey, raising her horned staff above her head. "If I did not have more pressing matters to attend—" Her threat dissolved into a tumble of arcane words. Szigo screeched and clutched himself, shivering in agony. Mareshka cackled at the sight of her minion's writhing.

A tiny part of Ellasif was proud that Mareshka's timely appearance had proven her speculation so literally accurate. More of her was angry that the witch might deprive her of her vengeance.

"No, you don't," said Ellasif. She clambered to her feet, her limbs still wobbly from the constriction of her bonds. "He's mine."

With a crazed laugh, Ellasif stabbed Szigo. It was an awkward blow, piercing his back just above the buttocks. The warlock screamed, rolling onto his back. From its nest by the fireplace, Szigo's toad opened its mouth and gave vent to a matching, eerily human shriek. Ellasif turned and gave the creature a ferocious kick, sending it flying into the wall, where it hit the wood with a sick thump and lay still.

"Open up!" shouted Declan from outside the house. "Let us in, or we'll burn the place down."

"No," breathed Mareshka. "He must not see me like this."

"Hurry!" cried Ellasif. She swept Erik's blade down across Szigo's belly, then back the other way. His screams pierced her ears.

"Come," said Mareshka, grasping Ellasif by the shoulder. At the same moment, the white witch screamed, her hair suddenly filled with the wings and claws of a thrashing dragon. She slammed her staff on the ground.

Ellasif felt the familiar icy sheath surround her, but this time she also saw it cover both Mareshka and the tiny drake that vexed her. She felt the drowning sensation, the vertigo, and then the fall.

Chapter Fourteen
The Impossible Door

Szigo released his death rattle and lay motionless on the threshold. Outside in the Charnel Grove, embers dropped from the trees as fire climbed the oily boughs. The flames leaped from tree to tree, and soon a brilliant orange halo ringed the crown of the warlock's house.

Jadrek leaned into the candlelit interior for a look. An instant later he leaped out as a fiery branch crashed at his feet. "There's no one else in here," he said.

Skywing, thought Declan. *What do you see?*

There was no answer. Declan prayed that didn't mean the little drake had died after flying down through the chimney gap. He thought he would have heard some psychic cry if Skywing had been harmed, but instead the drake had simply vanished, perhaps to the same place where Ellasif had gone. With Jadrek's bulk blocking the entrance, he couldn't see for himself.

Perhaps that was best, he thought. A ridiculous scheme formed in his imagination.

"Jadrek," said Declan. "What else do you see in there?"

Flinching away from another falling ember, Jadrek squinted into the house. "There are a lot of candles, a fire pit. There's a table with—Great Gorum!" He kicked Szigo's motionless body. "What a monster!"

"Never mind that now," said Declan. "What else?"

"Look for yourself," offered Jadrek, stepping aside.

"No," said Declan. "It won't work if I see it first."

Jadrek opened his mouth but shut it again. He might lack Ellasif's cunning, but he was quick enough on the uptake.

"Bone fetishes, skulls hanging from ropes, armor and weapons along the walls," he said. "There's a trail of blood, and behind it . . . It looks like water on the floor."

"That's it," said Declan. He remembered the ice that had covered Majeed Nores in his steam bath, and the fragile shell that so resembled Silvana on the manor roof. "They've been transported to Whitethrone."

"How can you know that," said Olenka, "unless you are yourself a winter witch?" She had finished wrapping her wound and now held her sundered armor as if debating whether to replace or discard it.

"A wizard is *not* the same thing as a witch," Declan said. He ran to fetch his packs and brought them back to the grove. There was no surfeit of light there, but a growing firestorm swirled through the trees.

"We cannot stay here," said Jadrek.

"I know." Declan pulled out sheaves of parchment and dug through the pack until he came up with a stick of charcoal. "Now, fast as you can, describe the inside of that house again."

"But—" was all the protest Jadrek offered before giving in. "It is perhaps thirty paces long, the walls about three feet thick in most places. It is the same shape inside as out."

"Good, good," said Declan. "Faster. Tell me everything inside."

Jadrek repeated his earlier description, adding more detail like the round shield he had seen on the wall just inside the door, the skeleton grown half into the unruly roots of a pine on the far wall. Declan added each detail in a quick economy of strokes, adding a shadow here and there by smudging the pigment with his thumb. Olenka moved to watch over his shoulder. She leaned so close he could feel her hair upon his shoulder. He smelled the pungent odor he had begun to associate with the Ulfen warriors, but on her it was slightly different, less offensive—even oddly alluring. It reminded him of Ellasif.

He tried not to think about it.

"That is everything," Jadrek said at last.

Declan nodded, finishing the last touches of a drawing of the interior of a house into which he had never looked. If he had a moment more to admire his work, he would have been pleased with the result. Despite the appalling details of the chamber, it was a striking illustration.

"What is that?" asked Jadrek. He pointed at the icy portal Declan had drawn just beyond the fire pit. "I told you, there was only water on the floor."

"I know," said Declan. "This is the door through which they left."

"But there is no such door," said Jadrek. "Besides, look!"

Declan looked where Jadrek pointed. The top of Szigo's house blazed like the head of a torch. From inside, crashing boughs exploded on the floor, shattering glass and scattering the macabre contents of the room.

"Let's go," said Declan. He stuffed the map back into his pack and clutched it to his chest. He lowered his head and charged through the door.

Inside, he could barely see. The heat prickled his face, and smoke filled his lungs at his first breath. An enormous branch fell beside him, cinders flying in all directions. Hot pine needles stuck to his face, searing their outlines into his skin. He ran deeper into the room, ignoring the protests of the Ulfen warriors who followed him. In a moment he reached the fire pit.

A few steps beyond stood a gleaming oval of ice. It was already melting in the inferno. Declan saw an image of himself, Jadrek, and Olenka reflected in its surface. The surrounding flames cast him in silhouette, making him look like a lost soul trapped in the furnace of hell.

Sparing one last glance at his companions, he cried, "Follow me!"

Then he plunged into the icy portal.

The shock of glacial cold struck his heart a hammer blow. He shouted, but that only filled his mouth with water. He kicked and thrashed until his head breached the surface of a lake. All the golden light of the fiery grove had been replaced with a dim blue-white radiance. Most of it came from above, reflected off the glittering faces of a palace resting two hundred feet above on a white pillar of ice. Behind him, a sprawling, bone-white city glimmered in the moonlight.

Jadrek and Olenka emerged beside him, sputtering and cursing in their native tongue. "Hurry," said Olenka, kicking toward an icy shore some thirty yards away.

Declan tried to respond, but the cold sent tremors throughout his body. He felt the weight of his soaked packs pulling him down. He kicked, but he could no longer feel his legs. Just before he surrendered to the inevitable, Jadrek's massive arm reached around his neck and gripped him under the shoulder. The big warrior swam him to shore and lifted him onto the frozen bank.

Once on dry land—or frosty stone, Declan noted bitterly—Jadrek cursed while trying to throw a spark into the damp tinder from his pack, while Olenka held Declan close, shivering beside him as they shared their meager body warmth. She was not, after all, so much bigger than he, but her muscles were so thick and hard that he felt like a child cradled in her arms. It was not an altogether unpleasant feeling, but it made him uncomfortable. He felt as if he were breaking some sort of rule, betraying a promise he had never uttered. He could not say to whom he felt unfaithful, but he also could not escape the feeling. After a few moments he was warm enough to cast a spell.

Declan uttered one cantrip to dry the two volumes of his animated caricatures and then, with only the faintest regret, cast another to set them alight. The three companions crowded the tiny fire so close they touched shoulders as they knelt and leaned over the meager heat. As the flames died, they got to their feet and climbed a sharp, winding trail to the top of the cliff face that formed a natural barrier beside the river.

Declan looked back at the lake. The harbor was filled with islets joined by bridges and a white road leading across a tongue-like peninsula and then up a long, rising bridge to the palace atop the ice column. The lake's black surface rippled in the chill breeze for only a few thousand feet along the shore in an area surrounding the massive pillar. Declan looked away from that dazzling structure and let his eyes adjust to the night sky. Far above the white city he spied the Stair of Stars and followed the invisible lines of the constellation to Cynosure, the pole star. Doing so reminded him of his original purpose in traveling to Whitethrone: to find the astronomer Majeed Nores.

How often he had forgotten his master's plight in favor of vain dreams of rescuing Silvana and enjoying a hero's reward from the grateful kitchen maid! Yet until he fixed his bearings by gazing up at the night sky, his only thought had been to follow Ellasif through whatever magical portal the warlock had cast her.

And now that he saw Whitethrone with his own eyes, he wondered why Szigo had sent Ellasif there. Had she gone voluntarily, to find her sister? He doubted it, especially considering the state in which Ellasif had left the warlock. No matter what the reasons, somehow Declan felt that Whitethrone was calling to him and Ellasif both.

The rescue business was much more complicated than he had ever imagined.

Now that he had his bearings, Declan surveyed the city from where he now stood in the southwestern corner. It was all contained in a roughly hexagonal wall, broken only by a distant gate to the north, some rough gap in the west, and the open southern harbor on the lake. From the water's edge, the city sloped gradually upward to the north, flat except for a pair of hills in the northwest. Near the peak of the farther hill, Declan noted the distinctive dome of an observatory.

He pointed it out to the Ulfen. "That is where we must go."

"You think Ellasif is there?" said Jadrek.

"No," said Declan. "But I am fairly sure we did not arrive where she did. The portal I created was only a crude imitation of the arcane channel created by the spell that sent Ellasif here. Due to the melted ice you found at the warlock's home, I can only suppose she arrived somewhere in Whitethrone. I've seen this sort of ice-based teleportation twice in recent months, and when I consulted a colleague at the—"

Olenka cupped his mouth with her strong hand.

"Imagine that we are not witches," she said, "and that we do not understand such things."

Jadrek grunted his agreement. "Just lead us to Ellasif."

Declan nodded, and Olenka removed her hand. "I am not a witch, by the way," he said, holding up a reproachful finger. How much things had changed this summer, that he was now so eager to assert himself a wizard. "We go to that observatory," he said. "It's the most likely place to find my master, who was abducted from his home in Korvosa."

"Tell us more as we move," said Jadrek. "Something tells me we do not wish to linger on these streets at night."

Declan had to agree with that opinion. They were no longer dripping, but their wet clothing made them both susceptible to chill and more than a little suspicious. Even on the streets of Korvosa, their appearance would have provoked some hard questions from the local guards, as Declan knew all too well.

Declan began to explain the events that had instigated his long trek from Korvosa through the wilds of Varisia, and then north through the Lands of the Linnorm Kings. He had barely described his master and the fetching kitchen maid when they walked into the western quarter, where the many shops competed with each other in extravagant displays of layered woodwork. By the eldritch light of the street lamps, Declan saw more shades of white than he knew existed, and between them hues so subtle that they seemed the ghosts of once-living colors.

Soon they were no longer alone upon the streets. Streams of people flowed from an enormous stone edifice to the north, spreading out into the streets in all directions. Dozens of Whitethrone natives approached, most of them laughing or talking in voices that echoed down the streets. Most appeared quite human, although their hair and skin were fairer than Declan was used to seeing, often so blond or pale as to seem white at a distance. Some were as tall as Ulfen, though many of those who appeared to descend directly from that hearty northern stock behaved as servants and bodyguards, gazing at the ground or glowering into the shadows to dissuade any hopeful cutthroats.

The strange folks wore garments of thick linen and wool with capes of rabbit or seal pelts. A few fantastic collars rose high behind the heads of men and women with such delicate features and elegant jewelry that Declan assumed they were nobles. Their clothes were almost uniformly white, with a black muff, hat, or stole as a striking accessory.

The exception to the rule of fashion were a few groups of young men and women who laughed somewhat too loudly, walked with affected swaggers, or encouraged their fellows in choruses of the same songs again and again. They wore clothes of many colors, often garish or downright theatrical. Declan had seen more somber apparel on fools capering in holiday parades. He recognized several southern fashions: Varisian, Chelish, Taldan, and even some from distant Osirion and Katapesh. One young rake kept retrieving the enormous purple turban that fell from his head whenever he laughed at a joke.

"Jadwiga," Jadrek murmured.

"You can't mean everyone here is a witch," said Declan.

"Not all of them cast spells," said Olenka. "But all of them are witches, daughters and sons of Baba Yaga."

She spat after uttering the name, and Jadrek admonished her with a scowl. Declan was relieved to see that none of the jadwiga seemed to notice her gesture.

Declan kept to the side of the street, hoping to avoid awkward entanglements. Jadrek and Olenka followed in grim-faced imitation of the Ulfen bodyguards they had seen. Definitely quick-witted, Declan thought. He finally appreciated the southern penchant for Ulfen bodyguards. These northern warriors were far more than just physically formidable.

They passed the celebrants without incident, for which Declan was thankful. By the time the newcomers reached the huge theater from which the revelers had emerged, the crowd had already dissipated into the surrounding residential neighborhoods. As they traveled farther north, toward the twin hills, a different nocturnal congregation began to appear.

In twos and threes, sometimes accompanied by one of the strange pale humans the Ulfen called jadwiga—surely they could not all be witches, Declan thought, so the term must have more than one meaning—enormous wolves prowled the streets. Their eyes were blue flame, and Declan overheard two of them conversing in human voices as they padded across the street ahead of them.

"Winter wolves," said Jadrek.

"Dangerous, I presume," said Declan.

Jadrek and Olenka exchanged a glance that let Declan know he had no idea.

"One of them led the attack on White Rook the night Ellasif's sister was born," said Jadrek.

"Do not speak of that night." Olenka touched the hilt of her sword, drew the wings of Desna over her heart, and kissed her fingers.

"I want to know," said Declan.

"You have not finished your story," Olenka noted.

She had a point, so Declan continued to fill them in on his reasons for coming to Whitethrone. He emphasized his duty to his master, the astronomer, rather than his initial enthusiasm for rescuing Silvana and playing the hero. And he included the stories he'd heard from the Varisians of how the fierce little Ellasif had beaten the mighty Gisanto, even though he had not witnessed their bout.

They passed along a street full of windowed shops displaying a dizzying array of porcelain dolls. Declan thought that each was, for lack of a better term, perfect. Their faces, while not exactly lifelike, captured expressions one would associate with a little girl. This one was sweet, the one beside her petulant. Another knew a secret and was ready to tell it, while another had just drunk too much milk.

"Once we've found Majeed and Ellasif," he said, "I should buy one of those for my niece."

"No," said Jadrek, gripping him by the arm.

Declan stared up into the big man's face, surprised by his ferocious response. Jadrek's blue eyes were hard as stones, and Declan decided it was best not to demand an explanation.

"All right," he said, pulling his arm back.

But Jadrek did not let go. "The jadwiga make their dolls from the ground bones of captives," he said. "They attack our villages for plunder, but also they steal children, as they tried to kidnap Ellasif's sister."

"Tried? I thought they succeeded." Between Ellasif's grim look of determination whenever the girl was mentioned and her revelation that she, too, had someone to rescue in Whitethrone, Declan had managed to piece together that much of the shield maiden's story. Liv had clearly been stolen by the winter witches, and Ellasif was determined to get her back.

Jadrek refused to be distracted. "They tear out the souls of these children and place them within certain of these dolls. And then they place these dolls in the dancing huts that stand sentinel along our border."

"I understand," said Declan.

"You do not." Jadrek emphasized each syllable with a painful squeeze of Declan's bicep. "This is not a human city. This is a city of witches and monsters. Some of them may look like you, but they are not like you. Do not forget."

Declan looked to Olenka, hoping for a sympathetic face, but she returned only a solemn stare, nodding agreement with what Jadrek had said. "I won't forget," he said.

Jadrek released his arm. Then he punched him once, hard in the shoulder, to show they were still friends.

Declan knew that was going to leave a bruise.

When they spied the rent in the western wall and saw packs of winter wolves sitting vigil nearby, they turned east toward the center of the city to avoid the creatures. They could not escape all the monsters of Whitethrone, however. They passed a little group of snow goblins led by an ogre so foul that a cloud of stinging insects formed a black halo above its lumpy head. On one street corner, a pair of blue-skinned ice trolls took turns striking each other in the chest with fists the size of ale kegs. Only occasionally did the travelers spy a band of ordinary northern men, bulky Ulfen or flint-eyed Kellids. Always these moved furtively in groups of their own kind, or else were thralls marked by collars with runes indicating ownership, supervised by one of the pale jadwiga.

When they reached the central thoroughfare, Declan noticed the cobblestones were unusually large and uniform. After the third time he twisted his ankle on them, he knelt to examine them more closely.

They were human skulls, each filled with sand and mortared beside the tens of thousands of others that formed a road from the northern gate all the way down to the ice palace.

"The bones of our ancestors," said Olenka. "The countless dead who fell when Baba Yaga stole our land, and the countless more who died in the centuries since."

Realizing they stood on a path of skulls, Declan lost all interest in further stories. He wanted to get inside, preferably beside a fire with a cup of spiced wine and, if Desna smiled upon him, someone who had heard news of Majeed Nores. It seemed too good to be true, but the sight of an observatory gave him hope that the winter witches had abducted him for his knowledge. He only hoped the cantankerous astronomer did not treat his captors so disagreeably as he had his apprentice. If he did, Declan's chances of finding him alive were considerably slimmer than he'd hoped. On the other hand, if the man yet lived, his sour disposition might make his captors accept a more reasonable ransom, if only to escape his presence.

As they began to climb the winding path—formed, Declan was relieved to see, of ordinary stones—Declan realized that at this hour the best he could hope for was a servant or guard with whom to leave a message. As they approached the tin-shod door of the observatory, he prayed he would not have to return to the road of skulls to inquire about lodging. He tugged the bell pull and heard a chime inside the circular building. Unlike most of the nearby structures, its walls were constructed entirely of stone, with a domed roof of brass tarnished to a pale, streaked green. A wide slice of the roof was open to the sky, revealing the outer lens of an enormous telescope.

A hatchet-faced woman of Kellid origin opened the door and eyed them with curiosity.

"Good evening," said Declan. "I couldn't help but notice that this is an observatory."

The woman stared at him, and Declan realized she might not speak the common tongue. Not for the first time, he regretted skipping language lectures at the Theumanexus. "Maybe she speaks Skald," he suggested, tugging on Jadrek's arm.

"I understand your words," the woman said. "Why have you come?"

"I seek my master," he said. "An astronomer named Majeed Nores."

The woman frowned at the sound of the name.

"I know he was brought here, to Whitethrone, and I assumed—or rather, I'd hoped—that someone here might know what became of him."

With a suspicious glance toward the Ulfen, the woman opened the door and stepped back to admit them. They passed through two small antechambers, the second with open cloakrooms to either side, before entering the central chamber. Jadrek and Olenka gaped openly at the sight, and Declan felt his own jaw drop as he saw the great telescope.

The device was to Majeed's glorified spyglass what an ancient redwood was to a sapling. Mounted on a frame the size of a merchant caravel, the brass tube consisted of eight parts of diminishing diameters, the largest wider than the mouth of a well. Standing near the eyepiece at floor level, four elderly jadwiga listened intently to the lecture of a completely hairless man who peered through the eyepiece.

"Master Nores!" cried Declan. He ran a few steps before mastering his enthusiasm and walking the rest of the way toward the portly astronomer.

"At last," said Majeed. He dismissed his audience with an imperious gesture, and the jadwiga departed with a few scornful glances at Declan and his companions. "I had begun to think you were permanently lost, boy. And do not think for a moment that your months of absence do not count against your apprenticeship."

"Where's Silvana?"

"What?" said Majeed. "Who? You mean the kitchen maid?"

"She was transported the same night you were," said Declan.

"Ah," said Majeed. "That explains the confusion. Upon my arrival, I asked why my hosts had not brought along my assistant. The estimable Mareshka Zarumina explained that you would arrive eventually."

"Mareshka?" said Declan. He remembered Skywing saying that name back in Korvosa, but that was a question for later. "Never mind that for now. What happened with Silvana?"

"I really couldn't tell you," he said. "She wasn't much use here at the observatory. Perhaps someone took pity and brought her into some local household, but really, I doubt it. The locals aren't exactly welcoming of uninvited guests. Those without good reason to visit—or a heavy purse—usually end up in the Bone Mill."

"The what?" said Declan.

"The Bone Mill," Majeed repeated irritably. "It seems the bedtime stories we Korvosans tell about Irrisen are essentially true. Visitors who do not make themselves useful by bringing wealth or, in my case, a superior understanding of the astronomical arts, are eventually rendered useful in other ways."

"What are you talking about?"

"It's as they say about giants and witches who capture lost children," said Majeed. "They grind their bones to make their bread."

Chapter Fifteen
The Winter Witch

"Get away, you filthy little lizard!"

Mareshka flailed her hands in a vain effort to swat Skywing out of her hair. Her icy familiar chased the little drake, orbiting the witch's head like a frosty comet. The more she thrashed, the more Skywing clung, using her head as cover from the elemental and churning her white locks into a chaotic nest.

"Let go of him," said Ellasif. She reached for the drake. "You're only making it worse. You're scaring him."

At Ellasif's touch, Skywing leaped away and flew a circle around the room.

They had appeared not in the Spring Palace but in a room with tall windows of perpetual ice. Ellasif could see at a glance that they were high above the frozen river. They were somewhere inside the Royal Palace.

The ice creature continued to chase Skywing. He paused to hover above a basin in the center of the room, gathering a deep breath that puffed out his little belly in what might have been a comical sight under other circumstances. He blew a gust of frost at his foe. The icy particles sparkled in the air and left a swath of white against the wall, marred by a drake-shaped blur in the center.

Skywing flew on, his wings slapping the walls as he sought a way out. Half-whitened by the sprite's icy breath, he panted in terror. Ellasif had never seen him behave less than fearlessly, and the pathetic sound laid a cold hand upon her heart.

"Let him go!" she shouted.

"I'll have you ground to dust," Mareshka growled at the dragon as she raised her staff. The eyes of the bearded head of her staff glowed blue-white, and a nimbus of frost danced between the horns of its helm.

Ellasif knocked the staff aside just as a flash of ice shot forth. It missed Skywing by inches and shattered one of the ice panes.

Run, sent Skywing. *She will kill us both!*

"Wait," Ellasif said aloud. She was not accustomed to this mental communication. She changed her mind and thought, *Out the window!*

"Do not touch me again," Mareshka snapped at Ellasif. She turned back to find her target, but Skywing had already darted out the broken window and vanished into the night sky. The little elemental pursued him, but Ellasif did not think for an instant that the clumsy thing could catch a frightened house drake.

Ellasif couldn't bear to see Skywing harmed, but neither could she risk angering the woman who stood between her and Liv. She was relieved to see Mareshka finger-combing her hair back into place, breathing calmly as she regained her composure.

"I'm sorry. I don't know what made him behave that way," Ellasif said. "He must have been frightened by all the commotion at Szigo's grove." She surprised herself with the depth of her loyalty to Skywing, a creature she barely knew and over which she could claim no ownership. Perhaps she felt protective of him because he was Declan's familiar—or pet, or neighbor, or whatever he had called the little drake. That Ellasif should feel protective of Declan was still confusing. After all, in a few days she expected never to see him again, once she exchanged him for Liv. She had known that from the beginning, but now the thought made her feel queasy, and not only because of her guilt at the deception she had perpetrated.

"Perhaps," said Mareshka. "But there is no lasting harm done." She waved the head of her staff before the broken window. With an icy hiss, a film of water spread across the ragged gap. In an instant, veins of frost crossed the surface, and as they watched, the white lines faded to leave the window perfectly clear once more.

Ellasif glanced around the small room. A staircase occupied two segments of the hexagonal walls, a bone handrail following it down to the lower floors. Ellasif frowned as she noticed that the bones appeared to be both real and human. In the center of the room stood a pearlescent basin of clear water, from which emanated silvery light that shimmered on the walls and ceiling. The only other furnishings were three nearly identical chairs with cushions of red velvet. The center chair had a higher back than the others, lending it the appearance of a throne.

Ellasif saw that they were in one of many slender spires rising from the perimeter of the palace she had previously seen only from the shore of the city. Inside the central citadel dwelt Queen Elvanna, daughter of

Baba Yaga and a jadwiga of such power that Ellasif would count herself blessed if she never saw the woman, even from a safe distance.

"So I guessed right," said Ellasif. "You were spying on Szigo the whole time."

"Not the whole time, of course," said Mareshka. "I have many duties in service to Her Majesty. You were fortunate that I peered into my pool when I did. I knew Szigo was cross with you, but did not realize his anger was great enough to risk my displeasure."

"Thank you for your intervention," said Ellasif. She kept every trace of sarcasm out of her voice, for she knew that Mareshka's timing was far too good to be true, for a witch or anyone else. Doubtless she had known of Ellasif's capture for hours or perhaps even days, intervening only when necessary. She also remembered what the witch had cried out just before transporting them back to Whitethrone: *He must not see me like this.* She could only have meant Declan, but Ellasif did not understand what she meant by that. She had an inkling it had to do with the witch's ability to change form. After all, Ellasif had seen her arrive at Szigo's grove in the shape of a white raven. What other forms had she adopted?

Had Ellasif seen her before? The thought gave her a cold shiver. For an instant, she felt an impulse to drive Laughing Erik's sword through the witch's heart. The only way Ellasif could be truly safe from her magics was to kill her before she could cast an enchantment. That was the lesson she had learned from the elders of White Rook.

That was also the reason they had drowned her sister.

"Declan Avari is on his way to Whitethrone," Ellasif said. She swallowed to clear her throat, which had shrunk as she thought about the difference between killing Mareshka and killing Liv. "I have fulfilled my part of our bargain."

Mareshka smiled and traced a line in the water with her finger as she walked around the basin. "That is not entirely so," she said. "You agreed to bring him here, not to accompany him part of the way."

"I can go back and find him," said Ellasif.

"But as you say, he is already on his way here. Why do I need you to fetch him now?"

"He was fighting off trolls when I was attacked," said Ellasif. "Even after he leaves the Grungir, the sentinels along your border and the packs of winter wolves are bound to find him."

"And all have instructions to let him pass when they do." Mareshka waved a hand as if to dispel an unpleasant odor. "You are finished with that business."

Ellasif suppressed the urge to raise the sword she still clutched in her hand. Mareshka seemed far more dangerous than Szigo, and she doubted she could kill the witch before the woman could utter a spell or invoke the power of that staff of hers. Besides, killing her would eliminate the one person she knew who knew where to find Liv. She had to suffer the witch to live, at least a little longer.

"You bargain like a Chelish devil," Ellasif hissed. "I did what you asked, and it's no fault of mine that your servant attacked our caravan. For all I know, you ordered the attack yourself so you could renege on our deal."

"For all you know, I did," smiled Mareshka. "But in fact I did not."

"Then you never meant to honor your word," said Ellasif. "Among my people, we would nail the rune of falsehood upon your forehead."

"I find that easy to believe," said Mareshka. "Your people are savages, little better than the trolls, and no less odious."

"No matter what you think, they are still my people, and Liv's. We belong with them, not here among witches and monsters."

"Ah," said Mareshka. A sparkle of amusement glittered in her eyes. "Perhaps we should ask what Liv thinks of that?"

Mareshka led her down from the scrying pool through increasingly larger chambers in the tower. At the bottom, she nodded to a pair of footmen dressed head to toe in various shades of white except for their dark blue tabards that bore the image of a white raven.

The men escorted them over carpets of bearskin and through passages lined with many-layered panels of wood carvings. They passed halls in which young jadwiga listened to the lectures of their elders, who demonstrated spells cast before mirrors, over braziers, and beneath icicles dripping from the naked feet of hanged men. They marched through a parlor in which the chatting jadwiga all fell silent as Mareshka walked by. At last the servants opened a pair of white doors filled with gold filigree.

Inside they found a sumptuous parlor that eschewed the blanched colors dominant throughout the rest of the building. From the deep red carpet to the terraces of green foliage and bright flowers, the room was alive with color. All of the walls were lined with shelves on which stood silent ranks of books interspersed with crystal skulls, leather masks, wands, orbs, and countless other arcane implements. In the center was a ring of tables forming three quarters of a circle surrounded by chairs. Upon one of those chairs sat Ellasif's sister.

In the time they had been apart, Liv had transformed from a coltish girl to a young woman. She was still lithe, but the gentle swell of her breasts and hips had forever altered her profile, which was once slender as a willow switch. Her hair was more blonde than red, and the soft lines of her face far more feminine than Ellasif's, but no one who saw them together could mistake them for anything but sisters.

"Liv," cried Ellasif, running forward. She dropped Erik's sword onto the table and squeezed her sister half to death.

"I can't believe it's you," said Liv. "She said she would find you, but I thought you were gone forever."

Through her tears, Ellasif turned to see what Mareshka had to say for herself. Obviously she had not told Liv about her earlier visit. The witch merely smiled in a perfect imitation of maternal affection.

"I will leave you two girls to catch up," she said. She withdrew, and the footmen closed the door behind her.

Ellasif knew Mareshka's departure provided only an illusion of privacy, but she could think of no way to ensure they would not be overheard by a witch who could view and hear things happening hundreds of miles away.

"Are you all right?" asked Ellasif. "How are they treating you?"

"I'm fine," said Liv. "Better than fine, really. Don't you know where we are? We're in the Royal Palace! Have you ever seen such a fabulous place? Every day is like walking through a dream."

"I've seen it before," said Ellasif. "I came here a year ago, looking for you. Did you think I would let a day go by without trying to find you?"

The gleam of tears on Liv's eyelashes confirmed her suspicion that Mareshka had never told her of Ellasif's previous visit, nor of the bargain they had struck. Ellasif opened her mouth to explain what she had done, but stopped herself from speaking. How could she explain to Liv that she had come to trade another person for her?

It had seemed reasonable back when Mareshka first proposed it—a stranger's freedom for her sister's—and Ellasif would not hesitate to slay a hundred men to rescue her sister. During the journey from Korvosa, however, Declan had become more like a friend, no longer a hypothetical hostage to exchange. Ellasif was no longer certain she could go through with the deal, even if she could believe that Mareshka would honor it.

"We have to get out of here," said Ellasif quietly. She went to the entrance and peered through the crack between the doors. The footmen stood outside, guarding the way. It would be dangerous to try only to subdue them. Ellasif was confident she could slay at least one of them before the other could raise an alarm. The trick was to silence them quickly.

Ellasif retrieved Laughing Erik's sword. She would not be able to invoke its power to fly while remaining quiet, but all she needed was its keen edge. "I can kill one before he shouts an alarm," she said. "Can you distract the other? You call for them, and I'll wait behind the door there."

"Why?"

The question took Ellasif by surprise. "What do you think I've been trying to do for the past year? I've come to free you."

"You don't need to free me," said Liv. "I'm perfectly safe."

"But you don't belong here, Liv. It's not your home. It's nothing like White Rook."

"That's true," said Liv. "At White Rook, everyone wants me dead."

"No, they don't," said Liv. "They were just afraid you were a witch. We must show them they're wrong."

"They aren't wrong, Sif," she said. "I may not be jadwiga, but I am a witch."

Ellasif flinched at the affectionate shortening of her name. The last person who had called her that was Jadrek. "No," she said firmly. "You aren't."

"Not when I first arrived, perhaps," said Liv. "But I've learned so much since then. I can cast spells. Look."

She raised her hand, but Ellasif grasped it and pulled it down. "You don't have to cast spells," said Ellasif. "You can stop being a witch."

"It isn't a choice," said Liv. "It's what I am. You were the first to know, the night I was born. We didn't understand it before, but Mareshka has taught me so much since she brought me to Whitethrone. I was born to be a witch."

"That was the tiren'kii, not you," said Ellasif. "It's a curse, not who you are. We can find a way to remove it. I know a wizard—"

"No," said Liv. "The tiren'kii is a part of me. When I'm ready, I will call it out myself. It will be my familiar, just like Mareshka's ice sprite. You have to accept the truth, Sif. I'm a witch."

Ellasif scowled, aware that she was losing the argument but unable to think of another way to counter what her sister was saying. "At least don't call yourself that," she said. "Say you're a wizard or a sorcerer or something! It doesn't matter, as long as we get away from here. I've spent every day since you vanished trying to rescue you. I would have rescued you the day . . . the day of the river, if only I'd realized what they were going to do."

"I know," said Liv. "Red Ochme knew you'd give your life to protect me, so they waited until you were away. But you don't have to protect me anymore. I'm safe here. If I returned to White Rook, they would only try to finish the job."

"Don't say that."

"You know it's what they would do."

In all the time she had been searching for Liv, Ellasif hadn't truly faced the fact that she could never take the girl home. The death of Red Ochme changed nothing. Hers was not a lone voice calling for Liv's death. All of the villagers feared and hated witchcraft—as did Ellasif, if she was honest with herself. She made an exception for her sister because she loved her. None of the others at White Rook would ever do so.

"We can go south," said Ellasif. "We can live in Korvosa or Magnimar or any city you choose. They have summer there, all the seasons. You'll be free of this eternal winter."

"But this is where I'm free," said Liv. "Don't you understand? Just as Red Ochme chose you as her successor, Mareshka wants to teach me everything she knows. I can be like her, not just a weird village girl who frightens the neighbors because she knows someone is going to have twins. Here, the monsters don't come to capture me. They bow when I walk past. They treat me like a princess."

"That's good," said Ellasif, devising a new plan. "We can use that to get out of here. It's better if we don't have to fight everyone on the way out."

"You aren't listening to me," said Liv.

"That's because you aren't thinking clearly right now. I promise, once we get away from here, we'll talk about it more. For now, though, you need to trust me."

"Why can't you be the one to trust me?"

Ellasif felt her temper rising. "Because you're probably under some sort of enchantment," she said. "We can deal with that later, but right now, you need to let me rescue you."

"Is that so?" asked Liv, her own cheeks flushing to match Ellasif's. "I'm the one who wants to stay. Maybe you're the one who needs rescuing."

Olenka and Jadrek might think that was exactly what they were doing, but really they were only obeying the orders of the White Rook elders, who wanted to prevent Ellasif from returning with her sister. But then there was Declan. She knew as soon as she heard his voice in Szigo's grove that he had come to rescue her.

She was still not certain how she felt about that. Her first reaction was indignation. She was not Liv, a frail young woman who needed rescuing. And yet she felt a certain thrill that someone considered her worth saving for herself, not simply because the elders commanded it.

"Don't be insulting," said Ellasif, but she could not help wondering where Declan was now, and whether he truly was coming to save her.

Chapter Sixteen
The Bone Mill

Outside the walls of Whitethrone, the wind slipped a knife through the gap in Declan's sealskin cloak and slashed his shivering arms. He had borrowed the garment from one of the astronomer's "other" servants, too grateful to point out that he was not Majeed Nores' servant but his apprentice, a position for which he had paid handsomely and about which he was having the profoundest of second thoughts. How to deal with Majeed—who seemed perfectly content to have been abducted to Whitethrone and the most spectacular observatory he had ever seen—was a question Declan would answer after he had found Silvana.

Or her corpse.

He had to fight the urge not to seek out Ellasif first, but he had no idea where to begin looking for her. At least in the case of Silvana, the first place to look was not far from Majeed's new home. Declan tugged the cloak tight as he walked onto the windswept plaza. There he paused, seeing that Jadrek and Olenka lingered behind, hesitating at the edge of the compound. They had followed him here from the observatory, but one whiff of the place had them both shaking their heads, refusing to go further. Declan could hardly blame them. The atmosphere was foul, even in the brisk winter wind.

He shivered and went on alone, muttering curses about this land that never saw a spring, much less a summer or an autumn.

The open plaza lay just to the east of the great gate. It was paved in huge, irregular gray stones mortared in white, giving the ground the appearance of a shattered plate or a vast frozen cobweb. Across the fractured lines, workers swarmed between a variety of stations, each dedicated to a different function.

Some were scaffolds, built around huge cauldrons from which clouds of steam spilled over the sides and crept with menacing purpose across the ground. The pungent smell of vinegar brought tears to Declan's eyes, but the sweet stench of rotting flesh lying beneath it explained why this compound lay outside the city walls. Declan watched in revulsion as masked thralls drew chains on pulleys that raised boiled corpses from the soup. They dropped the gray bodies into carts, and ogres lugged them along to the next station.

There, human thralls with scarves tied firmly around their faces hooked the swollen cadavers with implements resembling fisherman's gaffs and pulled them onto long slabs. Already rent open by the rough treatment, the cadavers were then flensed to the bone, their overcooked flesh slopped into long, open, oval troughs at the base of each slanting slab. From there, the flesh and bones took separate paths.

Teams of goblins carried the troughs on their shoulders. Declan thought they resembled the pallbearers at a southern funeral, carrying the coffin to the gravesite. Unlike true mourners, however, the goblins jabbered and poked at each other, slopping organs and half-rendered fat from the trough to leave a horrid trail of offal in their wake. They arrived with what remained of their cargo at a bank of kilns where slaves in leather masks and aprons shoveled the gore into stone trays. These they shoved into the fire, while they pulled out other trays and shook the charred remains into baskets for more goblins to carry away to yet another station. On the other side of the ovens another team collected the fully rendered fat in large clay urns. A tall man moved among them, tallying their production and directing other workers in packing the urns onto carts, which they drove back into the city.

Declan followed the bones. These the goblins brought to a different set of kilns, where men arrayed them in a single layer on trays. Once the bones were baked dry, the men scraped off any remaining detritus and tied them into neat bundles. These the goblins took to their final destination: the mills.

The structures lay upwind of the more noisome stations, and Declan was not surprised that this was where he saw the most humans involved in the operation. Most were common laborers, likely slaves or peasants of this rough land, but a few held themselves with a bearing that suggested they might be of the nobility—though what would possess one of the witches or witch-kin to work here, Declan couldn't imagine. Perhaps there were multiple levels of aristocracy.

The buildings looked nothing like the sort of mill he remembered from Korvosa. Those back home were big, barn-like structures powered by waterwheels along the Jeggare River, some for grinding grain, others for sawing huge shipments of timber. Here, above conical buildings of bone-white stone and pine, the arctic winds howled through frames of sailcloth shaped like a gargantuan child's pinwheel. Beneath the incessant wail of the wind, Declan heard the mechanical clatter of gears and wheels inside. It was here that Majeed Nores told him he would find a record of Silvana's death, if she had come to the fate most common to unwelcome visitors in Whitethrone.

Declan walked among the mills, searching for someone who seemed to be in charge. A number of men carried shallow boxes in which they made notes after conferring with the workers. Those were likely the overseers, but there were so many of them that Declan suspected they themselves must report to a superior.

"Collection or appointment?" asked a man Declan had not noticed arrive beside him. His voice was muffled under his scarf, but he spoke in words Declan could understand.

"Sorry?" said Declan.

The stranger pulled the scarf down to his neck. "Are you here to collect a vial? Or are you arranging for one to be made?"

Declan realized he stood beside a mill through whose open doors he spied tables full of black felt shadow boxes. In each tiny nook rested a ceramic jar similar to the one his father wore around his neck. If these were the same as the one Nagashar Avari wore, then they surely contained the bones of the departed. Declan had found the practice distasteful when his father explained the nature of the memento, but to see them produced in such quantities was even more unsettling.

"Um, neither," said Declan. "Inquiry, I suppose." His mind was awhirl with possibilities. He had always known his mother was from the north, but his father had never offered specifics. Declan had assumed she was Shoanti, but his recent travels had opened his imagination to the possibility that she came from the Ulfen or Kellid people. Never had he imagined she could be one of the jadwiga.

"Yes?" asked the man. He had fair skin and high cheekbones, but he lacked the thick musculature of the stereotypical Ulfen. Here was a man bred to life in the city, not the wilds. Declan searched the man's face for some similarity to his own, but saw none. Perhaps if he could remember his mother's face better, but she had died when he was still just a boy.

"Silvana," said Declan.

The man threw an exasperated gaze to the sky and let loose a puff of frosty breath. "Of which family?"

"Oh," said Declan. "I don't know. It would have been in the past two months or so."

The man shook his head. "Silvana is a common enough name," he said. "Without the family name, it would be difficult."

"I see," said Declan. The man turned to go, but Declan said, "What about Avari? Pernilla Avari."

"Avari?" the man said. "I am certain there is no such family in Whitethrone."

"No, of course not," said Declan. "She took her husband's name."

"Oh," said the man. "In that case, let me consult the ledger. When would this have been?"

Declan did the arithmetic. "About fifteen years ago."

The overseer stared back at him, gaping.

Declan dug into his purse for a bribe, but the man frowned at him, as if insulted by the gesture. "I'm sorry," said Declan. "She was my mother."

The man considered that information. "And your name?"

"Declan Avari."

Again, the man hesitated, weighing choices in his mind. At last he said, "All right, come with me. This could take a little time, but we can at least step out of this wind."

Inside the building containing the little urns, the overseer showed Declan into a side chamber. There he fumbled with a lamp until Declan, impatient, reached over and lit it with a cantrip.

"Ah," said the man. "Thank you, sir. I'll be back as soon as I can." He made a little bow as he departed.

Declan noticed the change in the man's tone. Before, the overseer had been indulging him at best, but now Declan sensed he meant to please him. If Declan were half-jadwiga himself, and the natives of Whitethrone revered witches, then he could probably use that to his advantage. Perhaps he could persuade the man to make the effort to inquire into all Silvanas.

As he waited, Declan considered his next steps. If he should turn up no evidence that Silvana had been "rendered," as Majeed had so callously put it, he could be more or less assured that she had found employment as a servant. It could take days or weeks to find her, even if he were able to draw a decent likeness of her from memory—and his failure to conjure her face with the charcoal so far made that doubtful. It occurred to him then that he should do the same for Ellasif, and perhaps for her sister, whose image he had drawn from Ellasif's description.

He had had the foresight to bring along his satchel. It wasn't that he expected the servants to steal his spellbook, but he felt more comfortable having it near since he had been casting spells so much more often lately. Besides, after his magical drawing followed Ellasif's teleportation to Whitethrone, Jadrek had thought it best for Declan to have his drawing materials close at hand.

He removed a sheet of parchment and the last nub of his charcoal from the satchel and set to work. Within a few minutes he had a decent likeness of Ellasif on the page, but he continued to add detail, smudging lines and painting contours with his fingers. He lavished pigment on the tight braids of her hair, and he redrew her mouth twice, unsatisfied until he had captured the proud triumph he had seen when she drove off Jamang's imp.

The memory reminded him that he had not seen Skywing since the inferno at Szigo's grove. He had hoped the little drake had arrived in Whitethrone with him, but he had not heard so much as a psychic peep from him.

Skywing? he tried to call out with his mind. *Where are you?*

He received no reply, but as he finished the drawing of Ellasif and began one of Liv, he tried again. This time he thought he picked out a distant sound. It was not even a word, just a sensation of feeling lost and wishing to rejoin family.

Skywing?

Declan felt a pang of loneliness, and couldn't be sure whether it came from the dragon or himself. He did not miss his father, not exactly. He loved the man and their extended family of servants back at the inn, but he loved Isadora and Rose just as much, if not more. All the same, so long as he knew he could see them again one day, and help support his brother's family with a little money now and then, he was content not to see them soon. He felt a certain fondness for the friends he had made at the Theumanexus and the University, but his life would not be so very hard if he never saw them again.

But Ellasif was another matter. He wanted to see her again, and soon. He needed to be sure she was safe, and that he did all he could to reunite her with her sister, whom he knew Ellasif loved more than anything else in the world. If he could see them happily reunited, he would know he'd done a good thing.

Yet if he were very honest with himself, he hoped it would not end there. He would like Ellasif to remain a part of his life somehow, and that couldn't happen until he found her.

He finished the sketch of Liv and frowned at it. It was much harder to know how well he'd captured her image, since he was working from a memory of what he'd sketched from Ellasif's description. He decided the result looked like a younger, softer version of Ellasif, perhaps a little skinny but with a shy, girlish beauty. It might be enough to evoke memories of people in Whitethrone who had seen the girl in the past year or so. He wished he understood more about the situation that had brought her here. Ellasif had been stingy with details, and Jadrek and Olenka even more elliptical in their answers when he had asked them.

It must be one hell of a story, he decided.

Skywing? he tried again.

He heard a distant reply. *Stay there. Coming.*

Smiling, Declan stood and opened the door to peer into the mill. There was no sign of the man who had promised to help him. If this was going to take much longer, perhaps he would leave and return later. He decided to wait until Skywing arrived, then to fetch

Jadrek and Olenka and go off together to inquire about Ellasif and Liv.

In the meantime, he tried once more to sketch Silvana's face from memory. He traced the outlines, but then he realized he could not remember how she wore her hair. It was long and fair as spun flax, but had it fallen loose over her shoulders, or had she tied it in the back? He left that alone and tried to give the eyes some definition. That was even worse. Disgusted with the results, he scratched out the image to start again.

Here, sent Skywing.

Declan could feel the dragon was nearby. Shouldering his satchel and picking up his sketches, he left the waiting room and walked out of the mill. As his eyes adjusted to the daylight, a tall shadow loomed before him.

She was a woman of forty years, perhaps more. She was tall, but the shadow that had surprised him came from the head of a long staff carved to resemble the head of a bearded warrior, complete with a horned helm.

"Declan Avari," she said.

"Yes," he replied lamely.

Behind the woman, Skywing dove toward Declan. He veered away suddenly with a little screech.

Run, the drake sent.

"Why?" said Declan, repeating the question mentally as he tracked Skywing's path through the air.

The woman turned with a start, her gaze following Declan's. She hissed when she spied Skywing, her hand straying to her hair, as if checking to ensure he hadn't struck her with any droppings.

Silvana is gone, sent Skywing. *Run!*

Declan took a step back from the woman. "Who are you?"

"A friend," she replied. "My name is Mareshka Zarumina, and I have long looked forward to our meeting."

"Mareshka Zarumina." Declan recalled both Majeed's mention of the name and Skywing's earlier use of it in the altercation with the guards. "The wizard from Korvosa!"

The woman frowned, puzzled. "I have been to Korvosa, but my name is not known there. And I am no wizard but a witch."

Declan must have flinched at her last word, for she lifted a hand to wave away his fears.

"You are in no danger," she said. "Your well-being is paramount to me."

"Thank you," he said, fumbling to stuff the pages he had been drawing into his satchel so he could once more hold his cloak shut.

Mareshka noticed the drawings. "What are those?"

"Just sketches," he said. "Portraits of some friends I've been seeking. Well, two of them, anyway."

"May I?" she asked. Before he could answer, she plucked them from his hand. She nestled the staff in the crook of her elbow, and Declan realized she was completely unaffected by the bitter wind. He wished he knew a spell to protect himself from the cold. He knew such charms existed; he had simply never bothered to learn one.

"You say you are searching for these people?" Mareshka asked. She studied Ellasif's picture with a frown of concentration, then placed it on the bottom to look at the image of Liv.

"I'm looking for the first one," he said. "She arrived in the city only yesterday. She is searching for the second woman, her sister."

"You have met the sister?" said Mareshka. She raised one arched eyebrow in surprise.

"No," admitted Jadrek. "I drew that from Ellasif's description."

"Really?" said Mareshka. "You have a remarkable talent. The resemblance is striking."

"You know Liv," said Declan. His heart was pounding with sudden hope. "Do you know where to find her?"

"Indeed I do," said Mareshka, turning to the third drawing. Her expression fell as she saw the scribbled-out image of Silvana. "What is this?"

"It was a mistake," he said. "I was trying to draw a picture of my master's kitchen maid."

Mareshka managed to look down her nose at him, despite the fact that he was a few inches taller. "I see," she said icily.

"I can look for her later," he said. "I need to find Ellasif. Can you please tell me where to find her or her sister?'

Mareshka's good humor had evaporated, and looking past her Declan saw the reason why. A pair of blue-skinned trolls approached. Between the brutes shuffled Jadrek and Olenka, their wrists and ankles bound by manacles and chains of ice.

"I can do better than that, Declan," said Mareshka. "I can take you to them both."

Chapter Seventeen
The Crooked House

Mareshka did not return to them that night, but a captain with astonishingly blue eyes arrived with a contingent of six guards to escort the sisters out of the palace. When Liv demanded to know where they were going, the jadwiga politely explained that he had orders to convey them to comfortable lodgings in the city, where they would meet tomorrow with Mareshka Zarumina. He requested with equal politeness that Ellasif surrender her sword. She did not bother weighing her chances of winning past seven armed guards in the Royal Palace of Whitethrone. After their long conversation, she knew she could not count on Liv to aid in an escape. She only hoped the captain would remain nearby, so she would have a chance to reclaim Erik's flying blade.

Outside, Ellasif saw the courtyard of the fabulous ice palace. Its gleaming walls contained a galaxy of colorful lights, most of them dancing upon the curtain wall but others carried on batons like torches by servants of the jadwiga. The captain ushered them into a carriage drawn by four dappled gray draft horses, their shaggy fetlocks concealing their hooves. His men perched on the footman's steps while he escorted the vehicle out of the courtyard and onto the long bridge that sloped gently down from the palace into the city of Whitethrone.

Ellasif found herself gaping through the carriage window. The sight of the lighted city from above captured her breath. At such a distance, even the most monstrous denizens appeared as tiny planets moving among a thousand stars. She wondered what Declan would make of the sight, the reverse of his frequent stargazing.

For Ellasif's benefit, Liv named the landmarks as the carriage wheels clattered over the skulls of the Bone Road: the Floes, the four islets between the city and the palace; the Spring Palace, which Ellasif had first seen from the inside; and the market square with its surprising array of colors. Wherever they encountered foot traffic, it parted for them. Ulfen thralls and goblins knelt as they passed, and even some descendants of Baba Yaga doffed their caps and bowed toward the carriage. Ellasif saw Liv smile as she rotated her wrist in a tiny wave to some of the more elegantly attired residents.

They crossed the city core and entered the Twohill district, where the carriage climbed the winding path to the top of the first, lesser hill. Upon its crown stood the largest wooden building in all of Whitethrone, the Crooked House.

It was, Liv told Ellasif, home to the greatest woodworkers of Irrisen. While other lands might view their carpenters as mere laborers, no nonmagical craft was held in higher regard in the land of perpetual winter.

In Irrisen, no felled trees could be replaced without significant effort, so the witches had to import most of their lumber. Once the commodity became precious, however, the demand grew even higher and more particular. Thus, in Whitethrone—with the notable exception of the palace itself—there was no greater sign of wealth than a house constructed entirely of wood.

The Crooked House appeared to have run amok and consumed a hundred lesser houses, adding them to itself as it sprawled over the hilltop and spilled down onto the slopes with extensions and annexes, all in different architectural styles. The one element common to every wing and nook, however, was the style known as gingerbreading. The multi-layered carvings that decorated so many of the city's homes were a point of pride among city residences, and only the poorest shared the same design with others. Most of these were first created by the master carvers of the Crooked House.

"Why is she sending us here?" asked Ellasif.

"Mareshka is a close friend of the mistress of the Crooked House," said Liv. She explained that she had visited the place many times, but she too was surprised they had come here. Mistress Tatyana Rekyanova had left Whitethrone weeks earlier on a journey to Magnimar, in Varisia. The master woodworker often went on such trips so that she could personally select the finest lumber to bring back to Whitethrone.

When the carriage arrived, the woodcrafters of the house welcomed the captain as if expecting their arrival. The guards led Ellasif and Liv inside and through a bewildering maze of halls and corridors until they reached a sumptuous bedroom deep within the house.

"Perhaps she thinks we'd never find our way out of such a labyrinth," Ellasif mused. Liv stuck out her tongue, and the expression reminded Ellasif how much her sister was still a child. Until the treacherous day at White Rook, she had lived a sheltered life, without benefit of the discipline Ellasif had gained from her warrior's training.

At last they were left alone with a pair of guards standing outside their door. Ellasif noted there were no windows, and one glance up the chimney flue was enough to realize they could never squeeze through that narrow aperture.

Not that Liv had any intention of leaving Whitethrone, at least not yet. Ellasif assumed she had until morning to persuade Liv on that count, but first she endured her younger sister's tour of the clothes that had been left for them. The nightgowns looked comfortable enough for sleeping, but Ellasif had no interest in trying on the white and pastel dresses she had seen on the women of Whitethrone's streets. Liv might feel like a princess here, but Ellasif would rather walk about in sackcloth than look like one of these witches.

At least she relished the hot bath the servants had prepared. She sank down to her chin in the steaming water while Liv sat nearby and told tales of her arcane studies, the queer customs of the jadwiga, and comic anecdotes about servile goblins and ogres. Ellasif could hardly believe her ears. These were monsters, the same savage beasts that had harried White Rook all of her life, foes she had trained to kill before they could reach the mothers and children. She hid her disgust, but could not stand to listen to such foolish prattle. She nodded occasionally, pretending to listen to the rest of Liv's stories as she concentrated on a course of action.

When the time came, she would drag Liv out of this wretched place whether or not she had come to her senses. They would set a course straight for the Grungir Forest, and if Lady Luck had ever heard their names, they would spy Declan coming from the opposite direction. It would take days, at least, before he could reach Whitethrone from Szigo's grove, but there was no point in waiting for him to arrive. Ellasif did not wish to spend an hour more than necessary here.

The warm water soothed Ellasif's sore muscles, and her eyes drooped shut. She woke to the sound of Liv's laugh. "Sif! Wake up before you turn into a dried prune!"

The hot water had leached away the last of her strength, what little had survived her captivity in the cannibal's house. She stepped unsteadily out of the bath and let Liv dry her with towels so soft and warm that they could have been the first breath of summer. By the time she donned a nightgown and lay her head on the pillow beside Liv's face, she was fast asleep.

Ellasif awoke to the feeling that an intruder approached. She leaped out of bed so suddenly that she nearly caused one of the two chambermaids who had arrived with fresh linens to die of fright. Even after the shock subsided and she realized she had slept for hours past dawn, Ellasif fought fiercely to retain her clothes, which she suspected the fastidious maids intended to burn. Her one concession was to accept a thick woolen cloak of deep crimson. It was warm, and at least it wasn't white.

Liv and Ellasif dined on pickled herring and biscuits. The bread was so dense that after a single bite, Ellasif set hers aside, trying not to think of the stories of witches grinding bones to make their meal. Even the damned food in Irrisen was white, she thought. Her feet itched to run away from this ghastly place. She let

Liv finish her food before broaching the subject of their escape.

Before Ellasif could say a word, the door opened and the guard captain informed them that they had been summoned. Fearing that she had missed her best chance for escape, Ellasif followed the man down another serpentine confusion of corridors and up three flights to what appeared to be the top floor of the house. She eyed Erik's sword, which hung at his hip in a new sheath beside his own sword. She wondered whether he carried it as a trophy of her capture or for some other purpose. Perhaps he meant to turn it over to Mareshka.

They entered one of two doors near the end of a long, oval hall flooded with light spilling in from spacious windows and skylights. To one side was a grand double door, and across the hall another pair of doors similar to the ones through which they had entered. Before them lay a white bearskin rug, the huge head of the beast pointed toward the windows; its twin sprawled on the floor on the other side of the room. Between the rugs, a dark rectangle on the wooden floor showed where a table usually stood, the ghost of the shadow that preserved it from the bleaching sun.

Between the windows hung framed landscapes of meadows overflowing with wildflowers, waterfalls that spilled into deep green pools surrounded by sun-dappled ferns, and deep forests in which bright fungus ringed the trunks of mossy trees. The illustrations were not painted but composed of many fragments of paper, hand-torn and pasted to a framed board. Much of the paper was coarse, with prominent threads of striking color running through the pulp, but somehow the artist had selected the conjoining pieces so carefully that they formed the effect of a unified shade even though each piece separately looked a different color. Other scraps were dyed in bright colors, apparently undiminished by the ample sunlight in the room. The lands depicted in the papercraft were of no place near Whitethrone, and each conveyed a feeling of longing for an as-yet undiscovered place. A fairy grove. A promised land.

The captain offered Liv the comfort of a plush divan, one of many throughout the room, all situated to offer the best view of the mounted artwork. He directed Ellasif to stand at her sister's side nearest the door. Suspicious, Ellasif walked around to the other side of the divan, but the captain seemed satisfied.

"Wait here," he said. "Do not approach those who enter from the other doors, and do not speak until you have been addressed."

"You mean now?" said Ellasif.

"What?" The man looked more perplexed than cross.

"You just addressed me, so shall I speak?"

Liv giggled, and for a moment Ellasif felt as she had in the years before they had both left White Rook. Then Liv had been as much a daughter as a sister to her, and nothing delighted Ellasif so much as the sight of Liv's smile or the sound of her laughter. Liv would be angry once Ellasif took her away from this illusion of happiness. Yet in time, Ellasif knew Liv would forgive her, knowing she had done what was best.

The captain did not waste his breath on a reply. He only frowned at Ellasif before walking across the room and opening one of the far doors.

In walked a tall blonde girl just a few years older than Liv. It took Ellasif a moment to recognize her as a servant from the house of Declan's master in Korvosa. It took a few seconds longer to recall her name, which she had learned only after Declan had mentioned it. It was Silvana.

"What are you doing here?" asked Liv. Ellasif was surprised that Liv recognized the servant, and more surprised still that Silvana answered by raising a finger to her lips. She smiled at Liv as if enjoying a secret that would soon be revealed, but when her gaze passed over Ellasif, the smile vanished. At a sound from the double doors, she put her smile back in place and smoothed her pale green skirt.

"Ready, Mistress?" asked the captain. He moved to the center of the room.

Silvana nodded.

"Now," said the captain.

The doors opened, and two footmen stepped in and moved to either side. Behind them, a pair of guards moved in and did the same. Behind them came Declan Avari. He blinked in the sunlight, and then he caught sight of one of the papercraft landscapes. He stared at them, mouth open and eyes moving from one to the next until his gaze fell upon Ellasif. A broad smile creased his face. He took a step toward her, and she saw her name upon his lips.

Ellasif could hardly believe her eyes. She had thought to find him on the western plains, assuming he continued his journey to Whitethrone. She wondered how he could have arrived so soon, but the explanation seemed less important to her than the proof that he had reached Whitethrone alive and well.

"Declan," said Silvana before he could speak. He turned, his expression caught between joy and wonderment.

Ellasif scowled when she saw who followed Declan into the room. There were Jadrek and Olenka, the last two people she wished to see again. Her feelings at the sight of them were complicated by the thick manacles of ice that bound their wrists and ankles, and the double rank of guards who stood behind them, swords drawn and pointed at their backs.

After a moment's hesitation, Declan ran forward and grabbed Ellasif by the arms. "Thank Desna and all your northern gods you're all right," he said. "By the time we got inside the house—"

"Declan," Silvana repeated.

Declan beckoned the girl to join him, still talking and holding Ellasif's arms, his smile beaming into her face.

Silvana's voice was insistent, but Ellasif was not interested in her. She looked over Declan's shoulder to see Jadrek gazing back, his expression a mixture of guilt and some sort of expectation. What was it? Hope that she would forgive his treachery? If that's what it was, Ellasif thought, he would be waiting a long time for it. Declan kept talking, and Silvana said his name again, this time in the petulant whine of a spoiled girl. All their chatter was becoming annoying, and all Ellasif wanted to do was—

Without thinking, Ellasif grabbed Declan's hair and pulled his lips to hers. He released her arms and drew her into a full embrace, kissing her back with such unexpected passion that she closed her eyes, releasing Jadrek from the death stare she had cast toward his heart.

Their lips parted for a moment. *That should do the trick*, she thought, but it was hard to think of Jadrek with Declan's mouth so close to hers. Then he was kissing her again, and with each second it became more and more difficult to think of spiting Jadrek, or of anything else at all. The clamor of voices in the room faded away, and she and Declan lost themselves to the kiss.

Someone tugged at her arm and kept tugging, and at last Ellasif turned to face the interruption.

"Sif!" said Liv admiringly as she looked up at Ellasif. Then she stole a glance toward Jadrek and exclaimed reproachfully, "Ellasif!"

The room exploded with voices.

"I never should have pulled him from the lake—"

"How could you come all this way only to kiss that—"

"Mistress, how should I—?"

"I told you we should have gone straight back home after the warlock—"

"I'm her sister, you must be Declan—"

"Silence!" The command came from Silvana, but it was no longer the voice of the young girl. Everyone turned to watch as her youthful guise melted away to reveal Mareshka Zarumina, clutching her tall staff in a white-knuckled grip. Her hand shook, and as the staff trembled, thick bony horns grew up out of her scalp to form the rugged peaks of a crown through her silver hair. "I will not be mocked!"

"Who are you?" said Declan. "Are you Silvana? Or are you someone pretending to be Silvana?"

"Yes," said Liv, shaking her head at Mareshka. "It's her favorite guise for when we tease the young men at the Spring Garden."

"You two-tongued cheat," said Ellasif to Mareshka. "You went to Korvosa after sending me to fetch him. You never intended to honor the trade."

"Trade?" Declan asked, puzzled. Then his face reddened with sudden understanding. "A trade! You were going to trade me for your sister! I should have realized! It was all too good to be true."

"Why are you here?" Liv asked Jadrek, ignoring Declan. "Did you come to help Ellasif?"

"Yes," said Jadrek. Olenka struck him with her elbow. "Well, no," he said. "Not exactly. I came to explain—"

The guards prodded them forward with the tips of their swords, herding everyone but their mistress onto the same side of the room. Flanking their captain, they formed a line between Mareshka and her guests, willing and otherwise.

"Jadrek was the one who lured me away from protecting you," spat Ellasif, stepping in front of Liv as if to protect her from him as he approached.

Liv stared at Jadrek in disbelief. "I can't believe Jadrek would ever do anything to harm—"

"Liv is right," said Olenka. "Only three people were unaware of what would happen that day: you, Liv, and Jadrek."

"That's impossible," said Ellasif. But even as she said it, she knew it had been completely possible. All that was required was that she be so angry that she didn't care to go back and demand an explanation. All that was required was that she be a fool.

"It was my fault," said Olenka. "I'm the one who told Red Ochme about the tiren'kii. She asked me to tell her when you and Jadrek would be away."

"Why?" said Ellasif. "Because you wanted Jadrek for yourself?"

"No," said Olenka. "Well, yes, I did. But that's not why I told her."

"None of these trifling personal dramas interest me in the least," said Mareshka. She straightened her back and seemed to grow three inches taller. "What is important is that Declan left his home and traveled all this way to be with me."

"To rescue Silvana," said Declan. He shot Ellasif a sideways glance and clipped his words, as if afraid more might spill out unbidden. "And Majeed, of course. But there is no Silvana, is there?"

"Of course there is," said Mareshka. "And I am she. Such is the power of my magic that I can appear in any form I choose." Her voice lowered, became sultry. "Or that *you* choose."

"But this is your real form, isn't it?" said Ellasif, waving vaguely at Mareshka's head. She wanted to stand up for Declan somehow, to win back the trust she had lost. But to be honest with herself, she had to admit she also wanted to spite the witch who had kidnapped her sister. "With the . . . ah, the horns."

Mareshka started. She reached up to feel the horns that had emerged from her head. She squinted in concentration, and the horns subsided into her hair. Her voice seethed with disdain as she said, "That is merely an effect of this staff." She looked directly at Declan. "Your mother's staff."

"What?" Declan's face blanched. "You can't mean that you're my . . . my . . ."

"No!" shrieked Mareshka. "Imbecile! Your mother was my teacher. She bestowed her staff on me when she chose to leave Irrisen. I never saw her again, until your father returned with her bones."

"You see, Liv," said Ellasif. "There's at least one witch who was wise enough to leave this forsaken place."

"I don't care," said Liv, crossing her arms.

"Why have you gone to so much trouble to bring me here?" Declan asked Mareshka. He seemed only then to notice how close he was still standing to Ellasif. He spared her only half a glance as he stepped away, as if avoiding an unpleasant smell. Even in the heat of all the accusations and recrimination, Ellasif felt her heart sink at his reaction. It was all the worse because she knew that she deserved his scorn as much as Jadrek deserved hers.

Or perhaps Jadrek deserved better, if Olenka had told the truth.

"Your mother had a rare knack for both art and magic," Mareshka replied to Declan. "You appear not only to have inherited her talent, but to have gained something else, some ability that's like no magic I've seen. Ever since my spell captured your master instead of you back in Korvosa, I have watched your progress through my scrying pool, and seen you do things not even your mother could match. Under my tutelage, your abilities could transform the face of Irrisen—and maybe more. Imagine redrawing a raging battlefield so that only one army remained."

"Could you really do that?" asked Liv. Her voice was tinged with resentment. Ellasif hoped that meant she was jealous of Mareshka's attentions to Declan. If so, that feeling could drive a wedge between Liv and this witch.

"I'm a map—" Declan began, but then he thought better of it. "I'm wizard, not a witch. Thanks all the same, madam."

"Madam!" cried Mareshka. "How old do you think I am?" Liv began to answer, but Mareshka shouted, "Quiet!" Her lips quivered with fury. She raised her staff, its eyes glowing frost white.

Liv blurted out a warning.

Ellasif took one look at vain, humiliated Mareshka and laughed in the witch's face.

Erik's sword leaped from the captain's hip, scabbard and all, and flew into Ellasif's hand. She charged forward, drawing the blade. She made it almost to the line of guards before a wall of ice hissed and crackled into existence before her, sealing the room from wall to wall and ceiling to floor. Ellasif put out a hand to keep herself from crashing face-first into the barrier.

"I can endure no more of this, Captain," said Mareshka. Her words were muffled through the wall of ice. "Have your men secure the doors behind them."

"It is done. But madam, the sword—"

"The next person who refers to me by that honorific will spend the duration of Queen Elvanna's reign frozen in a block of ice in the Floes. Do I make myself understood?"

"Yes, mistress!" the men said in unison.

"What about them?" asked the captain.

"They can cool off here while I consider how best to dispense with these ungrateful . . . foolish . . . *reeking* barbarians." She stalked out of the room, trailing guards. The captain paused for one last resentful look at Ellasif and then slammed the double doors shut.

Ellasif stared after them until the frost from her panting breath obscured the image on the ice. She turned to face the others.

"This will make it more difficult to rescue Liv," she said.

"I don't want to be rescued," Liv protested.

"We came here to rescue you," Jadrek said to Ellasif.

"Well you can take that thought and . . ." Ellasif let the insult drift off. Could she really have hated Jadrek all this time because of a mistaken assumption? "I can take care of myself. I certainly don't need you to rescue me."

Olenka shook the icy chains that bound her hand and foot. "Is there no one here who wants to be rescued?" she demanded.

Declan raised a tentative hand. "I do."

Chapter Eighteen
The Wolf Gate

Declan concentrated on controlling his breathing while the others dealt with removing the ice bonds from Olenka and Jadrek. They fussed over who would wield Ellasif's enchanted sword, which, even in his distracted state, Declan recognized was not the same blade he'd seen her with earlier.

When at last Jadrek gave up his demand that Ellasif let him use the sword, he knelt beside one of the divans and laid the chain over the seat. Ellasif severed it with one sharp blow, but the squeal of steel on the magical ice was worse than the sound of chalk squeaking on a slate board. Declan moved away from them, holding his head as he tried to focus his thoughts. The past hour had brought so many revelations that he felt like an overstuffed rag doll, his head swollen near to bursting. He was angry, exhilarated, confused, and most of all frightened.

He was not frightened for himself alone. He had a feeling that he and Liv were in less danger from Mareshka's wrath, but the others were in serious trouble. The witch seemed particularly displeased with Ellasif, especially after that impulsive kiss. Mareshka had no right to be jealous. Discovering she was a much older woman—well, that was awkward, but the revelation that she'd known his mother made it that much more uncomfortable. It felt like some long-lost aunt had been trying to seduce him. What continued to puzzle him was that she seemed powerful enough in magic that she could have simply transported him to Whitethrone from the start. If that were the case, he didn't understand why she had instead allowed him to travel all that way on horse and foot. Was it some sick need for validation, for proof of his devotion to her—or rather to her illusory persona of Silvana? Whatever her reasons, from the moment Silvana appeared to him as an ordinary girl, flirting with him, she had misled and manipulated him. How could she possibly expect he would want to remain with her in Whitethrone after that?

Much worse was the realization that Ellasif had manipulated him in much the same way. He had long wondered why she had cleared his path to Irrisen, arranging for Basha to offer him a job that would take him exactly where he wanted to go—or rather, where both Mareshka and Ellasif had made him think he wanted to go. On the other hand, if what he believed about Jamang and his wretched little imp was true, Ellasif had probably also saved his life from the very start. Still, Declan understood that he was no use to her dead, since she needed to trade him for her sister's freedom, so that was also in her self-interest.

Declan breathed on the wall of ice and drew a rough outline of the lands he had traveled since leaving Korvosa. Then he marked his starting point and traced the route of his journey west, then north, and finally east into Irrisen. His initial suspicions about Ellasif had faded gradually as they traversed Varisia, and he had to wonder now whether that was because he was just that stupid. Like Silvana—he could not think of the lithe young blonde as Mareshka—hadn't Ellasif also seduced him in her way? The shield maiden wasn't even pretty, not in the way that so drew his eyes to girls like Silvana. Even Liv was prettier than her sister, if a little young for him.

When he considered the question, Declan realized that he did not regret kissing Ellasif, despite the trouble it had caused with Mareshka and the revelation of Ellasif's own duplicity that followed. He glanced back at her, thinking of the taste of her mouth and the warmth of her cheek. He looked away as soon as she looked back and caught him staring.

Declan felt that Jadrek was boring a hole through him with his own stare. The big man wasn't glowering, exactly, but he looked much less friendly than he had before. Declan had overheard enough of his reaction to Declan's kissing Ellasif during the earlier confusion that he realized Jadrek had—or thought he had—some prior claim on Ellasif's affections. In the short time they'd known each other, Declan had begun to like Jadrek. The big man had also saved his life, and Declan had no reason to believe he'd been deceiving him. If anything, Jadrek seemed more stunned by the recent revelations than Declan himself. If they had been friends in Korvosa who spotted the same lass in a tavern, Declan would gladly have stepped aside.

"Hello," said Liv. She appeared as if by magic at his elbow, but Declan realized he'd been lost in his own little world. A bear could have walked up without his knowing.

Declan greeted her with a weak smile.

"I can see why Mareshka was so taken with you," she said.

"What?"

"These past months, she's been mooning over her scrying pool, but whenever I asked her who she was watching, she dispelled the image. She said only that whoever it was was coming to rescue her as proof of his love, and that she had a surprise for him when he arrived."

"It was definitely a surprise." He swallowed uncomfortably, and might have said more, had not an excruciating squeal drawn everyone's attention to the ice wall.

Ellasif chipped at the barrier with her magic sword, and each blow caused another awful screech. Everyone shouted at her to stop, lest she disintegrate their teeth. Jadrek and Olenka had already thrown their considerable bulk against the doors, but they were locked tight, and the threatening manner of the guards earlier reminded them that they would only face a fight on the other side.

"Try the windows," suggested Declan.

"That won't work," said Liv.

Ignoring her sister, Ellasif struck one of the clear panes. It shattered just like ordinary ice, despite its uncanny clarity. She shot out a hip and said in a tone of triumph, "See?"

Liv crossed her arms across her chest and nodded at the window. As they all looked, a film of water ran down from the top edge, freezing immediately in place. "Just be glad you didn't try to crawl out first," she said.

"Tatyana had all the windows in the house permanently enchanted after a hailstorm six years ago."

"You weren't even here six years ago," growled Ellasif.

"I've been catching up on the family stories."

"They aren't your family!"

Families are complicated. Declan heard an echo of his own words in his memory. The squabble continued, but he tried his best to ignore it, both because he had no desire to step between the combative sisters and because an idea of how to escape was beginning to tickle his imagination. The problem was that he'd seen the entire room, and so far as he understood his burgeoning talent for drawing magical maps, his tricks were capable of altering only places he had not yet seen. The instant he looked up at the ceiling, he realized his mistake.

"Damn it," he grumbled. He had not shouted, but Liv and Ellasif ceased their argument and looked at him for an explanation. So did Olenka and Jadrek. Declan shrank under the impatient demands of their collective gaze.

"If only there were a closet in here, or a door we didn't know had guards standing on the other side of it, then maybe I could draw us a way out of here."

"Like the bridge at Brinewall," said Ellasif.

He nodded. "The trouble is that I've seen everything in this room. There's no 'unexplored territory' for me to alter."

"What are you talking about?" asked Liv. "Is this some special kind of witchcraft?"

"No," Declan said firmly. Then he realized he didn't know what it was. "At least, I don't think so. It might have something to do with my mother's talent for art. I'd be happy to tell you all about it in a tavern in Korvosa, or at least an alehouse in Jol. The important thing is that we get out of here."

"It is like what you did at the warlock's house?" asked Olenka.

"That's it exactly, only this time I wouldn't be trying to connect with another caster's spell. It should be much simpler just to make a path out of this room."

The red-haired warrior stepped forward and took him by the shoulders. She pulled him toward the window and sat him on one of the divans facing the wall. "I think maybe there is a trap door beneath the rug behind you."

Resisting the impulse to turn to look at the floor, Declan instead smiled his thanks up into Olenka's face. He pulled the drawing materials from his satchel and set to work. A few minutes later he had sketched out the room from memory, adding a few details like the finer grain of the wooden doors and a few strokes to suggest the subjects of the papercraft landscapes, which he had immediately recognized as his mother's work. He even included the ice wall that Mareshka had conjured, as well as the bearskin rugs he had barely glimpsed upon entering. When he was satisfied that he had captured the room as he had seen it, he traced the outlines of a trap door.

"Ready?" Jadrek asked from behind him. Declan imagined him bending down to pull the rug up from the floor.

"No," Declan said emphatically. "We need to get out of this house, not just out of this room." He continued drawing, this time drawing light lines down from the floor to represent the staircase he wanted to exist directly beneath his imagined trap door. He drew the faint borders of rooms beneath theirs, adding floors beneath them until he was sure the stairs reached the ground floor. Then, trying to remember the approximate size of the outer walls of the Crooked House, he drew a narrow corridor, like a servant's passage in a Korvosan manor home, leading out to a side entrance.

Liv leaned over his shoulder to appraise his work. She clicked her tongue, unimpressed. "There is no such—" she began, but Olenka clamped her hand over her mouth.

"Let go of her," growled Ellasif.

"Please, Ellasif," Jadrek said. He reached toward her, but she slapped his hand away.

"It's all right," said Declan, blowing the last of the charcoal dust from the page. "I'm finished."

Jadrek was still sulking from Ellasif's latest rebuke, but he looked to Declan for a nod before he swept away the heavy carpet.

Beneath the bear skin lay the trap door that Declan's art had created. Jadrek lifted it without prompting, revealing a wooden spiral staircase below.

"Let's go," Declan said.

He led the way down the stairs, glancing back only to see Jadrek and Ellasif vying for second place. The heat in their mutual scowls was unmistakable. It was not hatred, and it was not just rivalry. Declan turned away, a queasy jealousy congealing in his stomach. He could at least dispel the gloom of the stairway, so he drew his sword and cast a cantrip along its blade. Green-white light filled the passage. The spell would not make his sword as fantastic as Ellasif's new weapon appeared to be, but at least it would light the way, and perhaps it would make a guard hesitate, thinking it was a powerful enchantment. Declan hoped the rest of the spells he had set in his mind that morning would prove as useful.

They crept down three floors to emerge in a narrow corridor, just as Jadrek's map had depicted. If all of the magically rearranged passages worked as he intended, the nearest door led outside, on the western side of the Crooked House, as far from the front entrance as possible.

Declan moved toward the door, but before he could put his hand on the latch, he heard a shout of alarm from above. He could barely make out the words, but it was clear that the guards had entered the gallery and found the conjured door in the floor.

"Outside," he said, pulling the latch and stepping through the back door. The bright afternoon sun dazzled his eyes, and a cold wind blew his cloak up around his shoulders. He sheathed his sword and held the door open as the others ran out, blinking and shading their eyes.

"I'll hold the door shut," said Jadrek. "The rest of you get as far away as you can."

"We stay together," said Declan and Ellasif simultaneously.

The look she shot him told him she was in charge, but he shrugged it off. They could all hear the running steps of the guards descending the stairs. He said, "Shut the door, and stand back."

Ellasif frowned, but then she nodded, noticing the drawing he still held in his hand. She pulled her sister along by the arm. Liv did not struggle so much as she resisted, dragging her feet and jerking her shoulders at every step to show her displeasure. Once they were all outside, Declan smudged his thumb along the stairway he had drawn.

Inside, the men screamed. Their voices pierced the intervening walls and rose above the howling wind. Declan hesitated, shocked by the effect of his action. He had meant only to prevent pursuit. There was no time to weigh the cruel effects of his spell. He had to escape and ensure that all the others made it safely with him. Even if these men did not seek to kill them, their capture would surely lead to death for some. Wincing at the tormented wails of the men trapped inside the walls of the Crooked House, Declan rubbed out the outer door on his drawing, and the real portal wavered and vanished, leaving only the smooth outer wall.

Jadrek pointed west and slid down a snowy hill to the street below. Liv balked until Ellasif gave her a shove, whereupon the girl leaped straight away from her sister and into the open air.

Ellasif cried out her name and reached for her, but Liv only laughed. She uttered a few arcane syllables that Declan recognized, then floated gently down to the street below. Ellasif plunged down the snowy hill after her, as did Declan. He felt a faint pang of jealousy at Liv's effortless display of magic, but he nodded and said, "Nice."

He would have liked to have followed Liv's lead if he'd had the foresight to prepare the same spell, but the last time he'd needed one, Skywing had been there to cast it for him. He wondered where the little drake had gone and called out for him mentally.

Skywing, he thought, and repeated the psychic call as they continued their descent down the hill. There was no reply.

Jadrek had assumed the lead, slowing his pace as they reached the streets west of the Twohill neighborhood.

Declan hurried to catch up to him but then paused to look back at the higher of the two hills and the observatory that perched atop it. Majeed had made it plain the night before that he had no interest in returning to his "inferior" facility in Korvosa. The astronomer's reaction had come more as a relief than as a surprise. Declan had come to accept that he'd traveled so far not for his master but for Silvana, yet even before the disturbing revelation that the fetching kitchen maid was only the guise of a scheming winter witch, his romantic notion of rescuing the maiden fair had evaporated. And yet he knew he had not come all this way, endured such perils, for nothing. He believed there was a purpose to his journey.

He just didn't have time to figure out what that purpose was.

"Stay behind me," said Declan. When Ellasif and Jadrek jutted defiant jaws, he explained, "Liv and I look more like the jadwiga. You three are our guards."

Liv smiled and moved up to slip a hand into the crook of Declan's arm. Her touch was surprisingly warm, and he noticed that she did not shiver in the cold air despite lacking a heavy cloak. That was another spell she had that he didn't. For an instant he hoped she would decide to come away with them. Not only would that please Ellasif, but Declan looked forward to learning how Liv's presence affected her sister's tough demeanor. Already he had seen them squabbling like sisters, but he believed there had to be more to their relationship.

"Only until we leave the city," cautioned Ellasif.

"I'm not leaving the city," Liv said. "But I will see you safely outside the walls."

"We'll see about that."

"Ladies," said Declan. He nodded toward a group of guardsmen in tabards depicting the image of a hut on chicken legs. Liv clutched his arm tight, and behind them Ellasif gasped.

"Royal guards," whispered Liv. "If they stop us, you'll never get away."

"What do we do?" Declan asked.

"If they ask, you're escorting me to the Frosthall Theater."

Behind them, Olenka and Jadrek fell into the same flanking positions they had adopted when they first dared to walk the streets of Whitethrone. Declan had to admit they looked convincing in the role, but taking up the rear position, Ellasif fixed such a disgusted expression upon her face that he almost laughed aloud, spoiling the illusion.

The guards eyed them as they approached. One whispered an inquiry to his commander, prompting the man to stare at Declan, who wondered what was wrong with the way he looked. He had sheathed the lighted blade of his sword, and surely his clothing was no more unusual than what he had observed on the young jadwiga the night of his arrival.

They came within ten feet of the other group. Just as it seemed they would pass without challenge, one of the guards pointed past Declan's head and gasped in alarm. Before Declan could turn to look at what surprised the men, Skywing plummeted once more onto his shoulder, clutching him tightly. Even through the thick cloak, Declan could feel the warmth of his body and the quick beat of his heart.

There you are, thought Declan. He was finally getting used to thinking rather than speaking his thoughts to the drake. *Where have you been?*

Skywing did not answer, but Liv squeezed his elbow. Declan returned his attention to the guards. Their commander looked him directly in the eyes. When Declan returned his gaze, the officer offered him a smart salute and led his men away.

As the guards departed, Liv leaned up toward Declan's ear and whispered, "See? Already the guards think you belong here. Perhaps you should stay and learn true witchcraft with me."

Declan smiled both to be polite and to mask his fear, but the way Liv smiled back at him made him think perhaps he was playing with fire. A glance back at Ellasif's disapproving countenance confirmed his assumption. He faced forward and continued walking west. The houses and shops they passed became less and less ornate as they approached the western wall. When it came into sight, he saw that a portion of the stone barrier had collapsed. Dozens of missing stones were embedded in the ground where they had fallen, yards away from the gap. Declan realized it had to have been some mighty force that caused the breach, not simply disuse or erosion. Judging from the weathered faces of the displaced stones, the sundering had happened hundreds of years earlier. For whatever reason, the custodians of the city had left the gap unrepaired.

"Wait," said Olenka. "Where are we?"

She stiffened, and Declan could almost see the hairs on the back of her neck standing up. He followed her gaze to the people in the area. They appeared to be tall humans at first glance, little different from those he had seen elsewhere in the city. Then he noticed they all had long snowy manes and their eyes were as blue as an alcohol flame.

"We're in the Howlings," Liv said. "Here the winter wolves walk on two legs. Do not be afraid. I have been here before."

"By yourself?" Ellasif's hand strayed to the grip of her sword as a group of white-haired men and women approached.

Liv hesitated before answering. "Well . . ."

"What have we here?" said a woman almost as tall as Jadrek. Her nostrils flared as she made a show of sniffing their scent. Her eyes surveyed the Ulfen, finally settling on the winter wolf tail that hung from Ellasif's belt. "There's an air of rebellion about this lot."

"Stand aside," said Liv. Her tremulous voice undermined the command. "If you interfere with us, I shall tell my mistress."

"And what shall you tell her, little one?" said another of the wolves. This one wore the shape of a man, and his voice was like the first crack in an ice floe. Something worse would break soon. "That you have been captured by your own thralls?"

Declan felt his bladder threaten to let go. He knew that any moment someone would attack, even weaponless as Jadrek and Olenka were. If they did, they would draw the attention of twenty or thirty more of these winter wolves in human clothing. They were everywhere, looking out of windows or pausing in their strolls to witness the confrontation.

"My mistress . . ." began Liv, but her voice trailed away. Declan felt her hand trembling upon his arm. Skywing's claws dug more deeply into his shoulder. He heard the scrape of Ellasif's sword leaving its scabbard.

"No," he said to Ellasif. She shot him a defiant look. *Tell her to trust me*, he sent to Skywing.

Done, replied Skywing.

"Well?" demanded the female wolf. Her lean body and arrogant posture reminded him of a combination of Olenka's intimidating physique and Ellasif's aggressive posture.

"Her mistress entrusted her to my protection," said Declan. He straightened his back in a desperate imitation of confidence.

The wolf in woman's clothing scoffed. "Is that meant to impress us?" She sniffed at Declan and a shadow of doubt crossed her eyes. "You are not jadwiga Elvanna. Who are you?"

The slightest hesitation would spoil his bluff, so he replied at once, "Declan Avari."

The wolves appeared unimpressed.

"Pernilla's son," he added. He lifted his chin with a confidence he did not feel.

The wolf woman repeated the name slowly, as if trying to remember where she had heard it before. Declan's heart sank. He had never known his mother's maiden name. If they should demand it, his ruse was done.

"Pernilla of the Crooked House," he said.

The wolves looked at him, their mouths half-open. For a mad instant, Declan expected their tongues to loll out as they panted. Instead, they stepped close and sniffed at him, their noses only inches from his body. Unlike the humans behind him, their breath formed no frost upon the air.

The winter wolves looked to each other and then turned back to Declan. "Forgive us, young lord," said the female. "It has been long since your mother left Whitethrone."

Declan did not dare to push his gambit further. He nodded, tight-lipped, and led his companions past the monsters.

They walked along in silence, passing through the broken wall and beyond the houses built outside the city. Outside, the winter wolves went on four legs more often than on two, although a few retained their human forms as they went about their business. Yet here there were no other guardians—no men, no goblins, no trolls. They stepped out onto the high bluff west of the city. Before them, a half-frozen stream ran south to spill over the cliffs into Glacier Lake, and nowhere in sight was anyone who might stop the group.

"That was brilliant!" said Liv. For a moment she seemed much younger than her fifteen years, but Declan could not help beaming at the praise.

"Yes," said Ellasif. She plucked Liv's hand off of Declan's arm and put her own arm around her sister's shoulders. "He is indeed cleverer than he looks, but we must put many miles between us and this accursed city before we rest."

Jadrek and Olenka murmured assent.

"You can go," said Liv. "I promise to do everything I can to mislead the guards Mareshka will surely send after you, but I'm not going with you." She shot a pointed glance at Olenka and added, "I'm safer here than in White Rook."

"We won't go back there," Ellasif promised.

"But you must, Ellasif," said Jadrek. "You are needed."

The big man's pleading tone tied a knot in Declan's stomach. The elders might have sent Jadrek to fetch

Ellasif, but he obviously had more personal reasons to want her back.

"Never," said Ellasif. "I'm done with White Rook. I go where I chose." She gripped her sister's arm and stepped out to lead the way west.

"What about Liv?" Declan asked. "Why doesn't she get to choose where she goes as well?"

Ellasif stopped dead. Her mouth worked silently for a few seconds before speaking. "You don't know what you're talking about. I'm her sister."

"As someone you tricked into traveling to Whitethrone to be handed over to the witches, I can tell you it doesn't feel like a friendly thing to do, much less the act of a loving sister. You say I'm cleverer than I look, but I must be an idiot to believe we had become—friends." His face was hot, and he choked out the last words before he humiliated himself completely. He turned to address the whole group.

"I'm not one of your people," he said instead. "You've told me only hints of what happened before Ellasif left the village, but it seems to me you'd all be a lot happier if you just stopped trying to make each other's choices. I'm going to assume you've given up trading me to the witches. Now stop trying to make Ellasif go home. Stop trying to make Liv leave *her* home. You're all supposed to be friends. Two of you are family. Act like it."

Everyone stood still. Jadrek moved toward Ellasif, but Olenka stopped him. When he turned to her, she whispered something Declan couldn't overhear. Whatever it was, it made the big man's shoulders slump, and tears appeared on Olenka's cheeks. Jadrek put his hands on her shoulders, and she pressed herself against his chest.

Liv pulled her arm out of Ellasif's grip, but she didn't walk away. She put her arms around her sister and whispered into her ear. They bent their heads together and hugged each other.

That's a start, thought Declan. *At least everyone has someone to hold. Everyone but me, anyway.*

Skywing squeezed his shoulder and curled his tail gently around Declan's neck.

Don't eavesdrop, Declan sent.

Couldn't help it, said Skywing, without a trace of apology.

Chapter Nineteen
The Last Laugh

Liv accompanied them as far as a high rugged hill near the cliff's edge. It provided shelter from the wind as well as from the eyes of any sentries with especially keen vision. Ellasif thought of the enormous spyglass she'd seen emerging from the observatory and wondered whether Mareshka could command it to sweep the surrounding land to spot them. She discarded the notion as a ridiculous fear, realizing the winter witch had far more immediate means of locating them. Mareshka had appeared so soon after Ellasif first arrived at Szigo's grove that she probably had to do little more than snap her fingers to reach them. It was only a matter of time.

"Here is where I leave you," said Liv. The words felt like knives in Ellasif's heart, but she understood now that it was wrong to force Liv to do anything she didn't choose. Still, the temptation to throw the girl over her shoulder and carry her out of Irrisen was strong.

"Will you look for me?" asked Ellasif. "Have you learned how to look through a mirror or a pool of water and see where I am?"

"Not yet," Liv said. "But I will."

"I only wish there was a way I could also see you."

Liv looked at Declan, who stood a short distance away scratching under Skywing's chin. "Perhaps if you ask, Declan will cast a spell for you. I imagine there is little he would not do for you, if you ask."

Ellasif scoffed, but the sound was unconvincing even to her own ears.

"That is, if you make up your mind before Jadrek pushes him into the lake."

"Liv!" Ellasif could not believe she would make such a joke after what had happened to her at the river.

"I suppose that was in bad taste," said Liv. "It all seems like a bad dream now. I can't even be angry with Olenka. I see now that she's just a scared and ignorant girl. If only she'd grown up in a city like Whitethrone, she would see things differently."

"I didn't grow up in Whitethrone," grumbled Ellasif. "And neither did you." She didn't like the way her little sister was looking down at her, even if she deserved it—*especially* if she deserved it. But she could no longer deny the obvious truth: Liv did not belong in White Rook, nor in any place where Ellasif was likely to feel at home. No matter how much she wanted her sister to be with her, Ellasif had to let her go where she willed.

They smiled sadly at each other, each finally seeing in her sister's eyes the understanding she had craved all this time. They embraced, holding each other tightly enough to squeeze out their breaths. At last Ellasif released Liv and kissed her cheeks.

"You will choose your own life," she said. "Make it a good one."

"And you do the same, sister. With whomever you choose to share it with." She winked and ducked away before Ellasif could respond.

Liv walked away without farewells to the others. Ellasif was not surprised she had nothing to say to Jadrek or Olenka, but she thought Liv had begun to warm to Declan. Perhaps that was the reason she didn't say goodbye to him.

Skywing called out a warning, and Ellasif caught it like an echo. The shadow of a bird passed over them, and then Mareshka's blue-white familiar plummeted down toward Declan. Its frosty breath blasted over his face and chest. Ellasif saw that the imp's true target was not the man but the dragon. Skywing leaped off Declan's shoulder and led the imp out over the gelid lake.

"Witch!" bellowed Jadrek. From the opposite direction, a white raven swooped and unfolded into the shape of Mareshka. Feet barely denting the snow, she moved slowly toward them with her staff above her head, shaking it to the sky. That blue-white expanse answered with a torrent of hail. Fist-sized chunks of ice beat Jadrek and Olenka to the ground and sent Declan retreating toward Ellasif.

Declan stopped and gestured as if smearing grease in an enormous pan before him. Ellasif saw the air shimmer for an instant, and then an invisible shield was deflecting the hailstones to either side of Declan's body.

Ellasif drew Erik's sword and ran a few steps forward, but Declan put out a hand to stop her. "Wait," he said. "The storm will pass."

It couldn't pass soon enough for Jadrek and Olenka. They covered their heads with their arms, but without shields they could do little to blunt the impact of so many icy stones. They crouched low, and the accumulated ice rose and collected around their feet, freezing them in place.

Skywing swooped past, and Declan nodded as though some silent message had passed between them. Ellasif overheard nothing this time, but as the sprite followed the little drake's trail, Declan summoned a little blob of greenish yellow goop into his hand and hurled it toward the imp. The elastic ball widened as it flew toward its target, splashing with a hot sizzle all over the tiny monster. The elemental screamed with a sound like shattering ice.

The moment she saw the tide of hail subside, Ellasif ran toward Mareshka.

"Don't kill her!" Liv shouted. "Please, Sif!"

Ellasif leaped at the witch, sword swinging high. Mareshka raised her staff in both hands, catching the blade on the wooden shaft. Where the weapons met, a blast of blue light shot out, dazzling Ellasif and sending her tumbling high into the air. Mareshka laughed and thrust the staff upward, launching spears of ice toward Ellasif.

Liv shouted again, this time a torrent of indecipherable syllables. A blast of wind flew from her hands and scattered the ice spears before they reached Ellasif. The missiles sank deep into the frozen ground.

Ellasif fell hard. A sharp stone caught her in the side, and she felt a rib break, maybe two.

Behind her, Jadrek and Olenka battered the ice with their fists. *If only they had fetched weapons before leaving the city*, Ellasif thought for an instant, and then she was focusing once more on the immediate threat.

Skywing shot toward Mareshka. She blocked him with her staff, but his barbed tail whipped around to strike her in the neck. She shrieked her anger, but he darted away before she could grab his wings. The elemental fluttered down, wounded and panting in frustration at chasing the swifter foe.

A sizzling sound approached Ellasif from behind. She moved even before Declan called, "Look out!"

A ball of fire the size of an ale keg rolled past her. Declan directed it with a gesture, making it circle Jadrek and Olenka. A few times they cried out, "Too close!" Declan adjusted accordingly, but melting them free was slower that way.

Ellasif ran back toward the winter witch. She feinted high but swept the blade low across Mareshka's knees. The staff was too slow to defend, but the sword's edge barely cut through the witch's robes, leaving only shallow wounds to bloom across the fabric. Like Declan, the witch had an invisible shield protecting her.

"Stupid barbarian," spat Mareshka. She made a claw of one hand, stabbing it toward Ellasif's belly. It felt as though a steely hand had reached into her body and clutched her guts, twisting them. The agony tore Ellasif's breath away and kicked the legs out from under her.

Liv lunged past her, reaching for Mareshka's staff. Ellasif tried to warn her of the danger of touching the weapon, but she could not speak. Mareshka cackled, and every utterance magnified the pain in Ellasif's body.

Liv grabbed the staff and pulled, but no ward stung her. She tried to wrench it from Mareshka's grip, but the older woman was stronger.

"Don't think that because you know a few spells you are a true winter witch," Mareshka said. "Stand back, girl, and watch what power can be yours if you remain obedient."

A low roar grew louder as Jadrek rushed forward. As Mareshka turned to face him, she winced in the face of the full-throated battle cry of an Ulfen warrior. She pulled at the staff, but Liv clung tight, denying her the use of the weapon.

The witch's icy familiar flew straight into Jadrek's face, biting and clawing. It was far too small to divert the warrior's charge, but it blinded him long enough for Mareshka to step aside and conjure a spell independent of her staff. With a flourish of one ringed hand, she blew across her palm. Her breath turned to fog, and the fog shot forth in a glacial blast. It lifted Jadrek and hurled him over the cliff's edge.

Olenka screamed, still struggling to free herself from the half-melted bonds.

"Skywing!" shouted Declan.

Skywing shot out over the cliff and plunged after Jadrek. It was a futile effort, Ellasif knew. The little drake could never hope to lift him, much less catch him from a fall.

Declan thrust his hands toward the witch's sprite and made hooks of his fingers, which he swept over his face as though tearing off a mask. The elemental took one look at him and shrieked, flapping away as fast as his damaged wings could carry him.

"You bloody-handed bitch!" screamed Olenka. She flung a chunk of jagged ice the size of a goblin's head toward Mareshka. Her aim was perfect, but the witch dodged just enough to avoid decapitation. The sharp edge of the ice left bright red scrapes across her face.

Mareshka hissed. She pushed Liv to the ground and regained control of her weapon. She swept the butt of the staff upward. Motes of frost sparked along the shaft, and a sheet of razor-fine slivers of ice sang across the air to bury themselves in Olenka's chest and belly. The barbarian screamed in impotent anger as a dozen fresh wounds spurted and oozed in the cold air.

"Now to finish this." Mareska raised her staff and whirled it twice around her head as she turned toward Ellasif. Frost danced along the length of the staff, congealing into heavier and thicker particles before lengthening to form sharp icicles. The witch whipped her staff toward Ellasif.

Liv threw herself between them. "Don't—"

Blood splashed across Ellasif's face. She blinked and wiped her eyes clear. Before her stood Liv, wobbling like a drunk. Her fragile body was transfixed by sword-long shards of ice, all of them dripping blood.

Ellasif heard screams all around her, the voices melting into an infernal chorus. Time slowed, as did the beating of her heart. As through a frosted window, she saw a vague image of Declan throwing himself at Mareshka. The witch lifted her staff to fend him off, but he grasped it tight. No spells threw him back, but the horned head glowed brighter and brighter. He was screaming at Mareshka, who was screaming back at him, but Ellasif could not understand their words. Her gaze followed Liv's ruined body as it fell gently into the snow beside her. She reached for her hand. Liv's head turned toward her.

"Sif," she said. "Listen."

Above them, the light of Mareshka's staff outshone the sun, blotting out its golden light in a blue-white nova. The explosion knocked Ellasif's head upon the ground. She raised it again to see Declan, clutching half of the witch's staff in either hand, flying over the cliff.

All of the men are gone, she thought. *And all the women are dying*.

Liv's eyes followed Declan's plummeting arc, and she breathed a few words after him. Her eyes closed, and she died with a faint, sad smile upon her lips.

"No," said Ellasif. Liv's last words had been for her, not Declan. Why had the girl wasted them?

Ellasif climbed awkwardly to her feet. If the witch's spell still worked on her, she could no longer feel the pain. There was nothing left inside her but a cold gray void, the winter wind whistling through a hole where her heart had been. She could not feel her legs, and she dared not take a step lest she fall on her face. She raised Erik's sword and said Mareshka's name, although all she could hear was a constant dull ringing.

The witch turned toward her. Mareshka's face was burned red, and a bright torrent of blood spilled down from a wound beneath her hairline. She sneered at Ellasif, revealing black gaps where the blast had knocked out her teeth.

Ellasif threw Erik's sword. The blade scraped by Mareshka's ear, severing the tip. Both women stared in surprise as the little flap of flesh fell away from her head. When it struck the ground, Mareshka laughed.

Blood bubbled out between the witch's broken teeth. Ellasif fell to her knees, numb to the impact. She watched as the witch tottered toward her, chortling as she drew her knife from its sheath.

The laughter got inside of Ellasif. She felt it bubble up in a geyser, hot and sudden, like the child who giggles during a funeral, not knowing how her emotions became so tangled, helpless to correct the insane reaction and dreading the inevitable reprimand from her parents, or the gods. She laughed because she had finally released her unwanted grip upon the one she loved most, only to watch her die at the hands of the woman she had chosen over Ellasif. She laughed because she understood the cruel irony of Lady Luck, who laughed as often as she smiled.

But also Ellasif laughed because she knew Erik's sword would hear her.

Mareshka choked and fell silent. Her knife dropped from nerveless fingers as she looked down at the full length of Laughing Erik's sword protruding from her chest. She turned to meet Ellasif's gaze, but by then her sight had faded with the laughter. The winter witch fell forward onto her face and died.

Chapter Twenty
The First Star

Declan did his best to comfort the wounded with the materials at hand. Most of his remaining spells were of no use, but with a few cantrips he began a small fire. Lacking better fuel, he used pages from his sketchbook for kindling and ignited Mareshka's broken staff. He tried not to think about the sounds that had filled his head as he wrestled Mareshka for control of its magic. As soon as he touched the staff he had heard a hundred demonic voices and the whispers of a thousand damned souls; he tried not to think about how much one of them sounded like his mother. The broken staff burned for hours, providing much more heat than Declan would have expected from so little wood.

It was Jadrek who did the hard work. With his bare hands, he formed blocks of snow to build a barrier against the wind. Declan thought it the height of irony that the men, who had both fallen to seemingly inescapable death, had suffered the least harm.

After Skywing caught him with his gentle falling spell, Jadrek had drifted safely down to the ice on the edge of the lake. By the time he touched the cliff face to begin climbing, Declan plummeted down after him. They gaped at each other for a timeless moment before the spell Liv cast with her dying breath cradled Declan in the same gentle hand, lowering him to earth. Once he saw that Declan had also landed safely, Jadrek clambered up the precipice. Thankful that this, at least, was a contingency he'd prepared for, Declan cast a spell and used its magically imbued expertise to clamber up the cliff face as nimbly as a spider. He reached the top first, but by then it was all over.

He gasped with relief at the sight of Mareshka's impaled corpse, but fell silent when he saw Liv's sundered body. Declan flinched, realizing the witch's elemental was nowhere in sight and could swoop down at any moment. When Skywing perched on his shoulder, gagging and coughing out clouds of ice particles, he knew the sprite would trouble them no further.

He spotted Olenka's bloody figure just as Jadrek crested the cliff. The men ran toward her, but Jadrek reached her first. One look at him revived Olenka, and it took all of the big man's strength to pry her arms from around his neck and force her to lie still while he bound her wounds.

Ellasif was less injured, at least physically. She moaned and banged her head against the ground next to Liv's body. Declan left her alone for as long as he dared, but as dusk approached and the temperature dropped, he knelt beside her and spoke gently. Nothing he said made a bit of difference, and he winced at the sound of the same tired platitudes he had heard men and women utter every time a neighbor lost a family member. By the time he finally persuaded her to come to the foot of the hill for shelter, he could no longer recall which words had done the trick. Whatever they had been, they were more potent than any spell he knew.

When Ellasif closed her eyes to rest, Declan returned to the bodies. He stripped away Mareshka's cloak and laid it tenderly over Liv's body. After retrieving Ellasif's sword, he tore the witch's robes into strips and rolled them for bandages. He took her dagger and searched for any other useful belongings, then rolled her corpse to the cliff's edge. He kicked it over the side, watching as it struck the ice once and then splashed into the dark water, where it sank into oblivion.

The uncanny fire sputtered and died shortly before dusk, which was both blessing and curse. It was good because the howls of winter wolves soon persuaded them that they were better off not risking the light, yet the night was brutally cold. Declan and Jadrek shivered as they covered the women's bodies with their own. They moved often, changing places and turning their faces outward or inward when the cold became too much to bear on one side.

Long after dark, as Declan strove to prevent his teeth from chattering, Ellasif pulled him down and took his place, sheltering him with her warm body. She ignored his protests, and he had little enough strength to resist. Later, Olenka did the same with Jadrek, although she required Ellasif's help to twist the big man's ears painfully until he obeyed. They continued through the night, sheltering each other from the cold as long as their bodies could bear it.

They rose soon after the eastern sky began to pale. They had no food, and no one dared suggest slipping back into Whitethrone for supplies. Their only hope of survival was speed. Only after they returned to the

Lands of the Linnorm Kings could they expect to forage with any success. Even Declan knew that fact, and he doubted they could reach them before he or one of the wounded women succumbed to the constant winter of Irrisen.

Declan drew one more map before they left the hill. On the side they had not yet reached, he sketched a good, deep grave. He and Jadrek carried Liv's body around to place it inside, and no one was surprised to discover a grave where none had been. No one had looked over his shoulder as he drew. None of them needed to ask to know what the others were thinking or feeling. It was as if they could all communicate like Skywing.

After they said their silent goodbyes to Liv, Declan thumbed the grave shut by smearing it away on the parchment. The sunrise glared brightly over the grave, leaving only a glimmer of virgin snow. Ellasif had finished with her tears, as had Olenka, but Jadrek turned his face skyward, blinking. Declan felt waves of sorrow radiating off of Skywing, who wrapped his tail a little too snugly around Declan's neck. Declan didn't mind. The pressure soothed the lump that had formed in his throat.

They trudged westward at a modest speed, following Jadrek. Declan did not know whether the big man set a modest pace out of respect for the women's injuries or Declan's inferior endurance, but he was too drained to protest that he would keep up. Besides, the warriors of White Rook might be able to run for days at a time, but Declan would be lucky to last an hour on foot beside them.

Skywing launched himself from Declan's shoulder. The sudden motion made Declan queasy, and the dizziness refused to pass. Instead, he began to see an image of Whitethrone as if from a high vantage. He paused and closed his eyes, thinking, *Skywing, what's happening?*

Sharing my sight with you, said the little drake.

How?

Familiar, said Skywing.

The revelation stole Declan's breath. He had performed no ritual, never consciously called for a familiar. And he was pretty sure that most wizards couldn't see through their familiars' eyes anyway. How, then, was this possible?

A gift from your mother's staff, sent Skywing, as if that explained anything.

Skywing's aerial scouting allowed them to avoid two Whitethrone patrols, one of them composed of a troll, two ogres, and a swarm of goblins large enough to raze a town. Each time, Declan warned the others to wait, describing what Skywing had seen. No one questioned that what he told them was true. All distrust had fallen from them.

Once they were out of sight of Whitethrone, Jadrek led the way in a wide arc, turning north, then east, and finally south into the heart of Irrisen. When they came all the way around to follow the edge of Glacier Lake to its easternmost point, they made another simple camp beside the water. Jadrek broke a hole in the ice and lowered a hook on a long line of catgut. He checked the line periodically, but even by the following morning, nothing had bitten.

So they continued, hiding when they heard the howl of winter wolves, turning away whenever they saw giant tracks in the snow, and always moving southwest, toward White Rook. Twice Jadrek proposed attacking small groups of patrols from Whitethrone, and Declan surrendered his sword to the big man, but ultimately they decided against risking a fight. Olenka's wounds were mending, but she grew weaker by the day.

Twice Skywing knocked out snowy hares with his stinger, leading Declan to the sleeping bounty. After the drake had led him to the second hare, Declan began dreaming of flight. When he awoke on the fourth night, he was not sure at first whether he was a man or a dragon.

By the time they reached the western border, Declan could feel all his ribs, and he could see them on the others as he helped change the dressings on their wounds. They took an unusually long rest as Skywing flew a long patrol and flew it again to confirm what he had seen. A pair of huts on enormous chicken legs stood sentinel between them and the nearest green plains of the Lands of the Linnorm Kings. They spoke more that day than they had since facing the winter witch, but all toward deciding whether it was better to wait for night or else creep between the two guardian huts in daylight. Eventually they took the latter course, crouching low as they hurried through the scant cover provided by snow drifts.

Once they put the snows of Irrisen behind them, they fell upon the land like ravenous beasts. Skywing hunted and felled prey more quickly than Olenka could gather it. Declan filled his satchel with mushrooms, and Jadrek spent the rest of the afternoon dragging pike out of a stream. The greatest pleasure came when they lit a proper campfire with deadwood Ellasif had gathered. Even just a few miles away from the land of the winter witches, the night had become summer once more, and the heat of flames stirred something that had frozen deep inside their bodies.

They gorged their appetites and lingered for an hour after sunrise before continuing their journey. Still they walked in silence, and so they continued until they met the first patrol from White Rook. A pair of men revealed themselves from their hiding places among the trees. One unleashed a mighty cheer at the sight of Jadrek and Olenka, but sobered when he received only nods in acknowledgment. One of them ran ahead to alert the village, while the other accompanied them, chattering questions about what had happened to them. When none of the others would answer him, the man turned to Declan.

"Is it true you are a witch?" he asked.

Before Declan could answer, Olenka clouted the man on the back of the head. "There are no witches among us," she said. He rubbed his skull and jutted his jaw ruefully as Olenka added, "There never were."

The villagers welcomed their returning heroes, although Declan felt their eyes upon his back whenever he turned away. He used Skywing's sight to watch them when they thought he wasn't looking. He could not understand what they said in their own language, but whenever he was included in the conversation, his friends insisted on speaking the common tongue. He noticed Jadrek and Olenka speaking intently to several groups of their closest companions, sending them out to spread word throughout the village. When Declan asked what they were doing, Olenka told him, "We're making sure you don't fall into the river." He did not need the details to understand her meaning.

If he were ever in peril from the villagers, Declan never felt it. The village girls were almost as solicitous as the young Varisian women had been, but he had neither the strength nor the inclination to return their flirtations. He accepted their gifts of food and sweet mead, but he did little to satisfy their requests for tales from the south. When they asked what had befallen them in Irrisen, he imitated Jadrek's stony stare. That stopped the questions, but not the girls' attentions. The idea that he might be dangerous appealed to them, as it did to foolish girls everywhere.

Olenka and Jadrek were also the focus of great attention from the young men and women, but each of them firmly rebuffed the advances. They seemed more quiet than they had when Declan first met them, and somehow much older.

Ellasif was spared this part of the homecoming, but Declan noticed she was often called away by old men and women to confer alone in a smoking hut near the village mead hall. Virtually all other activities seemed to take place out of doors, at least in these balmy summer days, so Declan supposed she was party to some grave consultation. He sent Skywing to eavesdrop from the roof, but it was no use. They spoke not a word of his language inside.

Outside, Declan eventually relaxed enough to enjoy the constant feasting and even engaged in trifling conversation. Along with the food and endless mead came offerings of clothing and weapons. Jadrek returned Declan's sword when the village smith presented him with his best warhammer. The big man showed the first signs of returning cheer as he savagely demolished lengths of firewood to demonstrate the quality of his new weapon.

On the third night, the elders gathered around a great central fire in the village. Ellasif stood among them, her garments all exchanged for a long cloak of winter wolf pelt, the beast's massive head lolling back like a hood. One of the elders presented her with an enormous greatsword inscribed with runes. Declan could not help but smile when he pictured Ellasif with the monster's head raised like a helm, the giant blade above it. How fearsome she would be in battle.

Beside him, Olenka whispered a translation of the proceedings. Ellasif had been given the sword of Red Ochme, one of the greatest heroes of the village, and their last great battle leader. The elders praised and anointed Ellasif, and after a mercifully short ceremony including prayers to Gorum and Torag, the lords of iron and warfare, they declared her the new battle leader of White Rook and placed themselves under her command.

The pronouncement should have shocked Declan, but somehow it did not. Upon learning the full extent of Ellasif's deception in Whitethrone, he had felt hurt and betrayed for only a few hours before the full weight of his affection returned. He would not be afraid to say now that he loved her, and loving her, would never try to force his will upon her. She would make her own choices, and he would be happy for her, whatever they were.

Still, after the feasting and drinking, Declan's heart shrank when he saw Ellasif go to Jadrek and take him by the hand. She drew the big man away from the fire, and they walked out into the summer night beyond the village. A few of the young men joked and struck each other playfully, nodding as the couple departed. The women whispered and cast sympathetic glances toward Olenka, who stared stoically into the fire.

Declan focused on her disappointment to avoid facing his own. He fetched a mead skin and filled her cup. They sat side by side, never speaking while the others chattered and laughed and left them alone. At last, Olenka slipped her hand into Declan's and led him away into the dark. They found a soft bower and lay down without so much as a kiss. They simply lay together, their breathing gradually matching each other's rhythm, and they slept.

They woke late the following morning, not to the light, which had come hours earlier, but to a commotion of angry voices in the village center. They ran to find the entire village gathered around the ashes. Ellasif stood atop one of the split logs that served as a bench and shouted down the arguments. Jadrek stood beside her, for once his head lower than hers.

Olenka whispered a translation as Ellasif shouted down the crowd.

"It is not only my right, it is my final decision," said Ellasif. "I choose Jadrek as White Rook's battle leader. Like Red Ochme before me, I go to wander the world, perhaps to fight and die upon the deck of a dragon ship as she did." Her eyes found Declan standing in the crowd.

Declan felt his heart rise to stop his throat. Blinking, he turned to see Olenka's reaction to the news. Her face twitched, torn between joy, sorrow, and disbelief. When another man shouted to Olenka to add her voice, she shook her head. She replied to him in their native tongue and repeated for Declan, "I will not tell my sister what to do."

Ellasif presented Jadrek with the greatsword, and with a look of mischief thrown toward Olenka, kissed him hard upon the mouth before leaping down from her perch. As her cloak—her usual one now, not the wolf pelt—spread like wings, Declan saw Laughing Erik's sword at her hip. She grabbed a pack that had lain unnoticed by the log and ran toward Declan.

"I couldn't believe you were going to accept the honor," he said. "And then I couldn't imagine you'd give it up."

"The word of the battle leader is indisputable," she said. "Only by accepting the honor could I give it away again, and none can challenge my decision."

"You are very clever. But what about Jadrek? When you went off with him last night, I thought . . ." He shrugged.

"It is like families. What you said is true. It's complicated."

"So now you're free?"

"Yes. Will you come with me?"

Declan had been dying for her to ask. His answer was a lopsided grin. "Do you mind if I bring my familiar?"

As if in reply, Skywing plunged down from the trees to strike him hard in the shoulder and then hang there, his little claws pricking through Declan's clothes. *Not your familiar*, said Skywing. Declan saw from Ellasif's reaction that she had heard the thought as well.

But you told me you were my familiar, he protested.

Skywing shook his head in a startlingly human gesture. *No*, he sent. *I was telling you that you are mine.*

Ellasif laughed and took Declan's hand, pulling him along as she ran out of the village. Declan followed, noticing that as they fled, the argument behind them died, and the villagers bowed to Jadrek. Olenka had gone to stand beside him.

"Where will we go?" Declan asked. Ellasif made no allowances for his lesser endurance, and already he was panting with exertion. If she wanted to keep up this pace, he would fall on his face before another hour had passed.

"Tonight," she said, "let us look up at the sky and see what the first star has to tell us."

About the Authors

Elaine Cunningham lives in a fantasy world. Several of them, in fact. *The Serpent's Daughter*, coming in 2012, will be her fourteenth novel in the Forgotten Realms. She has also written novels and short stories in such diverse settings as Star Wars, EverQuest, Spelljammer, and Ravenloft. Previous contributions to the Pathfinder setting include "Dark Tapestry," a serial novella in the Legacy of Fire Adventure Path; and work on the Pathfinder Campaign Setting *Guide to the River Kingdoms*.

Dave Gross is the author of *Black Wolf* and *Lord of Stormweather*, among other stories set in the Forgotten Realms. His first Pathfinder Tales novel, *Prince of Wolves*, features Pathfinder and Chelish aristocrat Varian Jeggare and his hellspawn bodyguard, Radovan, whose earlier capers appear in the novella "Hell's Pawns" in the Council of Thieves Adventure Path and the web fiction story "The Lost Pathfinder," available for free at **paizo.com**.

Acknowledgments

Elaine

Most people, including Ellasif herself, would describe her as a warrior who's just one raiding ship away from Viking. While that might be true, she owes her existence to the generations of Slavic storytellers who passed along a rich legacy of trickster tales, and to the folklorists who preserve and translate these tales. Many thanks to Andreas Johns for his excellent book *Baba Yaga: The Ambiguous Mother and Witch of the Russian Folklore*, and to the folks at Paizo for including this iconic Slavic figure in the Pathfinder setting. Thanks also to James Sutter for his keen editorial eye, and to Mark Moreland and the dozens of others who make the PathfinderWiki a valuable tool and an interesting reading experience. And to Dave Gross, who helped Ellasif and Declan find their way, no thanks are sufficient. Many people write in shared worlds, but only a few manage to capture and portray the essence of a setting. As far as I'm concerned, Dave is the voice and the heart of Pathfinder Tales.

Dave

First and foremost, thanks to Elaine Cunningham for welcoming me on her journey to Irrisen. Thanks and kudos to Mark Moreland, the ever-present reference librarian of Golarion, for his stewardship of the invaluable PathfinderWiki. Grateful thanks also to James Sutter and Chris Carey taking the editing marathon at a sprint, and to Amber Scott for ninja proofing. Most of all, my love and eternal gratitude to Lindy Smith for failing to realize she's far too good for the likes of me.

Glossary

All Pathfinder Tales novels are set in the rich and vibrant world of the Pathfinder campaign setting. Below are explanations of several key terms used in this book. For more information on the world of Golarion and the strange monsters, people, and deities that make it their home, see the *Pathfinder Roleplaying Game Core Rulebook* or any of the books in the Pathfinder Campaign Setting series, or visit **paizo.com**.

Acadamae: Notoriously effective and amoral school of magic in Korvosa.

Avistan: The continent north of the Inner Sea, on which Irrisen, Varisia, and the Lands of the Linnorm Kings all lie.

Baba Yaga: Queen of all Witches, a strange being who came from another world to conquer Irrisen, and returns every 100 years to install a different daughter as its ruler.

Baslwief: Mining village along the Sarwin River in southern Varisia.

Blackravens: A force of Ulfen warriors that patrols the border between Trollheim and Irrisen, hunting down monsters from the Witch Queen's lands.

Bone Road: A main thoroughfare in Whitethrone. Paved with skulls.

Brinewall: Mysteriously empty and possibly haunted port in northwestern Varisia.

Bugbear: Large, humanoid monster related to the goblin. Extremely violent and ill-tempered.

Cantrip: A minor spell.

Castle Korvosa: Enormous castle in the center of Korvosa that houses the city's ruler.

Chelaxian: A citizen of Cheliax.

Cheliax: Devil-worshiping nation in southwest Avistan.

Chelish: Of or relating to the nation of Cheliax.

Crooked House: The largest wooden structure in Whitethrone, home to a long line of talented wood-carvers. Somewhat sinister in reputation.

Cyphergate: Strange arch of stone that stretches over the entrance to Riddleport's harbor.

Demon: Denizen of the Abyss who seeks only to maim, ruin, and feed.

Desna: Good-natured goddess of dreams, stars, travelers, and luck.

Devil: Fiendish occupant of Hell who seeks to corrupt mortals in order to claim their souls.

Divination: Spell that enables you to predict the future, learn secrets long forgotten, find hidden things, and foil deceptive magic.

Dwarves: Race of short, solid, and civilized humanoids that generally live underground. Frequently characterized as gruff and hardworking.

Elemental Planes: Four planes—Air, Earth, Fire, and Water—that surround the Material Plane as part of the Great Beyond.

Elves: Race of long-lived and eminently civilized humanoids.

Elvanna: Current queen of Irrisen.

Erastil: Stag-headed god of farming, family, hunting, and trade.

Familiar: Small creature that assists a wizard, witch, or sorcerer, often developing greater powers and intelligence than normal members of its kind.

Fey: Creatures deeply tied to the natural world, such as dryads or pixies. May also have ties to the First World.

First World: The rough draft of existence, which still exists behind the Material Plane. Original home of fey creatures and gnomes.

Flayleaf: Plant with narcotic leaves.

Floes, The: District of Whitethrone made up primarily of frozen islands.

Freyr Darkwine: Castellan of Trollheim.

Garund: Continent south of the Inner Sea, renowned for its deserts and jungles.

Glacier Lake: Large lake in central Irrisen.

Gnomes: Race of fey humanoids known for their small size, quick wit, and bizarre obsessions.

Goblins: Race of small and maniacal humanoids who live to burn, pillage, and sift through the refuse of more civilized races.

Golarion: The planet upon which the Pathfinder campaign setting focuses.

Gorum: God of battle, strength, and weapons. Also known as Our Lord in Iron.

Grand Mastaba: Four-sided pyramid that forms the base of Castle Korvosa.

Grungir Forest: Large forest in the southern part of the Lands of the Linnorm Kings, just north of Jol.

Halflings: Race of humanoids known for their tiny stature, deft hands, and mischievous personalities.

Harrow Deck: Deck of illustrated cards sometimes used to divine the future. Favored by Varisians.

Harrower: Fortuneteller who uses a Harrow deck to tell the future—or pretends to.

Harse: Village in southern Varisia that serves as a gateway to Korvosa's inland holdings.

Hell: A plane of absolute law and evil, where evil souls go after they die to be tormented by the native devils.

Hellknights: Organization of hardened law enforcers whose tactics are often seen as harsh and intimidating, and who bind devils to their will. Based in Cheliax.

Hellspawn: A human whose family line includes a fiendish taint, often displayed by horns, hooves, or other devilish features. Rarely popular in civilized society.

Hippogriff: Aggressive flying creature with the hindquarters of a horse and the clawed forelegs, wings, and head of a giant eagle.

House Drakes: Slang term for the tiny, intelligent cousins of true dragons commonly found in the rooftops of Korvosa, where they feed on lesser vermin and combat the imps that infest the city.

Ilsurian: Settlement located at the mouth of Skull River on Lake Syrantula.

Imp: Weakest of the true devils, resembling a tiny, winged humanoid with fiendish features. The most commonly found devil on the Material Plane. Often used as a familiar.

Inner Sea Region: The heart of the Pathfinder campaign setting. Includes the continents of Avistan and Garund, as well as the seas and other nearby lands.

Irrisen: A realm of permanent winter north of Varisia, claimed by Baba Yaga and ruled by her daughters. Currently controlled by Queen Elvanna and her bloodline, the jadwiga Elvanna.

Jadwiga: The descendents of Baba Yaga and the nobility of Irrisen. Most have only a tenuous, distant connection to the Witch Queen, and do not necessarily have any magical ability themselves. Every 100 years, a new bloodline is created or rises to power as Baba Yaga installs a new daughter as queen.

Jadwiga Elvanna: Direct descendents of Queen Elvanna. Currently the highest caste of nobility in Whitethrone, though the time of Elvanna's replacement draws near.

Jol: One of the major cities in the Lands of the Linnorm Kings, located in the rugged uplands south of the Grungir Forest.

Katapesh: Mighty trade nation on the eastern coast of Garund.

Kellid: Traditionally uncivilized and violent human ethnicity from northern Avistan.

Korvosa: Largest city in Varisia and outpost of former Chelish loyalists, now self-governed. For more information, see the Pathfinder Campaign Setting book *Guide to Korvosa*.

Lands of the Linnorm Kings: Northern kingdoms ruled by the Linnorm Kings. Sometimes called the Linnorm Kingdoms.

Linnorm Kings: Warrior chieftains who dominate the larger settlements of the Lands of the Linnorm Kings, each of whom must defeat a linnorm to claim a throne.

Linnorm: Immense, snake-like dragons with two forward legs and rudimentary wings.

Material Plane: The plane of existence on which Golarion resides—the "normal" world.

Melfesh: Korvosa's largest inland holding.

Mindspin Mountains: Mountain range that forms part of Varisia's eastern border.

Necromancy: Magic that manipulates the power of death, unlife, and the life force.

Nethys: Two-faced god of magic, pledged to both destroy the world and protect it.

Nolander: Of or relating to the region of the Nolands, or one of that region's savage residents.

Nolands: Unclaimed region in northern Varisia where criminals and outcasts war and raid in rough, violent bands.

Nymph: Beautiful fey guardian of nature's purest places.

Ogre: Large, half-witted humanoid monster with violent tendencies and repulsive lusts.

Opir Eightfingers: Linnorm King of Jol, who claimed his throne by presenting a rotted linnorm head, and whose rule is therefore tenuous.

Osirian: Of or relating to the region of Osirion, or a resident of Osirion.

Osirion: Desert kingdom ruled by pharaohs in northeastern Garund.

Pathfinder Society: Organization of traveling scholars and adventurers who seek to document the world's wonders. Based out of Absalom and run by a mysterious and masked group called the Decemvirate.

Pharasma: Goddess of fate, death, prophecy, and birth. Ruler of the Boneyard, where mortal souls go to be judged after death.

Pixie: Small fey humanoid with gossamer wings.

Ravenmoor: Settlement in Varisia along the Lampblack River.

Riddleport: Notorious Varisian port city full of mercenaries, thieves, bandits, and pirates.

Roderic's Cove: Settlement at the mouth of the Chavali River in Varisia.

Sable Company: Elite Korvosan military unit of hippogriff riders.

Sanos Forest: Large forest in Varisia stretching from the Storval Plateau to the Mushfens.

Shoanti: Indigenous peoples of the Storval Plateau.

Skald: Language spoken in the Lands of the Linnorm Kings and by most Ulfen. Can also mean a bard or minstrel.

Sorcerer: Spellcaster who draws power from a supernatural ancestor, and does not need to study to cast spells.

Spellbook: Tome in which a wizard transcribes the arcane formulae necessary to cast spells. Without a spellbook, wizards can cast only those few spells held in their mind at any given time.

Spring Palace: Bathhouse in Whitethrone fed by hot springs and open only to the nobility.

Storval Plateau: High, rocky badlands making up the eastern portion of Varisia.

Taldan: A citizen of Taldor.

Taldane (Common Tongue): Most widely spoken language in the Inner Sea Region.

Taldor: Formerly glorious nation, now fallen into self-indulgence, ruled by immature aristocrats and overly complicated bureaucracy.

Theumanexus: Magical college in Korvosa. Less prestigious than the Acadamae, yet also less stained by devil-binding and other questionable practices.

Thileu Bark: Bark of the Varisian thileu tree, exported as a spice and claimed by some to have a narcotic effect.

Tiren'kii: Word used in some villages of the Linnorm Kingdoms to describe strange spirits that sometimes inhabit children at birth. Poorly understood, but believed to potentially be a manifestation of a witch's inborn power.

Torag: God of the forge, protection, and strategy. Father of creation.

Transmutation: Magic that changes the properties of some creature, thing, or condition.

Troll: Large, stooped humanoid with sharp claws and amazing regenerative powers.

Trollheim: A currently rulerless Linnorm Kingdom on the border with Irrisen.

Ulfen: Race of Viking-like humans from the cold nations of the north, primarily Irrisen and the Lands of the Linnorm Kings.

University of Korvosa: Seat of mundane higher learning in Korvosa.

Varisia: Frontier region northwest of the Inner Sea.

Varisian: Of or relating to the region of Varisia, or a resident of Varisia. Ethnic Varisians tend to organize in clans and wander in caravans, acting as tinkers or performers.

Velashu Uplands: Region in northern Varisia extending from the Red Mountains to the Mierani Forest.

Vjarik: Strong spirit brewed in the Lands of the Linnorm Kings.

White Rook: Small village in the Lands of the Linnorm Kings, situated near the border with Irrisen.

White Witches: The granddaughters of Baba Yaga.

Whitethrone: Capital city of Irrisen. For more information, see the Pathfinder Campaign Setting book *Cities of Golarion*.

Winter Witch: A member of the jadwiga with magical abilities.

Winter Wolves: Large, intelligent white wolves that breathe out blasts of cold.

Winterfolk: Slang term for residents of Irrisen, generally used by Ulfen residents near the eastern border of the Lands of the Linnorm Kings

Witch: Spellcaster who draws magic from a pact made with an otherworldly power, using a familiar as a conduit.

Wizard: Spellcaster who masters the art through years of studying arcane lore.

Wraith: Shapeless undead creature born of evil and darkness, which hates light and living things.

Yondabakari River: A mighty, heavily traveled river in Varisia stretching from the Mindspin Mountains to the Varisian Gulf.

TALES

For half-elven Pathfinder Varian Jeggare and his devil-blooded bodyguard Radovan, things are rarely as they seem. Yet not even the notorious crime-solving duo are prepared for what they find when a search for a missing Pathfinder takes them into the gothic and mist-shrouded mountains of Ustalav.

Beset on all sides by noble intrigue, curse-afflicted villagers, suspicious monks, and the deadly creatures of the night, Varian and Radovan must use sword and spell to track the strange rumors to their source and uncover a secret of unimaginable proportions, aided in their quest by a pack of sinister werewolves and a mysterious, mute priestess. But it'll take more than merely solving the mystery to finish this job. For shadowy figures have taken note of the pair's investigations, and the forces of darkness are set on making sure neither man gets out of Ustalav alive . . .

From fan-favorite author Dave Gross, author of *Black Wolf* and *Lord of Stormweather*, comes a new fantastical mystery set in the award-winning world of the Pathfinder Roleplaying Game.

$9.99
ISBN: 978-1-60125-287-6

PRINCE OF WOLVES

Dave Gross

The race is on to free Lord Stelan from the grip of a wasting curse, and only his old mercenary companion, the Forsaken elf Elyana, has the wisdom—and the swordcraft—to uncover the identity of his tormenter and free her old friend before the illness takes its course.

When the villain turns out to be another of their former companions, Elyana sets out with a team of adventurers including Stelan's own son on a dangerous expedition across the revolution-wracked nation of Galt and the treacherous Five Kings Mountains. There, pursued by a bloodthirsty militia and beset by terrible nightmare beasts, they discover the key to Stelan's salvation in a lost valley warped by weird magical energies. Yet will they be able to retrieve the artifact the dying lord so desperately needs? Or will the shadowy face of betrayal rise up from within their own ranks?

From Howard Andrew Jones, managing editor of the acclaimed sword and sorcery magazine *Black Gate*, comes a classic quest of loyalty and magic set in the award-winning world of the Pathfinder Roleplaying Game.

$9.99
ISBN: 978-1-60125-291-3

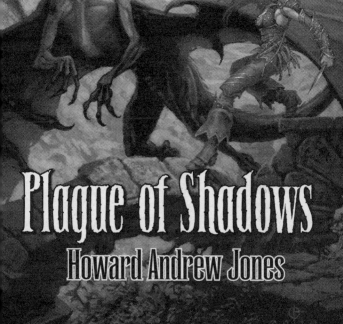

Plague of Shadows

Howard Andrew Jones

> "AS YOU TURN AROUND, YOU SPOT SIX DARK SHAPES MOVING UP BEHIND YOU. AS THEY ENTER THE LIGHT, YOU CAN TELL THAT THEY'RE SKELETONS, WEARING RUSTING ARMOR AND WAVING ANCIENT SWORDS."

Lem: Guys, I think we have a problem.

GM: You do indeed. Can I get everyone to roll initiative?

To determine the order of combat, each player rolls a d20 and adds his or her initiative bonus. The GM rolls once for the skeletons.

GM: Seelah, you have the highest initiative. It's your turn.

Seelah: I'm going to attempt to destroy them using the power of my goddess, Iomedae. I channel positive energy.

Seelah rolls 2d6 and gets a 7.

GM: Two of the skeletons burst into flames and crumble as the power of your deity washes over them. The other four continue their advance. Harsk, it's your turn.

Harsk: Great. I'm going to fire my crossbow!

Harsk rolls a d20 and gets a 13. He adds that to his bonus on attack rolls with his crossbow and announces a total of 22. The GM checks the skeleton's Armor Class, which is only a 14.

GM: That's a hit. Roll for damage.

Harsk rolls a d10 and gets an 8. The skeleton's damage reduction reduces the damage from 8 to 3, but it's still enough.

GM: The hit was hard enough to cause that skeleton's ancient bones to break apart. Ezren, it's your turn.

Ezren: I'm going to cast *magic missile* at a skeleton.

Magic missile creates glowing darts that always hit their target. Ezren rolls 1d4+1 for each missile and gets a total of 6. It automatically bypasses the skeleton's DR, dropping another one.

GM: There are only two skeletons left, and it's their turn. One of them charges up to Seelah and takes a swing at her, while the other moves up to Harsk and attacks.

The GM rolls a d20 for each attack. The attack against Seelah is only an 8, which is less than her AC of 18. The attack against Harsk is a 17, which beats his AC of 16. The GM rolls damage.

GM: The skeleton hits you, Harsk, leaving a nasty cut on your upper arm. Take 7 points of damage.

Harsk: Ouch. I have 22 hit points left.

GM: That's not all. Charging out of the fog onto the bridge is a skeleton dressed like a knight, riding the bones of a long-dead horse. Severed heads are mounted atop its deadly lance. Lem, it's your turn—what do you do?

Lem: Run!

NOW IT'S YOUR TURN . . .

CHART YOUR OWN ADVENTURE!

The PATHFINDER ROLEPLAYING GAME puts you in the role of a brave adventurer fighting to survive in a fantastic world beset by magic and evil!

Take on the role of a canny fighter hacking through enemies with an enchanted sword, a powerful sorceress with demon blood in her veins, a wise cleric of mysterious gods, a canny rogue ready to defuse even the deadliest of traps, or any of countless other heroes. The only limit is your imagination!

The massive 576-page *Pathfinder RPG Core Rulebook* provides all the tools you need to get your hero into the action! One player assumes the role of the Game Master, challenging players with dastardly dungeons or monstrous selections from the more than 350 beasts included in the *Pathfinder RPG Bestiary*!

The PATHFINDER ROLEPLAYING GAME is a fully supported tabletop roleplaying game, with regularly released adventure modules, sourcebooks on the fantastic world of Golarion, and complete campaigns in the form of Pathfinder Adventure Paths like Kingmaker and Serpent's Skull!

Begin your adventure today in the game section of quality bookstores, hobby game shops, or online at **paizo.com**!

Pathfinder RPG Core Rulebook • $49.99
ISBN 978-1-60125-150-3

EXPLORE NEW WORLDS WITH

PLANET STORIES®

Strap on your jet pack and set out for unforgettable adventure with PLANET STORIES, Paizo Publishing's science fiction and fantasy imprint! Personally selected by Paizo's editorial staff, PLANET STORIES. presents timeless classics from authors like Gary Gygax (Dungeons & Dragons), Robert E. Howard (Conan the Barbarian), Michael Moorcock (Elric), and Leigh Brackett (*The Empire Strikes Back*) alongside groundbreaking anthologies and fresh adventures from the best imaginations in the genre, all introduced by superstar authors such as China Miéville, George Lucas, and Ben Bova.

With new releases six times a year, PLANET STORIES promises the best two-fisted adventure this side of the galactic core! Find them at your local bookstore, or subscribe online at **paizo.com**!